MRS. WASHINGTON
AND
HOROWITZ, TOO

ALSO BY HENRY DENKER

NOVELS	PLAYS
I'll Be Right Home, Ma	*Time Limit*
My Son, the Lawyer	*A Far Country*
Salome: Princess of Galilee	*A Case of Libel*
The First Easter	*What Did We Do Wrong*
The Director	*Venus at Large*
The Kingmaker	*Second Time Around*
A Place for the Mighty	*Horowitz and Mrs.*
The Physicians	*Washington*
The Experiment	*The Headhunters*
The Starmaker	*Outrage!*
The Scofield Diagnosis	
The Actress	
Error of Judgment	
Horowitz and Mrs.	
Washington	
The Warfield Syndrome	
Outrage	
The Healers	
Kincaid	
Robert, My Son	
Judge Spencer Dissents	
The Choice	
The Retreat	
A Gift of Life	
Payment in Full	
Doctor on Trial	

MRS. WASHINGTON AND HOROWITZ, TOO

A Novel ××× Henry Denker

WILLIAM MORROW AND COMPANY, INC.
New York

Library of Congress Cataloging-in-Publication Data

Denker, Henry.
    Mrs. Washington and Horowitz, too : a novel / Henry Denker.
      p.   cm.
    ISBN 0-688-12466-6
    I. Title.
PS3507.E5475H63   1993
813'.54—dc20   92–32877
                                                CIP

Printed in the United States of America

First Edition

1   2   3   4   5   6   7   8   9   10

BOOK DESIGN BY LISA STOKES

To Edith,
my wife

Chapter 1

XXX

"WHERE TO, MISTER?" THE DRIVER ASKED ROUTINELY AS A NEW PAS-
senger stepped into his yellow cab.

"LaGuardia Airport," the man mumbled in a distracted, troubled manner.

The odd reply and the tone of distress in his passenger's voice
forced the driver to turn and stare at him. He was a man in his late
sixties, neatly dressed. But he appeared disturbed.

"I said, 'Where to, mister?' " the driver asked once more.

"And I said, 'LaGuardia Airport!' " Samuel Horowitz shot
back, irritated at having his thoughts interrupted.

"Mister, we are already *at* LaGuardia Airport. Now, if you
mean to say JFK Airport that's another matter."

Samuel Horowitz seemed to snap out of his distracted state to
reply impatiently, "Who said anything about JFK or LaGuardia? I
very clearly said, 'Central Park West and Eighty-fourth Street.'
And without any conversation, if you don't mind! Between cab
drivers and barbers a man can't get a moment's peace. Talk, talk,
talk."

Rather than argue, the driver joined the long line of cabs as
they began their slow bumper-to-bumper, stop-and-go, circuitous exit route from the airport. Annoyed at the slow pace,
Horowitz grumbled, "Takes longer to get out of this airport than

it takes to fly to Florida. If anybody was crazy enough to move to Florida in the first place."

The black man, in his mid-forties, bareheaded and dressed in a worn leather jacket, did not respond. But neither could he resist studying his passenger in the rearview mirror. Horowitz caught his glance, took it to be a hostile act.

Never one to back down in the face of what he interpreted to be an insult, express or implied, Samuel Horowitz challenged, "I'll bet this is the taxi company's idea! Costs four or five dollars on the meter just to get out of this damn airport. But to give a person a comfortable ride in a new taxi, oh, no! How old is this cab? Ten years, fifteen?"

"Four," the driver informed him.

"Only four?" Horowitz disputed. "From the way the springs in this seat are sticking into my backside, seems a lot older. The trouble these days . . ."

Before Horowitz could expound on his philosophy of modern life the black driver interrupted, "Look, mister, you obviously got some grudge against the world. Well, don't take it out on me."

"Grudge?" Horowitz disputed at once. "What makes you think I got a grudge?" Before the driver could respond, truth forced Horowitz to concede, "Okay, so I have a grudge. Not against you. Not even against this taxi. But against life. Imagine a man like Phil Liebowitz packing up and moving down to Florida. Must have been Rose. His wife. She can be a real *nudge*. You know what means a *nudge*?"

"Not exactly," the driver replied, more interested in concentrating on the heavy city-bound traffic than enduring his passenger's complaint.

In his present angry mood, Samuel Horowitz needed only a hint of encouragement.

"*Nudge* is short from the Yiddish word *nudnik*. Which means a person who can torture you to death with suggestions and ideas until you agree to whatever it is they want. Now, among *nudges*, Rose Liebowitz was a genius. Did I say 'was'? You see, Liebowitz and Rose are not in the air half an hour and already I have put them in the past tense. But a man like Phil Liebowitz who (now that he is gone, I can admit was really a damn fine pinochle player) is going to waste the rest of his life in Florida is a disgrace. How could he do such a thing to me? Every Thursday night, without fail, we had a game. Except for the time when I had a little—a little problem. Well, to tell you the truth, the doctors called it a stroke. Very minor. Even now you couldn't notice. Tell me the truth— when I stepped into your cab did you say to yourself, 'This is a man who once had a stroke'? Be honest with me. H'mmm?"

Not having paid any special attention, since Samuel Horowitz was his twenty-seventh passenger on this long day, the driver decided nevertheless to mollify him.

"No, sirree, never suspected it for a minute."

"You know why?" Horowitz asked, at once turning it into a rhetorical question by continuing: "You ever heard of Mrs. Harriet Washington?"

"Can't say that I have," the puzzled driver responded.

"Well, you should! A great woman. Great!" Horowitz extolled. "And you especially should know about her. Since she is also black. Or are you one of those who now likes to be called African-American?"

To avoid a potential argument the patient driver changed the subject by pointing out, "We're coming to the toll gate. You got it, or should I?"

Annoyed at having his harangue interrupted, Horowitz replied impatiently, "I got it, I got it," as he dug into his pocket to find two dollars and fifty cents for the toll.

After they had paid the toll and started south down the FDR Drive, Horowitz resumed, "Mrs. Washington is the person who made my miraculous recovery possible. Did I say miraculous? A small word for what she accomplished. She bullied me, tortured me from morning till night. But in the end she cured me. So that now not even you could tell that I once had a stroke."

"Fantastic," the driver extolled, hoping that would end the conversation while thinking, *However he feels about barbers and cab drivers, why is it that most passengers think that cab drivers are also part-time psychiatrists? People tell me things they would never tell their closest friends. And I have to listen. All for the price of a taxi ride and, if I am any judge, in this case a small tip.*

"Tonight," Horowitz continued, "tonight we are going to hear Itzhak Perlman. You ever heard him?"

"Of course," the driver replied.

Horowitz seized on the driver's response. "You are also a lover of classical music?"

"Classical?" the driver replied. "I only heard him play a jazz concert once. A charity up at the Apollo Theatre, in Harlem. Real jazz. None of that rock stuff. So he plays classical, too. Good to know."

"Does he play classical?" Horowitz replied. "One of the best. Isaac Stern, David Oistrakh, Itzhak Perlman. The three best in the world." Unable to resist at least a bit of chauvinism, he boasted, but in a tone he considered modest, "Goes without saying, all Jews."

"Is that so?" the driver pretended surprise.

For the first time Horowitz realized that the driver had been pulling his leg about Perlman. To outdo him he joked, "You know I wasn't always such a follower of classical music myself. When I first heard Mozart's full name I said to myself, 'Can't be. Must be the name of a law firm, Wolfgang, Amadeus and Mozart.' "

When he was not rewarded with a laugh or even a smile, Horowitz continued impatiently, "How come you steered me onto talking about violinists? What I was really saying, a man like Phil Liebowitz does not belong in Florida. What will he do there? Lie in the sun? Which every doctor will now tell you is bad for the skin. Or play shuffleboard? A man who never shuffled in his whole life? Or go for a slow walk? Or wait for the early-bird dinner to save a few pennies? A man like Liebowitz belongs here. In New York. Where the action is. Not always nice action. Or safe action. But there is life here. Excitement. Things going on all the time. Concerts, lectures, museums. Life! You know what I mean?"

"Yeah. Sure. Life," the driver said, easing into the right-hand lane as they approached the Ninety-sixth Street exit in preparation for heading west toward Central Park.

"Hey, what are you doing?" Horowitz protested.

"You said Eighty-fourth and Central Park West, didn't you? If we don't get off here, next exit is Seventy-ninth Street."

"I said Eighty-fourth Street and Central Park West?" Horowitz disputed. Then he conceded, "Maybe any other day I would have said that. But today, somehow, I don't feel like going home right away. So let's . . . Take me to Fifty-fifth and Eleventh Avenue."

Surprised, but not unused to occasional sudden changes in passengers' plans, the driver continued south, becoming sympathetic to the state of mind of his troubled passenger.

Chapter 2

XXX

THE CAB WAS HEADING WEST ON FIFTY-FIFTH STREET APPROACHING the Hudson River. An ocean liner in dock, its prow standing as tall as a ten-story building, loomed just beyond the West Side Highway.

The cab was halfway down the block when the driver turned to ask, "How far do we go?"

"Almost to the end," Samuel Horowitz directed. "See there, the building close to the river. The big sign where it says S. HOROWITZ AND SON. That's me. S. Horowitz. As for Son, no son. Not in the business. He is an important lawyer. With a big firm in Washington. Any white-collar crook you ever heard about, chances are my Marvin defended him. But an honest business like paper and twine was never good enough for him. Of course, nowadays it is no longer the paper and twine business. Now S. Horowitz and Son are packaging consultants. Means the same thing. Anyhow, pull up here."

The cab came to a stop in front of an old warehouse where a huge delivery truck stood backed into the loading platform. The name S. HOROWITZ AND SON was emblazoned on the truck's side. A crew of two men and a driver were hefting stacks of cartons, heavy cases of paper, twine and sealing tape into the cavernous vehicle.

As Horowitz stepped out of the cab, he dug into his pocket and pulled out a twenty-dollar bill. Though the meter read only sixteen seventy-five, Horowitz said, "Keep the change."

"Thanks," the driver said, but did not take off. Instead, concerned about his passenger's condition, the driver waited to make sure he was all right. Self-conscious at the driver's attention, Horowitz demanded, "Something wrong?"

"Nothing wrong," the driver said, though he felt that this was a truly troubled man, possibly even disoriented to judge from the way he had rambled on about unrelated topics, his sudden change of destination, his obviously strange state of mind.

Samuel Horowitz walked slowly past the huge truck, looked up but saw no familiar face there. He felt a slight twinge of disappointment. In other, earlier, years he would see Sol behind the wheel. Or Silvio, helping to load. Or Manuel. He knew every one of his drivers and helpers well, knew their families, their habits, their religious holidays, their weaknesses and their strengths. They were loyal to him and he to them. To see an unfamiliar face behind the wheel caused him to shake his head sadly.

Things change, yes. But everything? And in only six years?

It had been six years ago, right after his wife Hannah died, that Samuel Horowitz had turned the business over to Irving Stiner and Fred Brady, his two top men. Irving in the office, Fred in charge of salesmen. Together the pair took over the business as trustees for all the employees. Sam Horowitz believed that men who helped to build a business should profit from the business. Since his own son had no desire for it, instead of just liquidating it or selling out to someone else, he had decided to let it continue to make a profit and provide jobs for his loyal employees.

All he had asked for himself was that in good years he be paid out of profits a predetermined sum that would, in the end, leave the employees the owners of the business. Only one restriction did he insert into the agreement. That the business would always be called S. Horowitz and Son. He did not want to be forgotten in the paper and twine trade. Secretly, he hoped that from time to time, when the name crossed some customer's desk, that man would say, "Now, take Sam Horowitz, there was a man. Good as his word. When he said the stuff would be there on a certain day at a certain time it was always there. A man you could depend on, Sam Horowitz."

The day he had handed over the keys to the business to Irv and Fred he had said, "Boys, it's all yours now. I promise I won't come back to butt in. To tell you what you are doing right or wrong. The only time you will see me is at the annual company dinner, if you invite me."

Yet, after six years, on this day he was back.

The unfamiliar faces of the men loading that truck stabbed at him. *Sure, men retire, men die, but a whole new crew?* He wondered, *Do these men really remember, do they ever talk about me?*

He entered the office. It had been totally redecorated. At the new reception desk another new face. Instead of old Ida, he found a plump, pretty, dark-haired, olive-complexioned young woman, obviously Hispanic. He was surprised when she greeted him. "Oh, it's you, Mr. Horowitz!" She jumped to her feet in respect.

"You . . . you know me?" he asked. "How could you? You never saw me before."

"Your picture, Mr. Horowitz," the young woman explained. "In Mr. Stiner's office." She motioned to one of the doors be-hind her.

"My picture?" Horowitz remarked, curious. "And your name, my dear?"

"Filomina," she replied. "Filomina Cortez."

"Filomina," Horowitz repeated. "Nice name. How long you been here?"

"Oh, I was born here," she protested.

"I know, I know. I meant how long have you been working at Horowitz?"

"Year and a half," she replied, proudly.

"I should drop by more often," Horowitz said, a bit sadly. "Sit down, my dear, sit down. Relax." She slipped back into her chair. "Such a pretty girl. You married?"

"No."

"You will be," he said, patting her gently on her dusky cheek. "And Irving?"

"Mr. Stiner is in. Shall I buzz?"

"No. I want to surprise him," Horowitz said.

To himself he remarked, *In my day we called everybody by his first name. Even me. I was Sam to the office staff, the salesmen, the truckers, the warehousemen, the office boy. Now it's "Mr. Stiner." Nothing is the same.*

He reached the door, hesitated before opening it to prepare himself. Then he greeted Irving with a circus master's "Ta-rah!"

Stiner leaped from his desk chair. "Sam . . . Sam! What are you doing here?"

The now middle-aged, portly president of S. Horowitz and Son came across the room to embrace Horowitz and kiss him on the cheek. He leaned back to appraise his face. "Sam, you look better now than the day you retired. Why aren't you down in Florida? Or out in Arizona? What are you doing in this dirty, grimy, dangerous city? Come, sit down. Coffee? A drink? Miss Cortez! A coffee for Mr. Horowitz. Skim milk and no sugar. See, Sam, I remember."

The sound of the phone interrupted Irving Stiner. Horowitz almost lunged toward the desk to answer it. It could mean an order, a large order. In his day, Sam Horowitz would have been back at his desk and on that phone in a second. But very calmly Irving Stiner reached into his shirt pocket to withdraw a small flat black cellular phone that fit into the palm of his hand. He opened it, raised it to his ear and spoke into the other end.

"Stiner here."

While Stiner listened to the caller Horowitz thought, *Imagine, walking around with a telephone in your shirt pocket. In my day I was tied to my desk like a dog on a leash. Every time the phone rang I jumped to answer it.*

Stiner's conversation continued, giving Horowitz the opportunity to look around what had once been his own office. The first thing he noticed was the large photograph of himself on the wall behind Irving's desk. Just under his photo was a bank of computer screens.

Stiner continued to reply to the caller. "Uh-huh . . . got it . . . uh-huh . . . no problem." When he had heard it all, he said,

"Just a moment." He turned to the bank of monitors, punched in some numbers. On the screen there appeared a complete inventory of all stocks on hand and on order for S. Horowitz.

Stiner spoke into his cellular phone, "Ziggy, on the 48–6s, unlimited quantities. Between 48–9s in stock and on order we can deliver by the end of the week. Plastic sealing tape? No sweat. And as for heavy-grade brown wrapping paper, like always, if S. Horowitz hasn't got it, nobody's got it. All you can use. Listen, Ziggy, fax me the order now and you'll have delivery starting in the morning. Good. Good. Prices? Same as last time, Ziggy."

As Stiner returned the phone to his shirt pocket, he pressed a lever on the intercom on his desk. "Luther, before you go out to lunch, see me. We got a big order to put together before the end of the day."

Stiner now returned his complete attention to Sam Horowitz. "Yeah, Sam, so I was asking, what about Florida?"

"Too damp," Horowitz explained.

"Arizona?"

"Too far," Horowitz said, then asked, "Ziggy? Ziegenfeld? He's still in business?"

"His son," Stiner explained, then called out, "Where is Mr. Horowitz's coffee? Miss Cortez!"

In a moment the young receptionist entered, carrying a plastic cup of steaming coffee.

"Thank you, my dear," Horowitz said as he took the cup from her. She smiled shyly and withdrew.

"Sit down, Sam, sit down. Make yourself at home. After all, for how many years was this your home?"

"More than I like to count," Horowitz said, staring at the bank of computers. "With those you can keep track of the whole inventory? In my day I used to call, 'Hey, Luther, how many 48 by 6s we got up there?' "

"Not anymore, Sam. It's all computerized. Anything you want to know, just punch it in and up it comes. And, Sam, this is going to make you very happy. Since you left the business we have increased our volume three hundred and twelve percent. In only six years. Not bad, huh?"

"Not bad? Very good. Terrific!" Horowitz tried to enthuse.

Except that he did not feel enthusiastic. The business had done better without him.

Not exactly something to make a man jump for joy.

"So you also got a telephone that fits in your pocket and you can walk around with. And this office. All new. And very nice. Very nice. And a receptionist you call 'Miss Cortez.' "

"Have to," Stiner confided in a lower voice. "These days you call a girl by her first name she could claim you harassed her. So everything is very proper around here. Not like in the old days when you could make a joke with a secretary. Or give her a pat here or there. Now it's all Miss. I mean Ms. Very proper. Do you think I would dare ask her to get *me* a cup of coffee? Women's Lib wouldn't like it. But in your case, since you are the founder of the business and no longer a part of it, I felt free to ask her. Believe me, Sam, it's not like you remember. Changed, all changed."

"I can see that," Horowitz said sadly. "It was nice of you to at least put my picture up on the wall, Irving. I appreciate that."

"Why shouldn't your picture be up there?" Stiner replied. "Without you, no business. Sam, do you know how many families live off this business? Last Christmas when I was drawing up the bonuses I figured it out. Thirty-nine families live off S. Horowitz and Son. And if you add in the ones who have retired on the pension plan, it comes to fifty-eight. Yes, Sam, you can be very proud."

Horowitz was tempted to reply, *Then why do I feel so empty today, so sad? Was it just Liebowitz? Or did his leaving only point up something? And why did I come here today of all days? What did I expect, that Irv would beg me, "Sam, please come back. We need you. We can't run the business without you." They don't need me. They get along better without me. With all their computers and their walkaround telephones.*

"Yes, Sam, you should be proud. Very proud," Stiner repeated.

Horowitz attempted to belittle Stiner's praise. "Proud, *shmoud*, I didn't want to be bothered running a business anymore." Yet secretly wishing, *If only I did have someone to bother me now. Customers calling. Orders coming in. Giving instructions to assemble and ship. Like in the old days.*

The phone summoned Stiner again. He turned to the intercom on his desk to order, "Don't disturb me while Mr. Horowitz
is here." But a man's voice interrupted, "Mr. Stiner, we got a
problem."

One of the drivers was reporting by car phone that his truck
on the way to make a delivery in the Rockefeller Center area had
broken down. Stiner took the information. Gave the driver instructions, dispatched another truck to off-load the merchandise
and complete the delivery. All without leaving his desk or using
more than his nimble fingers. When he had dispatched help and
called the customer to inform him that the shipment might be an
hour late, he was free to turn back to Horowitz.

"Okay, Sam, where were we?" Stiner asked. "Oh, yes, about
being bothered with the business. I always thought it was Hannah—you know—her sickness. And after—I could see how that
would exhaust a man."

"Yes, Irving, Hannah's dying was part of it," Horowitz admitted. "Nothing was the same after that . . . nothing. Besides, I
felt, give the young fellows a chance. After all the years you put
in, the years Fred put in, the men in the warehouse, like Luther,
why should I stand in their way? They have kids to send to college. Maybe they would like a nicer home. A longer vacation. A
bigger car. As long as they run a good business they deserve it.
Besides, old Sam Horowitz could never have learned to handle all
these newfangled gadgets. Computers. And walkaround telephones. And car phones from the trucks. No, it would have been
too much for me."

All the while he thought, *Oh, if only I could be starting in
business now, how much more I could have accomplished. It's like being
an old man and watching all those girls with their skirts up to their
pupicks with their long legs with those beautiful thighs and thinking, If
only . . . Is that what the rest of my life will be? If only? Maybe life
wasn't meant to be so long. Maybe I have overstayed my time.*

After greeting and exchanging memories with some of the
older help, asking about their children and their progress in school,
about their wives, being surprised to learn that some of them now
had grandchildren, after all that, Samuel Horowitz took his leave

and started walking east along Fifty-fifth Street, the street on which he had spent so much of his life.

Though his visit had helped to refresh his contacts with his old friends and employees, it had only served to add to the deepening sense of depression he had experienced since saying goodbye to Phil and Rose Liebowitz as they passed through the boarding gate to the plane bound for Florida.

If he had not had his previous appointment with Harriet Washington for dinner and the Perlman concert at Lincoln Center, he would have gone home, fixed himself some simple dinner and spent the rest of the night feeling even more depressed.

He tried to console himself with one fact. Bernadine would not be waiting for him. Since he was going out, she had asked to have the evening off to attend a church festival. He was relieved to agree. For he had noticed lately that though she did her best to prepare dinner for him and succeeded quite well most times, he had little appetite. So she was always disappointed, which made him feel quite guilty. Tonight, dining out, he would not have to face her.

Terrible thing for a man to feel like a fugitive from his own home, Horowitz thought. It was only a reflection of his mood lately. For Bernadine had been a fine housekeeper, loyal to Hannah when she was alive and after Hannah died taking care of him with great concern. She anticipated his every wish, and many times anticipated wishes he did not even have.

Seeking some solace, some hint of pleasure on this day, Horowitz consoled himself: *At least tonight there is Mrs. Washington.*

It was thanks to Mrs. Washington he had become the Sam Horowitz of today. In his late sixties, self-sufficient, walking without a cane, and with only the slightest hint of the outward swing of his leg that most other stroke victims exhibited in more pronounced form. Only people who knew him well from long ago would notice any difference in him. And as for handling a knife and fork, no one could do it better. Despite the fact that he had resisted Mrs. Washington every step of the way, she had held her ground.

More than once he had said to himself, *That famous old animal trainer, Clyde Beatty, who tamed lions with only a gun and a chair, was nicer than Mrs. Washington once she ordered, "Pick up those buttons and marbles!" "Crumple that sheet of The New York Times!"*

And when she issued a warning by just saying, "Mr. Horowitz!," in that special voice of hers, it was enough to strike fear into the heart of any man. And that woman could cook. As well as Hannah. And some dishes, God forgive me for saying, even a little better than Hannah.

The only bright aspect in Samuel Horowitz's otherwise totally discouraging day was to look forward to seeing Mrs. Washington once more.

Chapter 3

×××

Samuel Horowitz stood before the door-length bedroom mirror that Hannah had had installed years before. Meticulously, he tied his tie as he had relearned to do under Mrs. Washington's firm instruction. Had she not forced him to pick up marbles and buttons in order to regain his hand skills, he would not now be able to tie a tie with, he liked to boast, the same skill as the men who trimmed the windows at Saks Fifth Avenue. He could even produce that crease in the middle just under the knot.

Dressing to meet Mrs. Washington would always be the ultimate test for him. God forbid that she should detect that his tie was the least bit off center or that his shirt was not properly buttoned. One time he had met her and his button-down collar was not buttoned. Her mere look of rebuke made him feel like a criminal or, worse, a disobedient child. Since that time he had never appeared in her presence in any way less than perfectly dressed.

Tonight especially, after this depressing day, the challenge seemed to demand more effort than usual. Nevertheless, Horowitz persevered. Shoes shined, and equally important, laces tied. Trousers fresh from the tailor. Shirt hand-ironed by Bernadine only this morning. Tie now properly tied and creased. Face smoothly shaved with the very same electric razor to which Mrs.

21

Washington had introduced him. The only thing missing was a splash of aftershave lotion, as they said in the ads in those magazines. Samuel Horowitz was now ready to meet his dear friend and severest critic.

Mrs. Washington, here I come!

That form of address sounded much more formal than their relationship actually was. It had resulted from the very first time that they met. Samuel Horowitz was then in the early stages of his recovery from a stroke. Like all stroke victims, he had been suffering from the depression and hostility that usually accompany the onset of that condition. When he had attempted to call her by her first name, as a demeaning tactic, she very promptly and firmly corrected him by laying down the law.

"Mrs. Washington, if you please! I was married to a fine man named Horace Washington. I don't intend to forget it, nor do I want anyone to forget it. So it is Mrs. Washington!"

And so it had remained even though their friendship had become warm and close in the intervening years.

They were seated in Enrico's, an Italian restaurant across from Lincoln Center on the Upper West Side of Manhattan. It pretended to have been inspired by the legendary Italian tenor of the early twentieth century, Enrico Caruso. In his day, Caruso was famous not only for his voice but for his gargantuan appetite as well. Enrico's walls were covered with faked antique photographs and lithographs of Caruso in his various roles. The most prominent was the huge photograph of the revered tenor in clown's costume and with tear-stained face in his most famous role in *Pagliacci.*

Horowitz and Mrs. Washington were seated below that particular picture at a table for two near the huge window that faced Broadway. Outside, the early-evening going-home traffic weaved north at its usual crawling pace, buses monopolizing the street while automobiles, like bugs, tried to skitter through momentary openings to race to the next red light.

Sam Horowitz studied his menu while Mrs. Washington peered over the top of hers, so that he would not suspect that he was under scrutiny. From the moment that he rose to greet her when she entered Enrico's she sensed something different about him this evening. He was one of the most sensitive of all the stroke patients she had ever treated as a physical therapist. On the surface gruff, easily angered, quick to feel accused, he was, in reality, an extremely vulnerable man. Tonight he appeared more so than usual.

They ordered dinner. Horowitz was careful to avoid his favorite dish, eggplant parmigiana, since it contained loads of cholesterol-rich cheese of which Mrs. Washington would not approve. He even made an obvious point of asking their waiter for margarine instead of butter. These amenities out of the way, Horowitz asked, "So?"

Between them that single syllable was not merely a preamble but an entire speech. It was Horowitz's way of asking, "So tell me. How is your grandson Conrad doing at Columbia Grammar School? And what about his sister, Louise?"

That was always his first question. For he was enormously fond of both children.

In addition to insisting on paying their tuition at the fine private school they attended, in gratitude for what Mrs. Washington had done to ensure his recovery from his stroke, he had grown to know the children well, having shared many a dinner and Sunday outing with them and their grandmother in the last six years. He had watched them grow and develop well.

And why not? he often thought. *Raised by a hardworking widowed mother and a very exacting grandmother, why shouldn't they be bright, have good values and do well in school?*

Conrad had already sent out his applications and his transcripts to four of the best universities in the East.

"Conrad hasn't heard, not yet. But then it's still early," Mrs. Washington reported.

Even more impatient than she, Horowitz demanded, "Not yet? What are they waiting for? With a record like his they should answer the next day!"

"With so many applications they have to wait till they are all in."

"Believe me, if I was the admissions man in one of those colleges I'd grab a boy like Conrad before some other college gets him!" Horowitz declared impatiently.

Mrs. Washington noted, in addition to her first impression this evening, that Mr. Horowitz was even more impatient and quicker than usual to anger. Sure now that there was something wrong, she decided to apply a test of the symptomatology of what she had come privately to call the *Horowitz Syndrome*. It was a test more revealing of the Horowitz Syndrome than a CAT scan or an MRI is of physical disease.

Pretending it was a chance remark and—to make it appear even more casual—staring out at the evening rush-hour traffic, she said, "I was reading in *The New York Times* this morning—"

By now the Samuel Horowitz she knew would have interrupted with a brisk, brusque, sarcastic comment on that revered newspaper. For he always disagreed with the *Times*. On any and every subject. The economy. Foreign policy. Taxes. The election, any election. City, state or national. The Supreme Court. The Congress. Crime. Morals. The president. Religion. There was no subject the *Times* covered on which Horowitz did not hold forth, always in disagreement. Sometimes loud, sometimes acerbic, sometimes with a mere grimace of his expressive face. Sam Horowitz was never a man to be found wanting an opinion, a strong opinion, on any topic. Nor did he confine his belligerent opinions to the *Times*. More than once when she was taking care of him during his recovery, she had had to warn him against shouting back at the commentators on the television news, fearful that he might precipitate a heart attack or another stroke.

Tonight, when she mentioned *The New York Times* and Horowitz did not interrupt her at once, she decided to venture further.

"I was skimming through and on the Op-Ed page I found this article about how the Supreme Court said the Son of Sam law is unconstitutional. Invasion of First Amendment."

Surely, Mrs. Washington expected, *now I will get one of Sam Horowitz's choice tirades. At the very least. "Supreme Court? Idiots!*

All of them. Where does the First Amendment say that if a man commits murder it is the job of the courts to make sure he earns a million dollars as punishment!"

But this evening, no complaint from Sam Horowitz. Not a word. He simply continued to sip the single Scotch and soda he permitted himself before his evening meal.

Most disturbing, Mrs. Washington concluded. *This is not the Samuel Horowitz I know so well. Something is wrong. Terribly wrong. He will bear watching. And if I am not mistaken, he has lost a little weight since last time.*

She made two more attempts to spark a critical response from him. She was disappointed both times.

They sat in Avery Fisher Hall listening raptly to Itzhak Perlman playing his Stradivarius with emotion as well as dazzling virtuosity. From time to time Mrs. Washington's gaze strayed from Perlman to glance at Horowitz. It was now obvious, beyond question, he was a troubled man. But about what? She determined to discover before this evening was over.

During intermission, when they went out into the lobby for a cup of coffee (at such a late hour decaffeinated, of course), Mrs. Washington decided to express her concerns head-on.

"Mr. Horowitz," she began.

"Yes, Mrs. Washington?"

"What's wrong?"

"Wrong? Who said there was anything wrong?" Horowitz disputed.

"I miss your feistiness. The belligerence in your voice. Something is wrong. And don't deny it. You couldn't fool me before and you're not doing it now. *So?*" she demanded, using his form of interrogation.

"So *what?*" he evaded.

"So tell me, or else."

"Or else what?" Horowitz defied.

"Or else I will no longer tell you anything about Conrad and Louise. I will no longer accompany you to any concert or lecture or museum. I will not even come to the telephone when you call."

"You wouldn't!" Horowitz protested at once, then, recalling her iron will of earlier times, he conceded, "Yes, you would. I remember. Only too well I remember." He was silent a moment, took another sip of his coffee, then, "So?"

To which Mrs. Washington responded, "So?"

Grudgingly, unwillingly, hoping the dimming lights would come to his rescue by signifying that intermission was over, Samuel Horowitz began.

"Today, a day that will live in infamy, Phil Liebowitz and his wife, Rose, departed from, or should I say deserted, New York City. Just flew off. To Florida. Imagine a grown man in his right mind moving to Florida. If that isn't enough to depress a man, what is?"

Too wise to be so easily misled, Mrs. Washington added, "And with Liebowitz went one of the best pinochle players in the Western world. Right?"

"Best?" Horowitz scoffed, then granted, "Pretty good. Maybe even a little better than pretty good. But 'best'? Not Liebowitz. Let us just say . . ." Horowitz searched for the exactly correct word. He settled for one he recalled from theater reviews in the *Times*. "Let us just say 'adequate.' "

The lights in the foyer blinked several times, warning that the second half of the Perlman concert was about to resume. Horowitz was relieved to start back to their seats in the hall.

After the concert, over more decaffeinated coffee and bagels at the coffee shop across from Lincoln Center, Mrs. Washington gleaned her most crucial insight into Sam Horowitz's condition.

He had been lamenting how things had changed in the city. The rude attitude of people toward one another. The rising rate of crime. Kids being shot to death outside schools. People afraid to even go into the subway.

"But, my dear Mrs. Washington, worst of all, the way people have disappeared. That's the only word for it. Disappeared. Was a time when I was young, when Hannah was young, everybody lived in New York. Family. Friends. All lived in New York. People stayed. Sure, some moved from the Bronx to Manhattan.

Or from Brooklyn to the Bronx. But the only time they left New York was when they died.

"In those days if you needed ten men for a *minyan*—you know what is a *minyan*, Mrs. Washington?"

"Ten men to hold a proper prayer service," she responded at once, having learned much Yiddish and many Jewish customs when years before she had worked as cook and housekeeper for a Jewish family while she studied to become a nurse.

"Well, in those days," Horowitz continued, "if you needed a few Jews to fill in the ten you could go out on the street, any street, and find them. Today, you would be afraid to even go out on the street. And if you did and found a few men, they would be too busy to come in for half an hour and be part of the service. I tell you, Mrs. Washington, things are not only bad. They are going to get worse."

Accustomed to such talk from almost all New Yorkers, Mrs. Washington took Horowitz's plaint to be no more than the usual dissatisfaction of people in all large cities in these times. But she was startled when, as he started to spread the margarine on his bagel, Horowitz said, "You know, only this evening when I was getting dressed to meet you I thought to myself, why not go out to San Diego and visit my daughter, Mona, for a few weeks."

That statement caught Mrs. Washington with her coffee cup halfway to her mouth. She set it down with such unaccustomed brusqueness it caused Horowitz to ask, "Something wrong, Mrs. Washington?"

"Oh no, nothing wrong. My cup just slipped."

But at the same time she realized, *If Sam Horowitz is even considering going out to visit his overbearing, domineering if loving daughter for as long as a few weeks, and it is not even an important Jewish holiday like Passover, then he must surely be depressed. Only in the most dire circumstances would Samuel Horowitz contemplate such a move.*

Mrs. Washington observed him as closely as she could without arousing his suspicion.

Something has truly gone out of this man who used to battle me every step of the way during his treatment. What's happened to him? Can it be merely Phil Liebowitz's leaving? Or was that only the precipitating factor in his present depressed state? Is there more lurking just below the surface?

What he told me about visiting his old business today and discovering it was more efficient and bigger now than in his day, that must have been a shock.

All in all, there is reason for him to feel depressed on such a day. But what about tomorrow? Or worse, what about Thursday night when he would have got his usual call from Liebowitz's wife, Rose, to come to dinner and a few hands of pinochle, but there is no call?

How will he fill in the time? By watching television? A man can't spend his life railing at The New York Times *or talking back to those television commentators.*

Very dangerous situation. I have seen patients become depressed to the point of giving up and eventually losing the will to live.

Something must be done. And soon!

The next day, unannounced, Harriet Washington dropped in at the office of Dr. Herman Tannenbaum, specialist in geriatric medicine, and doctor to Samuel Horowitz. She explained the signs she had detected. All Tannenbaum could add to the situation was that, yes, Horowitz had lost weight, but his vital signs, blood pressure, pulse, heart action, neurological reflexes, were normal for a man his age. Tannenbaum never pretended to be a psychiatrist, but he had observed a sufficient number of elderly patients to agree with Mrs. Washington. Depression in the aging had become a serious condition. Virtually a disease in this time of dispersed families, perhaps a terminal disease.

Tannenbaum readily agreed, something must be done for Samuel Horowitz. But he had no solution to offer.

Puzzling over the matter, Mrs. Washington arrived at the conclusion that whatever was to be done, it must be something that made a man of great pride like Samuel Horowitz feel wanted, important.

Possibly if I talked to Irving Stiner, explained that Horowitz needed to be needed, he could figure out something for him to do. Possibly invent some crisis that would demand his return to the business. No, that wouldn't do. A man like Sam Horowitz would know it was merely makework. What this calls for is something truthful and genuine. Something that would stand up to the scrutiny of Horowitz's naturally suspicious mind. It must be a situation that really needs his efforts, his interest and his compassion. Despite his grumbling and faultfinding, at heart he is a good, kind, charitable man. There must be some way to channel his virtues into some good purpose.

"Something must be done," Mrs. Washington called to her daughter, Elysse Bruton, who was in her bedroom getting dressed to go on duty as night supervisor of nurses at the hospital up in Harlem.

Meantime, Mrs. Washington was overseeing dinner for her grandchildren, Conrad and Louise, before they went off to do their homework.

"Your milk, Conrad," she urged, then called to Elysse, "Like all stroke victims, he was naturally depressed about his affliction. And if I hadn't bullied him and given him the will to overcome, he would have wound up a crippled old man."

By that time Elysse had come into the kitchen, slipping into the navy blue sweater she always wore over her crisp white uniform.

"Mama, as long as you're solving everyone else's problems, work on mine. Nurses! Where do I recruit nurses with the limited budget I have?" Elysse complained, as she bent down to kiss Louise goodnight, adding a soft but urgent "Don't forget your math, baby. Got to bring up that grade." Then, noticing, she said, "Conrad, your milk."

"Milk!" Conrad replied, "Didn't you or Grandma read the latest? Doctors say that milk's no good for you."

Mrs. Washington intervened at once, "Not 'doctors.' Only *some* doctors. And they were talking about whole milk. That is skim milk. So drink it!'

As Conrad grudgingly lifted his glass as if it were filled with hemlock, not nourishing milk, Mrs. Washington turned to Elysse.

"Sure he shows sparks of life when he's with me. But lately,

I think, instead of his friend, I have become his crutch. I can't let that happen. Something must be done."

"Mama, who in the world are you talking about?" Elysse asked.

"Mr. Horowitz, of course."

"Of course. Sorry, but I've got only one thing on my mind. Nurses. Trained nurses. How do I attract them? What do I say? 'I can offer you long hours. Short pay. Hard work.' What nurse in her right mind is going to volunteer for a job like that?"

Mrs. Washington seized on the word. "That's it!"

"What's it?" Elysse asked as she turned from the mirror where she had been brushing her jet-black hair.

"Volunteers," Mrs. Washington said.

"Volunteers can't take the place of registered nurses or even of practical ones. It takes experience, more experience than any volunteer would have," Elysse pointed out.

"Not volunteer nurses. Your volunteer baby corps," Mrs. Washington corrected.

"For Mr. Horowitz?"

"Why not?"

"You think a man so short-tempered would have the patience for such duties?" Elysse doubted.

Protective of the man as always, Mrs. Washington replied, "He may *appear* to be irritable and at times short-tempered, but that's only because he is so sensitive."

"Mama, Mama, you are always defending that man. Sometimes I get the feeling that you might even be in love with him."

"Don't be ridiculous! If I have any special feeling for him it is because he reminds me of your father. Who was also a kind, very sensitive man, who died of a broken heart. Because he could never overcome the prejudice. Never get to be the man he had the ability to be. Perhaps now, in these times, he might have had his chance. But back then . . . ." Mrs. Washington's eyes welled up with tears, her voice broke slightly.

Elysse respected her mother's moment of grieving. Soon Mrs. Washington felt able to continue.

"I see the same signs in Sam Horowitz that I used to see in your father. So I feel it is my duty, both as a friend and professionally, to see what I can do to help him. After all, I didn't get him over his stroke just to see him give up now. If getting him involved in volunteer work will do it, that is exactly what I am going to do."

"Mama, I don't want to see you work yourself into a frenzy and then be disappointed if it fails."

"It won't fail!" Mrs. Washington insisted, more firmly than she actually felt. For with a man like Samuel Horowitz, who was now no longer predictable, one should be prepared for disappointments.

The next morning, on her way to treat her new patient, Harriet Washington stopped off at the hospital to consult Catherine Flaherty, administrator of volunteer activities.

Yes, Ms. Flaherty admitted, she could always use more volunteers to care for the unfortunate babies in her nurseries. Yes, she did feel confident of being able to handle a sensitive man, even a man as sensitive as this Mr. Horowitz whom Mrs. Washington was describing. It was at least worth interviewing him, Flaherty agreed.

The only question now confronting Mrs. Washington was *How do I get Samuel Horowitz to volunteer?*

Chapter 4

XXX

SAMUEL HOROWITZ SAT IN HIS FAVORITE ARMCHAIR IN HIS LIVING room overlooking Central Park. He was halfway through the Anthony Lewis column on the Op-Ed page of *The New York Times*. Instead of his usual sarcastic growling at the opinions expressed by that columnist, Horowitz was merely grumbling vaguely, a sign of his desultory mood. His telephone interrupted.

Damn it, Horowitz thought, *who could be calling at this hour of the morning? Someone with news of yet another friend dying? Happens too often these days. In fact, at the rate things are going I will soon have to buy a new navy blue suit. Just for funerals. On the other hand, maybe it is only a call from yet another charity.*

Some people resented such calls. But Horowitz was forced to admit that these days, on the rare occasions when his phone rang, it was a welcome sound. Even if it was his daughter, Mona, calling from San Diego. Some days even a call to come join a *minyan* in some strange home where there had been a death was a relief.

Better that, he thought, *than the silence, those hours when the phone just sits there and seems to stare back at me.*

"Hello?" he greeted in his desultory manner.

"Hello! Samuel Horowitz" came the brisk and confident voice of Mrs. Washington.

At once he tried to brighten in response to her briskness.

"Ah, my dear, to what do I owe the pleasure of your dulcet voice at this early hour of the morning? Perhaps to compliment me on my aftershave lotion last night? It does leave a haunting fragrance, as they say in those TV commercials where naked people dance around in the shadows."

Mrs. Washington was not deceived. He might do his best to sound lighthearted but the real fun was missing. He was like a singer enunciating the lyrics but singing the melody badly off key.

He is in even worse condition than I suspected. I had better get to it quickly, she realized.

Adopting a tone of great urgency, Mrs. Washington began at once. "Mr. Horowitz, I'm afraid I am forced to ask a favor of you."

"Anything. A character reference for Conrad, granted! A contribution. Name the amount. Advice? Have you ever known me to be bashful when it came to giving advice? Whatever it is, just ask!"

"This time, I'm afraid it is going to take more than money, more than advice."

"It's that serious?" Horowitz asked, alarmed. "Tell me! Quick! There must be something I can do."

"There is."

"So?"

"I don't know how to ask . . ." Mrs. Washington pretended to be at a loss for words.

"Since when have you had trouble talking to me? We are, after all, friends. Very good friends. And between friends there should be no problem communicating. Or even just plain talking. So, take a deep breath. Then speak slowly. And then tell me."

Mrs. Washington deliberately paused before continuing. Horowitz anticipated the worst of calamities.

"Does this have to do with the children? Louise? Tell me already. What happened?"

"This has to do with Elysse," Mrs. Washington began. She paused again to give Horowitz the opportunity to jump to his usual conclusions.

"Aha!" Horowitz exclaimed. "Some crazy patient in the hospital went berserk and attacked her? Right?"

"Wrong."

"Then she was mugged on the street on her way to the hospital. How is she? Where is she?"

"She has not been attacked. She has not been mugged."

"Then what is the crisis? What can I do for her? Never mind. Whatever she needs, just tell me. What?"

"She needs volunteers," Mrs. Washington said.

"Volunteers?" Horowitz asked, puzzled. "What's the matter, there's a war on someplace? We are maybe stopping more Arabs from being killed by other Arabs?"

"This has nothing to do with Arabs. Or with wars. It has to do with the hospital," Mrs. Washington corrected.

"Oh, the hospital needs volunteers?" Horowitz realized. "I'm not a surgeon. Or even a plain doctor. What can I do?"

"Babies, Mr. Horowitz. Babies!" Mrs. Washington explained.

"What do you want me to do? Volunteer my semen? You ask me, there's already too much monkeying around with nature these days."

"No, Mr. Horowitz, that is not what I had in mind. Now, instead of interrupting or assuming, just listen."

"Okay, so I am all ears. Plus a little curious, if you don't mind. Speak!"

"These days babies are being born with problems of all kinds. Low birth weight due to being premature. Some born to young teenagers. Some little ones born drug-addicted.

"I know, I know," Horowitz commiserated. "I read about it in the *Times* every day."

"The point is, the hospital nursery is full of babies separated from their mothers. They need care. Attention. But with all the new budget cuts there is just not enough staff to give those poor babies the care they require. So the hospital needs volunteers."

At once, as was his habit, Horowitz jumped to a conclusion. "Aha! Naturally volunteers must be fed, need money for subway fare, cab fare. So how much is required? And don't stint yourself. After all, what good is money if it can't be used for some worthy purpose?"

"Actually, this isn't a matter of money," Mrs. Washington replied. "It's a matter of time."

"Time?" Horowitz repeated, puzzled. "What means time?"

"*Your* time," Mrs. Washington pointed out.

"*My* time?"

Mrs. Washington could already sense his reluctance. She would have to talk quickly and very convincingly. Using her most professional attitude she ordered, "Samuel Horowitz, instead of standing there talking, get dressed! Get into a cab! Meet me at the hospital!"

"You mean, right now?" Horowitz equivocated.

"If not sooner!" Mrs. Washington ordered in the same way she used to bully him during the early days of his stroke therapy.

"Well, if you say so . . . But frankly, I don't see what I can possibly do."

She interrupted, "No time to talk! I will meet you at the hospital. Half an hour!"

"If you take time away from your therapy to meet me, it *must* be important," Horowitz conceded.

"So stop talking. Get dressed. Be there!"

"Okay, okay. You know, Mrs. Washington, you have a very annoying habit of nagging. From the first day I ever met you."

She interrupted once more, "Be there!"

"All right already. I'll be there. I'll be there," he promised.

Then he shouted into the phone, "Tyrant!" After Mrs. Washington had hung up, of course.

Half an hour later, to the minute, breathless and perspiring, Samuel Horowitz raced into the main building of the hospital complex in Harlem. Good as her word, Mrs. Washington was waiting for him, and staring at her wristwatch.

"I am not late!" Horowitz defended even before being accused.

"No time to argue. Follow me," Mrs. Washington commanded crisply. She charged in the direction of the elevators. Horowitz had no choice but to follow, trailing along, hurrying to keep up with her swift stride.

* * *

The crowded elevator stopped at every floor to drop off or admit staff members, visitors and others. Finally it brought them to the eleventh floor. Without a word, Mrs. Washington stepped out of the car. Dutifully Horowitz followed. He found himself staring at a sign that read NURSERY, with an arrow pointing to the right. Mrs. Washington turned swiftly in that direction, Horowitz trailing behind, trying to keep up.

At the entrance to the Nursery, a nurse in white uniform sat in charge. Mrs. Washington said only, "This is the man Ms. Flaherty spoke to you about. His name is Samuel Horowitz."

"Oh, yes," the nurse said, as if she had been prepared for his arrival. Curious as Horowitz was about what had been said about him, he had no chance to ask, for the nurse said, "Take him in. She is waiting for him."

Samuel Horowitz was suddenly reminded of a book he had once read by an author named Kafka, in which a man was arrested, held and tried, but without any idea of why or for what crime. Now people discussed him, expected him, had plans for him, and he had no idea why. Mrs. Washington did not give him time to dwell on his predicament. She started briskly through the entryway and down a long corridor. Dutifully, if confusedly, Horowitz followed.

They passed several rooms, the glass walls of which revealed that they were Neonatal Intensive Care nurseries. In each of them there were a number of isolettes containing tiny infants, some hours old, some days old. Tiny infants lay squirming in pain and discomfort, with tubes and wires attached to their pitiful bodies. Nurses hovered over those unfortunate newborns, rendering what care and solace they could. In some instances a single distressed infant was attended by several nurses and a doctor as well.

No wonder, Horowitz thought, *no wonder there is a shortage of nurses. The care even one of those little ones needs just to stay alive.*

But in his haste to keep up with Mrs. Washington he had no time to stop and stare.

Finally they reached another nursery, which seemed a quieter, less hectic place. Mrs. Washington paused at the desk outside this nursery. The nurse looked up from making entries in a chart. She recognized Mrs. Washington at once.

"Ah, Mrs. Washington," the nurse greeted warmly, then stared at Horowitz in a manner he judged to be critical. He was sure of it when she said, "So, he is the one."

Horowitz could endure no more, for he responded sharply, "I am not 'he.' I am Samuel Horowitz, if you please."

She ignored his protest as she said, "Yes. I was warned." Before he could respond, she spoke to Mrs. Washington. "I hope he is all you said he is. Otherwise . . ."

"Otherwise *what?*" Horowitz interrupted.

"Otherwise you might not qualify," the nurse said frankly.

"Me? Not qualify? Samuel Horowitz has never failed to qualify for anything in his entire life!" he declared.

"We shall see," the nurse responded calmly. Turning to Mrs. Washington, "I'll take it from here."

"Do be considerate of him," Mrs. Washington said. Without another word, she left.

Horowitz was about to call after her, but the nurse took charge of him with an officious "Follow me, please."

She at least said please, Horowitz consoled himself as he followed along, feeling as he had years ago when he was in grade school and the teacher would lead the class to morning assembly. In those days he used to go rebelliously. He felt even more rebellious now. But now, as then, he followed dutifully. The nurse led him to a closed door on which was inscribed in faded gilt lettering: VOLUNTEER SERVICES. She opened the door to allow Horowitz to enter, calling after him, "This is the candidate Mrs. Washington mentioned."

So now I'm a candidate. Horowitz fumed silently. *I am not running for anything. In fact, if I had a brain in my head I would be running away from something.*

"Ah, yes," the woman behind the desk said, rising to hold out her hand.

Finally, a person with an ounce of courtesy, Horowitz was relieved to admit as he shook her hand.

"Well, Mr. Horowitz, let's become acquainted."

"My dear young woman, I would like very much to become acquainted. Since you are the first person here who has treated me with even a—as they say—a modicum of courtesy and respect. Even in the old days when there was a Soviet Union the KGB was more considerate of a person's feelings. So before we become acquainted, just tell me what this is all about."

"This, Mr. Horowitz, is the first step in your being accepted as a pediatric volunteer."

"I have to be 'accepted'? What's the matter, you think I wouldn't measure up? You don't know Samuel Horowitz!"

"This is your first step in the process. Your interview."

"Okay! Fire away! Ask any questions you want. I have nothing to hide!" he defied.

"Then sit down. And let's begin," Catherine Flaherty said.

Still bristling, Sam Horowitz sank into the chair across the desk from a woman who appeared to be in her early forties, with hair that had once been a rich auburn and was now tinged with slight streaks of gray.

Unaccustomed to volunteers who were so feisty and combative, she sought to moderate his attitude by lowering her voice and asking softly, "Mr. Horowitz, may I ask what stimulated you to come here and apply."

"My dear Miss . . . Or is it Mrs. . . . or, God forbid, Ms.?" Horowitz began, pausing for the information.

"Catherine Flaherty," the woman informed. "It was once Miss, then Mrs. and now is Ms. So take your choice."

Horowitz stared at her for a moment, attempting to determine whether she was joking with him or being serious. And if so, he had to make a choice. Which he did.

"My dear Ms. Flaherty . . ." He studied her eyes to see if he had made the proper choice. She did not react beyond betraying a provocative sparkle in her bright green eyes. He continued: "To answer your question, what stimulated me to come here was the world's greatest tyrant and bully, Mrs. Harriet Washington. How a woman could be so understanding and sympathetic one moment and such a bossy tyrant the next I will never know. But when she says 'Go' I go. She said to come here so here I am. What else do you want to know?"

Faced with more response than she had bargained for, Ms. Flaherty took a moment before she continued: "You understand that this activity is purely voluntary."

"So I figured, since it calls for volunteers," Horowitz replied, feeling that he had scored a point.

"What I mean is, this is an activity in which we depend on the *attitude* of the volunteer to a greater degree than in any other."

"Are you saying you don't like my attitude?" Horowitz demanded. "I get up early this morning, I shave, shower and dress. I don't even finish my *New York Times* so I can rush up here to be on time, and you don't like my attitude? Maybe I don't like your attitude, did you ever think about that, my dear Ms. Flaherty?"

If she were not so amused, Ms. Flaherty would have terminated the interview. But she had been prepped by Mrs. Washington: "Challenge him! Challenge him!" So she continued. "The importance of attitude as I was using the word is that we are dealing here with newborns who for one reason or another are deprived of the care and nurturing that all infants require from the moment of birth. They need the closeness of other human beings. They need to be held, cuddled, talked to, fed, handled tenderly. If not, they can suffer a form of infantile depression called 'failure to thrive,' which can be fatal. What happens to them in their earliest days can play a great part in shaping their lives from then on."

"Did I say I was against that?" Horowitz demanded. "After all, I am a daily reader of *The New York Times*. I keep up with all the latest developments of medical science. Between the 'Science' section of the *Times* every Tuesday and the *Reader's Digest* every month I know more than most doctors. So we agree on the babies. Now, you mean to tell me that an infant only a few weeks old—"

Flaherty interrupted, "A few weeks, even a few days old in most cases."

"A few weeks, even a few days, what difference?" Horowitz demanded, impatient to get on with his own thesis.

"In the first place, the infants you may be dealing with will mainly be only days old," she pointed out.

"You don't have them in different sizes?" Horowitz asked. "I mean when they are so little, like scrawny three-pound chickens, they are very difficult to handle," Horowitz said. "I remember when my Mona was born, she was premature, three pounds seven ounces. But so loud. I could not believe that so much sound could come out of anything so small. And, I might add, things haven't changed with her. But I couldn't—I mean, when it came to changing her or even holding her—I was not very comfortable. So maybe if that's what it takes, you don't want me."

He was prepared to leave at once.

"Mr. Horowitz, we do want you. We need you. But we want *you* to have the right attitude."

"Back to attitude!" he replied in frustration. "Can't we get past attitude and find something I can do?"

"The reason we stress attitude is that young as they are, helpless as they are, sometimes sick as they are, or drug-addicted as they are, they are extremely sensitive. Even without your being aware of it, the attitude of the volunteer transmits itself to the infant. The *way* you do what you do for them transmits either love and caring or else fear and disapproval. We want our infants to know they are loved."

" 'Loved,' " Horowitz scoffed. "If they were loved they would not be here but home in their mothers' arms, nursing from their mothers' breasts, you should excuse the frankness. You think it is right to fool such little ones by making believe they are loved?"

"Now, Mr. Horowitz, you have put your finger on the crux of the situation. *Not* to fool them. But to really love them. For as long as they are our responsibility they must be truly loved. And that will be your responsibility. If you are accepted."

"*If* I am accepted?" Horowitz considered for the first time that he might not measure up. As Mrs. Washington knew, nothing stimulated Horowitz more than a challenge. Nothing started his adrenaline surging faster. "And what makes you think I might not measure up, my dear woman?"

"Attitude."

"Oho! Again attitude." Horowitz was becoming impatient with this persistent woman. "So test my attitude! You got some kind of X ray or one of those newfangled scan machines to test attitude? Use it! Or do you have some kind of intelligence test for attitude? I never flunked a test in my whole life! So do your worst, dear Ms. Flaherty, I am ready!"

She didn't reply in words but opened her desk drawer to produce an orange-colored card some eight inches wide and five inches high.

"Fill out this application card," she said. "There is a pen at the desk over there."

Samuel Horowitz took the card and started toward the desk, muttering to himself about the officiousness of women in this strange new world.

Chapter 5

✕✕✕

SAMUEL HOROWITZ STARED DOWN AT THE ORANGE CARD WITH THE
words printed in heavy black type: VOLUNTEER SERVICES. He peered
through the lower half of his bifocals to read the information
required across the next line of the form.

MEDICAL REFERENCE. SECURITY. UNIFORM. LOCKER. PARENTAL
CONSENT FORM. WORKING PAPERS.

He lowered the form, turned to Catherine Flaherty.

"This," he announced, "does not apply to me."

"Why not?"

"Because in the first place for me to get my parental consent
you would have to hold a séance. In the second place, as to working papers, the last working papers I had were fifty-nine years ago.
Maybe more. This form is for children, not for people like me. I
can see I don't belong."

He rose, approached her desk and handed back the form.

"Mr. Horowitz, do you have free time?"

"Do I have free time?" he repeated sadly. "Yes, I have free
time. Too much and too often."

"And do you want to perform an act of human compassion?"

"Nobody, absolutely nobody has ever accused Samuel
Horowitz of not having compassion. I give to all kinds of causes.
UJA. United Way. Federation. Catholic Charities. Salvation

Army. Red Cross. I spend half my time writing checks to worthy causes."

"What do you do with the other half?"

"Other half?" Horowitz asked, puzzled.

"The other half of your time," Ms. Flaherty said.

"My dear Ms. Flaherty, you are undoubtedly looking to start an argument," he accused, leaning across her desk. "Well, don't start up with Sam Horowitz. Because once you unleash me I am like a hurricane."

"Is that what you do with the other half of your time? Give imitations of hurricanes?"

"What are you, President of Women's Lib? Or NOW? Were you put on this earth just to torment perfectly nice, reasonable men? I'll bet your mother wasn't like you. She had respect for your father. And she knew when to hold her tongue!" Horowitz fumed.

"My mother was a young widow. She worked at two jobs to support me and my two brothers through school and college. And she didn't take lip from anyone, man or woman."

"And she brought you up the same way, I can see," Horowitz bemoaned.

"She also brought me up to expect a civil answer when I ask a civil question. So, Mr. Horowitz, I ask you again, what do you do with the other half of your time?"

Since she had asked the question in a very soft, noncombative voice, Horowitz felt compelled to reply in kind.

"With the other half of my time I try to find things to occupy my time," he confessed. "Now, look, can we go at this in another way? I mean, can you be less hostile, not so quick to argue with every word I say?"

Though he had transferred all his shortcomings to her, Ms. Flaherty seized the opportunity. "I am sorry. I shall try my best to be nicer from now on."

Taking that as an apology, Horowitz replied, "That's better. Now just tell me what to do and I will do it. As you can see, I am not an unreasonable man. But I like to be treated like the nice human being I am."

"We all do," Ms. Flaherty agreed, "so fill out this card and let's get going."

Horowitz took back the card, stared at the small type that requested routine information about him. He began to fill it out. *Last Name. First Name. Home Address. Telephone Number. Social Security Number. Employer's Name.*

There he stopped.

"Employer? I have not had an employer for forty-seven years. I have been in business for myself. And after that retired."

"Then just fill in those spaces that *do* apply to you."

He continued scanning the card. *Date of Birth:* Easy. *Referred by:* Even easier. Mrs. Harriet Washington, who had got him into this mess in the first place. He read on. *Reason for Selecting This Hospital:* He was tempted to write in *I did not select it; Mrs. Washington did.* But he continued. *Education and Training:* He stopped once more.

"Mrs.—I mean Ms.—Flaherty, I had very little education. I came here an immigrant kid, had grammar school, that's all. Then I had to go to work. You see, my father, he had consumption. I guess today you call it tuberculosis. So when he was sent away to the Jewish Home for Consumptives I had to go to work. If education is a requirement for this kind of work, I wouldn't fit in here. Especially where it asks for training. I never had any training. I went to work for Crown Paper and Twine as an office boy. Nobody trained me. All they said to me was 'Hey, kid, get this' or 'Hey, kid, go out for coffee.' Or sometimes 'Hey, Sammy, where the hell are those order forms?' But no training. I learned the business by being called 'Hey, Sammy!' And sometimes, I am sad to say, by being called, 'Hey, Jewboy, where were you yesterday? Another one of your Jew holidays?' Those were different times, Ms. Flaherty. But if a boy was smart, he watched, he learned. And the thing you learned was to save your pennies until you had enough to take a chance. Then go into business for yourself. Succeed or fail on your own. That's the way it was back then. And if you are smart, it still is. Now how do you expect me to put all that into this tiny little box where it says *Education and Training?*"

"Just ignore that and go on, Mr. Horowitz," she suggested.

He resumed studying the card. The very next box was titled simply *Languages.* He pondered a moment before speaking.

"English I speak. But if you mean foreign languages, there is Yiddish. Does that count?"

"Put it down. It may come in handy sometime."

He continued down the form. The next box called for *Special Skills and Interests.* He pondered that for a moment, then, "You know, Ms. Flaherty, I think we may be off on a wrong track here."

"Oh? Are we?"

"It asks here, *Special Skills and Interests.* My special skill and interest is in only one thing. Paper and twine. Which of course in these days also includes shipping cartons, sealing tape, all kinds of materials like bubble plastic, and even popcorn. So instead of talking about babies, why don't we talk about that?

"I don't understand," she replied.

"What's to understand? I am an expert on such matters. And this hospital, big as it is, must buy a lot of such merchandise. I bet you I could go into your Purchasing Department and save this hospital thousands of dollars a year. Just turn me loose. I know all the tricks of the game. What do you say?"

"I do not think they use volunteers in the Purchasing Department," Ms. Flaherty replied.

"They should. I could be a gold mine for this hospital," Horowitz protested.

"Mr. Horowitz, let's just stick to babies."

"You are a very unreasonable woman," Horowitz said. "But okay. The babies!" he conceded grudgingly.

"Just continue filling out the card, please."

He returned his attention to the card. At first he bypassed the space marked *Work Experience.* Then he went back and printed in THE BEST! He continued, until *Now Under Medical Care?* Here he hesitated. The next question was even more troublesome. For it asked, *Physical Handicaps?*

"My dear Ms. Flaherty, some of these questions—they are, what shall I say, not exactly definite. I mean, take for example a question like *Physical Handicaps?* After all, what is the definition of a physical handicap? Is it serious? Does it get in a person's way? Does it keep him at home? I mean, physical handicaps is such a broad term it could mean almost anything. Right, Ms. Flaherty?"

Aware of his medical history, via Mrs. Washington, the administrator was able to reply, "Mr. Horowitz, to my eye you do not seem to be a man with any physical handicaps. Certainly not any handicap that would keep you from holding an infant, cuddling it, feeding it. So, I think you can very truthfully state, *None.*"

"Good!" he replied.

He proceeded to the next question, which read *Recent Illness?* This took a bit of pondering. So he asked, "My dear Ms. Flaherty, if I was to ask you to define for me the word *recent,* what would you say? I mean, yesterday is recent. No?"

"Very recent," she agreed.

"Last week?" he asked.

"M'mmm. You could certainly call that recent."

"Last month?" he asked.

"Still recent," she replied.

"Now, question. What about a few years? Recent? Or not recent?"

Since she knew precisely which question had stumped him, she took her time as if pondering before replying, "Well, if there was an episode—"

"Exactly the word the doctors used." Horowitz seized on it. "An episode."

"If the episode left no serious effects or disabilities, I think you would be justified in responding no to that question."

"A very reasonable suggestion, my dear woman," Horowitz said.

He went on to complete the rest of the information until finally he came to *Family Physician? Name and Address.*

Again Horowitz had to carefully consider his response.

That doctor of mine, Tannenbaum, is always stressing how sick the patient is. So it makes him look like a hero if he saves a perfectly healthy person from imminent death. If they ask him, he will make it seem like I am at death's door and he is barely keeping me alive. He will make me out to be an invalid.

Finally and with great reluctance he wrote in the name *Dr. Herman Tannenbaum, 945 Park Avenue.* He could not resist adding *Not only the high-rent district, but the high-fee district, also.*

Catherine Flaherty stared at the orange-colored card. Especially at the last comment about Mr. Horowitz's physician. She hesitated before broaching the next subject.

"Mr. Horowitz, you realize we will have to get in touch with Dr. Tannenbaum."

"Lots of luck! I try to reach him on the telephone and it takes hours, sometimes seems like days before he gets back to me. You got a better chance that the president of the United States will call you back."

"Fortunately, we do not have to call him. We have a standard form that we send to physicians to fill out. So I will need your permission."

"A form . . ." Horowitz had not considered this unexpected development. *Oh, that Tannenbaum, he could make a little sniffle sound like triple pneumonia.* So he replied, "My son Marvin, the lawyer, always says before I give permission for anything I should read it over carefully. So can I see this so-called form?"

"Here is the 'so-called' form, Mr. Horowitz," Ms. Flaherty said, passing him a printed sheet.

Horowitz adjusted his glasses to get a closer view of the form, then cleared his throat officiously before proceeding to study the required information. The first lines were not disconcerting. They were addressed to the doctor, with a blank space for his name. They stated that his patient had applied for volunteer service at the hospital, that the New York State Health Code demanded certain information prior to his commencing work. Would the doctor please supply the following information.

After a routine question as to how long the doctor had known the patient, it got down to business. Despite Horowitz's effort to control it, he felt the paper rustle in his now damp fingers. He readjusted his glasses, cleared his throat once more. Then he spoke.

Preceding his words with what he intended to be a casual if not debonair chuckle, he said, "My dear Ms. Flaherty, if this is all you want to know, don't bother a busy man like Dr. Tannenbaum. Because if I know him he will send you a bill for consultation. I personally can answer all those questions. Even better than he can."

"Mr. Horowitz, we need a doctor's signed statement."

"You want a signed statement, *I* will give you a signed statement. Look, I'll fill it in right now. You got a pen?"

"Mr. Horowitz, please . . ."

"Don't bother. I got my own pen." Out of his inside jacket pocket he took the gold-encrusted and revered pen that Hannah had bought him for his sixtieth birthday. He unscrewed the cap ready to fill in the spaces on the form as he read them off.

"I quote, Ms. Flaherty. 'Does the applicant have any impairment which might represent a potential risk to themselves, patients, the hospital?' The answer: Definitely not! I quote again, 'Or otherwise interfere with the performance of his or her duties?' I am glad to see, my dear Ms. Flaherty, that you do not slight the women's movement. His or her duties. Very nice. Now to answer the question. Samuel Horowitz has no health impairment. So it goes without saying it could not interfere with the performance of his duties.

"Now, as to the other questions, this next one about being addicted to nonprescription drugs or alcohol, let me tell you, my dear woman, I am not addicted to anything. As for alcohol, a drink of Scotch and soda before dinner. Which is on recommendation of the very same Dr. Tannenbaum. But it does not affect my behavior. If anything, it makes me what they call in the commercials 'mellow.' Even more pleasant than I usually am."

"I would hope so," Catherine Flaherty replied, making a mental note to discuss this candidate with Mrs. Washington.

"Now to continue. The date of my last physical? Exactly two weeks and four days ago. And my condition? Perfect! Blood pressure 110 over 72. Perfect even for a man fifty years old. Maybe even forty years old. So you don't have to worry about me. Now the last two questions: 'May applicant work directly with patients?' Who better? And as for the very last question, that, my dear Ms. Flaherty, is what we used to call in Brooklyn, when I was a kid, a hanger. A basketball shot that could not miss. A sure thing. Listen as I quote: 'May applicant transport patients in wheelchairs or stretcher?' My dear woman, you are talking to an expert. After my stroke I was in a wheelchair for weeks. I can turn a wheelchair on a dime. I can guide it between the sofa and the armchair in my living room, with only inches to spare. If you are looking for a wheelchair expert you have come to the right man. If you don't believe me, ask Mrs. Washington. She can tell you!"

"Oh, be sure I will certainly be talking to Mrs. Washington. And at the very first moment."

Ignorant of the warning lurking in her words, Horowitz said, "Then there is obviously no reason to bother a very busy doctor like Tannenbaum. And no need for this."

He started to fold the form preparatory to tearing it when Ms. Flaherty held out her hand. Reluctantly, he handed the form back to her.

"And now?" he asked forlornly.

"I will have to send this to Dr. Tannenbaum," she confirmed.

"Well, since we have disposed of that, is there anything else you want to know about me?"

"I think I know all I have to know, Mr. Horowitz."

"So?"

Puzzled, she responded, " 'So'?"

"So what is the next step? What do I do now? I am ready to go to work."

"Well, first I have some paperwork to do on your case. And some consultation. Then I will call you."

"How long will that take?" he asked.

"Several days at least."

"That long?" Horowitz considered. "Well, I waited sixty-nine years. I can wait several days longer."

As soon as Horowitz departed her office Catherine Flaherty picked up her phone and asked for the home number of head night nurse Elysse Bruton.

"Elysse. Is your mother at home?" Flaherty asked.

"No, she's on a new case with a stroke victim. Why?"

"I have just had a most—uh—shall I say, interesting or stimulating interview with a man she recommended."

At once Elysse replied, with a slight groan, "Don't tell me. I know. Samuel Horowitz."

"Exactly. Samuel Horowitz," Flaherty confirmed.

"I think you had better talk to my mother before you decide anything," Elysse said. "Shall I have her call you?"

"The sooner the better."

By the end of the day, after completing her work with her newest patient, Harriet Washington stopped by Catherine Flaherty's office at the hospital.

Throughout Ms. Flaherty's recital of her interview with Sam Horowitz, Mrs. Washington continued to nod her head. When the harried administrator finished, Mrs. Washington said, "Perfect."

"What do you mean, 'perfect'?" the astounded Ms. Flaherty replied.

"Let me explain about this man," Mrs. Washington said. "He is a softhearted human being whose only protection is appearing to be argumentative and arbitrary. He will resist anything new. But if you can overcome his initial resistance, he has a pride of accomplishment that makes him twice as good as most people at anything he is determined to do. If you handle him right, you will have a volunteer who has the ability, and what is more important, the desire, to help."

"What if he should become frustrated with one of the babies?" the administrator asked.

"He won't," Mrs. Washington assured.

Flaherty equivocated.

"I know the man. I spent months with him. Saw him recover from a bitter, defeated patient in a wheelchair to the man you saw this afternoon. I can vouch for him," Mrs. Washington insisted.

"Well, once I get this form back from his doctor . . . Uh, by the way, this Dr. Tannenbaum, is he really the ogre that Horowitz says he is?"

"Of course not. Like in everything else, Mr. Horowitz has a tendency to exaggerate. Tannenbaum is a very fine doctor. He is also very busy these days because he specializes in geriatric medicine. With more and more people living longer and longer, naturally his caseload is quite heavy. But he will find time to respond to your call. As for Mr. Horowitz, after what you've told me, I *know* he is ready."

*   *   *

Four days later, Samuel Horowitz received a call from Administrator of Volunteer Services Catherine Flaherty.

"Mr. Horowitz, would you come up to the hospital tomorrow for instruction?"

Chapter 6

XXX

During the entire bus ride uptown to the hospital Samuel Horowitz kept repeating the word that had nagged at him since Ms. Flaherty had used it yesterday. It had troubled him then; it annoyed him even more since.

Instruction.

The woman had the nerve to ask him to appear for "instruction." If she thought that Samuel Horowitz was going to sit in a classroom like some eight-year-old kid and be instructed, she had another thought coming.

Besides, what kind of instruction did it take to pick up a baby, feed it from a bottle, hold it a little, talk to it a little, and then put it back in a crib? He had done that with two children. Marvin and then Mona. And they turned out very well. So what was the big deal?

Of course, that Mona turned out to be such a driving over-achiever could take a little explaining. And Marvin, a fine man. A top lawyer in a Washington firm. His name in the papers every so often when one of his clients pleads guilty to some white-collar crime. But a man who reflects well on his parents and his up-bringing. The father of two such fine human beings does not need "instruction" on how to handle a baby.

Prepared to resist any suggestion she might make, Samuel

Horowitz presented himself at the office of Catherine Flaherty. She greeted him formally and then said briskly, "Follow me."

Again? Horowitz thought, *Ever since I first came to this hospital people have been saying, follow me. What do they think I look like, a natural-born follower? Not Samuel Horowitz. In the paper and twine business I was known as a leader. Twice president of the Paper and Twine Trade Association. So I am not a follower! Not me!*

However, he did follow Ms. Flaherty as she led him through what was now a familiar corridor. Until he found himself once more in the nurseries area. There, Flaherty slowed her pace, going from one glass-walled nursery to another, evidently seeking a particular person. Finally she stopped at the last small nursery, which held four cribs.

"Ah, yes," Flaherty said. "Follow me."

Again. Horowitz thought rebelliously. Nevertheless he entered the room behind her. He noticed a small woman, attired in a neat yellow smock, sitting in a rocking chair. She held in her arms a tiny infant, its black face almost hidden in the folds of a white blanket. The woman rocked back and forth in a slow, gentle rhythm while she held to the infant's mouth a small bottle filled with cream-colored formula.

"Mrs. Mendelsohn," Catherine Flaherty said. "We have a new volunteer who requires instruction. Would you mind if I left him in your charge?"

"Why should I mind?" Molly Mendelsohn replied cheerfully. "I would be happy to help."

To herself, Catherine Flaherty said, *Don't be so quick to be happy. You don't know this irritable curmudgeon.* But aloud she said, "Good. This is Mr. Samuel Horowitz."

"How do you do?" the pleasant woman greeted.

"Fine," he replied. "And you?"

"Likewise," she responded.

"Well, I'll leave you two to become acquainted," Ms. Flaherty said. "When you are done, Mr. Horowitz, drop by my office before you leave."

As she turned to go, Horowitz asked, "This is it? The instruction?"

"What did you expect?" Flaherty asked.

"No classroom, no teacher?"

"Mrs. Mendelsohn will be your teacher," the administrator said, and was gone.

Horowitz stood there, feeling ill at ease. He watched as Mrs. Mendelsohn held the little bottle to the black infant's lips. It appeared to be asleep, its eyes not merely closed but clenched. Yet as she gently introduced the nipple into its mouth the infant began to suck. During the process Samuel Horowitz had an opportunity to study not only what the woman did and how she did it, but the woman herself.

A small woman, he thought, *but then she is sitting down, so how can one be sure? Maybe she only seems like a small woman. And with a—how shall I say?—with a kind face. If not exactly a beauty, there is a certain feeling of warmth there. Her age? Possibly middle sixties. Give or take. Yes, middle sixties, since her hair, while neatly arranged, is gray. Obviously not a dye job. One thing Hannah never did was to dye her hair. "Let Nature take its course," she used to say. "Besides," she would say, "who are we going to fool?" A good sign of a woman's character, not to dye her hair.*

When Molly Mendelsohn finished feeding the infant, she rose and began to pace, cooing, "Pretty girl . . . pretty . . . you will grow up to be a beautiful woman. Smile for me . . . come now, smile. Pretty, pretty girl."

Horowitz belittled her attempts, thinking, *Anyone who knows babies knows that babies only a few days old don't smile. It is a good thing to talk to an infant. But at least make sense. This woman has a lot to learn about babies. And she is going to instruct me? Ridiculous!*

After Mrs. Mendelsohn had held the infant over her shoulder and burped it, she carried it back to its crib. Carefully she undid its blanket, changed it from its tiny shirt, which had become moist during feeding, into a fresh, clean one. She wrapped the infant in its blanket, making sure it was tight around the infant. Then she returned the carefully wrapped bundle of humanity to its crib. She leaned over the crib and whispered, "Sleep well, Clarissa, sleep well."

Horowitz had observed the entire procedure but not without some silent comments of his own.

Not bad. This is a woman who knows how to handle a baby.

Almost. Feeding? I give her an A. The way she held the baby when she burped it? B-plus. Changing the shirt? Also B-plus. Cooing and talking? Possibly a B. But that last part? Clearly a D. Maybe even an F. She wrapped that blanket too tight. And she is going to instruct me? I will give her a little "instruction" first. I will let her know I am not a Johnny-come-lately in this business. She is not dealing with any amateur here.

So, as she came away from the infant's crib to turn her attention to him, Horowitz resorted to what he considered his most diplomatic manner. "Mrs. . . . uh . . . I forget the name. But if you don't mind a little constructive criticism . . . no, let's not call it criticism. Let us just call it, say, an observation."

"The name is Mendelsohn," she replied. "And now your 'observation'?"

"Being a father, and even a grandfather, I do not come to this situation without some experience. What they call in the media nowadays a little 'hands-on' experience," he stated as preamble. "I have found that it is not the best thing to wrap up an infant so tight. Like she was two pounds of hot corned beef that was going on a long trip to the country. A blanket should always be loose. Relaxed. So a child has a chance to breathe."

As if hanging on Horowitz's every word, Molly Mendelsohn repeated slowly, "Loose. So a child has a chance to breathe."

"Precisely. Just an observation," Horowitz said, to ease his reproach, which he thought he had delivered as considerately as possible.

"Tell me, Mr. Horowitz, when was the last time you took care of an infant?"

He was about to demand, "What difference does that make?" Instead he controlled his impulse and replied, "Certain things, like swimming or riding a bicycle, once you learn them you never forget. Besides, babies are not like automobiles; they don't change the model every year. They are still born the way they always were. They suck the same. They sleep the same. So they should be wrapped the same. Logical? No?"

The little woman stared up at him but did not respond to his questions. Instead, she said, "Follow me."

Again, follow me, Horowitz rebelled silently. Still he followed her out of the nursery, muttering to himself. *Very touchy woman.*

*Some people don't know how to take constructive criticism. I hope they
are not all like her here.*

Mrs. Mendelsohn led him into a small room outside the nursery. It contained only one piece of equipment. A sink. With a tap
but no visible controls to turn on the water.

On the wall across from the sink was a line of metal hooks on
which hung smocks of the same color and kind as the one she
wore.

She pointed to the sink. "Wash, please."

Horowitz stared at the sink. Then turned to her. "How can a
person wash when there is no way to turn on the water?"

"Try the floor," she suggested.

He glanced down, discovered two pedals. He tried one. Cold
water flowed from the tap. He tried the other, producing a flow of
hot water.

"Wash, please." Mrs. Mendelsohn requested.

Horowitz kept the water flowing, while by habit he reached
for a cake of soap only to discover there was none. "If I may be so
bold as to point out," he said, "a person cannot properly wash
without a piece of soap."

"Try the bottle," Mrs. Mendelsohn suggested.

He looked to the narrow shelf alongside the sink. There he
discovered a clear bottle labeled ANTISEPTIC SOAP. He threw a resentful look in Mrs. Mendelsohn's direction, picked up the bottle,
prepared to squeeze some of the solution into his hands.

"Don't you think you had better take off your jacket?" Mrs.
Mendelsohn suggested.

"I have washed my hands millions of times without taking off
my jacket, thank you," he pointed out.

"Above the wrists?" she asked.

"Why above the wrists?" he challenged.

"You'll see," she replied, at the same time gesturing firmly.
Take off your jacket!

With an impatient sigh and a shake of his head, Samuel
Horowitz slowly and laboriously unbuttoned his jacket, took it
off. He looked around, found an empty hook among the hanging
smocks. His jacket off, he turned back to the sink, ready to wash,
when the woman intruded once more.

"You won't risk getting your cuffs wet if you roll up the sleeves."

"How far do I have to wash? Up to the elbows?" Horowitz demanded. Realizing he had raised his voice, he modulated it to add, "Okay. As you have noticed, I am not an unreasonable man. I will roll up my sleeves."

"That's better," she said.

He forcibly restrained himself from making any response, but set about using the pedals to start the water, at the same time squeezing some antiseptic soap onto his hands. He washed quickly and was rinsing his hands when she suggested, "A little more wouldn't hurt."

Horowitz bristled. "What am I, a surgeon getting ready to do brain surgery?"

"You are a volunteer, getting ready to take care of some infant who is subject to all kinds of diseases that, without knowing it, you may bring with you into the nursery."

"Samuel Horowitz does not bring all kinds of diseases into anyplace. Let alone a nursery," he replied angrily. "I will have you know I am a clean and proper person."

Rather than engage in controversy, Molly Mendelsohn replied simply, "Just wash, please."

He repeated the procedure, this time deliberately exaggerating his every movement, examining his fingers, his fingernails, holding them off to stare at them critically. Then, he held them out to her. "Well, 'teacher,' do they pass inspection?"

She ignored his taunt to say, "They will do."

With especial sarcasm he replied, "Thank you, my dear woman." Then he added, "Last time I did that I was nine years old and in third grade. Every morning we had inspection. Hands. Nails. And hair. She was looking for lice. Well, I had no lice *then* and I do not have any *now*." He made the point by adding, "Or would you like to look?" He leaned toward her, turning his head from side to side. Which was not necessary due to the sparseness of his hair.

"Very nice, Mr. Horowitz," she said.

Feeling he had complied with all her orders, he reached for his jacket but the woman interdicted, "Not so fast."

"Look, lady, *I* decide when I put on my jacket."

"Not when you are going into a nursery to handle an infant. Certainly not when I'm around!" she declared.

"What more do you want?" Horowitz demanded, feeling exasperated beyond enduring. "I am a reasonable person but too much is too much."

"Instead of putting on your jacket, slip into one of these smocks." She indicated the pink garments hanging on the wall.

"You mean to say I have to wear one of those?" Horowitz asked. "Such a lady's type garment? On you it doesn't look bad. But on a man . . ." He shook his head adamantly.

"Mr. Horowitz, please?"

"All right, all right. Nag, nag, nag. Your husband must be very glad when you leave the house to come to the hospital. Tell me the truth; he was the one who suggested you should do volunteer work, right?"

"I am a widow," Molly Mendelsohn said simply.

"Oh, I'm sorry," Horowitz said.

But he thought, *Another widow. God save me from widows. I had enough of them right after Hannah died. They wouldn't leave me alone. They wanted to cook for me. They invited me to dinner. To lunch. They even wanted to make breakfast for me. Widows! My luck. But at least this one is easy to hate. I must ask Ms. Flaherty if I have to put up with this one any more after today.*

By that time he had taken a smock off the hook and was slipping it on when she pointed out, "You slip into it from the back."

"From the back?" Horowitz demanded resentfully.

She turned to indicate that her own smock opened not from the front but from the back, where the strings were neatly tied.

"I see," Horowitz said. "Like a hospital gown. I'm going to be a patient again. With my . . . my behind sticking out. You should excuse the expression. I had enough of that when I had my stroke." Having blurted out more than he intended, he added, "Of course, nowadays no one can tell. Thanks to Mrs. Washington. You happen to know her?"

"Harriet Washington? Yes. She's the mother of the night supervisor of nurses."

"That's her. A fine woman."

"Yes, she is," Molly Mendelsohn agreed. "Now, slip into that smock, please."

He turned the gown around, slipped both hands into the sleeves, then stopped abruptly. "Something is wrong," he declared.

"What's wrong?"

"The sleeves. Closed. I can't get my hands through."

Using her own cuffs as a model she pointed out, "These sleeves are held tightly with elastic in the cuffs so that nothing above that line can reach the infant. That's also why you have to scrub above the wrists. Your hands and any part of you that can touch the infant must always be antiseptically clean."

Horowitz had no rejoinder to that. So he carefully worked his hands through the sleeves, past the elastic cuffs and into the open. He tried to tie the sash behind him but could not. So, without a word, she did it for him.

"You have to follow this same routine each time," she instructed.

"Okay. Each time," Horowitz acknowledged. "And now?"

"Now I suggest that you return tomorrow." She paused, then added, "And probably the day after. So you can watch some other volunteers work. Observation is the best way we teach and the way new volunteers learn."

"Tomorrow and probably a day after." Horowitz considered her choice of words. "When I went to school in Brooklyn we had what we called 'slow learners.' They put them in a special class. Is that what I am? A slow learner?"

"I didn't say that," Mrs. Mendelsohn replied.

"You said, 'Come back tomorrow,' and then you added, 'and probably a day after.' Which to me means that others could do it in another day, but me, I might take longer. So? Am I a slow learner?"

"Mr. Horowitz, you are slow, but also too quick."

"Slow *and* too quick?" Horowitz challenged. "Slow is slow. And quick is quick. Make up your mind."

"If you insist. You are too slow to learn because you have too much resistance. And too quick to take offense, even though no one has offended you." She stared up into his eyes, defying him.

Caught off guard and with no ready response Samuel Horowitz stared back. Then he left the room, muttering, "Widows."

When he found Ms. Flaherty in her office she was on the
phone, saying, "Yes, I shall have to make other arrangements for
him tomorrow."

Aha, Horowitz surmised, *around here is like the CIA and the
FBI together. You say one word to someone and right away it is all over
the hospital. Well, two can play that game.*

When Ms. Flaherty hung up her phone and asked, "How did
it go today?," he was ready with his answer.

"My dear Ms. Flaherty, I am usually an easygoing man."

"Yes, I know. Mrs. Washington told me."

He could not immediately determine if the woman was toy-
ing with him or being straightforward. But he continued: "That
woman, that Mrs. Mendelsohn, she may seem like a very nice
person. And it is certainly good of her to volunteer her time to
care for the babies. But she is very stubborn. The worst thing
anyone can do is try to help her. To correct her. Especially when
she is wrong. Such a sensitive woman, it is difficult to carry on a
conversation with her."

"For example?" Ms. Flaherty invited.

"Well, I made a harmless little suggestion. Mind you, not for
my benefit but for the benefit of the baby. And right away she
resented it."

"What did she say?"

"She turns on me, asks me, 'When was the last time you took
care of a baby?' Now it must be obvious to any sensible person
that I am not a new father. Or even a new grandfather. So I know
a thing or two about caring for babies."

"This 'harmless' suggestion, what was it?"

"Ms. Flaherty, you won't believe this. But when she put the
baby back into its crib she wrapped her very tightly in her blanket."

"And when you disagreed?"

"That woman turned on me and said, very snippy, mind
you—"

"Snippy? Mrs. Mendelsohn? I doubt that," Flaherty corrected.

"Then what other reason for her to ask when was the last time I took care of a baby?"

"Because, Mr. Horowitz, since the last time you took care of a baby, things have changed. The world has changed."

"But babies have not changed!" Horowitz insisted, sure that he had scored a telling point.

"Mr. Horowitz, you saw some of those infants in that nursery. Black. White. Brown. All equal in one way. Not born into this world under what we would call usual or normal circumstances. Some are born drug-addicted. Some are the offspring of single mothers as young as twelve or thirteen. Some born premature for the same reasons. They are not babies born after a normal nine-month pregnancy during which the mother had good prenatal care. Not babies born into this world with a decent chance at life. A good family. A fair start. So with no sense of security. Many of them never will be returned to their mothers. Some because their mothers are drug addicts. Some because their mothers are prostitutes or otherwise unfit for motherhood."

Horowitz nodded sadly.

"What every infant needs—" Ms Flaherty continued.

"I know, I know," Horowitz interrupted, "being held, loved, talked to, fed, cared for; most of all they need the closeness of another human being. You explained all that the other day."

"Most of all," Ms. Flaherty pointed out, "in this early stage, they need a sense of security. Which unfortunately we cannot give them twenty-four hours a day. So when we put them back into their cribs we fold their blankets close around them to in some small way take the place of the human arms that held them during feeding."

"You mean . . . You actually mean Mrs. Mendelsohn was doing the right thing?" Horowitz was forced to consider.

"Yes, yes, she was."

"I see," Horowitz replied, uncomfortably. "Therefore you also mean that I . . . I was wrong."

"Rather than right or wrong, let's just say it was a matter of experience or lack of experience," Ms. Flaherty said, since he was obviously ill at ease with his discovery. "I'll tell you what. Our volunteers have established a custom. A coffee corner. The hospital supplies a coffee urn and the volunteers supply the coffee and cake. It makes a nice break when they come off duty. Why not join the group today? Perhaps you will find some other volunteer with whom you prefer to train tomorrow."

A coffee corner, Horowitz considered. *I can just imagine. A group of widows gathering around to have coffee and cake. And what else do they do? Gossip, of course. And what will they have to talk about today? Only one thing. That Mrs. Mendelsohn will tell them about Samuel Horowitz who made such a fool of himself. Who spoke too quick again when he was wrong. Like she said, too slow in some things, too fast in others. Well, I won't give them the chance to laugh at Samuel Horowitz.*

The possibility of that forced him to say, "Thank you for the invitation, Ms. Flaherty. But no thanks. I do not think I am cut out for this kind of work."

He rose and started for the door. Catherine Flaherty made no attempt to stop him.

Chapter 7

XXX

"WHAT DO YOU MEAN, HE QUIT?" AN OUTRAGED MRS. WASHINGTON asked when she was informed by Catherine Flaherty of Samuel Horowitz's decision.

"Simply said, 'I do not think I am cut out for this kind of work.' And just walked out."

"And you *let* him walk out?" Mrs. Washington demanded. "Didn't you realize you were dealing with a depressed man at a very difficult stage of his life?"

"Also," Ms. Flaherty pointed out, "a man who could not get along with anyone here. Not even a nice woman like Mrs. Mendelsohn."

"You mean he had trouble with *her*?" Mrs. Washington asked.

"Which gives you some idea of the problem he's been."

"It also gives me some idea of how much he needs our help."

"Mrs. Washington, may I remind you that I am running a volunteer service for the benefit of deprived infants, not for old men suffering depression," Ms. Flaherty pointed out.

"Catherine," Mrs. Washington replied in her most stern of stern attitudes, "when you get to be as old as I am you will learn that sometimes a health professional has duties that extend beyond those printed on some organizational chart. We have a duty to

63

both ends of the life cycle. I want that man restored to the volunteer service."

"If he can't get along with the other volunteers—" the supervisor started to protest.

Harriet Washington was in no mood to abide protestations
from anyone. "Catherine! You will find some job for him to do
that will be in keeping with his idea of dignity and importance."

"What kind of job?" Ms. Flaherty asked.

"There must be something. And it must sound important
enough to merit his respect and enthusiasm," Mrs. Washington
dictated.

"Well, I'll think about it." Ms. Flaherty conceded.

"And so will I!" Mrs. Washington said with considerable
determination.

Not quite three hours later, Mrs. Washington was instructing
her new stroke patient in hand-dexterity exercises. As part of the
therapy she was having him try to open his mail, a challenge that
caused him to force his stroke-impeded fingers to their utmost. He
could not quite bring it off and ended up breathless from the
effort. She opened it for him. The contents turned out to be from
the hospital. But this time, instead of a bill it was a printed questionnaire requesting his opinion of the services that had been ren-
dered him during his stay in the hospital. Together they began to
fill it out. Mrs. Washington asked the questions, the patient answered. By the time she had filled in the answers to all the questions, she herself had the answer to the nagging question that had
been troubling her since morning.

During her patient's rest hour, she used his telephone to
punch in the hospital number. She was greeted by a recorded voice
that instructed her, "If you have a touch-tone phone and wish to
inquire about a patient's condition, please press key one. If you
wish to speak to a staff physician, please press key two . . ." The
voice continued for a full four minutes before it finally came to, "If
you wish to reach Volunteer Services, please press key one, then
key six."

During this long period of recorded instruction Mrs. Washington thought, *If things improve just one more electronic step, no two human beings will ever again be able to talk to one another.* Dutifully she punched in numbers one and six. She was rewarded by the real live efficient voice of Administrator Flaherty.

"Volunteer Services."

"Catherine, it has just come to me," Mrs. Washington said.

"What has just come to you?" a puzzled Flaherty asked.

"What to do."

"What to do about what?"

"Not about *what,* about *whom.* Samuel Horowitz. You can stop worrying about him right now."

"Mrs. Washington, if you think that is all I've been worrying about today you are quite wrong."

"No matter. You will call him. You will offer him a new area of volunteer work," Mrs. Washington instructed.

"Oh, I will, will I?" Ms. Flaherty bristled.

"Yes, you will," Mrs. Washington insisted. "You will offer him a job . . . No, not a *job,* a *position* as . . ." She hesitated while creating a fit and proper title that might appeal to Samuel Horowitz. "You will tell him that due to certain staff changes you are in desperate need for a new Volunteer Coordinator in Charge of Patient Relations."

"A *what?*" Ms. Flaherty almost shouted back.

"A Volunteer Coordinator in Charge of Patient Relations."

"And exactly what does that title mean?"

"You know those forms hospitals send out to discharged patients asking for their reactions?"

"Yes. Of course. To help us respond to patients' comfort and needs in the future," Ms. Flaherty said.

"Somebody has to send those out, don't they?"

"Of course."

"Well, whoever does that is Coordinator in Charge of Patient Relations. For now that will be Mr. Samuel Horowitz," Mrs. Washington ruled.

"Well . . . I suppose . . . I suppose that could be arranged," Ms. Flaherty considered.

"Catherine, remember when your mother died, the trouble you had, we all had, with your father? Unfortunately, we did not succeed then. But we have a chance now to do something for a worthy but defeated man. Let's do it. What do you say?"

"For you, Mrs. Washington, I will try," Catherine Flaherty replied.

The next morning Samuel Horowitz rose very early as was his custom. He showered, shaved, and was dressed in the event the rabbi or the sexton called. A tenth man might be required to comprise a *minyan* for early morning services to enable mourners to carry out their religious duty and still report to work on time. The rabbi knew one man he could always count on. Sam Horowitz. Many mornings that call would come. Today it did not. So Sam Horowitz sat in the living room in his comfortable old armchair which he had not allowed to be reupholstered since Hannah's death, despite Bernadine's protests. Every indentation and crease in the faded upholstery fit his body as if molded by a sculptor. This morning he scanned his *New York Times* with listless interest. His combative attitude of former times was missing. He was an old warrior who had withdrawn to his tent to brood in silence. The news on the front page, distressing as it was, no longer evoked his usual reactions of concern, anger or condemnation. He skimmed through the editorials unmoved. He even read the Anthony Lewis column without experiencing rage or pity. He did not trouble to consult the financial section. He had no interest in whether his stocks had gone up or down. If up, he felt no richer. If down, so what? His grandchildren would inherit less. Which might be a good thing. They were too spoiled as it was. As for Mrs. Washington's grandson, Conrad, and his sister, Louise, no matter what the market did, the money for their college education was safely invested in tax-free bonds. Let the market go to hell, who cares?

Feeling thus, and the hour having passed when the rabbi might call, Horowitz treated the ring of the telephone as an unwelcome intrusion on his solitude. He answered it grudgingly.

"Sam Horowitz here. Who is there?"

"Mr. Horowitz?" Catherine Flaherty greeted him.

At once he recognized that voice.

"Aha! Ms. Flaherty, if I am not mistaken?" he challenged.

Realizing that he was still in his combative attitude of two days before, and with Mrs. Washington's insistent plea in mind, Ms. Flaherty decided to mollify him in the best way she knew. "Mr. Horowitz, I'm afraid I must ask a favor of you. And I will understand if you refuse. After all, I can't say that the other day we treated you as well as we should have."

"Not you, Ms. Flaherty, but that nasty Mrs. Mendelsohn."

Flaherty decided not to take up Molly's defense at the moment. "What I need has nothing to do with her."

"Good! So what is the problem? I ask, since I am a problem solver from the old times."

"A new duty has just been imposed on the Volunteer Services department of the hospital."

"Possibly to help in the Purchasing Department?" Horowitz suggested hopefully.

"More important than that," Ms. Flaherty said.

"Ms. Flaherty, I can tell from the tone of your voice and the choice of your words that you are a little shy to ask. Don't be. You will find me a man who does not hold grudges."

"Perhaps if you came up to the hospital we could talk face-to-face."

"Face-to-face is the way I always like to deal. What time?" Horowitz asked crisply and now very businesslike.

"Say two-fifteen?"

"You say. I will be there," Horowitz responded.

Promptly by two-fifteen Samuel Horowitz had entered the hospital, boarded the elevator to the eleventh floor and was striding through the corridor of nurseries. He glanced through the various glass walls, noted a number of volunteers at work feeding, caressing, changing the infants. He passed one room where Mrs. Mendelsohn was caring for another infant. As if to add insult to injury she was just bundling it firmly into its blanket. Horowitz ignored her and trudged on toward the office of Volunteer Services.

Ms. Flaherty was waiting for him. After a proper exchange of greetings, Horowitz settled down in the visitor's chair and opened the proceedings with a businesslike "So what's your problem?"

Ms. Flaherty explained the hospital's policy of maintaining good patient relations. That to do so demanded knowing patients' complaints as well as approval of their hospital experience. To do that required contact with them after they had been discharged. To carry out that activity demanded someone who could oversee the mailing out of forms that each patient was requested to fill out. It was a service of benefit not only to the hospital but to patients as well. For it would not only serve to improve the comfort of patients but speed their recovery as well.

"You are telling me!" Horowitz replied. "When I was a patient during my last . . . unpleasantness . . . when I had the good fortune to meet Mrs. Washington, believe me, if the hospital had asked me, I would have given them a few suggestions."

To which Ms. Flaherty responded silently, *I am sure of that.*

Aloud, she said, "Then you can see the importance of this work."

"I certainly can!" Horowitz agreed wholeheartedly.

"Mr. Horowitz, the question is, do you feel up to taking on the assignment of Volunteer Coordinator in Charge of Patient Relations?"

Samuel Horowitz greeted her question with what he considered the proper degree of gravity such a title demanded. After a significant pause he responded, "Ms. Flaherty, I believe you have found your man!"

"Then I will issue you a volunteer–identification photo. It will admit you to the hospital at all times," Ms. Flaherty said.

Late that afternoon, when Mrs. Harriet Washington returned home from her daily therapy sessions with an elderly woman who had recently suffered a stroke, she called Catherine Flaherty at the hospital.

Once she had identified herself, Mrs. Washington asked, "So?"

"It worked, Mrs. Washington. Worked perfectly. He seems not just willing but enthusiastic to take on the work."

"Good! And thank you for being so cooperative. I'm sure you won't regret it."

"I hope you're right."

Just before they said good-bye, Ms. Flaherty asked, "Mrs. Washington, did you ever notice that at times you sound exactly like Mr. Horowitz?"

"I do?" Mrs. Washington asked in surprise.

"The way you ask 'So?' and expect people to know exactly what you have in mind."

"Really? I never noticed," Mrs. Washington replied.

"You two have a great deal in common. Has that ever occurred to you?"

"Catherine Flaherty, if you are hinting at what I think, you are wrong. Oh, I have plans for him. But not that," Mrs. Washington said, hanging up before Flaherty could pursue the subject.

But while her hand was still on the phone, she thought, *Is what we have in common that I can see myself in his situation not too many years from now? Conrad will be off to college soon. And Louise is already so grown-up she needs me less and less.*

Chapter 8

XXX

On Tuesday morning, the day that Samuel Horowitz was due to commence his volunteer work as Coordinator in Charge of Patient Relations, he was most meticulous about selecting his wardrobe.

He had considered his navy blue suit but discarded that as too formal for a hospital setting. He gave fleeting thought to his gray herringbone jacket with a pair of dark slacks, but decided such an outfit was too sporty for the title Coordinator of Patient Relations. He finally settled on his medium-gray suit, which he considered combined good taste with a proper degree of importance.

To brighten it up with a touch of color, he selected a maroon tie with matching pocket handkerchief.

Thus attired, he stood before the full-length mirror in his bedroom, striking various poses. Finally approving of his own excellent taste, Samuel Horowitz was ready to embark on his new position.

He was on his way to the front door when his phone rang. Somewhat harshly, it seemed to him. He was seized by a suspicion, a disturbing suspicion. It must be Mona. Even at this hour, when it was only seven o'clock in the morning in San Diego, his overachieving daughter would be calling. The woman never slept. Before the sun rose in the morning she was up and on the go for one of the many charities she presided over. And as if by electronic prescience, whenever Mona called, Horowitz's phone did not merely ring, it seemed to clang. His hunch proved correct.

"Dad!" he was greeted so effusively that he thought, *My daughter does not need a telephone. An open window would do, even all the way from San Diego.*

The conversation followed its usual routine. She inquired about his health. About his activities. Somehow he had a sneaking suspicion that, as was her frequent habit, she had talked to Dr. Tannenbaum before she called him. Horowitz protested that he felt fine. Better than in a long time. And no, he did not have any plans to come out to San Diego.

"In fact, my darling Mona, I could not come out there now if I wanted to. You see, I have just taken on a most responsible executive position with a hospital up in Harlem. I am Coordinator in Charge of Patient Relations."

"Really, Dad?" Mona sounded impressed. But only until her paranoia took charge. "Dad! You can't do it!"

"Why not? I have all the qualifications. The hospital said I can. Ms. Flaherty, a tougher woman you never met, she says I can. So who are you to say I can't?" he demanded.

In that tone of voice Mona adopted when she was no longer his daughter but took on the role of his mother, she lectured indulgently, "Now, Dad, you listen to me. A man your age who has had a stroke cannot take on such a taxing job. I will not have it! I will talk to Dr. Tannenbaum at once."

"Mona darling, if you call Tannenbaum, I will leave home, I will become one of the homeless on the streets of New York. Without a telephone. You will never be able to find me again!"

"Dad! You wouldn't!" she protested, aghast.

"Mona, if you know your father, you know he never makes idle threats."

Because she did know him, was aware of his sometimes perverse tendencies, she was forced to yield. But she was far from finished.

"Now, Dad, if you insist on going through with this, I do not want you riding buses."

"You want me to walk? Okay."

"Walk? Through those Harlem streets? You could be mugged!"

"The last time I was mugged was right here on Eighty-fourth Street. Not up in Harlem."

"Dad, please! If you insist on going up there, promise me you will take a cab."

"Okay. Okay. I promise." He had absolutely no intention of carrying it out. For he believed there were two kinds of promises God did not insist a man honor. Promises made under threat of death. And promises made to a daughter like Mona. "Now, if I don't want to be late, I better go," he said.

"Okay," she said. "Love you, Dad."

Love you, Horowitz repeated silently. *Ever since this fad began that every television show must end with a son or daughter telling his father or her father, I love you, nobody could end any conversation these days without that little "Love you." It sounded no more sincere than a commercial. "Love you." "Love you." The more times you said it the less it came to mean.*

But, he said to himself, *on to bigger and better things, Mr. Coordinator in Charge of Patient Relations!*

For the first time in weeks, instead of greeting his doorman with a grumpy "Morning, Juan," Horowitz said, "Ah, good morning, Juan. Nice day, hey?"

The doorman was so surprised that he watched Horowitz all the way down the street to the corner until he saw him board the uptown Number 10 bus.

Samuel Horowitz presented himself to Ms. Catherine Flaherty with a cheery "Ah, good morning, my dear Ms. Flaherty. Let us begin!"

Prepared for his arrival, she escorted him to the entry room outside her office. There, on a neat desk, was a box of envelopes, a stack of questionnaires and return envelopes, and a batch of printed labels.

"Mr. Horowitz, each former patient listed on these mailing labels is to receive one of these. You fold the form neatly, place it in the envelope, insert a return envelope, then place the label on the outside. The labels are self-adhering so there is nothing to do but strip off the backing and stick them on."

To prove himself the apt and alert student he was, Horowitz repeated crisply, "Fold form. Insert. Return envelope. Label. Right?"

"Right," Ms. Flaherty said.

"Good as done," Horowitz said, and sat down at the desk to commence his duties.

For two weeks Samuel Horowitz presented himself at Ms. Flaherty's office every Tuesday and Thursday. Each time he repeated the same procedure, efficiently inserting questionnaires, return envelopes, affixing mailing labels. Each of the four days when his work was done he reported to her. Each day she thanked him and looked forward to seeing him again on his next appointed day.

Each time he left, his journey to the elevator took him past the nursery area where he could not help but sneak a look at the volunteer women who were engaged in tenderly feeding, holding, walking and talking to tiny infants whom they carried gently, like precious little bundles in their white blankets.

He felt superior to all of them. While they were part of a group, he was the sole volunteer who had what one could call an executive-type position. He was now an important part of what newspapers and television had begun to call the Health Care System. Those very words made his work important.

As he strode past the glass-walled nurseries he wondered if those other volunteers realized who he actually was. Well, if not yet, one day soon the word would spread, that that man Horowitz was doing an important job. And doing it well.

When he spoke to Mrs. Washington on the phone, as he frequently did, he tried to sound casual as he bragged. "Even back in the days when I was running my own business I always said the right man in the right job is worth his weight in gold. I am not saying I am exactly gold. But I will do until someone better comes along. If ever."

Mrs. Washington was pleased to note his acceptance of his

new situation. It fit quite well with her other plans. So it was a
matter of great surprise to Catherine Flaherty when Mrs. Washington presented herself one day as a potential volunteer for baby
care.

"You, Mrs. Washington?"

Mrs. Washington came prepared with a quite credible story.

"Between Conrad and Louise's schoolwork and their activities, they don't get home now until time for a late dinner. Which
gives me a spare hour or two on most late afternoons, once my
own professional duties are over. Rather than waste that time I
have decided I might as well put in a few hours a week taking care
of some of our unfortunate babies."

Since Mrs. Washington had been a registered nurse before she
became a stroke therapist, there was no question of her superior
ability to give the little ones all the care, love and attention they so
desperately needed. So Flaherty was quick to agree.

Mrs. Washington did lay down one condition. She was not to
be assigned to the same hours or days as Samuel Horowitz. That
was easily enough arranged since his work was confined to late
mornings of Tuesday and Thursday.

For several weeks the arrangement worked quite well. Samuel Horowitz arrived Tuesday and Thursday to put in his volunteer hours. Mrs. Washington arrived late every Tuesday and
Thursday, never earlier than four o'clock. Each performed his or
her duty without ever crossing paths with the other.

On evenings when Mrs. Washington and Mr. Horowitz met
to have dinner and attend a lecture at the 92nd Street YMHA or
the Ethical Culture Society, or to see one of the newer films in a
movie complex on Third Avenue or the Upper West Side, he
talked freely and at length about his work at the hospital.

But Mrs. Washington was quite careful to give no hint of her
own volunteer activity.

She was gratified to note the improvement in his attitude. But
she was still sensitive to those moments when, feeling he was not
under observation, he betrayed traces of a sadness still deep within
him. In his eyes. In his posture as he sat across from her in the
restaurant, or when he sat alongside her at the theater or a lecture.

Nor did he yet exhibit his old feisty combative attitude on questions of public or political interest.

Most revealing of all, he seemed quite resigned to let *The New York Times* run the nation without any help or interference from him. Something was still wrong. She must hurry her plan.

She hoped there was still enough time.

Chapter 9

XXX

FOR SEVERAL WEEKS SAMUEL HOROWITZ HAD APPEARED EACH TUES-
day and Thursday at the office of Catherine Flaherty, supervisor of
volunteer services at the hospital.

Dutifully he had folded the questionnaires, making sure the
edges squared perfectly so that they would slip easily into the
envelopes. He folded each return envelope into three sections,
added it, and sealed the envelope. Once he had affixed the label on
each he placed them all in the outgoing bin on his desk, to be
picked up by the mail clerk.

His job done, he would feel free to leave for the day. In so
doing it was necessary to traverse the nursery corridor. Though he
pretended to move through that area without taking notice of the
activity there, on this particular day he noticed for the first time
that two of the volunteers engaged in that activity were men. One
of them black, one white. Both of an age Horowitz considered
elderly. Though the white man was Horowitz's age, and the black
man actually several years younger.

Obviously, he grumbled to himself, *men who have no pride, if
they can put up with the bossy kind of women in there, like that Mrs.
Mendelsohn.*

*Fortunately, I don't have to. I have my own work. I do it well. Ms.
Flaherty is very pleased. I am a man with a title that befits my experience.*

When the replies come back I will be in a position to influence the way the hospital treats patients in the future. In fact, I can safely claim that I am serving not only the hospital but the patients as well. But is that enough? No!

Next week I will talk to Ms. Flaherty about some changes that I would like to make in that questionnaire. There must be something wrong if we are not getting any replies. I will make my recommendations to her. And when she passes them on to the Board, or whoever, I am sure they will be incorporated. We will get new forms and start getting some results finally.

The day I was appointed Coordinator of Patient Relations will be a turning point in the history of this hospital.

Thus determined, Samuel Horowitz left the hospital carrying in his breast pocket a folded questionnaire which he would study for the next two nights to discover its shortcomings. Thursday he would present the improvements which would, in his considered opinion, produce the desired results.

He looked forward to his Thursday morning session with Ms. Flaherty.

Thursday was one of those mornings when his phone rang early.

He knew it was the rabbi or the sexton at the synagogue calling to ask him to fill in for the *minyan*. It was a duty he never shirked. For it also afforded him the opportunity to say *kaddish* for his dear Hannah. Even though it was no longer required except on certain holidays and the anniversary of her death, it gave him comfort to do so.

He had fulfilled his function at the synagogue and was back at his front door when he heard the phone ringing. He unlocked the door and hastened to the phone, saying to himself, *Why am I rushing so? Just listen to that ringing! Who could make a phone ring like that except my Mona?*

He was right, of course. It was Mona.

She greeted him with an excited "Thank God I found you!"

"Why? Was I lost?" he asked.

"Dad!" she exclaimed in annoyance. "I meant I was glad that I found you before you went off to that hospital."

"And what is wrong with 'that hospital,' may I ask?"

Again, exasperated with his attitude, she replied, "Dad! Please! I have been thinking it over. I don't like it. I simply do not like it."

"Do not like what?" Horowitz asked, as if he did not know.

"That hospital!"

"Mona darling, the only thing wrong with that hospital is that they don't know how to get replies to their mail campaign. They need a little lesson in direct mail. Which, starting this morning, I am about to give them."

"You refuse to understand, Dad. I do not like the idea of your going up to Harlem to that hospital twice a week."

"Why not? I am doing some good and I am keeping occupied. What's wrong with that?"

"Nothing."

"So?" Horowitz demanded.

"All I am saying, find some other hospital to do it at. Some nice hospital in Midtown. Or across town."

"Mona darling, do you mean some hospital that is not up-town in Harlem?"

"Well . . . yes," she granted reluctantly.

"Mona darling, you know, for a woman who is always taking up with liberal causes, who fought so hard for busing and school integration in San Diego, who is on every committee for the underdog, it is not nice to say you don't want your father working as a volunteer in a hospital just because it is in a black part of the city. Not nice at all."

Reaching the apogee of her exasperation she replied, "Dad! My public activities have nothing to do with my concern about my father! I do not like the idea of your going up, exposing yourself—"

"I go up there fully dressed!" Horowitz protested.

"Dad! This is no time for jokes. I do not want you to expose yourself— I mean I do not want you to endanger yourself. As for doing volunteer work, I am sure you can find something to do at some nice hospital closer to home."

"Mona darling, please don't excite yourself over nothing. Your father is completely safe. It is a short bus ride up there. I like the work I am doing and I will like it even more once they put into effect some of the improvements I will suggest. So you go about *your* life and *I* will go about mine."

There was a momentary silence from Mona's end of the line. Which caused Horowitz to wonder, *For the first time in human history is my darling Mona speechless?* If she was, it was not for long.

"Well, Dad, at least promise me you will come out to visit us for a while. And soon."

"I promise. And soon," Horowitz said. But after he hung up he muttered, "The 'soon' applies to the promise. Not to coming out there."

Poor Mona. I know she loves me, worries about me. And I appreciate that. But she can't run my life. I am a grown man with a mind of my own. Come to think of it, no wonder both her children chose to go to college in Boston, three thousand miles from San Diego.

But he had no more time to devote to Mona. He was now ready for his bus trip uptown to present his suggestions to Ms. Flaherty.

He waited until Ms. Flaherty returned to her office from her inspection visits to the various nurseries. Horowitz knocked politely on her door. When admitted, he said a respectful and formal "Good morning, Ms. Flaherty. I wonder if you have time to discuss a matter of great importance to the Patient Relations agenda?"

He had adopted the word "agenda" from *The New York Times* and all the Sunday morning discussion shows on television.

Surprised, wary, but by this time accustomed to Sam Horowitz's vagaries, she granted, "Of course I have time."

Whereupon Horowitz settled into the visitor's chair opposite her.

"My dear Ms. Flaherty, does it strike you that something very peculiar is going on around here?"

"No, not really," she responded, even more puzzled than before.

"Well, for several weeks now, twice a week, I have been sending out forms and return envelopes to, by my count, over four hundred former patients of this hospital."

"And doing a very good job, I must say," she complimented.

"Thank you," Horowitz replied with his idea of a due sense of modesty. "But that is of no importance."

"We think it is," Flaherty started to protest.

"The problem is with this." Horowitz drew the folded questionnaire form out of his pocket. By now it was no longer the neat, unwrinkled sheet it once had been. It was wrinkled and marked up at those questions he had found faulty, and for which he had noted suggested improvements.

Ms. Flaherty reached very gingerly for the form.

Meantime, Horowitz continued: "Hasn't it ever occurred to you, my dear Ms. Flaherty, that we send out forms by the hundreds and as yet have had not a single reply?" Horowitz displayed the insinuating inflection of a prosecuting attorney.

"Oh," Ms. Flaherty replied, once she realized to what Horowitz referred. Rather than argue or, at this stage, even explain, she simply asked, "What did you have in mind, Mr. Horowitz?"

"That!" Horowitz said, pointing to the form she now held. "There is something wrong with the form we have been using. So I have made a few, well, more than a few, suggestions to improve it. Then we will begin to get some replies. Otherwise we are, as they say, spinning our wheels. You ever heard that expression, Ms. Flaherty?"

" 'Spinning our wheels,' " she repeated.

"What else, if we are sending out forms and never getting any answers?" Horowitz continued: "After all, how can we improve the hospital if we don't even hear from the former patients?"

Ms. Flaherty paused while trying to find the most diplomatic way to impart the facts to him. "My dear Mr. Horowitz, you are making an incorrect assumption."

" 'Incorrect'?" he challenged. "Do we or do we not send out forms by the hundreds?"

"Yes," she granted.

"And have we yet to receive a single reply?" Before she could respond, he continued: "Now, it happens that during my many years running S. Horowitz and Son I had the occasion to run several direct-mail campaigns. And I might say with very good results. So I know what could be considered a good direct-mail response. And we, I am sorry to say, are not getting a good response. Or even any response at all."

"Mr. Horowitz, I think you may be under a misapprehension."

"My dear Ms. Flaherty, I am not a man given to misapprehensions."

"In this instance I think you might be," she started to explain. "You see, while we send out the questionnaires, the replies go to the office of the hospital administrator."

Horowitz was silent for a moment as that fact sank in. Then, to make perfectly sure, he asked, "You mean, Ms. Flaherty, that all I am doing is filling envelopes with forms, with return envelopes, then sending them out. And that is the end of it?"

"I wouldn't put it quite that way." She tried to ease the shock.

"What other way is there, if I do that and I never see any of the answers?" he demanded. "In that case I am not doing any more than I used to hire high school kids to do when I ran my business. Fifty-cents-an-hour work it was in those days. Is that what I come here twice a week to do?"

"Mr. Horowitz, please understand—"

"What is there to understand? I am a mail boy. A fifty-cents-an-hour envelope stuffer. Except I do it for nothing."

"But it is a valuable service to the hospital," she protested.

"I can see it now, my dear woman. You have made a fool of me. You gave me a title but with no responsibility. I am very disappointed in you, Ms. Flaherty. And after I bragged so to Mona. And to Mrs. Washington," he admitted sheepishly.

"Mr. Horowitz, all I did was try to keep you involved in volunteer activities," she explained.

"Keep me involved . . ." he muttered. "Ms. Flaherty, you have misled a man who had only the best of intentions by coming here in the first place. I'm afraid I must resign my title and this entire volunteer work."

"I'm very sorry that you feel this way, Mr. Horowitz."

"However, as you may have noticed by this time, I am not a

man who leaves a job undone. I will complete my work for today. But you may assume that I have handed in my resignation as of right now."

So saying, Samuel Horowitz rose and strode from the room, a man who, though his pride had been severely damaged, still carried himself with dignity.

Catherine Flaherty stared at the closed door for an instant before she lifted her phone. She called Elysse Bruton at home to inquire as to the whereabouts of her mother. She reached Mrs. Washington at the home of her patient. Though disturbed at being interrupted in the middle of a therapy session, once Flaherty told her what had happened, Mrs. Washington understood.

"Find some way, any way, to hold him there. Keep him involved," Mrs. Washington insisted.

"Under the circumstances, I don't see how I can do that."

"You have at least an hour to find a way. Start thinking! Unless you want my entire plan to go down in flames."

"Entire plan? What entire plan?" Ms. Flaherty protested.

"If you can't keep him coming back, you will never know!" Mrs. Washington warned.

Chapter 10

XXX

Samuel Horowitz sat at his desk dutifully folding his last batch of questionnaires, inserting them into envelopes. As Ms. Flaherty passed his desk on her way out, he pretended to ignore her, a silent but obvious indication of his hurt feelings. It served to make her burden of guilt even heavier. Which gave further impetus to her mission.

She started down the corridor that led past the nurseries, the same corridor Samuel Horowitz would have to traverse on his way to the elevator when he left.

She arrived in the nursery area. She glanced hurriedly through the glass walls of the various rooms, seeking one particular volunteer. If memory served her, Thursday morning was the time Homer Wesley was scheduled to be on duty. Since her memory of Sam Horowitz's encounter with a female volunteer was fresh in mind, she realized her only chance to redeem the situation lay with Mr. Wesley. Her first quick view of the situation was disappointing. Wesley's lean, friendly black face was nowhere to be seen, not in any of the nurseries. Usually she could find him walking some tiny infant about the room, singing to it in his soft bass voice, smiling, revealing the gold tooth just to the side of his upper row. But not this day.

She might yet be forced to give this crucial assignment to a woman. Risky at best, after today's disappointment it might prove disastrous to entrust Sam Horowitz to a woman. Since she had no choice, she finally acknowledged, better a woman than to let him leave, never to return. She had reached that conclusion when she noticed Homer Wesley hurrying through the double doors, calling to the nurse at the reception desk, "Sorry, Maria, but you know the damn buses in this city. Four on a block, and then there's not another one for half an hour."

Catherine Flaherty rushed to greet Wesley. Taking him by the elbow she led him aside for a quiet word. He went willingly, though protesting, "I didn't start out late. I just arrived late. I'm sorry. It won't happen again, Ms. Flaherty."

Once she had reassured him his tardiness was not the cause of her concern, she explained what she wanted him to do.

Startled at first, Homer Wesley was intent on making sure. "You want me to stop this man? Put him to work here?"

"Exactly," Ms. Flaherty said.

"Well, I don't know," Wesley replied. "The way I feel, if a man doesn't volunteer, we don't want him here. Least I don't want him here."

"Take my word for it; Mr. Horowitz wants to do it. He just doesn't know that yet."

The tall black man shook his head dubiously. Then conceded, "If you say so. What'll I tell him?"

"I'll leave that to your good judgment."

"He'll be coming through when?"

"Figure half an hour."

Homer Wesley went about his routine with an eye to the glass window past which this man Horowitz must pass to reach the elevators. Wesley scrubbed carefully between the fingers on his thin, graceful, skillful hands. He had earned his living with those hands for more than forty years during which he had owned and run a small hardware and locksmith shop up on Amsterdam Avenue near 116th Street. He also did the odd repair jobs that proved too difficult for most handymen in the buildings in the neighborhood.

A man who had worked hard all his life, and had no aversion

to it, he had been forced into retirement by staggering increases in rent for his modest little store. Now he filled in his time with volunteer work at the hospital and at his church.

Having lost his wife almost ten years ago he looked to his daughter and her children for family relationships. But he would not move in with them. He was a man who liked his independence. Even if a goodly share of loneliness went with it.

He was a thin man, so thin that sometimes people wondered how he kept his slacks up, for he seemed to have no hips. His coffee-colored face was so lean that he had a wrinkle down each cheek so deep that was where the sweat would flow.

In his high school days he had been a football player, and now before he scrubbed he always removed his wristwatch and the ring he had won when he played on a city championship team.

Once finished scrubbing, Homer Wesley slipped into one of the smocks he took from the wall rack. He did all this without taking his eyes off the corridor beyond the glass wall.

He entered the nursery, went to the crib of the infant who had been assigned to him for his first hour. Carefully he lifted the tiny baby into his arms. Smiling, he whispered, "My, what a strong little feller you are." Holding him gently, he bent slightly to read the chart at the foot of the crib. As he had suspected from the infant's tortured squirming, this one had been born addicted.

Poor child, he thought, *you poor little child. To come into this world with such a handicap, and through no fault of your own.*

Wesley picked up the bottle that was waiting in the child's crib, went to the rocking chair, sat down with his fragile bundle in his arms. He had difficulty coaxing the nipple into the mouth of the restless infant. Finally he succeeded. After a few moments the infant began to feed. But soon it seemed to lose interest and slipped off into sleep.

At least it has given up twisting and squirming, Homer Wesley thought.

He held the sleeping infant, rocking slowly back and forth in a soothing rhythm. He was doing that and keeping his eyes fixed on the glass wall when he noticed a man appear. He realized this must be the Horowitz whom Ms. Flaherty was so intent on retaining in volunteer work. Homer Wesley rose, moved quickly to the crib, was about to put the sleeping infant down, but changed his mind. Instead, he went to the door. Using his free hand to open it he called, "Say, friend, got a minute?"

Minute? Sam Horowitz thought, *Friend, I got all day and the day after, and all the days after that. So if this man needs a minute, why not?*

"A minute I got. What can I do for you?"

Pretending to shyness, Homer Wesley lowered his voice. "I got a little problem I think a man of your age would understand."

"Such as?" Horowitz asked.

"Here I am in the middle of taking care of this little one and I got to go. Frankly, I would rather not ask one of the women. You understand?"

"Prostate trouble?" Horowitz suspected.

Homer Wesley was quick to nod, two aging men understanding and commiserating with each other. "So I wonder, would you take over for me? Just for a few minutes?"

"I'm not scrubbed . . . I'm not really ready—" Horowitz started to protest.

"Then go ahead, wash. I can wait that long."

Horowitz hesitated, until Homer Wesley urged, "Please, I can wait but not too long."

"Okay, okay, give me a minute," Horowitz replied.

"Take a little more, two minutes for each hand," Homer reminded. "And be careful around the fingers and nails," he called after Horowitz who had started to the scrub room.

In five minutes, Samuel Horowitz, scrubbed and wearing a yellow smock he detested, presented himself at the nursery. Homer Wesley very carefully passed the sleeping infant into Horowitz's hands.

"The bottle is in his crib," Homer Wesley said, then slipped out of the room.

Samuel Horowitz held the infant as if it were a fragile but valuable artifact. As the infant woke and started to squirm once more, Horowitz made his way to the crib, picked up the bottle and held it to the infant's mouth. The infant did not accept it. It squirmed even more, and with greater strength than Horowitz expected for a child only days old. He held it more firmly, yet was careful not to squeeze it. The child began to cry. But it was not the cry of a days-old infant. It was surely not the kind of crying Horowitz could recall from his own two children or his grand-children. It was higher-pitched. More torment than simply com-plaint. Unable to make it feed, or do anything to still its strange crying, Horowitz began to feel extremely self-conscious and un-comfortable. He feared he might have done something wrong. Or, as bad, that he might be *accused* of having done something to injure the child.

That black man, where is he? What's taking him so long? He should be back by now. He said only a few minutes. Meantime there is something wrong with this little one. I have never seen or heard one who cries like this one. If only there was something I could do to help. Nothing hurts worse than to hear a child cry and not be able to help. Especially with one so young who can't tell you what's wrong. Can't be hungry because it refuses the nipple. Can it be hurting? Where? Why? Maybe I better call one of the nurses. Oh, do I wish that black man would get back here already!

During the time that Samuel Horowitz was tormented by the discomfort of his tiny charge, Homer Wesley was on the phone, out of view of the nursery, talking to Ms. Flaherty.

"He's in there. With one of the crack babies. It may be the wrong way to get him started, but I had no choice."

"Give him enough time, then go back in and relieve him."

"Will do, Ms. Flaherty, will do."

Samuel Horowitz had one anxious eye on the glass partition and one eye on the child. He was desperately torn between watch-ing for the black man and at the same time trying to soothe his tiny bundle. Once more he tried to make it feed from the bottle. When it did not, he gently forced the nipple between its faint pink lips. This time the infant responded. Its lips seized on the nipple. In moments it ceased crying and began to suck.

Finally, a greatly relieved Sam Horowitz thought, *finally it has stopped crying and started feeding. Thank God.*

Reassured, he recalled the first time he had seen a volunteer at work, that Mrs. Mandelbaum, no, Mrs. Mendelsohn, she sat in a rocking chair when she fed the baby. Maybe he should do the same. Very gingerly he made his way to the rocking chair, eased himself into it carefully so as not to disturb the sucking infant. He started to rock. Slowly. Very gently. The infant continued to feed.

He studied the tiny white face, pinched, thin, only days old but already suffering. He shook his head sadly. He knew that every baby who was in here was in difficulty of some kind. For some reason it could not be with its natural mother. He wondered, *What is the story behind this little one?*

He felt considerably relieved when finally he saw the black man enter the room. Homer Wesley said not a word but gingerly parted the white blanket to stare into the infant's face. He observed how well the little one fed.

"Man, you have the touch," he said to Horowitz.

"Touch?" Horowitz asked. "What touch?"

"Man, don't you realize this is a crack baby?"

"Oh, I see," Horowitz said, but actually he did not appreciate the full import of Wesley's remark.

"These crack babies, they are especially tough to handle. Cry in strange ways, at strange times. Twist, turn, squirm. And they don't eat like other babies. And here you got this one quieted down and feeding. Yes, you sure got the touch."

"You really think so?" Horowitz asked, experiencing a sudden surge of restored pride.

"Definitely," Homer Wesley reassured.

"You want him back?" Horowitz asked, ready to surrender the little one.

"Hate to disturb him, since he is doing so well in your care," Homer Wesley said. "But I wouldn't mind watching. Okay?"

"Why not?" Horowitz said, proud to show off his newfound skill. He rocked for a moment, then felt called on to explain, "Experience. Nothing like experience. Had two of my own. You?"

"Just one. A girl," Wesley replied. "She's a school principal. Of a high school over in Queens. Very capable."

"Talk about capable," Horowitz responded, "if my son-in-law wasn't so well off financially my Mona would be president of the whole Board of Education. As it is, I'm surprised he hasn't bought her her own school. Mind you, she does a great deal of good. If only she did it without being so pushy. Has to run everybody's life."

"My daughter too. Thank God she's got that whole school to worry about. Takes the pressure off of me."

"I know what you mean," Horowitz commiserated. "By the way, here we are talking like this and we don't even know each other. I mean our names. Horowitz, Samuel Horowitz."

"Wesley, Homer Wesley," the black man replied.

Horowitz felt awkward for the moment. "I guess we should shake hands, but mine are full at the moment."

"Couldn't be put to better use," Wesley said.

"Tell me, Mr. Wesley," Horowitz asked, "how often you come here?"

"Twice a week. Tuesdays and Thursdays."

"Me, too. That is, I *used* to come here Tuesdays and Thursdays."

"*Used* to?" Homer Wesley questioned.

"Mr. Wesley, I am a person who believes in the truth. I tell the truth. *And* I expect to get the truth in return. I am not an unreasonable man."

"You mean to tell me someone in this hospital lied to you? I don't believe it!"

"Mr. Wesley, if I told you the trick they played on me, you wouldn't believe me, believe me."

The tall black man pressed his forefinger to his lips in a thoughtful manner before he spoke again.

"Horowitz, you notice something strange about this conversation?"

"Strange? What is strange? Two men meet in a hospital. They have a little conversation. For two old men what does our talk turn to? Our children, naturally. What is so strange about that, Mr. Wesley?"

"What I mean is, I keep calling you Horowitz."

"Why not? That's my name."

"Well, my name is Wesley. But you keep calling me *Mister* Wesley. Why? Are you afraid you might hurt my feelings because I am a black man? So you patronize me? That's no way to do. You really want us to be equal I will call you Horowitz and you just call me Wesley. Okay?"

"Okay! Wesley and Horowitz. Hey! Like those vaudeville teams years ago. Tell me, Wesley, you old enough to remember vaudeville when it was really vaudeville?"

"Do I remember? Best thing ever, vaudeville," the tall man replied, a broad smile on his lean black face, in memory of old times.

"Remember those old teams? Block and Sully? Lewis and Doty? How funny they were?"

"No. But I'll never forget Buck and Bubbles. Not only funny black men but great dancers," Wesley recalled. Then he added, "You know what is strange? Two kids growing up in the same city. One with only white memories, one with only black memories."

"It is sad. That men have to reach our age before we can talk like this. The kids of today, it'll be different for them, I hope." Suddenly he became aware of the tiny sleeping infant in his arms. "Hey, seems we bored this little one to sleep. You want to put him back?"

"He's kind of used to your touch. Why don't you do it?"

"Okay. I will."

Very carefully, Samuel Horowitz rose from the rocking chair, cradling the infant in both his arms. He went to the crib, where there was a fresh shirt waiting. He slipped the damp shirt off, careful not to waken the little one. Then he drew on the fresh dry shirt, very gingerly slipping its weak arms into the sleeves and gentling down the shirt around its very thin body. He opened the blanket and folded it around the tiny body which suddenly shook with a tremor. Horowitz paused, glanced toward Wesley, who indicated this was not an unusual or dangerous moment. So Horowitz very firmly folded the blanket about the infant as he remembered that Mendelsohn woman doing that day.

"You see, Wesley," he remarked, "wrapping them like this, it gives them a feeling of security."

"Yes, it does," Wesley agreed.

Horowitz covered the infant with the light blanket lying in the crib. He stood back, looked down to observe his tiny charge.

When he was satisfied that it was sleeping peacefully, he said, "Done."

"Done," Homer Wesley agreed. "And I can't thank you enough for spelling me. You know the old prostate. When it says go, you got to go."

"Glad to help you out, Wesley," Horowitz replied, turning to depart.

"I'll be seeing you again, I hope," Wesley ventured.

"I'll . . . I'll think about it."

"Be a waste if you didn't. Because, Horowitz, you sure got the touch for it," Wesley said.

"We'll see . . . We'll see," was all that Horowitz would concede before he held out his hand and said, "Whichever, it was a pleasure to meet you, Wesley."

"Same here," Wesley said, as he shook Horowitz's hand.

Wesley's firm grip made Horowitz aware of the championship ring on his hand. He held Wesley's hand, turned it palm down and realized, "Hey, this is an athletic ring. You won a championship?"

"High school team," Wesley admitted.

"Basketball, no doubt," Horowitz assumed. "I figured, seeing how tall you are."

"Football," Wesley corrected. "In my day, basketball players were all Jewish or Irish."

"Sure," Horowitz agreed. "Remember the Original Celtics? Some name for a team of mostly Jewish boys. And short ones. Man, how things have changed."

"They sure have," Wesley agreed. "When I was a kid I was considered tall. Now, with players seven feet tall I would be considered a midget." Then he added, "So, will I be seeing you here again?"

"We'll . . . we'll see," Horowitz replied.

Samuel Horowitz sat on the half-empty Number 10 bus as it made its way slowly down toward Central Park West.

He kept repeating to himself, *Horowitz, you sure got the touch for it.*

*   *   *

That evening, when he met Mrs. Washington for an early dinner before attending a play at an Off-Broadway theater down on West Forty-second Street, he said, "You know, up at that hospital there are not only women volunteers, but some men too."

"Yes, I heard," Mrs. Washington agreed.

"What I mean is, a man could do his volunteer work up there without even talking to a widow," Horowitz said, then added, "Mrs. Washington, you understand, when I talk this way about widows I am not including you. *You* are a special-type widow. But the rest of them . . . Ahhh!"

Mrs. Washington nodded, pretending to agree.

"So, I have been thinking, maybe it wouldn't be so bad if I did go up there, say an hour or two every Tuesday and Thursday. I think tomorrow I will call that Ms. Flaherty and say I forgive her for the trick she played on me. And I will be willing to be a baby volunteer starting Tuesday."

"A very generous act on your part," Mrs. Washington affirmed.

Thus reassured, Mrs. Washington decided, *Time to put Phase Two of the plan into operation.*

Chapter 11

XXX

FOR TWO WEEKS SAMUEL HOROWITZ HAD GONE UP TO THE HOS-pital in Harlem every Tuesday and Thursday midmorning. He spent several hours in the nurseries, wherever his services were required.

He had taken care of black babies, white babies, babies of Hispanic descent. Some were crack babies, some were otherwise addicted. All were separated from their mothers by some need. Some mothers were not physically or otherwise able to give them the care every newborn child needs for a healthy start in life. Some mothers were prostitutes, some drug addicts, some young enough to physically bear a child but too immature to care for it.

He had found that regardless of color or parentage the little ones were all alike in one respect: *Need*. They all needed to be fed. They all needed to be kept warm. They all needed to be changed. They all needed a sense of closeness and security that could only be imparted to them by a caring individual.

Horowitz also learned much about his own impatience, not with the little ones but with the adults who were responsible for their condition.

He would mutter to himself, or say it aloud to Homer Wesley, "Children having children. What kind of world has this become?"

Each day he appeared he not only faithfully practiced the sanitary requirements of the job but improved on them.

It was during the Thursday of his second week that he was accorded what he considered a special honor, to which of course he felt entitled. Ms. Catherine Flaherty herself was waiting for him when he arrived.

"Mr. Horowitz, I wonder if I could impose on you for a favor?"

His first reaction was *I think you have imposed on me enough, young woman*. But in what he deemed his most gracious manner, he replied, "My dear Ms. Flaherty, I am here as a volunteer. Anything I can do to help this hospital I am eager to do."

"Thank you, Mr. Horowitz."

"Now, what can I do for you, my dear?"

"Would you mind instructing a new volunteer?"

"Instructing a new volunteer?" Horowitz considered, flattered by the request. "I think I can handle that."

"I'm very relieved to hear that," Ms. Flaherty replied.

"Just—just answer me two questions. . . ."

"If I can."

"This new volunteer, is she a widow?"

"He's a man."

"Good!" Horowitz said. "Nothing sexist, you understand, but I would feel more, shall we say, comfortable not dealing with any widows."

"I understand. And your second question?" Ms. Flaherty asked.

"You don't have to tell me, if it is confidential information, but did you ever before ask a volunteer who was only here two weeks to instruct a new volunteer?"

"No, Mr. Horowitz, I have not."

"Well, it proves you have an eye for talent, my dear Ms. Flaherty. Bring on your new volunteer."

Benjamin Pringle was a man in his early sixties who had been offered, and accepted, early retirement from a large computer company that was slashing overhead by cutting down on jobs through attrition rather than firings.

A widower who lived on the East Side of Manhattan, he found himself with much free time and unprepared for a retirement he had not anticipated. Like many retirees he indulged in all those activities he had yearned for during his working life. But he soon discovered that early dawn voyages on fishing boats off foggy Long Island no longer held the charm they did when viewed from the perspective of a man who had a daily job. Golf, which he used to enjoy on Sunday mornings, became a chore now that he was able to play four and five times a week.

Mainly, he had to admit to himself, he missed a place where his presence and his contribution were valued, as they had been during his working years. His priest had suggested that he look into volunteer work at some hospital. Upon application and investigation he proved to be a likely candidate, and was about to experience his first instruction under Samuel Horowitz.

"Pringle, glad to meet you," Samuel Horowitz said, extending his hand. "In fact, as they say in the navy, nice to have you aboard. Wesley is not here today. A personal obligation. But you will like him. And here we do not call each other Mister. It is Wesley, Horowitz and now Pringle. And we do not have differences of color, religion or financial status. Here, everybody is equal."

Pringle nodded, though a bit puzzled by this prologue.

"Now, as they say, to get to the business of the meeting. First off, I guess you have already studied the Volunteer Guidelines."

"Yes, yes, I have," Pringle replied

"Very important," Horowitz said. "Scrubbing. How to hold an infant. How to feed them. How to change them. How to practice eye contact. All very important. All of which you will learn if you watch me very closely. Now, first, scrubbing."

With a knowing and confident gesture of his head, Horowitz directed the new recruit toward the scrub room. Once inside, Horowitz made a ceremony of removing his jacket and hanging it up. He held out his hands, turned them palms up, then palms down.

"And now to begin!"

He made a point of displaying the foot pedals, starting the flow of water from the tap, while holding his hands up to demonstrate. He pointed to the bottle and said, "Antiseptic soap. You may not know, Pringle, but ordinary soap is not antiseptic. Certainly not antiseptic enough to protect the little ones. Now, watch closely as I scrub. See? Use the brush very briskly. Between the fingers, like this. Then around the nails. And above the wrists. Very important. The way I look at things, we have to be as careful as a surgeon scrubbing for an operation."

As he continued to wash and apply the brush, he asked, "Tell me, Pringle, you remember the Doctor Kildare pictures?"

"Oh, sure," a puzzled Benjamin Pringle replied.

"I don't mean that series on television. That was for the kids. Those young whippersnappers—they think Richard Chamberlain is Doctor Kildare. Ridiculous! Chamberlain was an impostor. The real, I mean the real real Dr. Kildare was Lew Ayres. The genuine article. And as for Gillespie, there was only one real one. Barrymore. Lionel Barrymore.

"*Now,* I like to think, there is also Horowitz. After all, didn't Barrymore play Doctor Gillespie in a wheelchair? And didn't I exist in a wheelchair until Mrs. Washington, my torturing angel, showed me how to recover so I walk the way you see now?"

By that time Horowitz had completed scrubbing. He turned to the wall, took one of the smocks from its hook and slipped his hands into the sleeves. While forcing them through the tight wristlets he pointed out, "See? The way the sleeves are made so that your own clothes do not come in contact with the little ones."

Having donned his smock and tied it very carefully in the back, he said, "Follow me!" He led the way into the nursery to which he had been assigned for the morning.

As he approached the crib closest to the window he looked at the chart hanging on the foot of the crib. One glance and he said, "This one I know. Yes, Pringle, I have taken care of this one before. Cute little fellow. Not a very good eater. And he moves a lot. Squirms. If you know what I mean?"

"Frankly, Mr. Horowitz—" A reproving look made him correct his manner of address. "Frankly, Horowitz, I *don't* know what you mean."

Sadly, and shaking his head, Samuel Horowitz said, "Crack.

This poor little one was infected, addicted, even before he was born. That is why he has been here longer than most. Poor little one. Well, that is why we are here, Pringle. Let us get to it."

Horowitz lifted the infant out of its crib very carefully, following the instructions and pointing out to Pringle, "See? Support the infant very carefully. His back. And also the back of the head. While keeping the blanket wrapped around him. Warmth. They need warmth."

Holding the infant carefully in his right arm, he picked up the bottle in his left hand and started for the rocking chair. He slipped cautiously into the chair so as not to disturb the little one. But that motion alone was enough to waken it and it began to squirm.

"You observe what I meant, Pringle?"

Hovering over them, and studying the unfortunate infant, Pringle nodded, his sympathy evident on his face.

Horowitz gently slipped the nipple into the baby's mouth. Soon it began to suck. Once that started, Horowitz began to rock slowly back and forth. Eventually the infant ceased to squirm and seemed content to feed.

"Notice, Pringle, how he trusts me? I think he knows me. He has confidence in me. That is a good feeling, Pringle. A very good feeling. Which you yourself will soon come to know."

After the infant had gradually drained the bottle of its formula, Horowitz said, "And now for what we call Infant Stimulation. Very crucial. Establish eye contact. Look into its face and into its eyes. Let it know you are here. And you care. Even if you think they don't know you, make eye contact. And then, watch this carefully, Pringle—touch. Hold its little hand. Let the fingers curl around your finger. Touch the toes. Play with the toes. The human touch, Pringle. The human touch. Then try to make the eyes follow your hand. Or hold something in your hand to get their attention and get them to follow that. Let's see, can it work this time?"

Horowitz tried to attract the little black infant's attention. The tiny clenched eyes opened, then closed. Opened again, then closed once more. Then opened and remained open for a brief time but did not follow the slow movement of Horowitz's hand.

Sadly, Horowitz admitted, "No. Not this time either. One of the problems with crack babies. They do not respond like other babies do. Maybe next time."

But Pringle sensed that his instructor had little hope of evoking a genuine and promising response from this particular little one.

After Horowitz had carried out the remainder of the routine, talking to the infant, singing to it softly, he placed it back in its crib, emphasizing the need for wrapping it securely to give it a sense of security.

"So that is it, Pringle. The whole *shmear*. I mean the whole routine. It may not seem like much to you, but believe me, most of these babies get a great deal out of it. You will enjoy the work. As I do."

"Thanks, Horowitz, for taking the time," Benjamin Pringle said.

They shook hands.

"Oh, one thing I forgot to mention because it did not come up today. When you change diapers, you must always use plastic gloves. I think that protects you as well as the little one. Something to do with AIDS, I think."

After Pringle returned to report to Ms. Flaherty, Horowitz went to the nurses' desk to pick up the chart and discover his next assignment. He went on into another nursery to pick up another infant and give it care and attention. When he was done he returned to the first nursery, went to the crib nearest the window, stared down at the little black baby, weeks old, who writhed and strained and seemed to rebel against the fate that had been dealt him even before he was born.

Oh, you sad little one, you poor—what is the name on your chart?—you poor little Cletus Simon. What is going to happen to you? What? Horowitz asked silently.

Before he could bring himself to leave for the day, Sam Horowitz dropped by the Office of Volunteer Services to see Catherine Flaherty. She interrupted her work to greet him.

"I must say you made a very good impression on Mr. Pringle

today. I think you have found us a very enthusiastic new volunteer."

"Thank you, my dear Ms. Flaherty. But I did not come here to gather rosebuds, as they say. Flattery is very nice, always welcome. But I have a problem today."

Ms. Flaherty's first impulse was to respond. *And when haven't you had a problem?* But she replied, "If I can help in any way, just ask."

"Ms. Flaherty, what happens?"

"What happens? When? To what?"

"Let me say there is a little one in the nursery and his mother is, say, addicted, and the little one is suffering from the same. And then this infant improves a little. I notice some little ones are here one day and gone a few days later. Where do they go? What happens to them? What would happen to such a little one as is in there now?"

Ms. Flaherty gestured Horowitz to sit down opposite her. Then she explained, "We are of course a temporary facility. We take care of infants during the time it takes to dispose of them."

" 'Dispose of them'? Is that what they call it?" Horowitz asked, prepared to be indignant.

"What is meant by that word is that eventually they must either be restored to the family, or else put into foster care until such time as they can be reunited or put up for adoption."

"You mean they just give such a baby to some foster family?" Horowitz asked.

"Mr. Horowitz, they don't 'just' do anything with one of these little ones. All the facts in the situation are considered. Then the city's Human Resources Agency does what it thinks best for the infant. Why do you ask?"

"Well," Horowitz replied, "there is one little one in there I worry about. I have taken care of him several times now. And I have watched him struggle with his addiction. He seems to get better. Not much. Just a little. But better. I think by now he recognizes me. I mean, I can feel that he is different toward me now than he was last week. I think in some way he knows my touch. My voice. He seems . . . I know you are going to say it's foolish of me to think so, but he seems to welcome my coming. And I worry about what will happen if suddenly he is in the hands of strangers. You know what I mean?"

Catherine Flaherty had witnessed this phenomenon before. Wherein a volunteer formed an attachment to a particular infant and was reluctant to see it move on in the normal procedure.

"Mr. Horowitz, you must always remember that we are merely a brief interim step in a process that is not within our control. We volunteers give what help we can at a time when there is no one else to do so. We derive our satisfaction from the fact that we were there to serve when we were needed."

"Of course," Horowitz said. "I just thought I would inquire."

"And I appreciate your concern," Ms. Flaherty replied.

He started toward the door, where he stopped to turn back and ask, "So Pringle thought I was a good teacher?"

"He did indeed."

"Nice. Nice to hear," Samuel Horowitz said, and he left.

Next Tuesday, midmorning, Samuel Horowitz appeared at the nursery carrying a long, narrow package which was wrapped in bright paper colorful with myriad balloons of various sizes. There was no concealing that his package had been purchased at a toy store. The nurse in charge, Sally Haworth, who ran the day shift in the nursery, exercised strict discipline. She felt the fate of each child rested on her shoulders alone, so she challenged Horowitz at once.

"And what do you expect to do with that, may I ask?"

"A little toy. Well, not exactly a toy. A little form of therapy, shall we say?"

"Therapy?" Haworth challenged. "What kind of therapy, shall we say?"

"Well, there is on Fifth Avenue and Fifty-sixth Street a Doubleday bookstore. So, as they say, I chanced by there yesterday. And I was browsing through some books on Infant Care. One of them happened to catch my eye: *The First Six Years*. So in pursuit of our work here I naturally concentrated on the section "Day One to the First Three Months." And I find there an advice on how to stimulate the little ones. They mention a thing called mobiles. It also says black and white are the two best colors to attract such a young one. So, purely by accident, I happened to be going by this toy store up on Broadway later in the day—and it is not easy to find toy stores anymore, believe me. But there I am, and there is the toy store. So I happen to go in. And as luck would have it, there is such a thing there as a mobile toy. And by further luck, in black and white. So, I figure, what could it hurt to bring such a toy? Especially to that little Cletus Simon, for example. So I thought, why not? We will, as they say, give it a shot.''

Sally Haworth stared at him, disapproval in her sharp eyes.

He hesitated before asking sheepishly, "We don't give it a shot?''

"We do not go through the strict regimen of scrubbing, wearing protective smocks, making sure volunteers do not have communicable diseases and then introduce into the nursery a toy that may carry all kinds of bacteria and viruses.''

"Does that mean—''

"I'm afraid it does," Haworth said.

"But the instruction sheet that Ms. Flaherty gave me the first day says very clearly, 'Have infant follow an object. Use black and white objects.' And this object is clearly black and white," Horowitz argued, but softly this time.

"I'm sorry, Mr. Horowitz, but I must say no.''

"I can still take care of him though, can't I?''

"Of course.''

Horowitz surrendered the package to Ms. Haworth's outstretched hands, and proceeded to the scrub room to get ready. After his careful ritual he donned his yellow smock, entered the nursery, approached the crib nearest the window, and leaned over it and whispered, "Hey, Cletus Simon, look who's back. Uncle Sam." He lifted the infant into his arms, picked up the bottle and proceeded to feed the infant while whispering to him, "Good boy. Today we are going to finish the whole bottle. Right? You bet, right!''

Before long, Homer Wesley appeared. Horowitz looked up from feeding his tiny charge, to greet him. "Hey, Wesley, where have you been for ten days?''

"Jury duty," Homer Wesley replied, with a marked lack of enthusiasm.

"I know what you mean," Horowitz commiserated. "When I was running a business I was able to get off most times. But after I retired, I was a dead pigeon. Where did you serve? Criminal or Civil?"

"Criminal," Wesley said grimly. "No fun. No fun at all. Makes you lose faith in the future."

"Not like when we were young, right?" Horowitz replied.

"Right," Wesley agreed. He looked down into the little bundle Horowitz held, parted the white blanket and studied the tiny pinched black face.

"He looks a little better, doesn't he?" Horowitz asked, seeking confirmation.

And because he did, Wesley replied, "Yeah, yeah, looks better."

"Got to get him fed up, got to take the unhappiness out of his little face so he's ready to go when the time comes," Horowitz said, gently urging the nipple into the infant's mouth. Eyes clenched, the infant began to suck. "Meantime," he urged, "that's it. That's it, Cletus my boy. You eat well and you will get better. Take my word for it, you will get better."

But, he thought, *Maybe if I say it like I believe it, he will somehow believe it. After all, the little ones even days old can sense things.*

Each time after he had placed little Cletus Simon back in his crib Samuel Horowitz would proceed to the desk and ask Ms. Haworth which volunteer was scheduled to follow him on duty. If it was a volunteer whom he did not know he would linger until that person, usually a woman, arrived. He would instruct her as to how to care for his little patient.

Some of them resented his instruction, since they had had longer experience at volunteer baby care than he. But he was careful to explain that this was a special infant, in need of special care on which Samuel Horowitz was an expert, if not *the* expert.

Once assured that his suggestions would be followed, he left the hospital, for he had made it a rule not to join the "coffee corner." He would not partake of the coffee and cake that the other volunteers looked on as a social part of their activities. Some of them brought in pounds of coffee to keep the urn constantly going. Women volunteers made it a practice to bring in cakes or cookies that they had baked. Although at times, if one were alert to such things, one could discern that occasionally a woman would contribute a cake that was actually the product of her local bakery, first removing its original carton and presenting it as home-baked.

Though Samuel Horowitz did not participate in the coffee corner, when he noticed the coffee running low, he made it a point to bring in a fresh can. From time to time he also brought in a cake in its original bakery carton. Thus making a point of the subterfuge of those women who tried to disguise their contribution as of their own baking.

Nor would he engage in conversation with other volunteers as they gathered in the coffee corner.

That, he declared, though not aloud, was time-wasting gossip fit for widows. Not for a man like Samuel Horowitz.

Chapter 12

XXX

IF SAMUEL HOROWITZ SHUNNED THE COFFEE CORNER, MRS. WASH-ington never failed to appear at the late-afternoon gatherings.

Anyone who observed her closely during those informal sessions would have noted that she never took more than one cup of coffee, and never finished any piece of cake, though she sampled many. Even if they noticed, they would never have suspected that she was sampling the volunteers as well.

The coffee corner served a special purpose. Because the nurseries were small rooms, confined at most to four cribs each, they offered only a limited opportunity to mingle with other volunteers. Whereas, around the coffee urn and the pastry tray she met groups of women. And under circumstances that permitted her to pursue her plan.

For, in recent weeks, despite the satisfaction Samuel Horowitz derived from his volunteer work, she noticed that away from the hospital he exhibited his previous signs of depression. She could see it in his eyes when he looked across the table at dinner. Sense it in his very posture when he sat beside her in the theater or in a lecture hall. In conversation he did not exhibit the same old feisty combative attitude on questions of public and political interest.

* * *

They talk about the danger of "failure to thrive" in infants. I think it applies as well to older adults. I have seen some of them fail to thrive and, like some infants, die. I will not allow that to happen to this man, she resolved.

During her late-afternoon volunteer hours Mrs. Washington had made a special point of becoming friendly and familiar with as many women as she could. While feeding her infants or walking them, she would strike up conversations with the other woman or two in the nursery. She would show off her infant, asking, "My, isn't he cute? Only a week old and you can see the spirit in him. Eats like a hungry man. And sleep? He does everything but snore. He'll make it all right."

Thus she encouraged the other women to brag about their little ones. Before they knew it she had them engaged in conversation, unaware that she was collecting data on them, names, family ties, religion, especially marital status.

However, the coffee corner was the most fruitful and revealing way. Not only were there more women around the coffee urn, but since most of them were widows or single women without family obligations, they had the time and the inclination to relax and enjoy the camaraderie.

Whereas Samuel Horowitz always shunned the cakes and pastries the women contributed, Mrs. Washington sampled them all. Of which there were many. For, though the coffee corner had started as a simple refreshment break, it had evolved into a competition. Each woman strove to outdo the others in the art of baking. Which served Mrs. Washington's purpose perfectly, for it helped reveal their family roots and cultural heritage.

She discovered that Mrs. Veronica Brady, whose husband had been killed in the line of duty as a New York City policeman years ago, could always be counted on to contribute her Irish version of scones. Occasionally she also brought a loaf of home-baked potato bread, for which she supplied the jam as well.

Mrs. Holochek, whose family had come to this country following the Hungarian rebellion against Soviet tyranny in the 1950s, always brought in her *polichenken*, which were tasty, delicate, and very sweet.

However, Mrs. Washington suspected her of cheating, using

too much butter. Which to this group of middle-aged and older women and men was considered a breach of an unwritten law. One did not endanger her fellow volunteers by tempting them with high-cholesterol foods during the coffee break.

There was Mrs. Celia Klein, whose proud boast was her coffee cake, stuffed with cinnamon, raisins and chopped nuts. She was in competition with Ida Steinman, who also made a mighty delicious coffee cake.

Which was not to belittle Mrs. Braun, a woman of Viennese origin. From time to time she brought in a rich chocolate-covered Sacher torte. She always made sure to remind them that hers was based on the original recipe, which her mother had managed to extract from the chief pastry chef at Sacher's world-famous hotel. She also added a bit of spice, not to the torte, but to her legend, by implying that her mother had secured the recipe while having an affair with the pastry chef.

"Ah, Vienna, in those days," Mrs. Braun was often heard to say.

Mrs. Braun's name often led to confusion with Mrs. Edna Brown. Mrs. Brown was the widow of a man who had been in the fur business. He had died as a result of a heart attack brought on by having bought mink skins at the fur auction in a year when the price of minks dropped dramatically and wiped him out financially.

Mrs. Washington discovered that Mrs. Brown was a woman who had never been able to adjust to her now stringent circumstances. She talked almost incessantly of her past wealth with a longing that became tiresome to those forced to listen. Only when she cradled the little ones in her arms, fed them, crooned to them, did she seem to forget the past and fix her mind on the present and the future.

Mrs. Washington thought, *Here is one woman who gains more from the volunteer work than she gives to it.* She was not one of the women who fitted Mrs. Washington's exacting standards. For she had set down certain qualifications. Each woman must be Jewish. Unmarried. And, just as important, she must be a fine, giving human being. Each must respond fully and unselfishly to the little ones. So much so that, as sometimes happened due to unfortunate circumstances when some other volunteer was suddenly unable to appear, an urgent call from Ms. Flaherty could always bring the woman to the nursery in a hurry. Proving she adapted freely and patiently to unexpected circumstances. A requisite virtue in Mrs. Washington's plan.

Harriet Washington spent a number of such late afternoons at the coffee urn sampling all the delicacies, chatting with the women, learning their habits, their views of life, trying in her mind to match them and their attitudes with the idealized picture that Samuel Horowitz had painted of his beloved Hannah.

More than once Mrs. Washington asked herself, *Is it possible to find such a woman?* More than once she feared it was not. Yet she persevered, knowing that the future happiness, if not the life, of her dear friend Samuel Horowitz depended on her success in a search about which he was completely unaware.

Applying her strict set of standards, Mrs. Washington had narrowed her list of possibles down to three women. All three possessed the basic qualifications. They were Jewish widows and hence marriageable. They were of a proper age for Samuel Horowitz. They were evidently good homemakers. And, to judge from their tenderness and care with the infants, they were extremely kind, loving, indulgent and outgoing.

One of her select three was Ida Kohn, a woman who had great skill with butter cookies, even when made with margarine.

Second was Mrs. Selma Robbins, whose pineapple upside-down cake was delicious but sometimes left a little to be desired. However, she was a very nice, pleasant person.

So, Mrs. Washington argued silently, *life does not hang on pineapple upside-down cake. Surely she is handy in the kitchen with all other dishes.*

Third was Mrs. Molly Mendelsohn, whom everyone called Molly. She was an extremely fine woman, very cooperative. Bright, neat, pleasing to the eye, she also had an excellent touch with little rolled-up pastries which she called *ruggaluch,* filled with cinnamon, nuts and a dusting of sugar. Not only were her *ruggaluch* delicious, but she was one woman who did not hesitate to give her recipe freely to any woman who asked for it.

With these three in mind, Mrs. Washington was now prepared for her final test.

On the day that Ida Kohn had brought in a batch of her delicious butter cookies, Mrs. Washington tasted one, admired its flakiness and flavor. While savoring the taste, she used it as a pretext for asking, "Tell me, Mrs. Kohn, are you this good with other dishes?"

Making a pretense at modesty, Ida Kohn replied, "My Dave never had any complaints."

"Then you must have a good recipe for blintzes," Mrs. Washington suggested, since that was one of Samuel Horowitz's favorite dishes as made by his revered Hannah.

"Do I have a recipe for blintzes?" Ida Kohn beamed. "You have come to the blintzeh queen. That's what my grandchildren always call me."

"Would you mind . . ." Mrs. Washington appeared hesitant. ". . . I hate to ask. But I am giving therapy to an old man who is the crotchety type, and I can't seem to make blintzes to suit him. Would you mind very much giving me your recipe?"

"Well, I don't do this often. In fact"—Ida Kohn lowered her voice and drew Mrs. Washington close to whisper—"I never even gave this recipe to my daughter-in-law. Just so my Jerome would come visit me when he got lonely for a real homemade blintz as only I can make."

Whereupon Ida Kohn proceeded to give Harriet Washington her blintz recipe in precise detail. At the end of which, Mrs. Washington asked, "Are you sure? Jelly filling?"

"My Jerome wouldn't eat them any other way," Ida Kohn insisted.

"I see," Mrs. Washington said, trying to conceal her concern. For Mrs. Kohn's recipe was sharply at odds with the instructions in Hannah Horowitz's recipe file. If the two did not match on such a basic Jewish dish as blintzes, the chances were that they would clash on other basic dishes as well.

Still, she could not allow her important decision to rest on a single dish. So she persevered. "Tell me, Mrs. Kohn, this matter of the filling? Jelly? Not cheese?"

Ida Kohn anticipated her by interrupting very didactically. "My dear Mrs. Washington, it is obvious you do not have the faintest idea of what real Jewish-Hungarian cooking is like. Just take my word for it. Jelly. Jelly. And again jelly. The only filling for a decent, respectable blintz."

Ah, Mrs. Washington realized, *Hungarian. The problem here is that unlike Hannah Horowitz, Ida Kohn's culinary heritage evolves from a different culture and a different tradition. This does not bode well for any future relationship. Not with a finicky man like Samuel Horowitz.*

So, despite the fact that she liked Ida Kohn very much, she reluctantly crossed her name off the list, reducing her number of eligibles to two.

For the better part of one afternoon, Selma Robbins appeared to fit Mrs. Washington's qualifications exactly. She had brought in one of her pineapple upside-down cakes, rich and gooey from sugar and pineapple syrup. So soft and delicate was it that one had to hold the slice by the bottom to prevent it from crumbling. It was delicious, better this time than last.

Using that as an opening wedge, Mrs. Washington asked for the recipe, which Selma appeared somewhat reluctant to give. Not that she would refuse, but she enjoyed being coaxed. Which Mrs. Washington proceeded to do. From the recipe for cake, Mrs. Washington worked her way around to blintzes. A test that Selma Robbins passed with flying colors.

But when it came to lima bean, beef and barley soup, a dish Samuel Horowitz relished when prepared according to his Hannah's recipe, there, unfortunately, Selma Robbins failed. The crucial point of difference lay in the selection of the cut of beef.

"Do you always make yours with a brisket of beef?" Mrs. Washington asked, pretending mere curiosity to conceal the importance of the issue.

"I would never dream of using any other cut. My mother, may she rest in peace, and my grandmother before her, who I can remember from when I was a little girl, always said, 'If you can't get a good brisket, better not to make lima bean, beef and barley soup at all.' My mother and I lived up to that ever since. Any other cut of beef simply will not do. Not for any cook who is proud to trace her recipes back to the German-Jewish cooking, which is the best kind.

"Frankly, Mrs. Washington, if I may impart to you a little secret, we German Jews have never felt too comfortable with Jews from Poland or Russia. Their tastes are too—too primitive. Of course, we are all Jews. But there are Jews and Jews. You know how it is. I mean, you being black, or should I say African-American?"

"Either one will do," Mrs. Washington said.

"I am sure among your people there are standards, too. African-Americans that you approve of and those that you don't. Am I right?"

"Yes," Mrs. Washington said, but did not add what she was thinking, *There are also whites of whom I approve and some of whom I do not. Such as you.*

Thus Harriet Washington was reduced to one last candidate.

She engaged Molly Mendelsohn at the coffee urn on the afternoon when she had brought in her latest contribution of *ruggaluch*. She had carried them from her home on West End Avenue on a large platter securely covered with plastic wrap, then enveloped in a bright red-and-white-checked linen towel. Each of the little delicacies had been carefully arranged on the platter and remained intact during the bus trip up to the hospital.

So popular were Mrs. Mendelsohn's *ruggaluch* that by the time Mrs. Washington arrived at the coffee urn there were only three left. A tribute, Mrs. Washington realized, to the public acceptance of Mrs. Mendelsohn's art. As she hovered over the remaining three pieces, Mrs. Washington observed, "Lucky I got here in time. Another few minutes and your platter would have been empty."

"Next time, I'll bring more," Molly Mendelsohn replied. "It seems each time I bake more than the last time, but it's never enough. So what? What else have I got to do? Actually, Mrs. Washington, I find baking and cooking is fun. Don't you?"

"Oh, I do indeed," Mrs. Washington replied. "Nothing does my heart more good than to watch my grandson, Conrad, and his sister, Louise, gobble up my cooking."

"I wish I could have such enjoyment," Molly said. "But these days, with families so spread out, who gets to see their grandchildren often? You are a very lucky woman, Mrs. Washington."

At the rate they are growing up, I wonder how long I will be lucky, Mrs. Washington thought.

As she pretended to sip her coffee, Mrs. Washington peered beyond the rim of her cup to study Molly Mendelsohn. For the woman had just voiced a plaint that she had heard Samuel Horowitz utter from time to time. Like many grandparents these days, except for the times he went out to San Diego to visit his daughter, Mona, or down to Washington to visit his son, Marvin, he had rarely seen his own grandchildren. Even now, when they were all in colleges in the Northeast, they somehow never found time to come to New York to visit their grandfather.

A point of common interest between Samuel Horowitz and Molly Mendelsohn, Mrs. Washington noted. *A somewhat favorable sign. But on to the more definitive tests.*

"I wonder, Mrs. Mendelsohn, if you could help me out?"

"I could try. What is your problem?"

"I happen to be giving therapy to a Jewish gentleman who is very sensitive, most particularly about the food I serve him. In fact, at times he refuses to eat if I don't prepare certain dishes exactly the way he demands. Now, I would not impose on you except that eating substantial, nourishing meals is necessary to his recovery."

"What can I do to help?" Mrs. Mendelsohn offered.

"There are certain Jewish dishes for which he has a preference that I have not been able to cook to his satisfaction."

"Such as?"

"Well, take a good basic nourishing dish like lima bean, beef and barley soup," Mrs. Washington replied. "It seems there is some difference of opinion about that. When I make it with brisket of beef—"

As if Mrs. Washington had committed a breach of good taste, Molly Mendelsohn could not restrain herself from interrupting. "My dear Mrs. Washington, you don't mean to say that you use brisket in lima bean and barley soup?"

Pretending ignorance, Mrs. Washington replied, "Yes.

Why?'' Her broad black face did its best to simulate concern and great puzzlement.

Drawing Mrs. Washington close, making a confidante of her, Molly Mendelsohn lowered her voice. "Mrs. Washington, from what I have seen, I have no doubt that some of the ladies here would actually use brisket. Wrong. Completely wrong. Only one way."

"And that?" Mrs. Washington whispered.

"Short ribs," Molly whispered in turn.

"Short ribs," Mrs. Washington evaluated as if greatly surprised. That had been the first ingredient on Hannah Horowitz's recipe card. "Why short ribs?"

"The bones, the bones," Molly insisted.

"The bones?"

"The bones give a richness and flavor to the soup that brisket could never do. Then you cook the soup so long that the meat falls off the bones. Tender. Wonderful. Believe me, no man could resist such a dish. Surely my Phil was never able to resist it. Dear man. Such a dear man."

Tears flooded into her blue eyes. But she contained them.

A woman who has been happily married, Mrs. Washington observed. *Good.*

"Short ribs, then. For flavor and richness," Mrs. Washington repeated in her guise as a devout disciple. "It seems there is a similar difference of opinion on blintzes."

"Yes, I know," Mrs. Mendelsohn said sadly. "You won't believe it, but there are even some Jewish cooks I have heard of who think that jelly is the only proper filling for a good blintz."

"But you do not?" Mrs. Washington asked hopefully.

"Of course not," Molly Mendelsohn said. "You see, Mrs. Washington, there are blintzes and then there are blintzes."

"So I've heard," Mrs. Washington said.

"There are dessert blintzes and then blintzes as a main dish. Which must only be made with a cheese filling. Cottage cheese, farmer cheese, any white flaky cheese, enriched with sour cream, an egg, and if people prefer, a touch of salt."

Mrs. Washington repeated each ingredient as if committing it to memory, but was secretly delighted, since thus far Molly's recipe matched Hannah's in every detail.

"Of course," Molly Mendelsohn continued, "the pancakes you wrap the filling in are the same for both kinds of blintzes. All-purpose flour, milk and a touch of salt."

"Ah, so the difference is only in the filling, jelly being for dessert blintzes." Mrs. Washington pretended to learn this for the first time.

"Absolutely only for dessert," Molly affirmed.

So far, so good, Mrs. Washington thought. *Now, one final test.*

"Mrs. Mendelsohn, there is a kind of noodle pudding that this gentleman I told you about prefers. But somehow I have never been able to make it to his satisfaction."

"Oh, you must mean a *kigel.*" Mrs. Mendelsohn assumed.

At last, Mrs. Washington thought with relief, *at last. A woman who pronounces it the same way as Samuel Horowitz. Now if only she makes it the same way as Hannah used to.*

"Yes, that's what he calls it," Mrs. Washington said.

"Well, the recipe is very simple. You boil up your noodles, not thin but medium noodles, then mix in a raw egg, add salt and pepper to taste. . . ."

"Salt and pepper?" Mrs. Washington pretended to question.

"Surely, Mrs. Washington, you haven't been talking to Jewish cooks who make their *kigel* with sugar and raisins?"

"I'm afraid so," Mrs. Washington pretended to confess.

"Ah, yes," Molly Mendelsohn sympathized. "I know the type. They also pronounce it wrong. They say *kugel.* And they come from Hungary or Romania, mainly."

"I'm afraid so," Mrs. Washington confirmed.

"Well, as Phil always said, it takes all kinds," Molly Mendelsohn remarked a bit sadly. "But, believe me, *kigel* is the only correct pronunciation. Salt and pepper the only right seasoning."

Delighted with her findings, Mrs. Washington thanked Molly Mendelsohn profusely. "You have no idea how much help you have been to me."

"Anytime, my dear, anytime," Molly promised.

"We will talk again soon," Mrs. Washington said. "Very soon."

"It would be my pleasure," Molly said, then added very softly, "Look, please don't mention to any of the other ladies what

I said about jelly blintzes or about people who say *kugel* when they really mean *kigel*. No reason to stir up hard feelings."

"Depend on me, Mrs. Mendelsohn," Harriet Washington said. "Depend on me."

I think, she assured herself, *I have found the right woman. Now for a graceful way to bring them together. Considering their previous less-than-friendly confrontation that will take time, and great diplomatic skill.*

Chapter 13

XXX

SAMUEL HOROWITZ HAD STEPPED OFF THE NUMBER 10 BUS AND headed in the direction of the hospital. He looked forward to his hours of volunteer work since on his previous day he had been complimented by one of the staff pediatricians for his effort, especially with the one infant about whom the staff was most concerned, weeks-old little Cletus Simon.

The most precious words to Horowitz were the pediatrician's "This little one has begun to thrive, really thrive."

The magic word, Horowitz said to himself, *"thrive." Nobody is ever going to use that terrible phrase "failure to thrive" about my "little Cletus."*

Of course, there were other infants with whom he spent time during his two-hour stints every Tuesday and Thursday. Little ones of all colors, all in need, all helpless. Some reacted more quickly than others, some fed more hungrily, some slept more peacefully. Some seemed tired of life after only a few weeks, or even days. As if they had not the courage or the strength to take on that challenge.

Still, Horowitz consoled himself, most of the little ones welcomed his attention and his meticulous care. They even seemed to respond to him when he hummed to them. It was a song his mother used to sing to him in Yiddish when he was a small boy back in Europe. He sometimes detected, or thought he did, that some of them even tried to smile up at him. Let other people say that infants so young do not smile; Samuel Horowitz knew better.

He also looked forward to meeting Homer Wesley each time. Theirs had become a small, exclusive club, just the two of them. Wesley and Horowitz. The old vaudeville team, as they referred to themselves. They shared many ideas in common. Both knew how the city should be run. To say nothing of the nation. Both had the same disbelief in politicians. Both found fault with the media. Horowitz had his disagreements with the *Times,* Homer with the *New York Post.*

When they reminisced they both agreed that those "good old days" that people talked about were really not that good, after all. Today, with all its troubles, was better. If only they would let men like Homer Wesley and Samuel Horowitz run things.

On this day, Samuel Horowitz looked forward to getting Homer's reaction to the mayor's latest plan to balance the city budget without raising taxes or cutting expenses.

"How will he do it? By magic?" Horowitz demanded.

He entered the hospital, took the elevator up to the nursery floor, bade his usual greetings to Nurse Haworth at the desk and went directly to the scrub room. He worked assiduously at his scrub routine, which he had now expanded by a full five additional minutes. Feeling properly prepared, even for surgery, he donned his smock and was ready for work.

He started toward the nursery in which all four cribs happened to be occupied on this day. Wesley had not yet arrived. But there was another adult in the room. Not one of the volunteers. A young black woman.

Actually, Horowitz thought, *not even a young woman, only a girl. Sixteen? Possibly even only fifteen. What was she doing in there?*

She must have slipped in when Nurse Haworth wasn't watching. Maybe a nut of some kind. There are always stories in the papers and on television about nutty women who want babies and kidnap them right out of hospitals.

Well, she won't get away with it! And certainly not with my little Cletus!

Horowitz opened the door to the nursery with such force that the young black woman turned to face him.

"Young woman, what are you doing here? And who are you, anyway?"

"I am here to see my son," she replied. She started to tremble, which Horowitz took to be a confession of guilt.

"And just who is your son?" he demanded.

The young woman pointed to tiny Cletus, who lay asleep in his crib, oblivious of the conflict that was brewing over him.

"He is your son?" Horowitz challenged. "We will see about that. Do not leave!"

He went out to inform Nurse Haworth.

"Ms. Haworth, summon Hospital Security right away!"

"Security?" the baffled nurse replied. "What for?"

Leaning across her desk to speak in a confidential voice, Horowitz said, "We have here in our midst a kidnapper. One of those loonies who steal babies. Well, she won't get away with it. Not this time!"

"Mr. Horowitz, would you by any chance be referring to the woman in Nursery A?" Haworth asked.

"The very same," Horowitz declared.

"I should have spoken to you about her," Haworth started to explain. "She is the mother of the Simon baby."

"You mean— You really mean that she . . . But I was told the mother is a cocaine addict. Crack. That's why that poor little one is like he is," Horowitz said.

"She *was* an addict," Haworth corrected. "She's been in treatment. She's clean now."

"Clean," Horowitz scoffed. "How many times have I read in the papers or seen on television an addict who was supposed to be clean and then went right back and did the same thing all over again? I say, for the safety of little Cletus, get her out of there."

"I'm afraid I can't do that. It has been decided that after a period of training she is to have her son back."

"What?" an outraged Horowitz exploded. "You are going to give that defenseless little baby back to a dope addict?"

"Back to his mother," Haworth corrected once more.

"Mistake," Horowitz warned. "Bad mistake."

"It is the policy of the Human Resources Administration of the city to keep families together whenever possible."

"Families is one thing. But this—this girl and that baby—" Horowitz lamented.

"Mr. Horowitz, while he is still with us it is your job to instruct her in the proper routine to follow in caring for her infant."

"Me? Instruct her?" Horowitz demurred.

"Since you know that infant better than anyone else, I think you are the best person to do it. Don't you?"

"Well, I . . . I guess . . . maybe. Teach her everything?"

"Right from scrubbing to holding, feeding, changing. Everything."

"All right, Ms. Haworth. But remember, I warned you. And I am a longtime expert on human nature."

So saying, Samuel Horowitz went back to the nursery.

"Young woman, come with me!"

He led her to the scrub room to initiate her in the proper procedures. She listened, she nodded, she began to imitate Horowitz's actions, scrubbing with the same pretentious air that he exhibited. When she was finally clothed in a pink smock he led her back to the nursery.

"Now watch," he said. "And watch closely. Because this is a very special child. I suppose I need not say why," he remarked, pointedly referring to her prior drug habit. "Little ones like our Cletus here must be handled with great understanding."

He carefully lifted the infant from his crib, held him and spoke softly, "Hey, Cletus, here I am. Uncle Samuel. Ready for a little nourishment? A little walk around? Even a little music?" He glanced at the young mother, who was watching with great curiosity. "He likes my singing."

Carefully, explaining every step of the way, Horowitz pursued his usual routine with little Cletus. Feeding. Cuddling. Rocking. Walking. Crooning.

"You see, young woman, what it takes to give a baby a sense of security, a sense of being loved and wanted," he pointed out, making no secret of his disapproval of what he feared might soon ensue.

After observing closely as Horowitz sat in the rocking chair feeding the second half of the bottle to her son, the young woman managed enough courage to ask, "Can I . . . can I do that?"

Horowitz considered her request, then yielded, saying, "Careful, though. He is very very sensitive."

He rose and cautiously transferred the infant into the out-stretched arms of his mother. He assisted her into the rocking chair, passed the bottle to her and stood over her, a stern task-master waiting to pounce on her for making the slightest misstep.

When she raised the bottle to the infant's lips, Horowitz complained, "No, no, no. That's not the way. Not the way at all. Here. Watch!"

He took the bottle from her hand, very gently brought it to little Cletus's lips. When his tiny mouth did not open to accept it, Horowitz eased it in and held it there until the infant began to suck.

"See? That's the way," he said. "Now make sure he keeps eating."

Each step of the way he continued to criticize and correct everything she did. Until he realized that she was on the verge of tears. Only then did he relent. "Now, young woman, this is when I usually sing to him. He likes music. At least my music. So sing a little."

"What shall I sing?" the mother asked.

"Something your mother sang to you," Horowitz said.

"My mother never sang to me. I never saw her."

My God, poor girl, no mother to sing to her. Someone must have. "You had a grandmother, maybe?"

"Yes."

"Well, didn't she ever sing to you?"

"Sometimes," the young woman said.

"Then sing whatever you remember her singing to you."

The young woman hesitated a few moments, trying to recall a tune from long ago. She nodded her head, and began to hum softly.

Horowitz was forced to grant, "Nice. Very nice."

"You think he likes it?" she asked.

Horowitz leaned close to stare into the tiny black face of his own special patient. "He likes it. I can tell."

For the first time the young woman smiled up at Horowitz.

She spent the entire two hours in the nursery. While she tended her son, Horowitz took care of, fed, cuddled, changed and put to sleep the three other infants in the room.

His stint done, he was ready to go. He debated leaving, still suspecting what she might do once he was gone. For he had not yet dispelled his fear that she might make off with the infant. But he had no choice. His volunteer replacement had arrived, a woman named Mrs. Collins, a widow, naturally.

Still harboring some misgivings, Horowitz bade her farewell and started toward the door. The young mother called to him, "sir?"

He turned, alert and suspicious of her motivation. "Yes, young woman?"

"Thank you," she said. "Thank you for showing me how."

"You— You are welcome," Horowitz said softly, and left.

That evening, after Mrs. Washington had finished her volunteer tour at the hospital, had fed Conrad and Louise their dinner and made sure they were settled down to doing their homework, she met Samuel Horowitz at the movie complex on Upper Broadway to see a new comedy that had opened to good reviews.

Horowitz had already bought the tickets, and was waiting in the lobby by the time she arrived. They passed the lines of people who waited to buy popcorn, soft drinks, frankfurters, nachos and other foods.

At his grumpiest, Horowitz observed, "Was a time people came to the movies to see the picture. Now they come to eat. If they want to eat, why don't they go to a restaurant? Or else stay home? Of course, if they were home they would do the same thing. Watch television and eat. You would think a person couldn't eat without watching something at the same time."

"Yes, you would think so," Mrs. Washington agreed, but in her special ironic tone which had the desired effect on him.

"Okay, okay, granted. So when I was getting over my stroke I would only eat in front of the television set. But these are healthy people. I was sick."

"Of course," Mrs. Washington agreed, but thought, *Something is troubling him tonight. More than usual. I wonder what happened to him today?*

Over the coffee and cake at a restaurant on Broadway, Mrs. Washington got her first hint of the problem, when Horowitz asked suddenly, "How could Human Resources know if a woman is ready to be a good mother? I mean, is there some medical test? An X ray? A scan? Have you ever heard of such a test? I never have."

A bit of subtle probing eventually brought to light the cause of his current dissatisfaction.

Mrs. Washington realized this day's events had evoked far more emotion and concern in him than was justified. He had obviously formed a deeper attachment to this one infant than was wise. It only served to confirm what she had suspected. His volunteer service had become as much therapy for him as for his little charges.

Her plan would have to be accelerated. But by how much, even she did not appreciate on this night.

Chapter 14

XXX

IT HAD BEEN SOME DAYS SINCE LITTLE CLETUS SIMON HAD BEEN returned to the care of his young mother.

Samuel Horowitz continued faithfully to attend his duties at the hospital each Tuesday and Thursday. On occasion, when requested by Ms. Flaherty, he would substitute for one of the others who, because of personal reasons, could not fulfill his or her duties. Twice he filled in for Homer Wesley, who now was really experiencing medical difficulties that demanded his attention. Once he substituted for Mrs. Braun, who had to go out of town to stay with her daughter so she could be on hand when her first grandchild was born. Another time Horowitz was called early in the morning to fill in for Pringle, who had become involved as a witness in a street crime and was forced to go to court, eventually for days on end until his turn would come to testify. Before his turn there was a plea bargain, so Pringle never did testify. During his absence Horowitz and seven other volunteers had had to serve in Pringle's place, upsetting Ms. Flaherty's carefully arranged schedule.

But, as Horowitz often thought, and at times said aloud to Mrs. Washington, "At my age a person is lucky to be needed."

And she always agreed.

By substituting for others, he was not only exposed to more

infants, but also to other volunteers whom he did not meet during his regular Tuesday and Thursday stint. Twice he crossed paths with that Mendelsohn woman. They were both polite, but very reserved. Neither seemed able to forget the memory of their first early and abrasive encounter.

But filling in as well as attending his own hours did little to replace the infant for whom Horowitz had formed such a deep sense of responsibility. There were other infants, white, black, brown, all of them needing his care. But they were gone very soon. Foster homes had been found for most of them. The rest were returned to their natural parents. The turnover in the nurseries was frequent and constant. Which Horowitz understood was a good thing. So that a volunteer did not become too attached to any special infant. He had read too many times in his morning newspaper or heard on the television news about a foster family that had become so attached to a child temporarily placed in its care that when the child was taken from them, they brought lawsuits to overrule the decision of the Human Resources Administration. Sometimes such cases dragged through the courts for what seemed years. No, he decided, not a good thing to become too attached to any one child. Better to give each of them your best care, your devotion, comfort and closeness, knowing all the while that you would never see that child again. Love them all, become attached to none.

So he had weaned himself away from tiny Cletus and banished any further thoughts of him. After that, his service at the hospital was fairly uneventful. He came at his appointed hours, performed his duties, was courteous, if reserved, with the other volunteers and went on his way. During those occasions when he served an additional session as a last-minute replacement, he made it a point to be courteous even to the widows, while at the same time bearing himself with a reserve that discouraged familiarity. When talk turned to subjects that might involve more personal matters, such as a movie one of the women had seen and was excited to talk about, Horowitz pretended that he had not seen it, even if he had. When one mentioned a restaurant in which she had enjoyed eating recently and was eager to recommend it, he listened politely, said a simple "Interesting." That was the end of the conversation.

Though most volunteers became more familiar and friendly and took to calling each other by their first names, Samuel Horowitz deliberately refrained. Polite, yes, but not too friendly was his rule. Closeness was something to be avoided.

So it would have gone but for two events on which he had not planned. One was the direct result of a news story that he had seen on the late-night television news. Usually he no longer stayed up for the eleven o'clock news. But on this night he had attended a lecture in his synagogue at which refreshments had been served. By mistake he had poured his coffee from the regular pot instead of the decaf pot which did not bear the usual orange ring around its neck.

So he tossed and turned in bed until he finally turned the television set back on and watched. It was the usual run of late news in New York City. One crisis piled upon another. The subways were, as always, dirty and dangerous. The city was in a budget crunch. There were the usual snippets of film showing teenage hoodlums being hauled into police stations after the commission of some street crime. And, of course, there was the investigative reporter bringing to public attention yet another serious defect in the city.

Reruns, Horowitz complained. *Bad enough the programs are reruns, the news is also reruns. Same thing night after night. I'll bet they could run the news from last week, last month or even last year and nobody would know the difference. The only time it changes is when it gets worse.*

He was about to turn off the set when the next item caught his attention. Months ago he would have passed it off with a "How can people do such things? Animals! The world is full of animals!"

It was a story so often repeated in almost any large city that it had become a grim cliché. An infant had been returned to a parent who had previously abused it, only to end up being brought to a hospital either dying or already dead.

When questioned, a spokesman for the Human Resources Administration refused comment but said the matter was under investigation.

"That's the trouble," Horowitz shouted at his television set.

"Everybody is so busy investigating nobody has time to do anything right!"

On this night, Samuel Horowitz was not content merely to vent his anger and disgust; he turned off his television set, slipped out of bed, went out into the living room and began to pace back and forth, a very troubled man.

Little Cletus. How does anyone know whether this same thing could not happen to him? Those Human Resources people, what the hell do they know? The courts and those judges are no better. Who gives children back to their abusing parents? The judges and the Human Resources people! You can't trust them. I'll bet right now that little Cletus Simon is being beaten by that druggie mother of his. Or worse, by the man she is undoubtedly living with. Don't they all live like that so they can get welfare?

He could not sleep the rest of the night. He paced the living room, trying to pass the time. He tried to ignore his concern by leafing through old magazines. Finally he went out to the kitchen to warm up some milk, hoping that might induce sleep. It did not.

He was glad to see the dawn come up behind the buildings on the other side of Central Park. Because by then he had formulated a plan of action. If it took stealth and duplicity, so be it. With little Cletus's life at stake, a little chicanery was a small detail. Samuel Horowitz knew what he had to do.

His previous services in Ms. Flaherty's office proved very valuable. He knew more about the files relating to discharged patients than any other volunteer. He waited his time. When she was summoned to a meeting, he slipped into her office, searched her files and found the one labeled SIMON, CLETUS. It took only a moment to discover the address of his mother.

So armed, after he had finished his volunteer stint, Samuel Horowitz left the hospital and walked west to Lenox Avenue and north to 117th Street. Down that street he found the address. In the entryway he searched the mailboxes. Found the name SIMON. Apartment 3C. Then, to catch the young woman redhanded in her illegal and dangerous act, he did not ring but waited until an elderly black woman came out. Before she could allow the front door to close behind her, Horowitz slipped in. He ignored her call, "Hey, mister, where you think you going?"

He started up the dark stairway. He reached the apartment door, listened, then leaned close to press his ear against it. He heard voices. Not a single voice, but several voices.

Aha, as I thought! She is living with a man! A drug addict too, no doubt. I'll bet right now they are sharing—what do they call it?—a joint. No, that is for marijuana, which is mild for them. They are, I'll bet, sniffing cocaine. Or smoking crack. God knows what they have done to little Cletus. Neglect would be the least. He must have cried for attention and they beat him. Or even killed him. Must have killed him. Because I don't hear any baby sounds from in there. Only one thing to do. Break in! Catch them in the act.

Never before having committed a crime, he took a moment to debate his tactics. Ring the bell? Or force the door? Since to him timing was crucial, he decided on bold action. He pressed hard against the door. It did not give. He leaned even harder with the same result. Finally he decided to hurl himself against it. He stepped back two paces. Summoning up all his strength and more than all his courage, he hurled himself at the door. It did not yield. But the noise he created caused other doors on the floor to open suddenly. People peered out. Mainly black women who glared at him, grumbled and retreated behind their doors.

Finally the door to the Simon apartment opened. A black woman in her early fifties, dressed in a faded flowery wrapper, glared out and spoke at the same time.

"Rafe, how many times I told you, stay 'way from my daughter—"

She did not complete her thought. Instead, she glared at Samuel Horowitz for a moment, then asked, "Who are you? And who do you want here? I could have you arrested for trying to break into a decent person's house."

Abashed, embarrassed, as well as out of breath, Samuel Horowitz was speechless. He tried to pull himself together, to recover some sense of dignity. Finally he asked, "Is this the home of a young woman named Simon?"

"And if it is? You represent the city? Or the court? I thought we was through with all of you people."

"I am not from the city. I am not from anybody but myself. I am very worried about an infant named Cletus Simon. I insist on seeing him. To see if he is all right."

"You insist? Who the hell *are* you, mister?" the irate woman demanded.

"If you don't let me see that child I will come back with the police. Or even with a court order," Horowitz threatened. "We have too much child abuse in this city as it is!"

"You are the craziest white man I ever seen. And I have seen my share. Now, *you* get out, or *I* will call the police!"

She reached out with both her hands to shove him out. He was prepared to resist when he heard a voice from inside the apartment.

"Gramma, you got some trouble there?"

"No, baby, nothing I can't handle. Just some crazy man here, about to go on his way, whether he knows it or not!"

She was about to shove him again when the young woman came out of one of the rooms down the hall. In the dim light of the hallway Horowitz could not recognize her. But she, with younger, more perceptive eyes, identified him.

"Gramma, that's the man I told you about," the young woman said as she approached them.

Sam Horowitz recognized the mother of tiny Cletus Simon.

"He the man, the same one?" the older woman asked.

"Mr. Horowitz. He the one taught me how to handle little Cletus. He is a very good teacher. Though I have met nicer," she observed critically.

In self-defense Horowitz protested, "Teaching is the important thing. Nice is a luxury. Now I want to see him. The little one."

The older woman protested, "You have no right to come barging in here demanding."

"Gramma, please," the young woman intervened. "He was so fond of Cletus. I could tell. The way he took care of him. He was just like a grandfather to him."

"Well, if you think so . . ." The grandmother relented, granting Horowitz access to the place.

The young woman led the way to the small bedroom where

a crib stood among some old furnishings. Horowitz approached it, stared down. There he was. Tiny Cletus Simon. Asleep. Horowitz studied the infant, trying to determine if there were any marks or bruises on the little black face. He could detect none. Now the child moved in his sleep. His tiny lips began to make a sucking motion.

"Seems to me," Horowitz said, "our little Cletus is hungry again."

"I was just warming up his bottle," the young woman said, hurrying off to get it. When she returned, she started to lift the infant into her arms.

"Please, you wouldn't mind," Horowitz said. "I would like to feed him, just one more time."

The young woman looked to her grandmother for permission. Then she gave way to permit Horowitz to pick up the child.

He cradled the infant in his arm and gentled the nipple into his little mouth. Soon Cletus Simon was feeding hungrily.

"He eats well. Better than before," Horowitz conceded. He also observed that the infant exhibited no signs of neglect or abuse. His clothes were clean. His tiny body did not show any signs of tension. He seemed to have benefited from his time in the care of his young mother.

Once the infant had been fed and burped, Horowitz returned him to his mother. "Thank you, my dear."

He started toward the front door, the older woman right behind him.

Wants to make sure I get out of here, Horowitz thought. *And who can blame her?*

But at the door the woman spoke in a whisper, "I know. I came here feeling the same. That my granddaughter is back on drugs. Ain't so. 'Cause if she was, I take that baby away from her so fast it make her head spin."

"Yes," Horowitz confessed, "that's what I was afraid of. It's a great relief to know it's not true. And a great comfort to know she has a grandmother like you. Take care of that little one."

"Don't you worry, Mr. Horowitz, I will."

Chapter 15

xxx

Catherine Flaherty, administrator of volunteer services, re-turned to her office to find a large hand-printed sign not only on her desk but pasted to the frame of her desk lamp so that it would be the first thing she would notice when she opened her door.

CALL SOCIAL SERVICES AT ONCE!!!

Startled, she snatched the note from its mooring and crumpled it in anger. That anyone would invade her office was indignity enough. But to confront her with such an order was beyond en-during. She lifted her phone and, with considerable force, punched in the extension number of Hospital Social Services. She heard the three rings before being greeted angrily by Emile Perez. "Yes?"

"Mr. Perez?" Catherine Flaherty demanded. "Did you have the audacity to have someone stick this sign on my desk lamp?"

"No. I had the audacity to do that myself," Perez replied.

"May I ask why? And you damn well better have a good reason," Flaherty threatened.

"Oh, I damn well do!" Perez responded, barely holding his voice down to a controlled shout.

"And just what is that reason, may I ask?" Flaherty asked in her most icy tone.

"My dear Ms. Flaherty, do you, by any chance, have among your volunteers a person by the name of Samuel Horowitz?"

129

Before she responded, Catherine Flaherty thought, *Good God,
what has he done this time?* Aloud, and in her controlled official
voice, she replied, "Yes, we do happen to have a volunteer by that
name. May I ask why you inquire?"

"Oh, indeed?" Perez replied. "The reason I inquire is that he
is single-handedly trying to destroy this hospital's Social Services
Department. That's all."

"What are you talking about?" Flaherty demanded.

"Ms. Flaherty, this is not something to discuss on the phone.
Could you come down to my office?"

Before she responded she weighed the protocol involved and
the matter of status, then decided, "Mr. Perez, since this seems to
involve a volunteer who happens to be on duty at this time, it
might be more expeditious to meet up here."

Grudgingly, Perez agreed.

Within minutes Emile Perez, a small, roundish man with a
glossy black mustache and what Ms. Flaherty suspected was a
toupee, entered her office. Their exchange of greetings was clipped
and formal.

"Ms. Flaherty?"

"Mr. Perez?"

She was standing behind her desk in a most combative attitude. When she gestured him to the chair across the desk, he
remained standing.

"Now, what is this all about?" she asked.

"Do you know what that man did?" Perez demanded.

"I thought you were here to tell me," Flaherty responded.

"He went beyond, or should I say behind, the city's Human
Resources Administration to intervene in a case in which an infant
had been restored to its natural mother."

"What did you say?" Flaherty demanded, surprised by such
conduct, even from a maverick like Samuel Horowitz.

"Need I repeat?" Perez asked sarcastically. "He went to call
on, or shall I say intrude on, or should I say check up on, one of
the women who is a client case of city Human Resources."

"You mean he actually tracked down one of our babies in her
own home?"

"*His* own home," Perez corrected.

"His own . . ." Flaherty started to repeat when a thought struck her. More than a thought, a suspicion. The kind of suspicion that gives one little chills along the spine. For she had suddenly made the connection. Samuel Horowitz's affinity for the little Simon baby boy was well known in the nursery. He looked upon him as a protégé, a special infant in whom he took great pride, imputing to him qualities the infant likely did not possess, just as a grandfather will find unusual qualities in a perfectly average grandson. "Well, Mr. Perez, I can't say anything until I first check the facts."

"Are you doubting the city Human Resources Administration? Or is it me?"

"I am not doubting anyone. But I must get the whole story. And if what you say is true, you may be sure that I will take the proper steps."

"Bear in mind that this hospital depends on the cooperation of this city and its Human Resources Administration. To say nothing of the financial assistance we get for charitable cases. Such as"—and he paused before he accented—"our nurseries for unfortunate infants."

"I am fully aware of the budgetary facts of life," Flaherty assured him. "Now, I would like to get to Mr. Horowitz before he leaves for the day."

"By all means," Perez said, and started for the door.

Before he reached it, she called, "Mr. Perez, you didn't tell me how this all came to light. I assume the mother complained?"

Perez appeared to be embarrassed, for he hesitated, cleared his throat before he responded, "Well, actually, no."

"Then what *did* happen?" Flaherty asked.

"That does not change the fact that one of your volunteers exceeded bounds of his authority by intervening in a case that belongs to Human Resources," Perez declared.

"What *did* happen?" Flaherty persisted. When she received no immediate reply she pointed out, "I can't really discipline the man without knowing all the facts."

Perez started to blush, right up to the line of his black toupee. "No," he admitted, "the mother did not complain. In fact, she felt very good about his visit. That's how this all came to light. When the caseworker went to check up on how the client and the infant were doing, the grandmother of the client said how thoughtful it was of the hospital to send someone to follow up on the condition of her great-grandson. Well, as you can imagine, once the caseworker heard that, she raised all kinds of hell when she got back to her office. And her office raised all kinds of hell. With me."

"All because of a visit that the young mother did not complain about?" Flaherty observed.

"That is not the point! Rules must be obeyed. Without rules there is no order. And without order there is only chaos. And God knows we have enough of that in this city as it is. The man must be disciplined. In a very official and meaningful way."

"Meaningful way?"

"Get rid of him! At once!" Perez said, then left, slamming the door behind him.

Catherine Flaherty sank into her chair. She reached for her phone. Then stopped to consider how to handle what she knew would be a traumatic confrontation with a man as sensitive as Samuel Horowitz. There was also the personal relationship with the night supervisor of nurses, Elysse Bruton, and her mother, Mrs. Washington. Perhaps Mrs. Washington was the person to explain to Horowitz the reason for his termination. No, Flaherty realized, that would be an abdication of her own responsibility. But she decided to discuss it with Mrs. Washington before confronting Samuel Horowitz. Being responsible for recruiting him, Mrs. Washington was at least entitled to that courtesy.

When Harriet Washington appeared for her late-afternoon tour of duty in the nursery she found a note asking her to call Catherine Flaherty at once. She did so. They met over coffee in the hospital cafeteria. Ms. Flaherty explained the situation. Ending with the order Mr. Perez had given that Samuel Horowitz be terminated from any future volunteer services.

Mrs. Washington's first and immediate response was "Oh, no! You can't! It is absolutely necessary that he continue in volunteer service. Otherwise, it will ruin my whole plan."

"Plan? What plan?" confused Catherine Flaherty asked.

"Never mind that," Mrs. Washington said. "So you think you absolutely must get rid of him?"

"I don't 'think' I must get rid of him. If you knew Emile Perez as I do, you'd know I have no choice. He does not make idle threats. He is the perfect example of a nervous bureaucrat scared to death of losing his job."

"Must you do it right away?" Mrs. Washington asked.

"Wasn't it Shakespeare who said, 'That you would do, do quickly'?"

"Not according to my Bible. That was Jesus. At the Last Supper," Mrs. Washington said. "But in this case 'quickly' can be a matter of degree. Give me a few days. It is most important."

"I wish I could, but I've already delayed by not doing it today. So when he shows up on Thursday, that's it," Flaherty said.

Greatly distressed, Mrs. Washington shook her head in despair over this unexpected development.

"A beautiful plan, so carefully worked out . . ." was all she said before she left the table.

On Thursday midmorning Samuel Horowitz arrived at the hospital. As usual, he rode the elevator to the nursery floor. He passed Ms. Haworth's desk, which for the moment was untended. He went directly to the scrub room. He was in the middle of one of his favorite activities, his surgeon's scrub, when he was alerted by a knock on the glass door. He turned to see Haworth beckoning to him with a very officious forefinger.

Aha, he thought, *a special case. Some little one really in trouble. And it needs special treatment. Who else to call on but Samuel Horowitz. And who will respond with, as they say in the books, alacrity? The same Samuel Horowitz!*

He continued to scrub while smiling at her and nodding that he would soon be ready to confront the challenge. Haworth did not appear reassured. Instead, her gestures became more frantic and commanding. Finally he dried his hands and opened the door to declare, "Ms. Haworth, no need to get anxious. I'm ready, I'm ready."

"Mr. Horowitz, I'm sorry I wasn't at my desk when you came in. It would have saved a great deal of trouble."

"Whatever the trouble, I can handle it," Horowitz reassured.

"You don't understand," Nurse Haworth replied. "Ms. Flaherty wants to see you. The minute you came in."

"So that's your big excitement?" Horowitz commented. "As they say, no sweat. So I will scrub all over again after I see her."

Ms. Haworth did not respond, feeling it was not her duty to impart the bad news to him. She was relieved when he slipped his jacket back on and started in the direction of Volunteer Services.

Samuel Horowitz approached the partly open door of Ms. Flaherty's office. He paused, knocked softly, at the same time calling playfully, "Ms. Flaherty, are you decent and ready to receive company?"

Her words came back to him in a very sober, firm voice, "Do come in, Mr. Horowitz."

That should have proved a warning to him. But it did not. He entered with a smile, made a gesture toward the visitor's chair, in essence asking, "Will this take long enough for me to be seated?" Ms. Flaherty's face did not change from the stern look that had greeted him.

"Mr. Horowitz, I do not know the proper form to do what I am now forced to do. Because I have never had to do this before."

"Aha, so it's advice that you need. Well, one thing about Samuel Horowitz, he has never been short on advice. Though I must say some people resent it. Now, what is *your* problem?"

"Mr. Horowitz, I must ask you straight out: Did you or did you not visit the home of an infant named Cletus Simon last Friday?"

"Oh, that. Yes, of course. And am I glad I did. Believe me, I slept a lot better that night, seeing that the little one was in good hands. Not only is his mother in good shape, but she has a grandmother who is a tough cookie. Things there were very encouraging. In fact, if you would like a written report on my visit I would be pleased to give you one."

"Mr. Horowitz, didn't you realize that you were breaking the rules by doing that?"

"Rules, *shmules,* as long as the little one is being well cared for. That's the important thing," Horowitz insisted.

"Mr. Horowitz, you refuse to understand. Rules are made for a reason. And anyone who disobeys them can no longer continue to serve as a volunteer."

" 'Can no longer . . .' " Horowitz repeated, puzzled. "Exactly what does that mean, 'can no longer . . .'?"

"I mean, Mr. Horowitz, that I must ask you never to come back here again," Flaherty said, as simply as she could.

"*Never* . . . Never is a big word. It sounds so . . . so final. Admit it, Ms. Flaherty, you are really saying that to scare me so I won't do such a thing again. Right?"

"No, Mr. Horowitz. Wrong."

"You mean for such a little thing—" Horowitz wrestled with his stunned feelings. "But I can do so much good for those little ones, and they like me. I know you don't think they know one of us from the other, but believe me, they know me. They feel safe in my arms. They eat when I give them their bottle. They listen when I sing to them. They understand when I talk to them. Not the words, but the meaning. They know they have a friend in this world. No matter how you feel about me, you are not being fair to the little ones by keeping me away from them," Horowitz pleaded.

Ms. Flaherty wished that it was within her power to rescind the order that had been given her by Emile Perez, director of social services. For by now Samuel Horowitz's eyes were moist and she feared he might actually begin to weep.

To bring an end to the painful meeting, she said, "I'm sorry, Mr. Horowitz. But I have my orders."

"Yes . . ." he repeated aimlessly. "Yes, of course. You have your orders." Then he asked, "About today—"

"Mr. Perez said the order is to take effect immediately."

"Yes. Of course. Sure. Immediately."

As Samuel Horowitz turned to leave Ms. Flaherty said, "And I will have to ask you to return your identification pass, please."

                          *   *   *

Eyes misted over with tears, so deeply hurt that he did not
dare glance at anyone in the nursery area, Samuel Horowitz
trudged through on his way to the elevator.

He stepped out of the hospital building onto the Harlem
street. He was so dispirited that he did not flag the approaching
Number 10 bus. Since there were no other passengers waiting at
the bus stop it continued downtown.

Horowitz started to walk, slowly, shaking his head. How
could such a simple act become a crime? All he had wanted to do
was make sure little Cletus was safe, in good condition, being well
cared for. After all, wasn't that the purpose of the volunteer group?
Did a man's obligation to a helpless little infant end simply because
they removed it from the nursery? Didn't they realize that it might
be in more need of protection when it was out of the hospital than
when it was in?

He continued walking and thinking, arguing with the hospital, with Ms. Flaherty, with that Mr. Perez, with the whole unjust
world. Another Number 10 swept by him. This time he noticed
and made a late but futile gesture to stop it.

He gave up, thinking, *So, if I have to walk these streets? Who
cares? Mona? But not me. Let them mug me. It's the end of the world
anyhow.*

He continued walking, from time to time sniffling and having
to use his handkerchief, for which he blamed the New York City
air. *Pollution,* he decided. *Too much pollution.*

He only knew that he had not felt so depressed in a long time.
Worse even than the day he discovered that he was no longer
needed in the same business he had founded and which had been
his life for more than forty years.

Chapter 16

XXX

Mrs. Harriet Washington called Samuel Horowitz that very evening. When Bernadine interrupted preparing his dinner to answer the phone, Mrs. Washington knew how seriously things were amiss. For, in his usual hunger for conversation, Horowitz would have interrupted the very first ring.

"Good evening, Bernadine," she greeted.

"Evenin', Mrs. Washington."

Bernadine's dispirited response only confirmed how heavy a pall had descended on the Horowitz household, for she usually reflected Horowitz's mood. Mrs. Washington had her suspicion absolutely confirmed when she talked to Horowitz. Not once in the entire conversation, which was devoted to the usual inquiries about her family and his health, did he say a word about his confrontation with Ms. Flaherty or being banned from further participation in Volunteer Services.

She decided not to bring up the subject herself. But when she hung up the phone she was a greatly troubled woman.

Not only was her cherished plan now impossible, the fate of Samuel Horowitz was in jeopardy. Having taken so to the welfare of "his babies" and now being deprived of them, he was even worse off than he had been when Mrs. Washington first urged his becoming a volunteer.

As for the other part of her meticulously worked-out plan, that was now impossible, of course. All her carefully planned missionary work, ferreting out the background of those women, learning their cooking and housekeeping habits, all that was time and strategy wasted. With Horowitz now banned from the hospital, there could never be the seemingly chance meeting she had planned.

There was no doubt in Harriet Washington's mind that her meddling, yes, no matter which words she chose, it was meddling, had produced a far worse situation than the one she had sought to correct.

She tried to defend her strategy by recounting the benefits that had resulted from involving Horowitz in volunteer work. It had given him a new interest in life. A reason to be involved. A place where he had to go regularly. Where he was expected. Where his services were valued. An activity in which he had learned to take pride. Just to watch him scrub was a delight. To witness his devotion to his little charges was a lesson in dedication. Even Ms. Flaherty admitted that. To rob him of all that now was like throwing a life jacket to a drowning man, then snatching it away.

Yet Harriet Washington could not deny that he had brought it on himself. He had broken the rules. It was clearly understood that when the time came to give up a little one, volunteers, like foster parents, must do so with no strings or further contact. But this was Samuel Horowitz; no rules could limit or bind his conduct. He was a man who followed his instincts. Which, though almost always unselfish, were sometimes wrong.

Ironically, the man's instinct to protect an infant had become the cause of his downfall, and had turned her well-planned strategy and her careful detective work into a total disaster.

She did not sleep well that night. Or the next night.

After her third restless night, she had given up.

That morning, on her way to her current patient, she was sitting on the bus headed crosstown when she was nudged suddenly, not by another passenger but by familiar words.

"Harriet, child, this world is full of lemons. 'Specially for colored people. 'Less you are going to grow up to be a mighty unhappy black

woman, you better learn how to squeeze those lemons and when to add sugar to make lemonade."

Her grandmother's words. Exactly as she had used to speak them when Harriet was a child. They were the words that had guided and encouraged her all through her life, making it possible for her to overcome hardships and advance from being a cook and housekeeper to becoming a registered nurse and eventually one of the most sought-after stroke therapists in the city.

But why this jolting reminder now? she asked as she walked from the bus stop to her patient's house. *Lemons and lemonade. How to squeeze the lemon, when to add the sugar. So instead of lemons you have lemonade.*

She had a difficult day with her patient, forcing him to go out in public in a wheelchair for the first time. That made him testy for the rest of the day. But in her usual style, she forced him to perform all his manual-dexterity exercises. While all the time she kept thinking of squeezing lemons. And adding sugar.

By the time she was headed up to the hospital for some volunteer nursery duty, she had made up her mind whom to squeeze and how to add the sugar. Tomorrow she would make sure to get to the hospital early enough to cross paths with Molly Mendelsohn.

Harriet Washington was rocking to sleep a tiny infant who had arrived in the nursery only two days ago. It had been found abandoned in a hallway in a tenement building in the neighborhood of the hospital only hours after it had been born. Since, despite its abandonment, its physical condition was good and it had no need for neonatal intensive care, it had been sent to the nursery until identification and proper disposal could take place.

The little one had eaten with good appetite. It seemed placid enough to indicate that it had no special health problems, surely no drug problems. So Mrs. Washington was content to rock it and coo into its tiny pink ear. While she was doing so, Molly Mendelsohn, having put her infant to sleep in its crib, approached. She leaned over the infant to stare down at its little pink face.

"I took care of her yesterday when they first brought her in,"

Mrs. Mendelsohn explained. "Pretty little one. Saddens me to think a mother could abandon a little one like this. Terrible to live in these times."

"Yes," Mrs. Washington agreed sadly.

"Well, got to go. I expect a call from my grandson, Mark. Friday nights he calls usually around seven or eight o'clock."

"A very considerate grandson," Mrs. Washington said.

"Yale Law School," Molly Mendelsohn felt compelled to add. "He knows my schedule. Friday afternoons here. Then he expects I'll be home alone in the evening. And, the truth is, I always am. So he calls to cheer me up."

"That's a nice young man," Mrs. Washington agreed. She pretended to start to rise with the infant in her arms, then suddenly, as if feeling a twinge of pain, "Mrs. Mendelsohn, would you do me a favor?"

"Of course. Anything."

"Hold her. Just long enough for me to get out of this rocker. You know how it is, if you've ever had a bad back. You need both hands sometimes just to get up."

"Do I know," Mrs. Mendelsohn commiserated. "Bad backs and age go together. Sure, let me have her. And you take your time getting up."

Once the infant had passed from her arms into Mrs. Mendelsohn's, Harriet Washington rose from the rocker, pretending considerable more difficulty than she actually experienced. And once erect, she pretended to massage her lower back while remarking, "To bad, isn't it?"

"I wouldn't worry, Mrs. Washington. A healthy little one like this, a few weeks in foster care while they get the legal things straightened out and people'll be fighting to adopt her."

"I meant, too bad about Mr. Horowitz."

"Oh, God, what happened? Another stroke? He tries to cover it up, but I know he did have a stroke once."

"No, not another stroke," Mrs. Washington said.

"Then what? A heart attack? I heard once sometimes that can follow a stroke. Or did he— I mean, we have lost more than one volunteer in the last few years. And very suddenly. You see them here one afternoon and the next thing you know they're in *The New York Times*. On the obituary page. In those ads that families and charitable organizations run announcing a death. It's always a shock. Though at our age it shouldn't be. So how did it happen? Or should I guess? With his temper, he got excited about some trivial thing and just collapsed. Right?"

"He did not have a heart attack. He did not have a second stroke. He is in very good health."

"Then what's too bad?" Molly Mendelsohn asked.

"They want to expel him," Mrs. Washington said.

"Expel him?" Mollie asked, even more confused than before. "I didn't know he was going to school. What is he taking, night courses at Columbia or City College?"

"They want to expel him from the volunteer group."

"They can't do that! How can they say to someone, you can't volunteer?"

"They can. And they will. Unless someone does something about it," Mrs. Washington pointed out.

"What did he do that they want to expel him?"

Mrs. Washington proceeded to relate in full the details she knew of the crime of which Samuel Horowitz had been accused and found guilty.

"Oh, he shouldn't have done that." Molly Mendelsohn shook her head sadly. "Although I have to admit he was very attached to that little one. One time when I was taking care of him, Mr. Horowitz came back after his morning shift to try to instruct me on exactly how to do it. As if I wasn't the one who taught him in the first place. But he felt that little one needed special care. He took such pride in his little Cletus. He called him by his name all the time. Still, he should never, never have gone to check up on the mother. Definitely not."

"Then do you think for doing such a kind unselfish act he should be punished by being expelled? After all, he did do his job here very well."

"Nobody scrubs harder," Molly Mendelsohn agreed.

"Nobody is more tender or careful with a little one," Mrs. Washington added.

"He even wraps them in their blankets nice and close to give them a sense of security, just like I taught him," Molly Mendelsohn said. "Too bad, too bad."

"If only there was something one could do . . ." Mrs. Washington lamented. Then she seemed seized of a sudden inspiration. "Why not?" she demanded suddenly.

"Why not what?"

"Organize!" Mrs. Washington suggested.

"Organize?"

"A protest. After all, if they expel Horowitz today, tomorrow they can expel any of us. I do not think we should take this lying down. Do you?"

It took only a moment of consideration for Molly Mendelsohn to reply, "He may not be the easiest man in the world to get along with; still, he does have rights. Everybody has rights. In fact, these days, the more difficult people are to get along with, the more rights they seem to have."

Mrs. Washington was strongly tempted to remark, *Samuel Horowitz couldn't have said it better. How right I was to have picked this lady.*

Aloud she said, "This is not a matter of personalities but of principle. We can't let them do this to him. Can we?"

"We should take a lesson from the younger women. Become activists. I know. We will get up a petition! And we will confront Ms. Flaherty with it!"

Chapter 17

XXX

MOLLY MENDELSOHN LIVED IN AN APARTMENT ON WEST END Avenue and Eighty-second Street. She lived alone, in the same apartment in which she had lived all her married life with her husband Phil. She had raised her two children there, her son, Lawrence, and her daughter, Sybil. After her husband died she continued to live there for two reasons: At the time of her great loss she could not bring herself to leave the place that had been a comfort and a source of security for most of her life. The second reason was that her son, who was a partner in a large accounting firm, pointed out that with rent stabilization in effect, she could not find another apartment of smaller size and desirable location for anywhere near the same rent.

She also had the security that came with having a doorman as well as elevators still run by human beings. She also knew the tradesmen she dealt with, the grocer, the vegetable man, the kosher butcher and the local stationer, who also delivered the daily newspaper every morning.

Since Lawrence had moved to the suburbs to permit his children to attend school with a semblance of safety, and since her daughter lived in Philadelphia to accommodate her husband's business, Molly Mendelsohn lived quite alone most of the time.

Rarely did her entire family get together, except for mandatory family affairs, such as funerals of close relations, an occasional wedding, the graduation of one of the grandchildren and always the first night of Passover when the Mendelsohn family tradition was still observed. The first-night seder was always at Grandma's house.

For a whole week she would bustle about the neighborhood making preparations, ordering chickens and beef and breast of veal, eggs by the half-case, matzoh and matzoh meal for stuffing and for pancakes, sweet potatoes and carrots for the tzimmes, potatoes, salad vegetables, fresh green beans and peas, wine for the service, and above all the white horseradish, bitter herbs and lamb shank so necessary to carry out the Passover service.

For the entire day before the holiday she baked and cooked. Her own special honey cake that her Phil had loved and that her son, Lawrence, still loved so much he took home what was left after the evening was over. She prepared everything else so that it had only to be started roasting in the oven or cooking on the stove on the afternoon of the festival to be ready when her kids, as she called them, started to arrive.

Since Sybil, her husband and their two daughters came all the way from Philadelphia, Molly prepared for them some baked patties of mashed potatoes and browned onions to tide them over until dinner. Lawrence and his wife and their two children always arrived late for some reason and just in time for the start of the seder. Lawrence insisted on bringing the wine that was required for the service, since he considered himself a connoisseur. Privately, and never sharing her opinion with anyone else, Molly preferred the cheaper brands of wine for the Passover rather than the expensive ones her son insisted on. Those reminded her of the old days, when Phil was alive and had charge of all such things. Then they had kosher wines like Mogen David and Manischewitz. Not fancy names, but familiar. However, if it pleased Lawrence to bring wines with French or even Israeli names, let him enjoy.

Passover was the big event of the year for Molly Mendelsohn. Otherwise, she had made her adjustment to the single widowed life mainly by devoting her time to such activities as volunteer work at the hospital, the Women's Auxiliary at the synagogue, and serving as the collection lady for charitable causes such as the

Cancer Fund, the Heart Fund and Easter Seals. These required her to carefully print out, in her special script, envelopes for each apartment in her building and ask the elevator man to slip them under each apartment door. Then she awaited the return of those envelopes with a contribution enclosed. Most of the envelopes were never returned. But Molly Mendelsohn had done her duty.

The rest of her time was filled doing the crossword puzzle in *The New York Times* with her morning coffee, watching or listening to some talk shows on television or radio. One afternoon a week she went to an exercise class to which she had been introduced by watching Jane Fonda on television.

She was less enamored of the Fonda regimen when it became public knowledge that that famous woman had recently undergone plastic surgery to have her breasts augmented.

Molly Mendelsohn stood before her bathroom mirror and thought, *Not bad for a woman in her sixties. And I do not need augmentation like some movie stars and models.*

Some afternoons Molly Mendelsohn, in company with some widowed friends, or ladies from the synagogue, would attend a movie at senior-citizen prices.

But mainly there were the hours spent in sheer loneliness. Which unfortunately consisted of most of the hours of the day and night.

Of all her activities she enjoyed most her service at the hospital. When taking care of those unfortunate infants she could relive being young. In her arms the little ones felt like Lawrence used to feel when he had just been born, and Sybil when she was only weeks old. The satisfaction of holding such a delicate bundle was a pleasure beyond description. She too experienced some reluctance to let them disappear into that world from whence they came. To some fate that she never knew. But that was the way of volunteer work. You served your purpose and took your pleasure from having made your contribution.

Feeling that way she could well sympathize with Samuel Horowitz and what he had done. Foolish, even risky, as it was for him to have done so, she could understand why. And she resented his being punished for it.

All of which made her work with concentration and dedication on the sign she was now engaged in printing as she bent over her dining-room table to practice a skill in which she had excelled in school—precise, careful hand lettering.

With a stub-pointed lettering pen and black India ink she had already made up two cards and was working on her third.

SAVE A VOLUNTEER
OR YOU MAY BE NEXT

Below she printed in smaller but no less neat type the basic facts of the sad saga of Volunteer Samuel Horowitz who, because of his concern for a helpless little infant, a victim of its mother's drug abuse, was now being expelled from Volunteer Services.

SHOULD A MAN BE PUNISHED FOR CARING? were the words with which Molly's handiwork concluded.

By the time she had finished her third such description of victim Samuel Horowitz and his plight, she found herself forgiving him for his combative attitude during their first encounter. She had even endowed him with attributes that exceeded his natural qualities.

She held up her handiwork, all three cardboards, and found them good. She then affixed to each one by a string an inexpensive ballpoint pen for readers to use to sign their names in protest.

They were ready to be posted. One on the bulletin board beside the coffee urn, where every volunteer would be sure to notice it. The other two in prominent places.

As she admired her handiwork, she could not resist remarking to herself on the irony of the situation. The only volunteer who would not see her neat yet bold work was this same Samuel Horowitz.

Chapter 18

XXX

THE NEXT AFTERNOON, PRIOR TO STARTING FOR THE HOSPITAL, Molly Mendelsohn took one last look at her three posters before she covered them in brown wrapping paper.

She felt forced to admire her handiwork. It had not changed much from the last time she had done such an assignment as a sophomore at Julia Richman High School, in a class in what they called, in those days, Home Economics, which meant mainly cooking. She had been assigned the task of printing out for the class the basic recipes that would serve as the test questions for the final exam.

Her teacher, Miss Tolbert, had said, "Molly, you have the nicest, neatest handwriting in the class; you do the charts." And she had done them: bought the white cardboard, the India ink, the blunt printing nibs. She had done such an excellent job of it that Miss Tolbert excused her from taking the final exam and gave her an A for the course.

As Molly Mendelsohn tied the cord around the brown wrapping paper she said to herself, *Who would have thought then that Molly Lefkowitz would one day be doing the same thing, after a lifetime of marriage, of bearing children, raising them, becoming a widow. And now serving as a volunteer in a hospital. A whole lifetime dispatched in a single sentence,* she thought sadly. And yet it had not been sad. It

147

had been fulfilling. Her life with Philip Mendelsohn had been good, rich. In many ways.

Even in the early days, when they first started out and Phil was a hardworking designer with a manufacturer of petite-size dresses for young women. He worked six, and sometimes in the season seven, days a week. He took time off right before Christmas, which was between seasons for clothing manufacturers. And two weeks during the summer when the kids were too young to go to camp and they took them up to the country.

After Phil went into business for himself, things became even more hectic. He worked even harder, longer. Yet he managed to make a home, and a family, for her and with her. Of course there were times when friends of theirs went on trips and invited the Mendelsohns to come along. Trips to Europe. To the West Coast. Always Phil was too involved in the business. Always he promised, "Some day, when I slow down, or some day when I retire."

When Phil finally did retire it was due to his health. Since he never felt comfortable being too far from his doctors and the large New York hospitals he trusted, they never did take those trips or make those flights or spend that time in Florida or Arizona.

But, Molly assured herself, when she looked at her children, now grown up, successful, with children of their own, it was surely worth it.

The last thing she thought of as she picked up her neatly tied set of posters was what Miss Tolbert had always said, "Molly Lefkowitz, you are the neatest pupil I have ever had. I can always pick out one of your test papers from the neatness of your handwriting."

She felt self-conscious and even a bit childish that she cherished that memory to this day. Perhaps that accounted for the fact that, as a housewife and mother, neatness had characterized her life. People often complimented her on that very quality. Whenever large family occasions came about, bar mitzvahs or holidays like Passover, or important graduations from college or professional school, or important occasions such as when the two families of a newly engaged couple were meeting for the first time, the young folks always said, "Do it at Aunt Molly's. She always makes such a good impression." No matter the occasion, given a choice, her relatives, and Phil's too, always said, "Have Aunt Molly do it. She does things so nicely."

She felt forced now to caution herself: *I have got to stop thinking only about the past. Besides, if I don't hurry with these posters I will miss half the volunteers for today. And we need all the signatures we can get if we are to save that man Horowitz. I wonder, what makes a black woman like Mrs. Washington so concerned about him? What goes on there? Is it possible . . . No, it couldn't be. After all, she is not Jewish.*

Her posters proved a bit unwieldy to carry on the Number 11 bus, so on this day she decided to take a taxi despite the increase in cab fares.

Things in this city are getting out of control, she remarked to herself as she hailed a taxi on the corner of West End Avenue and Eighty-second Street.

She asked Mrs. Brown to hold up the poster on the bulletin board beside the coffee urn. "Higher," Molly said. Mrs. Brown obliged. "A little higher, so people will have to notice." Again Mrs. Brown obliged. "No, too high. Back to where it was." Then, while Mrs. Brown held the poster firmly in place, Molly Mendelsohn pushed the red-topped thumbtacks into the cork backboard to hold it in place. She took the cap off the ballpoint pen that hung from the red strand of wool.

"Now it's up to us volunteers," Molly said.

She posted the other two cards, one at the door to the nursery, the other alongside the supply closet, both areas no volunteer could miss.

Within the first hour there were enough signatures on the poster alongside the coffee urn to force people to sign in small letters that almost ran off the edge. The posters at the door and the supply closet did not fare as well but had a number of signatures.

Between babies she cared for, Molly Mendelsohn visited

each of her posters. She was quite satisfied with the results. Until she was summoned to· the office of Administrator Catherine Flaherty.

"Under normal circumstances things never would have gotten this far," Ms. Flaherty began. "But for most of the afternoon I have been at a staff meeting. Now, Mrs. Mendelsohn, do I understand that it was your idea, your handiwork that is soliciting signatures on behalf of Mr. Horowitz?"

"Yes, Ms. Flaherty," Molly spoke up forthrightly.

"Do you realize that this is against hospital policy?" Ms. Flaherty demanded.

"If it is hospital policy to punish a man for doing a very considerate thing, maybe the policy needs to be changed," Molly Mendelsohn suggested in her gentle but firm manner.

"So you took it upon yourself to change it," Ms. Flaherty remarked.

"Considering how many signatures are on those posters, I wouldn't say I took it upon myself alone," Molly pointed out. "Now, I understand the situation you are in. That Mr. Perez and his phony toupee, a man who spends more time waxing his mustache and protecting his job, is not easy to deal with. So I thought, we are all in this together, Ms. Flaherty and Mr. Horowitz and all us volunteers. Why not give her a little ammunition to use when she goes back to Mr. Perez to ask him to change his mind."

"You expect me to take these posters to Mr. Perez?" Ms. Flaherty asked, somewhat indignant.

"That would be better than having a staff of unhappy volunteers," Molly pointed out. While Ms. Flaherty considered that, Molly added, "Of course, if you'd rather, I'm sure the whole group of volunteers could go to see Mr. Perez in person." It was a threat made in the gentle manner that only a diplomat like Molly Mendelsohn could make.

Quickly Ms. Flaherty replied. "No, no, I don't think that will be necessary. It would be more effective for me to handle this in my own way."

*   *   *

Late that afternoon, all three posters were taken down after Catherine Flaherty made it known that the matter of Samuel Horowitz was up for review with Mr. Perez. By the end of the day Ms. Flaherty was authorized to call Mr. Horowitz and ask him to return for an interview.

The next morning when Samuel Horowitz entered the office of the administrator of volunteer services, he was greeted by three posters, each bearing the large, neatly drawn words:

SAVE A VOLUNTEER

OR YOU MAY BE NEXT

Horowitz had to lean closer to read the text that followed below. And he had to squint to read most of the signatures.

He turned to Ms. Flaherty. "They did this for me?"

"Yes, they did," Ms. Flaherty replied. "And because they did, I have been authorized to reinstate you on a conditional basis."

" 'Conditional basis'?" Horowitz questioned.

"The very next time you break any rule, you will be *out*. For good, this time!" Ms. Flaherty tried to sound as stringent as she could, as she handed back his volunteer pass.

"Oh, you don't have to worry about me," Horowitz assured. "From now on I am number one when it comes to observing the rules."

He turned to admire the posters once more. "Very neat work." Carefully he felt the cardboard. "Good quality. If it is not against the rules, who did this fine lettering?"

"Molly Mendelsohn," Ms. Flaherty informed him.

"That . . . that Mendelsohn woman! She did this! For me?" Horowitz asked, not only impressed but touched as well. "Well, I—I guess I should thank her for taking all this trouble."

By the time he had returned to the nursery area he found that Mrs. Mendelsohn had gone for the day. The next time she was scheduled to be on volunteer duty was Thursday. He decided he would stay late on Thursday, after his own hours, to thank her in person.

That evening, after Bernadine had given him his dinner, cleared the table, stowed all the dishes in the dishwasher and left for the night, Samuel Horowitz telephoned Mrs. Washington.

"My dear Mrs. Washington, how would you care to play one of our little guessing games?"

Aware that when he had some gem of news to pass on to her, especially one that reflected well on him, he would broach it in such a roundabout manner, she agreed.

"But this time you will pay up. No more double or nothing like you used to do whenever you lost to me in pinochle."

"Mrs. Washington," he proceeded in mock indignation, "are you accusing Samuel Horowitz of reneging on a gambling debt? Or any kind of debt?"

"Of course not," she granted at once, hoping to hurry him to his announcement.

"Guess what happened to me today?"

"I wouldn't know where to begin," Mrs. Washington said, fully intending to sound surprised when she heard the news.

"Today I was summoned. No, let me say, invited, to the office of Ms. Catherine Flaherty, administrator of volunteer services. I was informed that I am now reinstated as a first-class volunteer."

"My, that *is* good news!" Mrs. Washington said, hoping she exhibited the proper degree of surprise and delight.

With his usual need to embellish the facts, Horowitz said "Not only reinstated, but put on special status. And guess how it happened? I mean, aside from that Mr. Perez realizing what a valuable person I am in volunteer work."

"How did it happen?" Mrs. Washington asked.

"You would never guess. Of all the people in the world, of all the volunteers who would do such a thing . . . Don't even try to guess. I will tell you. That woman, that widow—Mrs. Mendelsohn. She made up the most terrific posters asking the other volunteers to protest in my behalf."

"You don't say!" Mrs. Washington pretended to react in sheer astonishment. "Imagine that! It just goes to show, you should never judge on first impressions."

"Haven't I always said that, Mrs. Washington?"

"Always," she agreed. "Of course you thanked her."

"Well, actually, I tried. But she had already gone for the day. So I'll see her on Thursday."

Thinking, *Time to add the sugar,* Mrs. Washington suggested, "You think it's wise? After all, suppose she's not there on Thursday? She gets a cold. Or has some family problem. You know how those things go."

"You're right, Mrs. Washington. Look, tell me, you think it would be too . . . too forward if I should call her at home and thank her? I am not so well up on those things any longer."

"Under the circumstances, and considering that you're only calling to thank her for a kind deed, I think it would be all right. Surely no woman would misunderstand such a call."

"Well, if you think so . . ." Horowitz procrastinated.

"Yes. I really think so," Mrs. Washington said more firmly. To make sure that he would act on her suggestion she added, "I remember hearing once at the hospital she lives over on West End Avenue. In the low Eighties. And when you look it up in the phone book, remember that a woman living alone in New York City usually doesn't list her first name, only her first initial."

"I'll remember that when I look it up," he promised.

Good, Mrs. Washington thought, *because that is how I found it in the Manhattan book. Mendelsohn, M. 643 West End, 726-0769.*

Twice Samuel Horowitz started to dial the number. Twice he faltered before completing it. He wondered why he felt so nervous and unsure.

Must be because I have to apologize to her. After all, I was not exactly the nicest man in the world the first time we spoke. And when I went in that day to suggest how she should care for little Cletus, she did not exactly take that too kindly. Still, the woman did a fine thing for me. And not easy, either, to make three posters like that with such care. I'll try again.

First though, better to know exactly what to say, especially for the opening. "My dear Mrs. Mendelsohn . . ." No. Sounds too familiar. I don't want to give her the impression that this is anything more than a thank-you call. So it would be proper to say, perhaps, "Mrs. Mendelsohn, this is Samuel Horowitz." Or would it be more proper to say "Mr. Horowitz"? Yes, that's it, "Mrs. Mendelsohn, this is Mr. Horowitz. It has come to my attention that you are responsible for the three posters that are responsible . . ." No, no, no! he interrupted himself, *too many words. Also I repeated the word "responsible." Make it simple and direct. "Mrs. Mendelsohn. I wish to thank you for the trouble you went to to draw up those three posters which are responsible for my being . . ." Again too many words. There must be a way, a simple way to say thank you. After all, thank you is only two words. Say it, and that's that,* he decided.

So armed, on his third try he succeeded in completing the number. He waited for the ring and actually felt considerable relief when she did not answer. He started to hang up the phone when he heard a breathy voice call, "Hello?"

"Hello. Mrs. Mendelsohn?"

"Yes, who is this?" she responded, sounding somewhat defensive and on edge.

"This is Samuel—I mean, Mr. Horowitz."

"Oh, Mr. Horowitz. Yes?"

"I am calling to thank you for the very fine work you did on those three posters, which you did on my behalf, and which have been responsible for my being reinstated as a volunteer at the hospital," he blurted out.

Oh, my God, all those words, he lamented to himself. *Too many, too fast. I am like a schoolboy reporting to his teacher. Why am I so nervous?*

"So you've been reinstated? I'm glad to hear that," Molly Mendelsohn replied.

"Yes, reinstated," he confirmed. "Thanks to your posters. You know you have a fine hand. I have seen lots of posters in my time in the business. And yours were among the neatest I have ever seen."

"Why, thank you, Mr. Horowitz," she replied.

"And the quality of the cardboard. I know. Because I was once in the business. Really in an allied business. But I am a maven on paper products. So I also know that in the average household one does not find such cardboard, or such India ink and lettering pens. Which you must have gone to great trouble and some expense to find."

"It was nothing, really," Molly Mendelsohn tried to belittle.

"These days there is no such thing as 'nothing really.' Everything costs too much. Especially for a woman who is a widow. I remember you said your husband was gone. So for a woman living on a fixed income, Social Security and such, I would like to repay you at least for the expense you went to."

"Please, it's not necessary," she protested

"But I insist. I would feel guilty, otherwise." Horowitz persisted.

"I would rather you didn't," she said, closing that subject for discussion.

"Then I'll tell you what," Horowitz compromised, "someday when we are both at the hospital somewhat around the same time, instead of the coffee corner, let me at least buy you lunch."

"Well . . ." Molly Mendelsohn considered, "someday."

"Good!" Samuel Horowitz said.

Within the hour, Molly Mendelsohn called Mrs. Washington.

"Mrs. Washington, you will never guess what happened," Molly began.

"What?" Mrs. Washington coaxed.

"Mr. Horowitz, he called. To thank me."

"Now, wasn't that nice of him?" Mrs. Washington replied.

"You know, on the telephone he doesn't sound like he does in person. I mean, he sounds very . . . very—"

"Very nice? Soft-spoken?" Mrs. Washington suggested.

"Exactly," Molly Mendelsohn agreed. "Also a little, how shall I say? A little nervous in a way."

"Really?" Mrs. Washington commented, as if surprised.

"Yes. But as you said, nice, soft-spoken. A very pleasant surprise."

"Well, what do you know?" Mrs. Washington said.

*   *   *

Three people on the Island of Manhattan all slept a bit better that night.

When she turned over in her sleep, Mrs. Washington murmured, *You were right, Grandma. Squeeze a little, add a little sugar, and you turn lemons into lemonade.*

Chapter 19

XXX

THE FOLLOWING TUESDAY, SAMUEL HOROWITZ HAD FINISHED HIS morning stint in the nursery, taking care of four different infants whom he called "My United Nations," one being white, one black, one Hispanic and the fourth a tiny Oriental infant who was born in stressed condition due to the dangerous early pregnancy experiences of its mother while making an escape from Vietnam on a rickety boat.

Based on his self-appointed status as an expert, Horowitz decided that the little one had a good chance at a normal life. In consultation, his associate Homer Wesley confirmed the prognosis.

This was a day when Samuel Horowitz needed all the confirmation he could get. For this was the day he decided he would stay on until the afternoon volunteers arrived. If his timing was correct, he would catch that Mrs. Mendelsohn before she had had lunch. So, instead of following his usual policy of avoiding the coffee corner, he waited not too far from the coffee urn. While others partook of coffee and pastries, Horowitz buried himself in a section of the *Times* he had not read before he left the house. Being a Tuesday this was the "Science" section. Which Horowitz brandished so that the others would see that he was a man of scientific bent, hence well qualified for pediatric volunteer work.

He was almost done studying the article on the latest technique for diagnosing exotic heart problems when Molly Mendelsohn appeared, carrying her colored plastic bag.

Too large to be a purse, Horowitz observed. *What could it be?*

His curiosity was quickly satisfied when she began to unload several baggies which contained a larger than usual contribution of those *ruggaluch* for which she was justly famous in the coffee corner. As she laid out the last of her fragrant delicacies she noticed him. Her smile was an invitation to approach.

"You . . . you make these yourself?" Horowitz asked.

"Of course. These days the way bakeries are run you can't get the real thing anymore," Molly Mendelsohn replied.

She knew the look that men have when they are tempted but too shy to ask. So she suggested, "Would you like to try one?"

As if the fragrance of cinnamon and vanilla had not tempted him, and trying to appear diffident, Samuel Horowitz replied, "Don't mind if I do."

He surveyed the entire tray and finally picked one of the small rolled pastries. With the air of a connoisseur he inhaled the aroma, then bit into it. The taste of the rich dough, the zesty flavor of cinnamon combined with the chopped walnuts and little golden raisins almost overcame his attempt to appear aloof and superior. He examined the second half of his *ruggaleh,* giving it what he considered his expert appraisal.

"Icebox dough?" he asked, with the air of the restaurant critic of the *Times*.

"Yes," Molly Mendelsohn replied. "How did you know?"

Instead of replying, he continued his diagnosis: "Cream cheese *and* margarine?"

"Yes," she conceded.

"Goes without saying, cinnamon, chopped nuts, raisins," Horowitz concluded.

"You certainly know your *ruggaluch,*" Molly Mendelsohn said with considerable admiration.

"Anyone can *eat* a *ruggaleh* but not many really know how they should be made. Mrs. Mendelsohn, may I say that you are the second best *ruggaluch* baker I have ever met," Horowitz replied.

"Of course," Molly assumed. "First best was your wife. Right?"

With a modest shrug Samuel Horowitz nodded.

"That's nice. Very nice," Molly Mendelsohn said.

Surprised, he asked, "You're not hurt, being only second best?"

"I know that with my husband I was always the first best baker in the world. So I understand," Molly said.

Chary, Samuel Horowitz thought, *This is either a very nice woman, or a very shrewd widow. She knows just what to say.*

Aloud, he said, "I am glad you understand. Now that you do, can we have the lunch we agreed on?"

"I'm sorry, but these are my volunteer hours."

"Oh," Horowitz replied, "I waited, thinking you might—"

"I am free tomorrow," Molly suggested.

"Tomorrow . . ." Horowitz considered. Though he had decided to accept her suggestion, he had to pretend he had affairs to attend. "Tomorrow. If I put off my meeting with my accountant— We are having a little tax trouble, and I will first have to call my daughter in San Diego. She worries if I am not home when she calls. But I can handle all that. Yes, tomorrow will be fine. Shall I pick you up?"

"It might be better if we met at the restaurant," Molly suggested.

"Of course. These days, a woman can't be too careful," he replied. "Do you know the little French-type restaurant on Broadway between Eighty-first and Eighty-second?"

"Oh, yes," Molly said.

"Shall we say one o'clock?"

"Shall we say," she agreed.

Just before he left, he scanned the tray with a hungry eye.

"Please. Help yourself," Molly suggested.

Samuel Horowitz selected one, bit into it, savored it. "Very definitely icebox-type dough, with cream cheese and margarine."

"Then have another. One for the road, shall we say?" Molly urged.

"Shall we say . . ." Samuel Horowitz replied, taking another of her *ruggaluch*.

*   *   *

It being a pleasant, early spring day, Horowitz arrived early
at the restaurant on Upper Broadway to reserve one of the out-
door tables. He took the seat that faced Eighty-second Street since,
aware of her address, he knew she would likely approach from
that direction. She appeared from around that corner and started
toward him.

From that distance she seemed smaller than he had thought.
But she carried herself with a dainty ease that befit her size. Some
women he knew walked with a gait and carriage that betrayed that
they either were greatly overweight or had been at one time. Not
this woman. He rose to greet her as she reached his table.

"Such a nice day. I thought we might eat outside. You mind?"
he asked.

"Of course not," she replied.

With a gallant gesture he had copied from early Cary Grant
movies, he invited her to sit across from him. Once she was seated
he snapped his fingers in the general direction of the waiter. A
Humphrey Bogart bit. When the waiter arrived, he asked for
menus.

"I already know what I want," Molly said, almost apologetic.

"Well, in that case, so do I," Horowitz said. "So?"

"I will have the omelet, made with the whites of the eggs, if
you don't mind. And some decaffeinated coffee. With skim milk,
please?" she ordered.

"And you, sir?" the young waiter asked.

"I . . . I will have the same," Horowitz said.

Once the waiter was out of earshot, Molly Mendelsohn said,
"Such a nice-looking young man. Another actor looking for a role
on Broadway, no doubt."

"These days you don't dare be sharp with a waiter. Next
thing you know his picture is in the *Times* entertainment section
because he's suddenly a movie star," Horowitz said. "Tell me,
you read the *Times*?"

"Every day," Molly Mendelsohn said.

"Very aggravating. Right?"

"Some days yes, some days no," Molly conceded.

"For me, every day," Horowitz confessed. Groping for some

subject in common, he reverted to the only one he was sure of. "That whole thing, about little Cletus. After all, considering his history, I mean his mother, the crack and all that, what was I to think? My only interest was making sure he was all right. Once I did, that was the end of it. Still it was very nice of you to protest on my behalf."

"Anyone would have done the same," she tried to diminish.

"Anyone *would* have, but you *did*. That is the difference," Horowitz pointed out. "And I would like to know why. Considering the circumstances of our previous meeting."

"Because I have the same feeling. You take care of a little one. Try to give him or her a sense of being loved, wanted. Then they disappear. You always wonder about a certain one. What will happen? Will they grow and be healthy? Or will they end up on the six o'clock news?"

She did not specify such an unfortunate infant's end but he knew to what she referred.

"One thing I admired about you, Mr. Horowitz—you did what I often thought of doing, but never had the courage."

"Why, thank you, Mrs. Mendelsohn."

They had exhausted that subject. A period of self-conscious silence descended on them. To revive the conversation, Samuel Horowitz asked suddenly, "Tannenbaum?"

Taken by surprise, Molly Mendelsohn glanced across the table at him, her small, nicely featured face showing her puzzlement.

"Your doctor? Dr. Tannenbaum?" Horowitz asked.

"No. Why do you ask?"

"I noticed when you ordered: omelet, whites only, decaf with skim milk. That's Tannenbaum's instructions for my breakfast. But just between us, at home I eat the whole egg. I don't believe in all this cholesterol business. Do you?"

She smiled. He noticed that the slight wrinkles in her cheeks gave way to dimples that made her appear even prettier than he had thought.

"Did I say something funny?" he asked.

"No," she confessed. "But home alone I do the same. I am only on my good behavior when I am out in public. Then I order exactly what Dr. Cleary prescribed. My doctor's name is Cleary."

"A Gentile?" Horowitz asked.

"Yes. And very nice. A young man. No more than forty. A client of my son. They went to college together."

"Your son is also a lawyer?" Horowitz asked.

"Accountant," she corrected.

Feeling that lawyers were by right of higher station than accountants, Horowitz could not forgo boasting, "My Marvin is a lawyer. With a big firm in Washington."

"That's nice," Molly Mendelsohn replied. Then added, "My Lawrence is a partner in an important accounting firm down on Park Avenue. They have branches in Washington, Chicago, Los Angeles."

"Wouldn't it be funny if somehow my Marvin and your Lawrence did business together on some case?" Horowitz suggested.

"Yes, yes, it would be funny," she conceded.

"Tell me, your Lawrence, his firm, do they by any chance have a branch also in San Diego?"

"I don't think so. Why?" she asked.

"Well, I have a daughter. Her husband, Albert, is very big in real estate in San Diego, one of the biggest, so I thought . . . But not if your Lawrence doesn't have an office there."

Fortunately the waiter arrived with their lunch. So they could spend the next minutes eating, while cautiously observing each other for idiosyncrasies and habits.

Horowitz observed, *She eats in small bites. Does she always do that, or is it just to pretend she is a delicate person? And her hands, small, but very nicely made, thin, not chubby. Hannah's hands were like that. Small, but very capable. She does not use any of that red stuff on her cheeks. Do they still call it rouge? No matter, she does not use it like some women her age who I have seen on the street or in a movie house or even at synagogue. Imagine a woman wearing rouge at synagogue. This woman uses just a little lipstick. And not too red. These days it is like a plague. Every woman, young or old, is wearing such red lipstick it looks like she is hemorrhaging from the mouth. And, notice, when she takes a sip of coffee she doesn't leave a big red mark on the cup. All in all, a nice, very decent woman of good taste. How could I have been so rude with her that first time? Of course, I regret to say, she is still a widow. And that is that.*

Having reached that conclusion, he resumed concentrating on his whites-only omelet. Until he glanced again and thought, *I wonder, how old is she? Not that it matters. But just out of curiosity . . .*

Molly Mendelsohn continued eating, in small bites, but occasionally raised her eyes almost imperceptibly to steal a glance at her luncheon partner.

He is not bad-looking for a man in his late sixties. Or is he already past seventy? No, sixty-eight, sixty-nine possibly. Of course, if he is in his seventies, he is in very good health. He has good color. And what I heard about his having a stroke, he doesn't show any signs. So he must have made a good recovery. Must be Mrs. Washington. They say she is a genius with stroke patients. One thing sure, what I thought about her and Horowitz together, that isn't so.

He is a neat man, nicely dressed. And he shaves well. I notice he does not have any of those long straggly gray hairs on his neck, or behind his cheeks like so many older men. A small point. But an indication of character, the type a man is, which would be important if a woman were looking around. But, thank God, I have my own life and I like it.

He eats like a man who likes food. Which is a good sign. Among the things I loved about Phil, that was one. He loved to eat, and he loved my cooking. Nothing upsets a woman more than to spend hours cooking and baking and for a man not to enjoy it. This Horowitz liked my rugga-luch, liked them even better than he let on. He is a strange man that way. Likes to conceal his feelings. I wonder, his wife, what was her name? Anna . . . ? No, Hannah. I wonder, when she was still alive, did he let her know how much he loved her? Or was it only after she was gone? The number of husbands of friends of mine who cried to me after their wives died, or left them, but never said a word when they were still alive or together . . . seems like hundreds. I wonder what he was like when Hannah was still alive.

The waiter appeared with a glass coffeepot with the telltale orange ring around its neck.

"More decaf, anyone?" the young man asked cheerfully.

"Mrs. Mendelsohn?" Horowitz inquired.

"Don't mind if I do," she responded.

"Likewise," Horowitz said.

They continued eating in silence, observing each other from time to time. Until by chance they both glanced up at the same time, and their eyes met. In embarrassment they both looked down at their food and continued to eat.

Chapter 20

XXX

ALMOST A WEEK LATER, SAMUEL HOROWITZ RECEIVED IN THE MAIL two tickets he had subscribed for to the Actors' Fund Benefit, an occasion when the cast of a hit show donates its services for one special Sunday night performance. The entire proceeds went to support the Actors Home over in New Jersey.

While Hannah was alive it was one of her favorite charities. She had been a devotee of the Broadway theater from her days in high school when she cherished ambitions to become an actress. Since that time she had always felt part of the theater. And she took her husband to many a play when he would rather have stayed home after a long day at S. Horowitz and Son.

Since Hannah's death, and in her memory, he never refused a request from the charity. During the past three years he had taken Mrs. Washington and she had been delighted to go. It had become an annual tradition with them.

This year, when the tickets arrived for a new play that she had expressed a desire to see, Horowitz was especially delighted to call her. Knowing she would be home by early evening, cooking for her grandchildren, and supervising their homework, he enthusiastically lifted his phone and dialed that very familiar number.

When he was greeted by her hurried "Hello!" he suspected that she was in the midst of cooking.

165

So he came to the point quickly. "My dear Mrs. Washington, the Actors' Fund Benefit. The date is May third. The time is seven-thirty. But first, dinner at Sardi's. Our usual table. Six o'clock. Unless, of course, you will permit me to pick you up at the house. Say the word."

Instead of the response he expected, he heard her respond, "Did you say the third?"

"Of course, the third," Horowitz replied. "Don't you remember? I told you to hold the date when I sent for the tickets. It's, like it says in the song from *Fiddler on the Roof,* a tradition with us."

"But the third is a Sunday," she replied.

"My dear Mrs. Washington, the Actors' Fund Benefit is always on a Sunday," he reminded.

"Of course. I should have remembered. But I'm afraid I now have a problem."

"Problem? What kind of problem? Sunday night Elysse is off duty, so she is home. And you are free. Problem solved! So, six o'clock, Sardi's. Right?"

"You don't understand. I promised the pastor of our church that I would help out at a special prayer service to console families who have lost children in the recent street violence. It's become a very serious problem."

"I know, I know," Horowitz commiserated. "You're sure he can't make other arrangements?"

"I would hate to ask, you understand."

"Of course. I understand," Horowitz said, obviously disappointed.

"Surely there must be someone else you can ask," Mrs. Washington remarked.

"Someone else . . ." Horowitz considered. "But it won't be the same. You and I have always gone together. And you're the only one who knows that I do this in Hannah's memory. You understand. Who else would?"

"I am truly sorry, but I can't leave my pastor in the lurch," she said.

"Of course not," Samuel Horowitz said, quite unhappy with her decision.

When Mrs. Washington hung up the phone and turned back

to her stove, her granddaughter, Louise, who had been puzzling over a trigonometry problem at the kitchen table, looked up and said, "Grandma, that is the first time I ever heard you do that."

"Refuse an invitation from Mr. Horowitz? That's not so, darlin'. Remember the time you and Conrad both had the flu and I had to take care of you that whole week?"

"I didn't mean that, Grandma. I meant, first time I ever heard you tell him a lie."

"Oh, darlin', that was no lie. That was a test," Mrs. Washington corrected.

"Telling him you have to help out in church when there ain't no . . . there is no such church activity. You call that a test?"

Mrs. Washington gestured her granddaughter to stand beside her at the stove while she cut some carrots and raw potatoes into the beef stew.

"Darlin', you've learned in biology class about how inoculations create immunity in a person. You give that person an injection of the germs you want to guard against. Then you wait to see if it succeeded."

"Yes. You wait to see if it took," Louise agreed.

"Well, I have just given Mr. Horowitz a shot that he really needs. Now I am waiting to see if it took," Mrs. Washington said.

"Why? You afraid he was going to get sick?"

"He *was* sick. I'm waiting to see if he's going to get well," Mrs. Washington said. "So it wasn't exactly a lie I told him. It was a shot. For his own good."

Left with two tickets to a very good play, Samuel Horowitz considered his possibilities. If Liebowitz were still here, he could have called and said, "Phil, how would you like to go to the theater with me? On a Sunday, when Rose likes to stay home and watch Angela Lansbury?" And Phil, always a bit of a *shnorrer,* would be delighted to get a free ticket to anything.

But Phil was gone. Florida. So who else? There was that woman at synagogue who had tried on several occasions to strike up a conversation with him. No, that would give her false hopes. The same with the widow Rubel right in the building. But that was too close for comfort. Given a little encouragement, and the next thing you know she would be inviting him for dinner, and God alone knew where that could lead.

Oy, Phil, Phil, why did you have to move to Florida? Phil . . . The name suddenly had new meaning. *Phil. Philip. Wasn't that the name that Molly Mendelsohn spoke of when she mentioned her husband? Sure. Philip Mendelsohn.*

He toyed with the idea. After all, he argued, she seems a very pleasant woman. What he remembered best and liked most about her was that she was not a pushy-type widow. She seemed shy. Especially that moment when their eyes met that one instant over lunch. Yes, a shy, sensitive woman. She would not misunderstand an innocent invitation to go to the theater. And possibly have dinner as well. An evening out. That's all. She would understand. Especially if he presented the invitation in the right way.

He hesitated a long time before summoning up the courage. First, he made sure that Bernadine had finished and left for the night. For some reason he could not explain he would feel very uncomfortable if she were to walk in on him when he was in conversation with a strange woman. He had not felt this nervous about making such a call since his early days in high school when he called Hannah for a first date.

Finally, he brought himself to dial her number. She answered with a cheery "Hello!"

He cleared his throat before saying, "Mrs. Mendelsohn, this is Samuel Horowitz."

"Oh, Mr. Horowitz," she greeted.

She sounds pleasant enough, he thought, *like she is almost glad to hear from me. Or is she just pleased to hear from anyone. Living alone, I know how that can be. However, this is the real test.*

"Mrs. Mendelsohn, I have a little bit of a situation. The way it developed, I am a long-time subscriber to the Actors' Fund Benefit. Well, to tell the truth, it was Hannah who was. And I carry it on in her name."

Sam, he cautioned himself, *you are talking too much again. Come to the point.*

Sensing his discomfort, Molly Mendelsohn said, "I think it's very nice of you to carry on such a worthwhile cause in your wife's memory."

Thus encouraged, Horowitz proceeded: "The point is, my dear Mrs. Mendelsohn, that I now hold in my hand two tickets in the sixth row for a very good show. And there is only one of me. So, what am I going to do, use the extra seat for my hat and coat? In May? Who wears a hat and coat in May?"

"Mr. Horowitz, am I to understand that you are asking me to accompany you to the theater?"

"Precisely. May third. Sunday night. I thought, if you were free, and had nothing else to do, that perhaps we could also have a little dinner first. It is a very good show, I hear. So we would pass a pleasant evening," he coaxed. "What do you think, Mrs. Mendelsohn?"

She thought a moment. For Samuel Horowitz a most uncomfortable moment, for he said to himself, *Mistake, Sam, bad mistake. To call, to ask.*

He was greatly relieved when he heard her say, "Why, I would like very much to go."

"Wonderful!" Horowitz replied. "I will pick you up at five-thirty!"

On May 1, Friday afternoon, when Bernadine did her marketing for the weekend, she found Samuel Horowitz sitting in his usual armchair looking out over the park, rattling his *New York Times* in frustration.

Thank God, he is his old angry self again. I was so worried before, Bernadine thought. *But these days things are almost back to normal. I will find out in a minute.*

"Mr. Horowitz . . ." She intruded on his mood.

"Bernadine! Did you read *The New York Times* this morning?" he demanded, ready to exchange angry views with her. Since he knew that she never read the *Times* he did not wait for an answer. "Bad enough when Tom Wicker was writing steady for the *Times*. Now that he is gone, things are even worse."

Bernadine waited out today's diatribe, which condemned not only the new columnist, but also an editorial, and even two letters to the editor as well. *He is in rare form today,* Bernadine thought. At the first break in his tirade, she asked, "Mr. Horowitz, what shall I prepare for you for Saturday and Sunday?"

"Prepare? Why prepare anything? I will no doubt lose my appetite when I read the Sunday *Times*. You know, I have often thought, with all those quick weight-loss diets, like you drink one glass of something and you lose fifty pounds practically overnight, the *Times* should put out a quick weight-loss edition. You read the editorials and Anthony Lewis and you lose your appetite for a whole month."

Having patiently endured his outburst, Bernadine persisted, "Mr. Horowitz, Saturday evening and Sunday evening, what would you like me to prepare?"

"Saturday and Sunday . . ." He considered for the first time. "Well, for Saturday night I think I would like something from the delicatessen. Which I will order myself. A little hot corned beef, maybe some center-cut tongue, with a few sour pickles, some mustard and cole slaw. However, since I am on a diet, no potato salad."

Bernadine always permitted him this flight into gastronomic fancy before she reminded him, "You know very well Dr. Tannenbaum is not going to allow you to have all that."

"Bernadine, you are as bad as Mrs. Washington was. Maybe even worse!"

"So what do you want for Saturday night and Sunday?" she persisted.

Calmed down and more realistic, Horowitz replied, "For Saturday, something I can heat up. Say, like chicken soup and boiled chicken. With noodles. And maybe a matzoh ball or two."

"And Sunday?" Bernadine persisted.

"Sunday I will be going out," Horowitz replied.

"Oh, so you have a date?" Bernadine observed.

"Who said anything about a date? I am just going out to dinner and the theater," Horowitz protested. "A very simple, ordinary thing to do. But it does not mean that it is a date!" he protested.

Surprised at the vehemence of his denial, Bernadine said softly, "Sorry. I didn' mean to step on any toes."

"Who said anything about toes?" Horowitz demanded. "If it isn't Mona, it's Mrs. Washington, and if not her, it's you! My whole life is run by women! If there is one thing I do not need, it is another woman in my life. I am going to dinner. I am going to the theater. And that is that!"

"Yes, sir," Bernadine said, departing the living room and thinking to herself in her feminine way, *Ah, so there's a woman in his life. Why else would he act so strange?*

Chapter 21

××××

Bernadine was just skimming the fat off the boiling chicken soup when Samuel Horowitz came into the kitchen late on Friday afternoon carrying in one hand a striped shirt and in the other his favorite tie.

"Bernadine, I wonder, would you mind before you leave to run an iron over this shirt? And also over this tie?"

She turned, a quizzical look on her black face.

"Something wrong?" Horowitz asked, more than a little self-conscious.

"No, nothing wrong, Mr. Horowitz," she replied in that tone of voice that refuted her words.

"So, please, just iron it."

"Can't," Bernadine said.

"What do you mean 'can't'?"

"Can't iron a shirt without washing it," Bernadine explained.

"It doesn't need to be washed. I haven't worn it since last time you washed it," Horowitz protested.

"Won't iron 'less it's damp," Bernadine explained.

"You mean you have to wash it, then let it dry and then iron it?" Horowitz asked.

"Only way it's going to come out right," Bernadine said.

"And," Horowitz considered, "it's already late on Friday. Look, let's forget it then."

"Can't," Bernadine said.

"Again 'can't'?" Horowitz replied, his irritation stimulated as much by his sense of guilt as frustration.

"I mean, can't forget it. 'F it's important to you to wear this special shirt, then I can't forget it. So leave it. I'll do it."

"Thank you, Bernadine." He turned to go until she mumbled something. "What did you say, Bernadine?"

"Just said, must be something special for you to want to wear this shirt and this tie, that's all," the woman explained.

She was making reference to the fact that this shirt was the one extravagance Samuel Horowitz had permitted himself since Hannah's death. He had been browsing in the new Charvet shop on Saks Fifth Avenue's men's floor when he came upon this shirt. It took his fancy. Despite the fact that it cost one hundred and seventy-five dollars, the silky broadcloth, the striping of alternate blue and crimson so intrigued him that he said to himself, *For once in my life I would like to know how it feels to wear something like this.* So he had bought it. Then he refrained from wearing it except on very special occasions. Once when he went down to Washington to attend the graduation of Marvin's son, Elliot, from college. The second time when he was himself honored as the only living retired prior president and dean of the Paper and Twine Trade Association.

The rest of the time the shirt lay in his drawer untouched. Thus it accumulated wrinkles, especially around the collar. He wanted it to look perfect for Sunday evening.

Early on Friday evening, when he went into the kitchen he found Bernadine at the ironing board pressing the shirt and muttering to herself.

"You said something?" he asked.

"I didn' say nothin'," she responded. "Only must be a very special 'casion to be wearing this shirt."

"It is no special occasion, Bernadine. I happen to be going to the theater Sunday night and I want to look decent, that's all," he protested.

"You got lots of shirts that look decent."

"Look, if you didn't want to iron it, all you had to do was say so!" Horowitz replied.

"I didn' say I didn' want to do it. I just said, seems like a special occasion."

"It is not a special occasion. Period. End of discussion!"

With that, Horowitz left the kitchen and went back to the living room where he attacked his newspaper with special animus. In minutes Bernadine came in, holding the hanger on which the freshly ironed shirt hung, its collar faultless.

"There," she said.

"Thanks," he replied gruffly.

"Still say it's a special 'casion." With that she said " 'Night. Have a good weekend."

He called after her, "It's no special occasion. Just going to the theater."

All the way uptown on the bus, Bernadine Vosper kept repeating to herself, *Got to be more. He ain't the same. Somewhere must be a woman in his life. First thing a new woman do is get rid of the maid. They don't want nobody around to be reminding them about how things used to be run. Seen it happen once to Florabel. And to Clara Dawkins. Time she was working for that man over on Fifth Avenue. Never works out. Never.*

Promptly at five-thirty on the bright Sunday afternoon of May 3, Samuel Horowitz presented himself at the home of Mrs. Molly Mendelsohn. She was dressed and ready to go so he did not have an opportunity to do more than catch a glimpse of her apartment. It appeared neatly kept and had the fragrance of a clean home. He expected no less of a woman so proper in her personal appearance.

He felt uncomfortable in the elevator on the way down, especially when the car stopped on the sixth floor and a woman entered who greeted, "Ah, Mrs. Mendelsohn! Nice to see you. Where have you been lately?"

All the while Horowitz felt himself under close scrutiny. The collar of his very expensive Charvet shirt felt tight suddenly.

This woman, he thought, *a jealous widow. Can't forgive another woman for having a date. Oy, did I say 'date'? This is not a date. It is merely so a perfectly good ticket to a good show for a good cause should not go to waste. It is only because Mrs. Washington couldn't make it. Go explain that to this obviously jealous widow.*

It was the longest elevator ride of his life.

They were seated in Sardi's facing each other across a table for two. As they studied their menus, Molly Mendelsohn remarked, "So many Italian dishes."

"They have other kinds. Chicken, steak, roast beef," he pointed out. "You don't like Italian food?"

"Oh, I love Italian food," she protested. "Just that I was thinking, when Jewish people go out to eat they always eat Italian food. Or Chinese. I wonder why?"

"Maybe because we have so much Jewish food at home we would like a change," Horowitz suggested.

"The Chinese eat lots of Chinese food at home but you don't see them eating in Jewish restaurants when they go out," Molly replied. "I wonder why?"

"Must be what they mean when they talk about the inscrutable Orient," Sam Horowitz said.

"I guess so," Molly said, concentrating on her menu.

During the play, Horowitz took the opportunity to glance at Molly Mendelsohn while her eyes were fixed on the action onstage. Since they were in the sixth row, if a little to the side, the light from the stage reflected on her face, permitting him the opportunity to study her. Like the woman herself, very neat. Small features. And her skin was smooth. Except, of course, where age had etched a few wrinkles.

To be expected, he thought, *a woman in her middle sixties. But somehow on her they seem so natural, like they belong. Not exactly belong but are graceful. That may not be the exact right word either. But there is something . . . Well, like with Hannah, she was not one of those women who went to a doctor and said, "Make me look like thirty-five again so no one would ever know." But everyone did know. And the woman didn't look any better for it. No, this woman is not given to such nonsense. Like Hannah . . . My God! Did I say like Hannah? Am I comparing this woman with Hannah?*

To avoid any further betrayal of the memory of his dear wife, Samuel Horowitz turned his eyes back toward the stage and kept them fixed there for the rest of the evening.

After the play, they had no difficulty finding a taxi to take them uptown. When they arrived at her house Molly invited him up for coffee and cake.

When he demurred because of the lateness of the hour, she tempted him with "*Ruggaluch.* I just made a new batch today."

"Thank you, my dear. But some other time," he replied.

"Of course, some other time," she said.

Once inside the apartment, her door triple locked in the New York habit, she thought, *He didn't like me. Something I did or said displeased him. Too bad, he seems like a nice man. And so lonely.*

Samuel Horowitz walked east on Eighty-second from West End Avenue to Broadway and then up Broadway to Eighty-sixth Street, across Eighty-sixth Street to Central Park West and down to Eighty-fourth Street. The reason for his circuitous route was to walk as much of the time as possible on wide, well-lighted main streets, a strategy thought to protect one against being mugged or killed in the world's greatest city.

His longer route also gave him much time to think. He had not yet got over the startling realization that he had committed a sin almost equivalent to adultery by comparing this woman, this virtual stranger, with his beloved Hannah. Could Bernadine's attitude, her suspicion, have some basis? Was he revealing to others feelings that he was hiding from himself? No, not possible! If he had any feelings about another woman he would know it. He could deny, very forcefully, that he had such feelings for this woman or any other than his own Hannah.

And, Hannah, my darling, listen to me. No other woman will ever take your place. No other woman!

Chapter 22

XXX

More and more in recent days Samuel Horowitz realized he was developing a habit that disturbed him.

He found himself talking to Hannah very frequently. As if she had come to life once more. She was a nearer presence than she had been since the early months after her death. In those days she seemed to be with him always. Watching over him. Giving him advice. Guiding him. Preventing him from moments of rash and impatient reactions to which he was prone.

As time went by, and especially after his stroke, Hannah had seemed to fade back into memory, a loving presence whom he called up from time to time. Now she seemed to appear on her own, surprising him at the oddest moments.

He often found himself thinking, and at times even saying aloud, *Hannah, oh, Hannah, remember how it used to be? Why can't it be that way again?*

The condition troubled him so that one day at the hospital, after he and Homer Wesley had completed their service, he asked, "Wesley, you got a little time?"

"Too much. Why, Horowitz?"

"Let's have a cup of coffee."

"Sure," Wesley agreed. "Mrs. Brown brought in some pineapple upside-down cake today."

"Mrs. Brown? Pineapple upside-down? I thought that was Mrs. Robbins's specialty," Horowitz pointed out.

"Seems last week Mrs. Robbins made some remark about Mrs. Brown's sponge cake. So now the war is on. Mrs. Brown is going to show up Mrs. Robbins. The biggest fight since Muhammad Ali and Joe Frazier in the Thrilla in Manila."

"Boy oh boy, was that a fight!" Horowitz concurred. "But I would like a little quiet time. Away from widows. Just us men."

"Sure. There's a little coffee place around the corner."

They had carried their coffee and cake from the counter to a table in the rear of the shop. Wesley passed the sugar container to Horowitz who refused. "Tannenbaum says cut down. Seems I gained maybe half an ounce since my last checkup."

"Dr. Yerby tells *me* it might do me good to gain a little."

"Wesley, it ever strike you how much like our little ones we are? We worry about them not gaining a few ounces. Our doctors worry about us gaining too many ounces. Is that the tipoff? Our babies are at the beginning of life. We are at the end, but doctors have the same concerns about us. You ever think about that?"

"Yes," Wesley agreed. "But I don't dwell on it. Thinking about things like that can only depress you."

Horowitz stirred his coffee slowly as he broached the subject of his concern. "Wesley, I am not a man to pry. I figure, like my mother used to say, everybody comes into this world with his own *peckle* of trouble. Which means his own bundle of trouble. We are no two of us the same. But I wonder if maybe you, being a widower longer than me, if you had such a strange thing happen to you as is happening to me."

"Such as?" Wesley asked, as he cut into his apple pie.

"Such as, did it ever happen to you that after the pain and the memories are not so sharp anymore, suddenly they come back even stronger than before. That ever happened to you?"

Wesley chewed slowly on a mouthful of pie, then downed it with a sip of coffee. As a psychiatrist might have done, the tall, gaunt black man considered: "The pain and the memories come back and stronger?"

"Yes. That happened to you also sometime?" Horowitz asked.

"Of course, there's times. Special moments such as when you see one of the grandchildren do something like, say, graduate from college, I find myself saying, 'Lydia, Lydia, you shoulda been here to see this. My, how you would have cried with joy.' That kind of thing, Horowitz?"

"That goes without saying," Horowitz agreed. "But I mean like she is with me all the time. Almost as if she was back."

Wesley searched his memory, took another bite of pie, sipped another swallow of coffee before shaking his head. "No. Far as I can remember, never had that happen. So that's your problem? Wish I could help. Thought about seeing one of those counselors?"

"Counselor?" Horowitz scoffed. "I don't need any counselor!"

"They say folks, especially when they get older, can get depressed and may need someone to talk to," Wesley suggested gingerly, aware of Samuel Horowitz's sensitivity.

"Folks, maybe. But not Horowitz." He disposed of the suggestion.

Wesley did not pursue the idea. They finished their coffee in silence, except for a few remarks about the still early baseball season and the Mets and the Yankees and George Steinbrenner. All of which Wesley ended with a grim forecast. "Horowitz, I have noticed over my long years of following baseball, when the management gets more publicity than the players, you got a losing team on your hands."

"Right, Wesley," Horowitz agreed.

But he was no closer to solving his own vexing problem.

More and more in recent days Samuel Horowitz experienced another disturbing phenomenon. In previous times when he had tickets to the theater, or a lecture, or there was a new exhibit at the Museum of Natural History or at the Metropolitan Museum of Art, he could always depend on Mrs. Washington to accompany him. If his preferred timing did not coincide with hers, he could accommodate to her schedule. At times he was delighted to take both her grandchildren with them. Somehow, things almost always worked out.

But lately, during the last two weeks, no matter how he juggled his time, things did not seem to jell between them. As kindly and cooperative as Mrs. Washington sounded, somehow she could never join him.

Once he went to Natural History on his own, but found it a very frustrating adventure. The need to share the experience was too strong. He even turned to a strange woman, trying to share his reaction to the exhibit of a new species of dinosaur. She glared at him and walked away to view the giant exhibit from another angle, continuing to stare at him through the simulated bones of the towering creature. Then when a man, whom Horowitz assumed to be her husband, had joined her, she whispered to him while pointing to Horowitz. He was so embarrassed that he skulked out of the museum.

Going to museums had lost its pleasure, a pleasure it was easier to forgo than attending a lecture or concert on a specific date where a specific pair of seats demanded his presence. One such evening involved a lecture at the 92nd Street YMHA. Usually not only were those lectures informative, ofttimes controversial, but the lecturers were almost always people who had been in the news. When the Y announced a lecture on Cultural Diversity by the woman dean of a midwestern university, Horowitz did not write for tickets but took advantage of a pleasant warm spring day to walk through Central Park to Lexington Avenue and pick up the tickets himself.

With tickets in hand, he called Mrs. Washington at home that evening.

"My dear and elusive Mrs. Washington," he began, making what he considered a humorous comment on her unavailability in recent days, "I am holding here in my hand a pair of tickets to a lecture which you, being of African-American heritage, will find most interesting."

"Really? And what might that lecture be, Mr. Horowitz?"

"Cultural Diversity on Campus," he announced.

"Oh, yes. Most interesting. What night are they for?"

"Next Tuesday," Horowitz replied.

"Tuesday . . ." Mrs. Washington repeated with some regret. "Wouldn't you know, wouldn't you just know!"

"Something wrong, Mrs. Washington?"

"Wednesday morning Louise has a math exam. So I'll have to be coaching her Tuesday night. You know how it is when they get to the last two years of high school. Every grade becomes important for college entrance."

"Yes, yes, I know," a disappointed Horowitz said.

"Surely," Mrs. Washington suggested, "with five days to go you can find someone to take."

"Yes, sure, of course," Horowitz agreed without much enthusiasm. "Well, maybe next time."

"Of course, next time," Mrs. Washington promised.

She hung up the phone with some regret but more determination. What disappointment he might feel now would be worth the happiness he would find later, if things worked out. *Meantime, she thought, I hope Molly Mendelsohn is not busy Tuesday night.*

Samuel Horowitz had hung up the phone. He sat there holding the two tickets in his damp hand. His first impulse was to tear them up. His recent days had only impressed on him the futility of trying to enjoy alone experiences of feeling and thought that were intended to be shared.

Hannah, oh, Hannah, if only you were still here. How you used to urge me: "Samuel, let's go to this play, let's go to hear a lecture at the Y." You were the one who decided where to go, when to go. The cultural side of our lives was in your hands. Since then, believe me, I have tried to do the things you always made me do. But it is not the same. For a time it was. When Mrs. Washington and I went together it was nice. Not like with you, of course. But nice. Another person to talk to, to share with. There is nothing worse than eating alone, listening alone, having no one to share thoughts with. I have begun to hate that word "alone." Five letters, two syllables, but what pain is contained in that little word.

Hannah, you wouldn't mind, I would like . . . I mean . . . Look, would you object, would you consider it a sin, a crime, if I asked that Mrs. Mendelsohn to go the lecture with me?

I have a feeling she is also lonely. Something she said to me about her grandson calling every Friday night, because he knew she was alone. That's very significant. Home alone Friday night means also Monday

*night and Tuesday night and all other nights as well. In a way, you could
say I would be doing an act of kindness and charity toward another person.
Like when you used to say to me, "Sam, as long as we're going to see that
movie, let's ask Mrs. Feldman to come with us. She is alone since her
husband died." Remember? And the times you used to say, "Sam, what
does it hurt to ask Mrs. Rubin to come to the theater with us?" Or when
you used to invite Abe Fogel to dinner and you would make such a fuss
over him. I could see the difference between when he walked in, so sad and
dragging, and when he left feeling so good, and it was more than your
cooking that did it. It was the way you cared, made him feel wanted and
not so alone anymore.*

*Yes, Hannah, it would be the same to ask that lonely Mrs. Mendelsohn to go to a lecture. After all, who could misinterpret an invitation
to a lecture? She would know it was not a serious thing.*

When he called, Mrs. Molly Mendelsohn was not at home.

The next day, after having had a restless night to work up his
courage, Samuel Horowitz finished his Thursday volunteer hours
in the nursery. But instead of leaving with Homer Wesley as
usual, to the black man's surprise he lingered at the coffee corner.
Consulting his watch often, despite the huge clock on the nursery
wall, Horowitz waited out what seemed interminable hours,
though actually it was only one hour and six minutes before neat
little Mrs. Mendelsohn arrived with her usual tidy package of
home-baked delicacies.

She seemed pleased to see him. "Ah, good afternoon, Mr.
Horowitz."

"Good afternoon to you, Mrs. Mendelsohn," Horowitz replied.

When she started to unwrap the aluminum foil that protected
her cake plate, he asked, "*Ruggaluch?*"

"Cheese strudel," she announced.

"Not *ruggaluch,*" he commented, disappointed.

"Not this time." She lowered her voice to a conspiratorial
level. "They were becoming jealous. My *ruggaluch* are the first
cakes to disappear whenever I bring them. I didn't want to stir up
any trouble. So, for a while, cheese strudel."

"Very thoughtful, very diplomatic," Horowitz replied with
the air of a sage.

"Would you like to try some strudel?" she invited.

"Don't mind if I do," he said, studying the plate for a piece that seemed not the largest, but not the smallest either. He picked it up, and with an expert's touch appraised. "Light. Very light. Such a fine dough."

"That's the secret of strudel. I learned it from my aunt, who, by the way, was also named Molly. She taught me."

"Very tasty filling, also," Horowitz decided after a lingering taste.

"The touch of lemon in the cheese makes the difference."

"A coincidence," Horowitz announced. "A very significant coincidence,"

"Oh? How so?" Mrs. Mendelsohn asked.

"Hannah—that is, my wife—she used to say the same thing. A touch of lemon can spice up the sweetest cake."

"She must have been a very good cook," Molly Mendelsohn said. "Else you would not be such a maven on cooking."

"You think I am a maven?" he asked, secretly pleased.

"The way you diagnosed my *ruggaluch*. And now with the strudel. Yes, I think you have been well trained by an excellent cook."

"Hannah would have been pleased to hear you say that," Horowitz replied. "Tell me, Mrs. Mendelsohn, by any chance—I mean if you are busy, just say so. But by any chance would you be free to go to a lecture at the Y on Tuesday night?"

"Tuesday night . . ." she considered, giving him a momentary qualm that she might refuse. "I could arrange to be free on Tuesday night. Yes, I would be delighted to go to the lecture."

"Very good. Shall I pick you up for dinner, say seven-thirty?" he asked.

"Say," she agreed.

He stared down at her strudel until she invited, "Have another. They are made with margarine."

He had bitten into his second piece when he paused, chewed a moment, then said, "So you had an aunt named Molly. Which is also your first name. Nice name, Molly. Nice."

Chapter 23

XXX

THURSDAY AFTERNOON MRS. HARRIET WASHINGTON APPEARED AT the nursery ready to fill in for any volunteer who was prevented from attending by reason of illness or some family obligation.

That her arrival coincided with Molly Mendelsohn's hours of service could have been charged to coincidence. Whatever the reason, this confluence of events gave both women a chance to chat while they cared for the little ones. Between feeding them, changing them, slipping them into fresh clean shirts, they managed to carry on their conversation. During which, Molly Mendelsohn confessed to Mrs. Washington that Mr. Horowitz had called to invite her to a lecture at the YMHA. Mrs. Washington greeted that news with what she considered a proper degree of surprise.

Later, while they were enjoying their coffee break, Mrs. Washington managed to subtly suggest that it might be a good idea if, instead of dining out that evening, Molly invited Mr. Horowitz to dinner at her home.

"Don't you think that would be considered a little too forward? After all, when a woman invites a man to dinner at her home it suggests that she has some designs on him."

"Mrs. Mendelsohn, I know that man. I have seen him through a difficult time. I also know Bernadine, his housekeeper.

As Horowitz himself would say, the greatest cook in the world, she isn't.''

"Yes, but—" Molly started to protest.

"No 'yes, but,' " Mrs. Washington ruled. "The man is tired of eating in restaurants, tired of eating Bernadine's version of his wife's food. He wants a good home-cooked meal.''

"A good home-cooked meal," Molly Mendelsohn considered. "The question is, what would be considered a good home-cooked meal?''

"Well," Mrs. Washington pretended to consider, "remember once you described to me your lima bean, beef and barley soup?''

"Yes.''

"What man could resist such a hearty and delicious dish?" Mrs. Washington asked. "And if for dessert, with a little decaf, of course, you served a plate of your *ruggaluch,* that would be perfect.''

"You think he would like that?''

"I have good reason to think he would like it," Mrs. Washington said with great assurance.

"To tell you the truth, I would like a good lima bean, beef and barley soup myself. But cooking for one, it always seems like too much trouble.''

"Do it," Mrs. Washington argued. "From just talking to you and tasting your *ruggaluch* and your cheese strudel, I know you are first-class *ballabusteh.*''

"Mrs. Washington, if you don't mind my asking, how do you come to know such a word as *ballabusteh?* And know what it means?''

"Years ago . . .'' Mrs. Washington began.

But Molly Mendelsohn anticipated her. "Yes, I remember, you used to work for a family named Rosengarten.''

"Exactly. And now that you mention the Rosengartens, I remember how Mrs. Rosengarten, when she served lima bean, beef and barley soup, since the vegetables were already in the soup, she would serve a nice spicy *kigel* as a side dish.''

"You think that might be a good idea?''

"As Mrs. Rosengarten used to say, 'Couldn't hurt!' ''

Early that evening, Molly Mendelsohn called the home of Samuel Horowitz.

"Mr. Horowitz, this is Molly, Molly Mendelsohn," she announced.

At once the thought flashed through his mind: *Aha, I should have known. She has changed her mind. She thinks I was too forward asking her to go to this lecture. Being stuck with that expensive theater ticket could be a one-time thing. But a second time? No, she must think I am making what they call these days a big move on her. Used to be a pass, now is a move. Same thing. It was a mistake. But if she doesn't want to go, I can't force her.*

Aloud he said, "Ah. Mrs. Mendelsohn, a pleasant surprise to hear your voice. What can I do for you?"

She began with noticeable hesitancy, "Mr. Horowitz, I . . . I was wondering if . . . if . . . Well, about . . . if . . . on Tuesday evening . . ."

Aha, I was right. Here it comes. But I am ready for it.

Anticipating her change of mind, he said, "Yes, Mrs. Mendelsohn, what about Tuesday evening? If there is any problem, just say so."

"Well, I wouldn't exactly consider it a problem. Unless *you* think it's a problem."

"And exactly what is the nature of this problematical problem?" Horowitz asked. "After all, between two adults, what is there that can't be handled by straight talk?"

He thought he had gone as far as he could to give her the opportunity to back out.

"Well, I was wondering if instead of eating out you might like to have dinner at my home," Molly Mendelsohn invited, greatly relieved that she had been able to get it all out in a single sentence. She awaited his reply, hardly daring to breathe.

"Dinner?" Horowitz asked, greatly relieved. "At your home? I don't see why not."

"Good!" she was relieved to confirm. "If the lecture is at eight, why not be here by six?"

"Six o'clock? Mrs. Mendelsohn, six o'clock it will be!"

He hung up the phone with considerable relief. As did Molly Mendelsohn.

*   *   *

On Tuesday evening, promptly at six, Samuel Horowitz presented himself at Molly Mendelsohn's West End Avenue apartment building. As bad luck would have it, he entered the elevator to find the same woman whom he had encountered the only other time he had been here. She smiled at him. A little too pleasantly, he thought. She had the gleam of a gossip vulture in her eyes when she said, "Ah, again, I see."

He smiled back, thinking, *Tomorrow it will be all over the building, all over West End Avenue, all over the whole West Side of Manhattan: Samuel Horowitz is having a date with another woman. A widow, yet.*

What compounded his discomfort was that he had stopped at a florist's on Broadway to pick up two red roses and a sprig of green. It was a hangover from his days as a child when his mother would say, "When you are invited to someone's house for supper never come empty-handed." In those days his mother always brought a box of Whitman's chocolates. The size depended on the relative financial situation of the Horowitz family.

In later times, with so many foods on the forbidden list for their contemporaries, Hannah always used to bring flowers. So he had stopped to buy two roses.

Is that a crime, he argued silently, *two measly little roses? The way this woman is staring at them you would think they are evidence of a murder. How long can it take this damn elevator to reach the sixth floor, where she will get off?*

He was a bit bashful about asking for a second helping of Molly Mendelsohn's noodle *kigel,* since he had already had just one more ladleful of that excellent lima bean, beef and barley soup. But she could tell by the glance in his eyes that he might just be persuaded.

He justified it by excusing, *After all, a woman goes to such trouble to prepare a meal for only two people, the highest compliment you can pay her is to ask for seconds. And such a meal certainly deserves a compliment.*

He thought he showed excellent restraint by limiting himself to only three *ruggaluch.* After all, they were rather small.

Throughout the meal, Molly Mendelsohn watched, commenting silently, *He seems to like the soup. Or is he just being polite? Does a man ask for seconds out of politeness? No, I think he likes my soup. Really likes it. About the* kigel, *Mrs. Washington was right. In fact, when I think of it, she is always right when it comes to this man. She knows him so well. They must be very close friends. Oh, now he is eyeing my* ruggaluch. *He's had two. Will he take a third? Yes! Now I am wondering has he eaten too much? Will he feel uncomfortable during the lecture? Or even fall asleep? Phil used to fall asleep at times like that. Too late to think of that now. Well, if he does fall asleep he won't wake up hungry.*

Samuel Horowitz did not fall asleep during the lecture. In fact, as the woman dean of that midwestern university continued to talk about diversity, bilingual and multiethnic courses, about Native Americans, African-Americans, Latinos, and why one must not use words such as Oriental when referring to Orientals, the more awake Samuel Horowitz became. Molly could feel that he was beginning to seethe in discomfort. At first she suspected he was suffering the effects of overeating. But as she heard him grumble, she realized he was growing angrier by the minute with this lecturer who was extremely dogmatic about her beliefs.

"Nonsense," Horowitz grumbled. "Dangerous nonsense!"

Soon people sitting close around them started to cast resentful glances in their direction. Molly began to feel self-conscious. Not so Samuel Horowitz, who continued to protest. He could hardly wait until the formal part of the lecture ended.

He began to feel a glimmer of hope when the dean said, "And so the net gain from these creative new improvements in education will be to give our students, in grade school, high school and university a knowledge of their own roots, their own history. They will know why they are different. They will have reason to feel pride and self-respect in their origins, their history and their original language. And now, if there are any questions . . ."

Before she concluded the word, Samuel Horowitz's hand shot up belligerently.

"Yes? The elderly gentleman on the right," the woman recognized him.

I'll give you "elderly gentleman," Horowitz thought, but launched into his question.

"Madam, or Dean, or whatever you like to be called, I have a question. Are you actually teaching such nonsense to your students in that university?"

With a condescending smile, the woman replied, "Ah, one of those," evoking a ripple of laughter from the audience.

Horowitz shot back, "I don't know what means 'one of those.' I am not a 'those.' I am a citizen of this country. Of course, since I was not born here I cannot claim to be a Native American. And since I was born in Europe I cannot claim to be an African-American either. But some things I do know from my own personal experience."

The woman attempted to interrupt. "Please, we don't have all evening."

"My dear woman, I listened to you for one hour and seven minutes. You can at least listen to me for five. Now, as I was saying, I speak from experience. Which you do not. When I came to this country as a small boy my father and mother had only one dream for me. To become an American. So they sent me to public school. In those days they did not have bilingual education. So they did not teach me Yiddish. Why should they? I already knew Yiddish. They taught me what I did *not* know. They taught me English."

"Sir," the speaker reprimanded, "that is not a question but a speech."

"So it's a speech," Horowitz granted. "Listen anyhow. You might learn something. They taught me, and all the other kids, English. When it came to history, just because I came from Poland was no reason to teach me Polish history. Another thing they did not teach me. Why we are all different from one another. Tell me, my dear Dean, what do you accomplish by pointing out to your students how different they are from one another?"

"Sir, it is obvious," the woman proceeded in her most icy tone of superior prejudice, "you are of the old school and no matter what I said it would not convince you." She turned her attention to another part of the audience.

But Horowitz called out, "Madam! It says in the program

you are a professor of history. Well, have you ever found any country in history that took in more millions of immigrants than this country did in the last hundred years?"

"Really, sir, there are other questions waiting and I don't have time—"

"Why? You are in a hurry to get back to that university and teach more nonsense?" Horowitz commented.

By this time some of the audience was beginning to protest. He turned his anger on them.

"Ask yourselves, does any country in the world have more experience turning immigrants into citizens? And that system, did it work? Better than any time in history! So why have we thrown out a system that works for phony ideas like bilingual education, and diversity and some of those other high-class nonsense words?"

"Quiet!" someone shouted from across the room.

Horowitz turned his attention and his defiance toward that part of the room.

"You tell me! Have we improved education in recent years? The test scores give you the answer. We have not. Why? Simple. You want a kid to know history? Teach him history. You want him to get good marks in geography? Teach him geography. don't teach him propaganda and call it social studies. My dear people, we have 'improved' education into a national disgrace!"

"Sir, sir," the speaker tried to interrupt.

But Horowitz swept on. "Don't waste time teaching kids where they came *from*. Teach them about where they came *to*."

His tirade evoked shouts and catcalls now from various sections of the audience. But they did not deter him.

"Please, someone in this big hall explain to me how it is going to help a black kid to get a job if he is taught all about Africa five hundred years ago? Or how a Spanish-speaking kid is going to learn how to speak good English from a teacher with a heavy Spanish accent?"

"My dear benighted man, I can see that you have come here with a heavy burden of old preconceived notions."

"And I," Horowitz countered, "can see that you, my dear lady, have come here with a heavy burden of the new *crackpot* notions!"

By now people in other parts of the hall were on their feet shouting at him. But to no avail.

"School used to be a place where kids of all kinds, all religions, kids from all over the world learned how to become Americans. Now it is a place where they come to learn how to be different. This country is no longer a melting pot. It is a battleground where different groups fight each other. And you call that education?"

By that time, at the dean's signal, two ushers had started in his direction. Horowitz refused to be silenced. He was still protesting when they carried him up the aisle with Molly Mendelsohn trailing alongside, protesting, "Don't you dare! You let that man go! You let him go at once!"

Out on the street, he was still shouting at the ushers. "Gangsters! That's what you are. Storm troopers of the New Left!"

Passersby stopped to stare at the irate elderly man who was accompanied by a neat little woman who was trying to mollify him and at the same time straighten his tie and his jacket, which had become badly disarranged during the altercation.

The ushers had retreated into the Y. Samuel Horowitz and Molly Mendelsohn were alone on Lexington Avenue. With no particular destination in mind they started walking south.

By the time they had reached the corner of Eighty-seventh Street and Lexington, Samuel Horowitz had calmed down sufficiently to say sheepishly, "I embarrassed you, didn't I?"

"No, not at all," Molly Mendelsohn denied.

"Admit it. I made a spectacle of myself," he confessed.

"I don't think you did. You had something to say and you said it."

"I have a confession to make to you. I am a man who sometimes lets his temper run away with him. I am what they call 'impulsive.' Hannah used to say, what's on my mind is on my tongue. And she was right. Frankly, how she put up with me I'll never know."

"I imagine you weren't angry all the time," Molly suggested subtly.

"Not all the time. But enough. More than enough. About

tonight I am very sorry. I just hope there was no one there who knew you."

"I don't care if there was," she replied.

"You don't care? You mean you didn't mind?" he asked.

"What you said is what I would have said, if I had the nerve. Even from the time I was in high school I was always too bashful to get up in class and recite. It was like agony. When I had to write a speech and deliver it, I was terrified. I think that's why I concentrated on drawing and writing. Things I could do in private by myself."

"Me," Horowitz said, "I had the opposite trouble. I was always first up with my hand. First with the answer. Not always right, but first. Now, you take Hannah, she was a shy one. Like you, I guess."

His sudden awareness that he had made such a direct comparison between Hannah and Molly Mendelsohn caused him to become silent. They continued walking.

When they reached the corner of Eighty-sixth Street Molly remarked, "There's a crosstown bus waiting. We can just make it."

"No, we will take a taxi," he decided.

"But it's such a waste of money. The bus goes practically to my door."

"A taxi!" he insisted.

They were at her apartment. As she was unlocking the door she asked, "Would you like to come in for some decaf?"

"I think I have given you enough trouble for one evening," he said.

"No trouble at all," she responded. "In fact, I am very proud that you stood up for common sense."

On his circuitous route from Eighty-second Street and West End Avenue to Central Park West and Eighty-fourth Street, he relived the events of the evening.

She said, "Don't you dare lay a hand on him! You let that man go!" That's what she said. She defended me. And she wasn't embarrassed. "Let him go at once!" she said. She defended me.

Chapter 24

XXX

THE NEXT AFTERNOON SAMUEL HOROWITZ FOUND HIMSELF CON-
fronted by a dilemma. It had never occurred to him before. But
when he was reading his morning *Times* he came upon a review of
a new film.

His instinctive and automatic reaction had always been,
*Sounds like the kind of picture Mrs. Washington would enjoy. This
evening I will call and ask her.*

But, it came to him, not this time. This time, for some reason
he could not immediately discern, his first reaction was *Molly
Mendelsohn might like this kind of picture.* Not only had she come
first to his mind but he had referred to her as *Molly.*

He was assailed by strong feelings of guilt. He reviewed his
conduct of recent days. Not once in the past several weeks had he
seen Mrs. Washington at dinner, or taken her to some lecture or
entertainment. Of course, twice during that time he had called
her, twice she had been busy with other things. So that he was not
entirely at fault. Still, his sense of guilt lingered. Tonight he would
call her and invite her to see that new movie.

He was dressing to walk down to his broker's office on Fifth
Avenue. Not that he intended to trade any of his modest portfolio
of stocks. But it gave him a feeling of importance to be asked by

his broker, "Well, Mr. Horowitz, how do you feel about the future of the market?" Thereupon he would hold forth on the market, as well as the national and international economies. It was an exercise, both physically and for his own sense of importance. The brisk half-hour walk was good, pleasant exercise. The opportunity to have his opinion considered was also stimulating.

He was tying his tie with great care and dexterity when his phone rang. He hurried to answer, hoping it was not Mona again. In the last week she had called twice, and for some reason he could not ascertain, her calls seemed to irritate him even more than usual. Of late there seemed to be a subtle rebuke in her tone of voice. It would never occur to him that her tone and her talk were no different from before. It was his perception that had changed recently.

Fortunately, it turned out not to be Mona. But he heard instead the gentle voice of Molly Mendelsohn.

"Mr. Horowitz?" she inquired softly.

To cover his pleasure at hearing her voice he tried to joke, "The president of the United States it isn't." She did not respond with laughter so he felt a bit embarrassed. "My dear, what can I do for you?"

"I just wanted to thank you for last evening. It was very exciting. And it has been a long time since I have gone to such a lecture."

"My pleasure, I assure you," Horowitz replied. "In fact, it was on my mind to call you. To thank you, not only for such an excellent dinner, but for defending me. That was very nice of you to do." Before he could inhibit himself he blurted out, "That's exactly what Hannah would have done." He reminded himself, *I did it again. Brought up Hannah's name. Nice as this woman is, she will never be another Hannah. There will never be another Hannah.*

"She must have been a wonderful woman," he heard Molly Mendelsohn say.

"She was, she was," he agreed at once.

"I know the feeling," she responded.

"Your Phil was also a nice person?" Horowitz asked.

"Yes," she replied.

"That's good. At our age all we have left are memories. What a wonderful thing to have good ones."

"I think we are both very lucky people," Molly said. "Well . . ." she continued, with that intonation that indicated she was about to conclude the conversation.

To prevent her from doing so he blurted out, "Mrs. Mendelsohn—Molly—there is a new film just opened up which was reviewed in the *Times* this morning. Sounds very interesting. I wonder would you like to go some afternoon?"

"Any afternoon I'm not at the hospital," she replied.

"Of course. I would never interfere with your volunteer work. So shall we say Wednesday?"

"I think Wednesday would be nice," she replied.

"Say, the three-fifteen show?" he suggested. "It's the Loew's on Broadway and Eighty-third."

"I will meet you there," she agreed.

Honesty forced him to confess, "Frankly I would like to come pick you up. But there is that woman I keep meeting in your elevator. Somehow she seems to know every time I am there. It's like she waits for me. So she can give me that nasty smile of hers. Personally I think she is jealous of you."

"That's Mrs. Berkowitz."

"She is also a widow," he assumed.

"No. But I think she wishes she were," Molly said. "Her husband is not exactly the finest man in the world."

"She *is* jealous," Horowitz concluded. "To see another woman enjoying life again."

"I didn't know it was so obvious," Molly Mendelsohn replied softly.

"Are you . . . I mean, did you mean—" Horowitz faltered in trying to ask.

"Did *you* mean . . ." Molly Mendelsohn started to ask.

"Did I mean *what*?" he asked.

"When you said, 'She is jealous to see another woman enjoying life again.' "

"*Are* you . . . enjoying life again?" he dared to ask.

"Lately, yes," she admitted, and sounded shy in doing so.

"You want to know something? Me too," he confessed.

There was a long silence, not of embarrassment but of realization. Their words, indirect as they had been, were an admission of deep feelings each of them had been experiencing, but were afraid to admit even to themselves.

Finally, to clear the air of mutual embarrassment, Horowitz said, "As long as we are confessing, I want to say that before, when I asked you to go to that 'film' I don't usually say 'film.' To me they will always be movies. Or moving pictures. 'Films' are for the young people who bring in food and popcorn, who talk during the picture, who think going to the movies entitles them to be rude and loud and vulgar. So from now on, when we talk about movies, let's agree to just call them movies. Okay?"

"Okay. And as long as we are making up rules, there is one more. Let's never compare grandchildren."

"I know what you mean. It's what I call Jewish Bridge. Each grandparent tries to outbid the other with the accomplishments of their grandchildren. And whoever's grandchild has the best record at Harvard or Yale or MIT is the winner."

"Oh, how well I know *that* kind of bridge," Molly agreed.

"So, tell you what," Horowitz replied, "as long as we are going to meet at the movies for the three-fifteen show, why not make an afternoon of it? There happens to be a little Continental-type café right down the street from Loew's."

"You mean the little place on Eighty-fourth Street west of Broadway?" Molly asked.

"Why not meet there for lunch? Say about one-fifteen? So we don't have to rush things," Horowitz suggested.

"A very good idea," Molly replied. "One-fifteen."

Samuel Horowitz had just hung up the phone, feeling a tingle of excitement such as he had not felt in a long time. It was the kind of anticipation he used to experience back in his high school days when he made a date with some girl whom he fancied.

He had to chide himself.

Horowitz, what do you think you are? A young boy? You are not even a young man. Or even, he admitted, *middle-aged. You are an old man. In your late sixties. What right do you have to feel this way? If tomorrow you were attacked on the street, or hit by a car, and it was reported on the* Times *or on television, they would say, "An elderly man named Samuel Horowitz was struck down, etc., etc., etc." That's what they would say: "An elderly man." So get hold of yourself.*

All that is happening is that on Wednesday, instead of having lunch alone, or going to the movies alone, you will be going with a rather nice widow. That's all. No big deal. No big gedillah. In fact, come to think of it, it is something you used to do quite often with Mrs. Washington.

Suddenly the thought struck him: Mrs. Washington! My God, what have I been thinking of? Wrong expression. "Not thinking of" is more correct. How could I have forgotten about her in all this? Not very nice, after all she has meant to me. It is almost as if suddenly this new person, this woman I didn't know until weeks ago has taken her place. Surely Mrs. Washington must have noticed. And her feelings must be hurt. Who could blame her? She deserves an explanation. No, she deserves an apology. I must call her. Right away. Soon as she gets home this evening.

On Wednesday evening, as he had arranged with her, Mrs. Washington met him at the Stanhope Hotel across from the Metropolitan Museum of Art. The dining room there was one of the best in the city, and also among the most expensive. But Samuel Horowitz thought that the seriousness of the occasion merited such surroundings.

They started the evening with a cocktail. After they had ordered, but before their food arrived, he began his planned explanation.

"I suppose, my dear Mrs. Washington, that you are wondering what is so special about this evening. As we say on Passover, why is this night different from all other nights? Well, a situation has come up. Well, not exactly a situation. Let us say a . . . well, situation is not such a bad choice of words, after all."

Mrs. Washington toyed with her frosted stemmed glass, concerned because he was having such difficulty putting his thoughts into words. Usually, Samuel Horowitz was very forthright. Often much more than forthright about his feelings and reactions. She was tempted to intercede and assist but she knew if she waited long enough he would come around to what was troubling him.

"The thing is, there has been a change, a change in the way—"

Fortunately for him, their first course arrived. Once it was served, he could avoid all issues by eating and remarking, "Excellent salad, excellent."

Mrs. Washington agreed but glanced across the table at him, coaxing silently, *Come now, you can tell me; no matter what it is, you can tell me. I have seen you through some of the worst moments of your life. Whatever it is, it can't be so bad.*

Suddenly she was seized by a chilling thought. She had had a therapy patient, early in her career, whom she had brought back from a serious stroke to almost perfect functioning. Only to be told by him months later that he had been diagnosed as having inoperable cancer.

God, I hope this is not one of those confessions, she thought, losing all appetite for food.

Horowitz noticed. "Mrs. Washington, something wrong with your salad? I will have the waiter change it at once."

"No, no, nothing wrong. Now, you were saying—" She urged him on.

"Well, this situation— You may have noticed that we, you and I, that is, we are not seeing each other as much as usual lately."

"Well, I have been busy, more so than usual," Mrs. Washington said.

"And I also have been busy, 'more so than usual,' " he commented. "The reason is, and I hope I do not hurt your feelings, because that is the one thing in this world I would never, never do. You have meant too much in my life for me ever to hurt you, or Conrad or Louise."

"I know that, Mr. Horowitz," she said to ease his obvious difficulty.

"The thing is there is this . . . Well, you know her, the woman from the hospital—Molly Mendelsohn?"

"Yes, yes, I think I do know her. A small woman. Very nice-looking. Always so neatly dressed. Excellent baker. I think she makes . . ." Mrs. Washington pretended to grope for a moment for the form of pastry. "Is it *schnecken*?"

"*Ruggaluch*," Horowitz corrected.

As if he had refreshed her memory, Mrs. Washington replied,

"Of course, *ruggaluch*. I should have remembered. What about her?"

"Well, Mrs. Washington, something very strange has happened. Something very unexpected. Remember how she got up those posters to get them to reinstate me on the volunteer service and you said I should thank her? Well, I did. And it led to, to a kind of . . . call it a friendship. I mean, the times when you could not go to the theater with me, and that lecture, I invited her. And it turns out we have . . . have certain things in common. Like the night at the lecture, where I was asked to leave. Well, actually I was thrown out, and she defended me. And tomorrow we are going together to a new movie at Loew's Eighty-third Street. So what I mean to say, is that, well . . ."

Since she knew he was going to have great difficulty articulating his new relationship, Mrs. Washington decided to assist him.

"I know, Mr. Horowitz. Things will not be the same between us."

"Oh," he protested, "things will be the same. Only they will be a little different. If you know what I mean."

"Yes, I know what you mean, Mr. Horowitz. There is a new interest in your life. And, frankly, I don't blame you."

"You don't?" he was both surprised and relieved to ask.

"We are friends. And will always be friends, I hope."

"Oh, we will, we will!" Horowitz insisted.

"But there are other relationships in life that are different from friendship. Closer than friendship," she suggested.

"No," he protested, "this is just a friendship with Mrs. Mendelsohn. I assure you that's all I intend. And all that she intends. Friendship, that's it."

Mrs. Washington made no effort to dispute him. Since her plan had worked so well up to this point, she felt quite sure it would continue. She attacked her salad with fresh appetite.

While Samuel Horowitz sat across the table from her and observed, *She took this much better than I expected.*

On her way uptown, Harriet Washington thought, *What we have between us, that is friendship. But he needs more. He is a man used to a homelife. He needs a woman, a wife. I think he is on his way.*

Chapter 25

×××

For several weeks Samuel Horowitz followed his new routine. Two mornings a week he served his time as a volunteer. He was pleased and took considerable satisfaction from his success with what he had come to call "My Babies." Between them, Horowitz and Wesley ran a very efficient and caring nursery. When it came time to train new volunteers, Ms. Flaherty knew she could depend on them.

For the rest of his time, Horowitz sought pretexts to invite Molly Mendelsohn to share his time. Any new exhibit at any museum, a new movie, some play about which he heard a good word, all served his purpose. But all ended the same way. At her door. And then he was alone again.

It took the attack on Mrs. Robbins to change things. She had been on her way to the hospital one afternoon, carrying her usual platter of pineapple upside-down cake, when she was attacked by three teenaged muggers. Fortunately, her cries attracted attention so the muggers ran off with only her purse.

She was brought to the hospital Emergency Service where her injuries were assessed as superficial and she was given a sedative. When word reached Ms. Flaherty she hurried down to Emergency to take charge of one of her most dependable volunteers. Though Ms. Flaherty offered to have her taken home by ambulance, Mrs. Robbins insisted on going up to the nursery and putting in her regular hours.

Word of the attack on Mrs. Robbins was the talk of the nursery for the rest of that day and into the next. Each shift of volunteers who came on heard the disturbing story. Each woman and man among them was both outraged and also a little more afraid. The hospital was located in an area where the crime rate was high.

When Samuel Horowitz arrived the next morning he was shocked and angered by the news. He could not wait for Homer Wesley to arrive to discuss the outrage with him.

"We have to do something!" Horowitz insisted. "After all, these are women. Defenseless women!"

"What can we do? Organize ourselves into vigilantes? We wouldn't have a chance," Wesley pointed out. "The trouble with men like us, Horowitz, we got the indignation of youth, but the weakness of old age."

Samuel Horowitz grumbled a bit, but finally had to give way to Homer Wesley's practicality.

"Remember, when we were young, such things didn't happen," Horowitz complained. "I remember when Hannah and me were starting to go steady. On a Saturday night we could go up to Harlem. By subway. We would go to the Savoy Ballroom, hear the best jazz bands in the world. And come home two o'clock in the morning, also on the subway, and feel safe all the while."

"Don't I know," Wesley commiserated. "Well, when our little ones grow up things will be better."

But neither man really believed it.

When it came time to leave late that morning, instead of following his usual routine, Samuel Horowitz volunteered to stay on. Even though no substitute was needed, he explained to Ms. Flaherty that it would give him more time with one special little one who was suffering the pangs of withdrawal.

She warned against a repetition of the attachment that he had formed to tiny Cletus. But Horowitz had learned his lesson so she need have no fear of that. He stayed on to give the struggling infant more rocking time, more walking time, more close singing time, singing his favorite, a Yiddish folk tune, to him. After he had fed and changed him, he bound him in his blanket and set him down in his crib. He hovered over him, watching, hoping that the little one would give up struggling and rest awhile. Improved as its condition was, it still exhibited vestiges of the involuntary twisting and turning so characteristic of withdrawal.

Damn you, woman, whoever you are, I wish you were here to see what you have done to your own flesh and blood, Horowitz railed inwardly. But there was no more he could do. He glanced up at the clock. It was almost two o'clock.

He slipped out of his yellow smock, put on his jacket and left. Instead of going across the street to wait for the Number 10 bus back down to Central Park West, he walked two blocks to the bus stop of the Number 11 line. There he waited. From time to time he glanced at his watch. From time to time he looked down the street in one direction, then in the other. Then he stared up the street once more, watching for the Number 11 to appear.

Surely she will be on it. How else would she come? After all, from West End Avenue she must walk to Amsterdam, take the Number 11 uptown which brings her here. Or maybe after what happened to Mrs. Robbins yesterday she is too afraid to come by bus and is taking a taxi? Or worse, maybe she decided not to come at all.

He crossed the street to the public phone. His first quarter was wasted. That phone had been vandalized. But his second quarter produced a dial tone. He pressed in Molly's number. It rang and rang and rang. No answer. She must be on her way. He started back to the bus stop when a thought struck. If she did take a taxi she could have come by a different route and he would never have seen her. He must go back to the hospital and see if she had arrived. And yet, if he went back and she was on the bus, he would miss her. He was in a sweat of indecision.

It reminded him of the time years ago when, as he approached his house, he sighted a number of fire engines on his corner. Central Park West was blocked off by police cars with flashing lights. No one was permitted to approach. He had started to run, thinking, Hannah, Hannah, there is a fire in our building and

Hannah is there. He had pushed his way through the police cars, brushed off one officer with a desperate, "I live here. My wife is up there! You can't stop me!" He broke away and reached the door to be greeted by the doorman who said, " 'S okay, Mr. Horowitz. Not our building. A building down the block.' " He could have kissed the doorman. Instead, he stood there drenched in sweat and breathing hard. He felt the same way now. Wet through, fearful and breathing hard.

He started toward the hospital entrance when he caught sight of the Number 11 just pulling up. He went to meet it. The door opened. To his great relief, Molly Mendelsohn stepped off the bus, carrying a plate of her own baked creations.

The moment she saw him she knew something was wrong.

"Mr. Horowitz . . . Samuel . . . What happened?"

"Fortunately, nothing happened," he replied.

"But you're so, so perspiring . . . And you look upset. Something must have happened," she insisted.

"I think something did happen," he confessed.

"What? Tell me. One thing I can't stand is suspense."

"Neither can I," Horowitz said with considerable relief. "Let me carry that plate for you."

Taken aback by what she considered an odd request, Molly replied, "I have carried this plate twice a week for more than two years. I can do it myself."

"This time, let me," Horowitz insisted. She surrendered the plate to him.

Once he was sure she was safely inside the hospital, he made her promise to meet him tomorrow. If it was a pleasant day he wished to take a walk in Central Park with her.

When he arrived home Bernadine was vacuuming the dining-room carpet. She greeted him with the usual "Ain't nobody called."

Horowitz stood in the foyer, staring out toward the park and contemplating the wisdom of his next urge. Finally, he decided on his course of action.

"Bernadine, tomorrow is Friday. And since Friday comes

before Saturday and Sunday, why not make it a long weekend?"

"Mr. Horowitz, what do you mean, long weekend? Who is going to prepare your Sunday evening dinner?"

"Don't worry about it, Bernadine. Just take tomorrow off."

"Whatever you say, Mr. Horowitz."

She continued to run the vacuum over the thick carpet at the same time mumbling to herself.

Horowitz came into the living room to resume reading his mail and his morning newspapers, which he had interrupted to go up to the hospital. But he was distracted by Bernadine's continuous mumbling.

She can drive a person crazy with her mumbling, Horowitz mumbled on his own. *I say if a person has something to say, come right out and say it. But not Bernadine. First she will drive you crazy trying to figure out what is wrong and then when she finally tells you it is nothing. Like that last time. When she was all upset because I went shopping at the corner supermarket and brought back 1 percent milk instead of skim milk. For two whole days she went around grumbling. All I could make of it were little snatches, a word here, a word there.*

"Ain't me done it everybody know. . . . Doctor blame me, ain't no fault of mine. . . . How anybody do that . . ."

Until I finally had to sit her down and ask her very directly, "Bernadine, look at me. If you have something to say, say it to me. Not away from me. Not into the closets. Not into the dishwasher. Not into the refrigerator. But right to me. Now, what's the trouble?"

He recalled how her black face had taken on a determined look as she steeled herself before she spoke. "Everybody know that a man in your condition . . . And don't you tell me you don't have no condition 'cause I know better. No such man should have one percent milk. Skim the only kind. But you bring back that other stuff. Then, if something happen to you, they going to blame me. Dr. Tannenbaum. Your son, Marvin. And most especially that daughter of yours. That Mona. I can see her now, crying and pointing the finger at me. Like I was the one killed you."

"Bernadine, I will leave you a written statement that I was the one who bought the one percent milk. Just stop mumbling and go about your work in a nice quiet fashion."

So that cataclysmic confrontation had ended on that day. Today, her grumbling was new. And absolutely without justification. All he had suggested was that she take a day off. How many employees ever complained about having a day off?

Perhaps it was time to have another face-to-face with Bernadine.

"Bernadine. Come over here if you please."

She approached, twisting her hands in that washing motion she adopted whenever she felt tense. He gestured her to be seated in the chair opposite his own.

"Bernadine, when you go around mumbling, something is wrong. Very wrong. Now, tell me, what is it? Something I have done?"

She did not respond at once, but sniffled, her lips twitching. She did everything but mumble.

"Well, Bernadine? What is it? You think you are being overworked? Or underpaid? Whatever, just speak up."

"Started with that shirt," she managed.

"Shirt?" He was taken totally by surprise. "What shirt? What are you talking about?"

"Moment you come in that kitchen and say can I press that shirt for you, I knew it was the end," she declared.

"End? End of what?" Horowitz demanded in puzzlement.

"You ain't going to want me around here no more."

"Who said?" Horowitz asked.

"*She* said," Bernadine declared.

"She? Someone talked to you? Who?" Suddenly it occurred to him, "Oh, boy, wait one minute. Tell me the truth. Did my daughter, Mona, call and talk to you?"

"Nobody call me. Nobody has to call me. I know from the minute you say, 'Bernadine, can you press this shirt for me?' "

"And exactly what is it you know?" he asked.

"She."

"Again 'she'?" Horowitz demanded. "What she? Who she? What are you talking about?"

"I seen it too many times, too many of my friends. Once the Mister starts up with another woman, first thing happens *she* wants the maid fired," Bernadine blurted out. "When you ask for that special shirt to be pressed, first I could see the handwriting on the wall. Then when I see this here change in you last few weeks, I could read the words. And now when you say, 'Take tomorrow off,' I know for sure."

"Know for sure, what?" Horowitz demanded.

"She coming here tomorrow, and you don't want me around."

For the first time Samuel Horowitz realized the depth of this woman's intuition. She had sensed his mind and his disposition even before he had. What it had taken him the trauma of Mrs. Robbins's mugging to realize she had sensed days ago, weeks ago.

"Bernadine . . ." He reached across and took her hand. "Bernadine, how long have you been in this house?"

" 'Leven years with Mrs. Horowitz and six years after."

"Well, you have my word," Horowitz said. "You can stay here as long as you want. Nobody is going to tell you otherwise."

She started to nod until tears began to trickle down her thin black cheeks.

"Now, you take tomorrow off and be back Monday morning, as usual. From now on in this house *everything* will be as usual. Okay?"

Sobbing, she nodded. But as she started from the room he could hear her mumbling again.

"Bernadine!" he called out. "No more mumbling! We got something to say, we say it! Right?"

She turned to confront him. She hesitated, wondering whether to dare. Then she spoke, very forthrightly.

"First thing, she going to want to recover the living-room furniture."

"Will you stop that?" he responded, barely controlling his irritation.

"And she be right. Living room ain't been redone in nine years now. I have wore out them chairs and that sofa just from dusting."

"Bernadine, when I need an interior decorator I will send for you. And when I do, don't mumble!"

He was so upset that he did not even finish reading his newspaper, but decided to go for a walk.

He was on his way down Central Park West, striding firmly and mumbling to himself.

Women, they know everything about everybody else's business. I had no idea of inviting Mrs. Mendelsohn up to my apartment. Tomorrow when I meet her and we go for a walk in the park, all I intend to do is explain why I met her bus. That's all. Nothing more.

Of course, if tomorrow by any chance it happens to rain, then what I have to say might better be said in the comfort of my own dry living room. That was the only reason I asked Bernadine to take the day off. That reason and no other!

Chapter 26

×××

SATURDAY MORNING SAMUEL HOROWITZ ROSE EARLY, WENT AT once into the living room, raised the blind on the picture window that gave him an unobstructed view of Central Park below and of the buildings on Fifth Avenue and farther east. Between those buildings the first rays of the rising sun assured him that today would be a fine late spring day. Excellent for walking in the park. And for talking.

He had his simple breakfast, consisting of one all-purpose vitamin pill, some orange juice for potassium as Dr. Tannenbaum insisted, a bagel with no-cholesterol margarine, and a cup of de-caffeinated coffee. With skim milk, thanks to Bernadine.

Some commentary on our life today, he complained. *Everything you eat or drink is censored. If not by your doctor, then by the stuff you read in the papers or hear on television. Oh, for the old days, when a man could eat a hearty breakfast. Bagels with butter and cream cheese. Scrambled eggs with smoked salmon and onions. Coffee, real coffee, with real cream. We have been defeated and enslaved by medical science!*

Someday, he threatened silently, *I am going to sneak off and have one of those old-time breakfasts again. Someday!*

He knew, of course, that he never would.

Certainly not today. Today he had other things to do. Important things. So important that he gave *The New York Times* only a minimum of his usual disdain.

He stowed his breakfast dishes in the dishwasher. Considered turning it on, but realized that in all the years that machine had been in his kitchen he had never learned how to run it. Let Bernadine do it on Monday, he decided.

He found himself glancing at his watch often, too often. He was waiting for the hours to pass. Yet in a way he dreaded the approach of the appointed hour.

What should I say? I know what I would like to say but how do I say it? The words. Strange. Samuel Horowitz can make long angry speeches about the economy, the president, Congress, the Times, *television commentators. But when it comes time to talk about his own feelings, he does not have the words.*

Seems almost like when I first went to school. I could speak Yiddish but not English. The teacher called on me but I could not answer. I stood there and started to cry. I did not have the words then. I do not have them now.

Of course back then there was that nice Gentile, Miss Corbin. Somehow she understood. When class was over she made me stay late. I thought, now I will really catch it. Instead, she took me by the hand, made me sit on her lap, said to me, "Samuel Horowitz, there is never a reason to cry because you don't know something. The time to cry is when you give up trying to know something. So, we are not going to cry. Because we are not going to give up. You will stay late every afternoon and we will practice new English words until you know them all."

She was good as her word. By the end of the term I passed, and with higher grades than some of the kids who started out speaking English.

Boy, could I use Miss Corbin now. To teach me how to say what is in my heart to say.

He began to practice various openings to his speech.

Molly . . . I know I am presuming to call you just Molly and not Mrs. Mendelsohn, but maybe I am presuming altogether by even talking to you this way. After all, I have no way of knowing how you feel. But that is a chance I must take. So I will tell you how I feel, and then, if you are so inclined, you may speak what is in your mind.

No, he decided, *too formal, too stiff. First, no need to apologize for calling her Molly. Just say it. See how she reacts. Does she call me Samuel or Mr. Horowitz? That will be the tipoff.*

Also, no need to say I have no way of knowing how she feels. Goes without saying I don't know how she feels. That is what this conversation is all about. To find out. And as for saying that I will tell her how I feel, you don't have to tell someone that you are about to tell them. Just tell them. And as for telling her that after I speak she can say what's on her mind, she will do that anyhow.

So what does it all come down to? That I still don't know how to start off what I want to say. As they say on the radio and television, back to square one. How to start.

He was trying out his fourth attempt at an opening declaration when the phone rang. Instinctively, he called out, "Later, Mona! I am busy!" After five rings he answered.

"Yes, Mona, darling?" he greeted.

"This is not Mona," he heard Molly Mendelsohn reply in a tense voice that warned him of unwelcome news.

"Oh, I'm sorry. But at this hour usually it's Mona." To himself he said, *She is calling to say she has changed her mind. She will not meet me today.* "Well, nice day for a walk in the park, no?"

"I hope you understand, but I am calling to—to say that I can't meet you this afternoon."

I knew it, I knew it, Samuel Horowitz concluded. *At the last minute she changed her mind. If there is any advantage to being Jewish it is that you learn to expect the worst. So you are never disappointed.*

"Well, today is only one day," Horowitz said. "There is tomorrow. And if not then, there is next week."

"We'll see," Molly Mendelsohn said with a troubled air that caused Horowitz to pursue it.

"Tell me, is there . . . is there something wrong?"

Her denial was quick, too quick, he thought.

"No, no, nothing wrong!" she replied. "We'll see about next week," she repeated. "So I'm sorry. Please forgive me." She hung up.

Samuel Horowitz stood there, phone in hand, distressed by this strange conversation which had ended so abruptly.

She misunderstood, he complained, *she was expecting something cataclysmic . . . something like who knows what. Marriage? No. Unless her mind was jumping far ahead of mine. No, it has to be more. Something in her voice told me it has to be more. Has to be.*

In a way, I almost wish it had been Mona. It would have been easier to deal with her than with what just happened. Oh, boy! Come to think of it, what would Mona say if I ever called her and told her that I was seeing another woman? I can just imagine the geshrei. *First, the outcry, then tears. Mona can be quite a crier when she puts her mind to it.*

But this call, this call from Molly . . . I don't like the way it sounds. If I did anything to upset her I better make it right.

He dialed her number twice, hanging up both times before it rang. He debated with himself: *Perhaps she doesn't like me. It could be that simple. She has seen me several times. She has thought about it. She decided she does not wish to see me anymore. She has a right. After all, she is a mature woman. With a mind of her own. If she decides she does not want to see me, that's it. Forget it, Horowitz.*

Forget it. . . . Easy to say. But it also means forget the pleasure, the excitement of having company at a movie, at a lecture, at a concert. Forget having someone to share a meal with? Go back to feeling as alone as I felt before I met her?

Of course, I still have my babies. Four hours every week that I have something helpful and constructive to do. Only four hours out of a whole week. Better than nothing. I will ask Ms. Flaherty if perhaps I can add another day to my schedule.

But nothing could stifle his need to discover the reason for Molly Mendelsohn's sudden decision. With greater determination he dialed once more, this time waiting for it to ring. He heard a busy signal. He hung up. Dialed once more. It rang. The second ring was interrupted by a pickup.

"Hello?" Molly Mendelsohn asked eagerly, as if she were expecting a call, but not his call. For as soon as he identified himself, her voice dropped to a lower and less expectant, "Oh, yes."

"Look, I don't want to make a nuisance of myself. But I want to know if I have done anything to offend you."

"Oh, no, it has nothing to do with you, believe me," she protested.

"It has to do with something," he insisted. "You never sounded like this before."

"No, really. I am . . . I am fine. Everything is fine," she insisted. "Look, I'll call you in a few days and we'll talk."

She sounded anxious to hang up, but because she did he could not permit it.

"Why can't we talk now?" he persisted.

"We can't talk because . . . because—" She broke down and began to cry.

"Mrs. Mendelsohn—Molly—what is it? What's wrong? Tell me." His plea was answered by even more tears. "Listen, you stay right there. I will be over in five minutes."

Through her tears she resisted, "No, please, please don't—"

"I will be there!" Samuel Horowitz said. Before she could protest again he hung up.

This time when he entered the elevator of Molly Mendelsohn's building it was unoccupied, thank God. He was in no mood to contend with any nosy jealous neighbors. When he rang Molly's bell she was slow in answering. His first look told him that she had been delayed by an attempt to powder away the result of many tears.

"You shouldn't have come," she greeted him.

"Does that mean you won't let me in?"

She realized that without being aware of it she was blocking the door. She stood aside.

Once seated in the bright living room, her eyes betrayed that she had been crying long before his call. He felt the same discomfort and helplessness he used to feel when Hannah had rare occasions to cry.

"My dear Molly Mendelsohn, if I have done anything to give you cause for tears I wish to apologize," Horowitz began.

"No, I told you, it has nothing to do with you," she protested.

"Because I insisted we make an appointment for today. A special kind of appointment. So you have every right to imagine all kinds of things that I might have in mind. I must confess to you that I am sometimes considered an impulsive man. In business, some people thought I was too quick to make decisions. Fortunately, most of my decisions were right. But with people I tend to make quick decisions that are many times wrong. The way I battled Mrs. Washington for the first weeks shows how wrong I could be. So maybe I have been wrong about you. If so, I am sorry. I would like to make a suggestion. If I have been a nuisance, I say let us not see each other for a while. Let us have, I don't know the expression for it—If people are married they call it a trial separation, but in our case let's just call it we don't see each other for a while. Does that make things easier for you?" he asked.

Instead of replying she commenced crying again.

"Please, Mrs. . . . Molly . . . please. It hurts me to see you cry. If it would help, rather than see you like this, I will leave and never bother you again."

Through her tears she managed to say, "I told you. It has nothing to do with you."

"It doesn't?" he asked skeptically.

"No."

"It must have to do with something," he insisted. "To make a woman cry like this."

"I . . . I have a problem," she confessed.

"A problem," he considered. "Thoughts, feelings, about your husband? Like I have sometimes about Hannah. You think that maybe you are being disloyal?"

"Mine is a very different problem."

"Evidently a very serious problem," Horowitz concluded.

She hesitated before conceding, "Yes. Serious."

"Then make it my problem," he blurted out.

"What do you mean, make it your problem?"

"Tell me what it is. I might be able to help. Make it my problem, too," he insisted.

"Make it . . ." she considered. "It wouldn't be fair."

"Fair is what *I* think is fair," Horowitz protested. Then immediately apologized. "You see what I mean. Impulsive. Let me put it another way. When people have a serious problem is no time to sit around asking what is fair and what isn't. Help is what's fair. Not talk. So tell me."

She was obviously very ill at ease. She had stopped crying. She dabbed at her eyes once, then with determination she set herself to confessing.

"Last evening, after dinner, I took my bath. Like my doctor

and all the commercials on television say, in the tub I do . . ." she hesitated, then, "I do a breast examination. Last night I . . . I thought I felt something."

"Something that wasn't there before?" Horowitz asked.

Molly Mendelsohn nodded. "So I tested again. And this time I could feel it even more."

"Well, we have to call a doctor, we have to make an appointment. You need a mammogram. Right away!" Horowitz took charge.

"I called. I have an appointment. For this afternoon."

"And so *that's* the reason you couldn't meet me," he realized.

"My doctor called his X-ray man. I have an appointment at three o'clock," she informed.

Then she admitted, in a whisper, "And I'm afraid. So afraid."

"There's nothing to be afraid of," he tried to encourage.

But she replied, "A man couldn't possibly understand. But when a woman feels, or suspects that she feels, even a small lump, the thoughts that go racing through her mind. She thinks of all the women she knew . . . all the women she even heard about . . . who started out this way. A small lump, then surgery, chemotherapy, and everything that goes with that word. It all flashes through your mind like a horror movie and you keep saying, 'Not me, not me. Yesterday I was feeling fine, everything was wonderful. I was looking forward to tomorrow, to many tomorrows. I have finally become adjusted to my life after Phil. How can this be happening to me now?' Then suddenly you can already see your own obituary. 'A member of the family said, "She died of cancer." ' "

She was trembling. Horowitz felt the sharp impulse to embrace her for support and courage. But he dared not risk such intimacy. He took her cold hand between his own, and assured, "Look, I am kind of an expert on medical things. From reading the *Times* 'Science' section and *Reader's Digest* I know a lot about this. First of all, the odds are in your favor. Most lumps are what they call benign, and even the ones that are not are not so dangerous anymore. I mean, with all the new treatments, if you catch it in time, it's a minor thing. Very minor."

He thought he had succeeded in reassuring her, at least a little, until she said, "I read too. And what you just said does not apply to me."

"What do you mean, doesn't apply?" Horowitz asked, almost indignant that his expertise had been challenged.

"My mother and one of my aunts, they also had it."

"Yes, that does change the odds," Horowitz was forced to concede. "Look!" he decided. "At three o'clock we will go. Together. You will have your mammogram and we will find out the truth."

"You want to go with me?" she asked.

"Yes, I want to go with you," he declared.

"Just before you called," she confessed, "I started to call my son. Because I was afraid to go alone. Then I hung up. He is such a busy man, what if I bother him and it turns out to be nothing?"

"Isn't that the way? We always want to save our children any worry or inconvenience. In a way I am glad you *didn't* ask him. You and I will go together. And on the way, since it is still early, we can even have a bite of lunch. That is, if you feel like having lunch."

She did not feel hungry but he prevailed on her to have some coffee with him. By a quarter to three they presented themselves at the office of the radiologist on Park Avenue and Eighty-eighth Street. As usual the waiting room was filled with patients, some alone, many accompanied by relatives, all waiting to be tested by one of many modern devices, X rays, sonograms, mammograms, CAT scans, magnetic resonance imagers. But, by whatever medical miracle, all of them had one thought in mind.

Will I be one who gets a death sentence?

Samuel Horowitz and Molly Mendelsohn sat on one of the sofas off in a corner of the large waiting room, affording them a bit of privacy so that they could speak softly without being overheard.

"Such a busy office," Horowitz said.

"Dr. Neary said he is the best X-ray man in the city."

"So he is worth waiting for," Horowitz tried to enthuse.

They were silent a while, until Molly whispered, "They go in. They get tested. They come out. They have to wait for the result. Then they get called in again. This time when they come out you can tell the ones who got good news and the ones who got bad news."

"I know the feeling," Horowitz said.

"You've been X-rayed?" she asked.

"No. But Hannah . . . Before she—well, in her last year she was X-rayed several times."

"Phil, too," Molly confessed. "What was your Hannah's problem?"

Before he could answer, a nurse came out and summoned, "Mrs. Mendelsohn?"

Molly rose. As she started forward, Horowitz reached out to grasp her hand, squeeze it for courage.

She's been gone a long time, he thought. From what he had read, mammograms, being noninvasive, were not supposed to take long. *Why was this taking almost half an hour? Did they find something? Are they redoing it to make sure? Or did the X-ray man have to talk to her own doctor before letting her go?* Horowitz began to feel a slight film of perspiration break out around his neck where his collar made contact. He picked up a magazine for diversion, only to discover that it was a battered copy of *Sports Illustrated* that was months old and featured football on the cover, though that season was long gone. He tossed the magazine aside, glanced at his watch again.

Forty-two minutes. What can be happening in there?

Never a man to abide frustration or uncertainty, he approached the desk.

"I am here with Mrs. Mendelsohn. Can you tell me what is taking so long? After all, it is only a mammogram."

"If you will be patient just a little while, Mr. Mendelsohn . . ."

"I am not Mr. Mendelsohn," he protested. "I am a friend of *Mrs.* Mendelsohn. And I would like to know what is taking so long!"

"Please, sir, the doctor is very busy. But he is also very

thorough. So it takes time. Now, do sit down. I'm sure your friend will be out soon."

Grudgingly, Horowitz retreated to the sofa, this time sitting on the edge to indicate his impatience. Some eight minutes later the door opened. Molly Mendelsohn emerged. He tried to read her face but it was a mask, which caused him to conclude, *The news is not good. So I will try not to upset her any more than she already must be.*

He rose to greet her, took her hand. She slipped down onto the sofa, sat there stiffly.

He could not restrain himself. "So? What did he say?"

"It wasn't a he, it was a she. His assistant."

"What do you mean, assistant? If you come to see the best X-ray man in the city you don't want to deal with any assistant."

"Shh," Molly said. "Don't make a fuss. She knew what she was doing. She is very capable."

"So what did she say?" he insisted.

"She wants to consult with him. Then they will let me know."

"So we wait," Horowitz agreed. "As long as you feel she is a capable doctor . . . Confidence is the main thing, to have confidence in the doctor."

He realized that having nothing of real comfort to say he was saying too much. He fell silent. A moment later he reached for her hand.

Her hand is cold, very cold, he realized. *Mine, too. I wish I could do something, say something. I wonder, is she thinking now of her husband, wishing he were here, not some stranger like me?*

The door opened once more. A different nurse leaned out to call, "Mrs. Mendelsohn, the doctor will see you now."

Molly rose to go. As he was about to release her hand, Horowitz changed his mind. He rose with her.

"We will go in together," he said.

They were shown along a corridor flanked on both sides by little dressing rooms, consultation offices, larger rooms with much complicated diagnostic equipment. Finally they were ushered into a semidark office, the only light source being one wall that consisted of backlighted opaque glass on which were ranged large X-ray films of various internal organs.

The female doctor who had conducted the test was there alongside the desk of a huge man in a white lab coat. He had a shock of white hair and a thick, graying mustache. He looked in their direction. "Mrs. Mendelsohn, Mr. Mendelsohn! Come in."

Neither of them interrupted to correct him.

"I understand from Virginia here that this is your first mammogram. Very careless. A woman your age, with your family history, should have had one every year, at least."

Molly Mendelsohn felt suddenly weak. Horowitz sensed it and gripped her hand to steady her.

"Look, Doctor," Horowitz intervened, "if you have something to show us, show!" He indicated the mounted X-ray films.

The doctor glared at him through the semidarkness. "Mr. Mendelsohn, these films have nothing to do with this. I am trying to make a point with your wife."

"Did you or did you not find something?" Horowitz demanded.

"Yes, we found something," the doctor said. "Fortunately—"

At the mention of that word, Molly Mendelsohn resumed breathing. Horowitz pressed her hand firmly.

"Fortunately, what we found is not serious. A cyst. Fibrocystic disease is unusual in women her age. It can develop into a malignancy. But is not dangerous if watched. Which is the point. Constant self-examination. Plus semiannual mammograms. Most women need a damn good scare before they take this advice seriously. Some days I think the most constructive thing I do is to scare the hell out of them."

And you do a good job of that, Horowitz was tempted to say.

"Now, Mrs. Mendelsohn, I will call Dr. Neary and give him my report. But remember what I said."

"Yes, of course, I will never forget," Molly said, greatly relieved.

"Don't worry, Doctor," Horowitz promised. "I will see that she gets here every six months!"

"Good, Mr. Mendelsohn," the doctor replied, waving them out of his office.

As they were leaving, Samuel Horowitz stopped in the doorway, turned back long enough to say, "Horowitz. The name is Horowitz."

Chapter 27

XXX

THEY HAD CROSSED FIFTH AVENUE AND STARTED INTO CENTRAL Park at Eighty-fourth Street. They passed the many-windowed Egyptian wing of the Metropolitan Museum of Art and continued walking west.

They had both been silent since leaving the radiologist's office, content to enjoy the deep sense of relief they felt.

"You don't mind walking?" Horowitz asked.

"On a lovely day like this, and after what happened, I could walk forever," Molly Mendelsohn said.

"I know what you mean."

"The sun has never seemed brighter. The sounds of the children never sounded more like music. It takes a scare like that to make you really appreciate life," Molly said.

They strolled along the path which led around a ballfield where students of two grade schools were playing a noisy softball game.

Suddenly Samuel Horowitz said, "They thought we were a couple. Not only the nurse. But the doctor also."

"Yes," she agreed, somewhat tense now.

"*You* think we look like a couple?"

"I never thought of it that way," Molly confessed.

"Funny thing," he said, then interrupted himself to suggest, "Would you like, maybe, to sit a while and talk?"

"Why not?" she agreed.

They had been seated on one of the benches for some minutes, had watched young mothers wheel their strollers by, watched more active children scrambling up the rock formations beyond the path. Once Horowitz rose to his feet to pick up a badly thrown ball and toss it back to some children who were playing catch.

After a long silence, and considerable preparation, Samuel Horowitz said, "Life is strange. Yesterday when I asked you to come for a walk in the park, what I had in mind to ask you was if you would object if I changed my hours at the hospital."

"Why should I object?" Molly remarked.

"What I had in mind was if I could pick you up every Tuesday and Thursday. Together we would take the Number 11 up to the hospital. That way you wouldn't be alone. Wouldn't get mugged like Mrs. Robbins."

"That is very thoughtful, Mr. Horowitz. I don't see why we can't do that."

"That was all I had in mind *yesterday*. But in the last few hours something has happened. Something I never expected."

"You mean being taken as a couple?" Molly assumed. "What is so strange? We are about the same age. We are both Jewish. We are nicely dressed. I am shorter than you. And you are more dominant."

"I am?" Horowitz asked, just a little resentful.

"You have a habit of taking over. Like Phil. He used to be the same way," Molly said. "So it is a natural mistake to take us for a couple."

"That is exactly the point," Horowitz said.

"What point?" a puzzled Molly Mendelsohn asked.

"Suppose it wasn't a mistake?" he asked, looking into her blue eyes.

She was suddenly tense, almost terrified by the thought.

Oh, this time I have really made a mistake. A blunder. I surprised her. Shocked her. I was too sudden. Especially after the scare she had earlier. To tell the truth, I am shocked myself. I never thought I would be suggesting such a thing. I must try to calm her down.

"I know it is sudden. Too soon. It is sudden for me, too. It came to me sitting in that doctor's office waiting for you. Each year there are fewer friends. They die, they move away. But always fewer than the year before. I thought, a man not only needs someone to depend on, even more he needs someone to depend on *him*. Else everything feels empty.

"From the minute you told me why you were crying and what you had to do today, I felt, no, it can't be. It can't be over. Here we have become friends. Maybe one day we might even have been closer than that. Yes, I must confess that lately some moments, like early in the morning when I am between waking and really waking up, thoughts cross my mind. I even . . . I have even talked to Hannah about you. Don't think I am crazy. I talk to her often."

"I know. I talk to Phil, too," Molly admitted. "I . . . I once mentioned to him what a nice man you are."

"You did?"

"Yes," she confirmed. "And I got the feeling that he was not too upset. Though in his lifetime he was very jealous. In fact, that was how we first started going together."

"He was jealous before you even went together?" Horowitz asked.

"In my day very few girls thought to go to college. So in high school I took typing and shorthand. Then I got this job in a company that specialized in junior misses' dresses. Phil was just starting there, too. As a designer of the petite line. One day a buyer came in without an appointment. The model was out. Phil was so anxious to show his new line that he asked me if I could model his line for him. Which I did. The buyer must have liked the line. Because he ordered not dozens but grosses of some styles. Of course, Phil was very excited. So was I. When I was done modeling I went into the dressing room to change back into my own clothes. But I could hear the conversation from outside.

"The buyer said, 'You got very good taste, young man.' And Phil said, 'Thanks, I appreciate that. If you knew how long I worked on this line . . .' But the buyer interrupted. 'Line, shmine, I mean that model. A beauty. And not a bad built, either. So?'

"And Phil said, 'So *what*?' To which the buyer said, 'I am in New York alone. I am free for the weekend. How about fixing me up with that girl?' For just a moment, a single moment, Phil did not answer. Then he said, 'I do not do business that way.' The buyer laughed. 'Come on, kid, don't play games with me.' That's when Phil took him by the coat and walked him to the elevator. He held him there until the door opened. He shoved him in, and yelled, 'Don't you ever come back here again!' Even though it cost him the biggest sale of that season.

"Then he came back to the reception desk to apologize to me. After that we started dating. And I became the model for his petite line."

"So you were a model?" Horowitz commented.

"In those days, if I may say so, I was rather pretty," she admitted modestly.

"And today? Sitting here in the sunshine. With that new brightness in your eyes since we left the doctor's office, believe me, you are still pretty."

"You really think so?"

"Yes."

"That is the first time since Phil that someone has said that to me," she admitted.

Embarrassed, she turned away, facing toward the setting sun that was disappearing behind the buildings of Central Park West.

"Look," Samuel Horowitz resumed, "I know that what I said was very sudden. You need time to think. So I should tell you something about myself to consider while you are thinking. First, I am not a well-educated man. You graduated from high school. I never even finished high school. It was 1935. The middle of the Depression. My father's little notions business failed. I had to get my working papers. Only fifteen years old and I had a family to help support. Bad as it was for me, it was even worse for my father. I think that's what broke his heart. You see, he had such plans for me. That was the reason he brought us to this country. To give me a chance to get a good education. To become a professional man. A successful man. Yet here I was, fifteen years old, and an errand boy in a paper and twine business down on Broome Street.

"I can't tell you how many times in later years I wished I could tell my father, 'Look, Pa, I ended up with a business of my own. S. Horowitz and Son. A well-to-do man. So you didn't have to be ashamed. We accomplished what you came here for.' But of course we never get the chance to say things like that to a dead father."

He felt uncomfortable having exposed so much of himself at a time when he felt he had burdened her with enough to think about.

"I don't mean to bore you," he apologized.

"I'm not bored. I feel like I'm just getting to know you," she insisted.

"All I am trying to say, I'm a simple man. I don't make any pretenses. I read a lot. I argue a lot. But that may be *because* I don't have much education. But I have lived an honest life. Ask anyone in the paper and twine business about the reputation of Samuel Horowitz and they will tell you. I was married to the same woman for forty-one years. We raised two very fine children. My Marvin—his name now is Hammond—of the Washington law firm of Hotchkiss, Stuart and Hammond, big lawyers. And my daughter, Mona . . . Well, about Mona, you have to understand. I mean there is nothing to apologize for. She is, after all, married to one of the biggest real estate men in San Diego. She has two fine children. Bruce and Candy Fields. The Fields is from Feldstein, which it was until Mona made her husband change it. She is that kind of woman. Mona gets her mind made up nobody in this world can say no.

"Like the Bruce and Candy. Bruce is from my father's name, which was Baruch. And Candy is from my mother's name, which was Chana. So Samuel Horowitz has two grandchildren named Bruce and Candy Fields. Some world. But that's my Mona."

He broke off, saying, "I didn't mean to tell you the story of my life. Which is not exciting, as you can see. I just wanted you to know the truth while you are thinking."

Molly nodded thoughtfully.

"Of course," Horowitz added, "to tell the whole truth, I want you to know that I am not exactly one hundred percent. I did have a stroke. But mostly I got over it. Thanks to Mrs. Washington. An angel, that woman. I should also tell you, if you haven't already suspected, I am a man with a temper. Never with Hannah, though. Mainly about the nation and how it is run. Let me put it this way: The easiest man in the world to get along with I am not. But not the worst, either. I guess you could say, average. A decent man. And now a very lonely man."

"I'm glad you told me. It helps to know. It really helps," she said.

"Good."

"To tell you the truth," Molly Mendelsohn said, "my story is no more exciting than yours. I, too, have two children. Lawrence, the accountant. And Sybil. Something tells me that Sybil and your Mona could be a little bit alike. Anyhow, Phil once went into business with a partner. Petites, Incorporated. They had good years and bad years. But we made out. The children went to camp. Then to college. And they are both doing well. What more can you ask of life?" Molly said.

"What more?" Horowitz echoed. "While we were waiting in that doctor's office I asked myself the same thing: What more can you ask? And suddenly I knew. The rest of my life. The rest of your life. Whether it is six months or six years or sixty years, I said, I don't care how long she has left. I want to spend it with her. Well, turns out we are lucky. You have not months but years left. Years. I want you to think about that. Years alone. Or years together. That is up to you."

Chapter 28

XXX

SAM HOROWITZ HAD A BAD NIGHT. ONE OF THOSE NIGHTS WHEN there was no comfortable spot in a bed to which he had been accustomed for years.

Usually he slept curled up on his right side. Not tonight. He tried his left side. Not tonight. He lay on his back staring up at the ceiling until he found himself, eyes open, studying the reflected light from the streetlamps that filtered through the slats of the venetian blind.

In desperation he turned on the radio. There were always all-night talk shows. In which men and women called talk-show hosts, who had hardly enough education or experience to form an intelligent opinion, pontificated on world problems, national problems and city problems.

A world of big problems and small minds, Horowitz lamented. *And they wonder why the country and the world are in such terrible shape.*

Which only aggravated his sleeplessness. He turned and twisted, and finally thought, *Whenever I read about such things they use the phrase "tossed and turned." Turned? Yes. But tossed? I have spent the hours from eleven o'clock until—what is it now?—three, four o'clock, turning and twisting. But tossing? No such thing. Where did that word ever come from?*

226

He finally gave up. He slipped out of bed. Went out to the kitchen. Warmed up some milk. He sat at the small breakfast table and sipped slowly. He was reminded of other times when he had sat in this kitchen in the early hours of the morning, unable to sleep, sipping warm milk.

There was the time Mona had fallen from the parallel bars in gym class and was rushed to Mount Sinai Hospital where she was hospitalized while the doctors tried to determine the extent and severity of her spinal injuries. And the night when Marvin was one of the boys in a Scout troop that was lost in a heavy fog in a climb up Mount Washington in New Hampshire. Two very frightening nights. There were others, too.

The difference between those nights and this one, Hannah was here then. They consoled each other. Now he was alone. As alone as he had been during the nights he spent while Hannah was in the hospital in what proved to be her last illness.

Hannah, Hannah, if only you were here. . . . Until it occurred to him that if Hannah were here now he would not have spent half the night fearing that Molly Mendelsohn would reject his precipitous, badly worded proposal. And spent the other half of this night worrying that she *would* accept it.

Either response created problems

If she accepts, Horowitz argued, *surely my life would be different, and better. She is a delightful woman to be with. I would recognize once again the comfort of a woman in the house, a companion, a friend. Someone whom I love, and who, if she doesn't exactly love me, seems to like me. She certainly liked the way I spoke up at that meeting. And she now thinks I handle babies very well.*

We seem to like the same kinds of movies. And food. She is easy to talk to. And she is intelligent. I mean she agrees with me. Most of the time.

She is also ballabatish. *She runs a nice clean home. She is a good cook. Almost as good as Hannah. A man is very lucky to meet such a woman at this time of his life. And she is interested in me, at least interested enough to even consider my proposal.*

Then, of course, he argued in a Talmudic frame of mind, *there is the other side. I can think to myself, she cooks almost as well as Hannah. But, if, in a moment of carelessness I were to say such a thing, that would hurt her. And who could blame her?*

There are other things as well, moments I remember from my life with Hannah that would cause me to make comparisons. Comparisons are not good.

If she were to say yes, we should make a rule, like we did about grandchildren, no comparisons. None. Yet who could live up to such a rule? Even with the best intentions.

There is also the day-to-day, Horowitz considered grimly. *The little habits people develop over the years. For instance, Hannah knew and respected the fact that when I sit in the living room reading my* New York Times *she was never to interrupt. Because, if she did, she might become the unintentional target of my anger against Tom Wicker and Anthony Lewis.*

Or in the morning, when I am shaving, Hannah knew to answer the phone quickly because if I tried I would most likely cut myself, especially on the neck near my Adam's apple. Of course, since Mrs. Washington converted me to an electric razor that is no problem any longer.

But there is always soup. Some men like their soup warm. To me, Samuel Horowitz, warm soup is like the wet kisses I got from my stout Aunt Shoshana on my bar mitzvah. To me, hot means hot. If it is too hot I want to be in charge of cooling it down to what I consider hot enough. What would happen the first time I have to ask Molly to take back the soup and heat it up? Will she take offense? After all, she is a very sensitive woman. God knows I discovered that today. That is another thing.

We are neither of us young anymore. One of us could get sick. Seriously sick. Would she want to tie herself down to a sick old man? Oh, it is one thing for her to say she knows about my stroke. It does not seem to frighten her that I might have another one. But saying it is not the same as living with it day after day. Who knows if next time even Mrs. Washington herself could repeat her miracle?

Mrs. Washington, he decided, *she is the person to talk to. I can be honest with her. And I know she will be honest with me. I will call her!*

That decision, more than the warm milk, allowed him to go back to bed and eventually fall asleep. He slept late. So that by the time he called, Mrs. Washington had already gone off to administer therapy to her present stroke patient. It was her grandson, Calvin, who answered the phone, since his mother was not yet home from her night shift at the hospital.

"Calvin here . . ." Calvin greeted.

"Son, is Grandma home?"

"Just missed her. Any message, man?" Calvin asked.

Man, Horowitz thought. *As a child he used to call me Uncle Samuel.*

"Yes. Ask her to call me. I'll be home all evening. And Calvin, now that the Mets have agreed to pay so many millions of dollars for some mediocre ballplayers, maybe you and me should go out to Shea some Sunday afternoon and take a look. What do you say?"

"Gotcha, man!" Calvin enthused.

Gotcha, man, Horowitz thought. *If this young fellow didn't have such a terrific record at Columbia Grammar School, I would think he doesn't know how to speak the English language.*

Horowitz hung up the phone. He had a long day to get through before he would be able to consult with the woman who had become his closest friend and confidante. He was tempted to call Molly and ask to see her today. But that would defeat the whole plan. He needed time to think, away from her. He needed to have the cool, intelligent advice of a woman like Harriet Washington, who, though she was gentle most times, could be quite severe and truthful when that was required.

God knows, if she had not been so strict with me, I would have ended up as a cripple. Or what they now call a disadvantaged person.

She had even helped him through that crisis when Mona was determined to uproot him from his own home and drag him out to San Diego, where he would surely have ended up in the Hebrew Home for the Aged.

The mere thought of Mona added to his woes of the day. If he and Molly were to agree to marry, how could he possibly break that news to his darling daughter?

Today was turning out to be a long day, a very long day.

Mrs. Molly Mendelsohn had a bad night. She could not find a comfortable spot in her large double bed. She tried sleeping on her left side, but could not. When she turned on her right side, she found herself sleeping in the position and the direction in which she used to sleep when Phil was in bed beside her. She turned back on her left side.

She considered getting up to take a Valium but decided
against that. Those pills were to be taken sparingly and only used
to counteract a minor irregular heartbeat to which she was prone
in times of stress. After some hours of turning from side to side,
she decided to turn on the television. She ran through the chan-
nels, found nothing but old movies that were no good the first
time around. She turned off the set.

She slipped out of bed, pulled her cotton robe around her and
started out to the kitchen. There she made herself a cup of hot
decaf. She sat at the table where she always had her breakfast. She
considered her situation.

Here I am, a sixty-eight-year-old woman, she thought. *I have
lived my life, I have made my adjustments. I have sacrificed enough for
Phil, and for the children. The two times that Phil's business was in
danger, once when the partnership broke up and Petites, Inc. became a
one-man business. Once when he was close to bankruptcy because the
styles he cut that year did not sell.*

*There was no income, though the expenses continued. He had to
support the house and the business from money he was forced to withdraw
from our savings. My own jewelry had to be put up for security for large
loans as well.*

*I have seen the children through the usual traumas and problems of
growing up. Fortunately neither was ever involved with drugs. But there
was the time Sybil moved in with a young man at college, which created
a great crisis with Phil. And when Lawrence got that girl into trouble at
college. The question was, should they get married and leave school? The
girl's father wanted no more to do with Lawrence, withdrew his daughter
from school, and forbade her ever to have contact with him again. It took
Lawrence the rest of the school year to recover from that because he truly
loved that girl. We never did find out what happened to her.*

*So my life has not been uneventful. But that is all in the past. I have
lived it, and by living it I think I have earned the comfort I now enjoy.
Believe me, it's far better to be a grandmother than a mother. Sure, it's
nice to have the grandchildren come to visit and stay over. I enjoy baking
and cooking for them. I certainly enjoy when they boast, "My grandma
is the best cook in the whole world!" That's all very good. As long as at
the end of the holiday or the weekend they leave. And I can lock my door,
take a nice, warm, leisurely bath, get into bed with my newspapers and*

my favorite magazines. I can turn on my television and watch my favorite programs instead of the grandchildren's loud, noisy MTVs with their headache-making rhythm and all those twisting half-naked girls and those young men who do everything but actually have sex right on the screen. And, yes, my solitude. Peace and quiet are wonderful things. Real civil rights, that a person earns by just growing old.

That was the question now. To give up that peace and quiet by completely changing her life? By including a man who, until after they had lived together for a time, would be a stranger?

There is no question, Samuel Horowitz is a nice man. He is polite. Or seems to be. It is in day-to-day living that tempers can wear thin. Phil was one man when business was good, but quite another man when he had a bad season.

Of course, Mr. Horowitz is no longer in business so he is not subject to the ups and downs of the economy. Which means he won't be subject to those stresses. But on the other hand, not having a regular business to attend, he would be home all the time. How well I know what happened when Phil retired and was suddenly home all the time.

First thing, he wanted a hot lunch every day. He was tired of eating in the cafeterias, delicatessens and restaurants in the garment district. He wanted the kind of lunch that only his Molly could prepare. It has been several years since I made lunch for anyone, except when the grandchildren came to visit. I wonder, the Samuel Horowitz who takes me out to lunch now, would he become like Phil if we were married?

I would be surrendering my freedom, Molly Mendelsohn thought. *Now I go to the beauty parlor when I decide. I go to bed and get up when I choose. I eat in when I like and out when I like. I don't have to depend on the tastes and desires of another person. Especially a stranger.*

That word troubles me. But how much can you really know about another human being without living with him day in, day out, night in, night out? Without living through illness with him? An overnight illness from some bit of spoiled food, or longer illnesses that are more serious. That is when character reveals itself, when the real person emerges.

Of course, these days, sometimes for economic reasons, sometimes for other reasons, older people don't marry. They just move in together.

No, I, Molly Mendelsohn, could never do that. Not for myself, not for what it would do to my children.

So, she pondered, *I have finally put my life together again since*

Phil died. Do I reopen it now to fresh problems? Maybe fresh wounds? Living alone has its advantages. Freedom is one, too much freedom to surrender at this time of my life.

She went back to bed. In time she feel asleep. She woke less than an hour later. Woke with a start. In her sleep she had turned on her right side and from old habit had reached out to put her arm around Phil. Emptiness had wakened her.

She lay in her bed, staring into the darkness, asking, *This freedom that I cling to, is it freedom or loneliness? How does one balance the two? Or can't they be balanced? Does a woman have to choose one or the other? Is there no in-between? Can't courtship just go on forever? Can't a woman have the best of everything?*

She tried to fall asleep again. But could not. She rose at dawn, still troubled, undecided.

Chapter 29

XXX

SAMUEL HOROWITZ SAT ON A PARK BENCH ACROSS FIFTH AVENUE from the building where Harriet Washington's current patient lived. From time to time, more frequently than he realized, he had glanced at his wristwatch.

She should be out by now, he fretted. *Unless she left early and I missed her. Maybe I should call uptown and see if she is already there. But if I go find a phone she may come out and I will miss her. This is like that day waiting for Molly. My whole life seems to be between deciding what to do, then not doing it. I will sit here and wait. She must come out.*

If not, they will take me for one of the homeless and drag me off to some shelter. Let them. How much worse off could I be than I am now? Do I or don't I want to marry this woman? I am like Hamlet. To be or not to be? Of course I am not exactly Hamlet. Or even Richard Burton. Who also could not make up his mind. Didn't he marry Elizabeth Taylor once, divorce her, then marry her again and divorce her again? I can't even make up my mind once, let alone twice. Mrs. Washington, where are you?

After twenty more agonizing minutes he saw the uniformed doorman open the front door. Out came Mrs. Washington. As always nicely dressed, she wore a light green print dress under a spring jacket of deeper green. Horowitz waved to her. She did not see him for she started toward the corner to head to Madison Avenue and the uptown bus. Horowitz hurried across Fifth Avenue against the light, heard an angry driver call out, "Hey, old man! You wanta get killed!"

"So kill me!" Horowitz shouted back.

It was his loud, defiant voice that forced Mrs. Washington to turn. She knew that voice, recognized that defiance. She was right. She stopped, glared until Horowitz caught up with her.

"What in the world are you doing crossing a busy street like this against the light?" she demanded.

To deflect her anger, he smiled and cajoled, "Did you notice, Mrs. Washington, how quick I was? No foot dragging. You have performed a miracle as great as Moses leading the Israelites across the Red Sea."

"Don't change the subject!" Mrs. Washington reprimanded. "And don't ever cross a street like that again! Understood?"

"Yes, Mrs. Washington, I understand," a penitent Samuel Horowitz said.

"Besides, what are you doing here anyhow?" she asked.

"We have to talk," Horowitz insisted.

"Talk? Now? I have to get uptown and make dinner for the children," Mrs. Washington reminded.

"Of course. So we take a cab up. Then we take the children out to dinner. At that restaurant, Sylvia's. After, when the children are doing their homework, you and I could have a quiet talk." While she debated the efficacy of his suggestion, he pleaded, "This is very important to me. Besides, you know how I love the fried chicken at Sylvia's."

"Since this sounds so urgent, yes. Let's do that," Mrs. Washington conceded.

They had eaten well at Sylvia's, the finest restaurant in Harlem. Conversation at the table had consisted mainly of Horowitz lecturing both Conrad and Louise on the necessity of maintaining good grades so that they could win early acceptance at college. Only at the best schools, of course.

"And remember," were his parting words before they went to their rooms to do their homework, "it will come in handy later on. When some smart aleck says to you, 'You only got here because of affirmative action,' you can say, 'Would you like to compare high school grades?' And you show them your record."

Once assured of privacy, Mrs. Washington and Mr. Horowitz could confront the emergent problem which had burned in him all evening.

As if preparing to deliver an oration, he graciously gestured her to a chair in her own living room. Then he began: "My dear Mrs. Washington, the problem I have now is different from any problem you and I have ever had before. I know, when I tell you, right away you will say, 'This is not my responsibility. Make up your own mind.' However, in a way it *is* your responsibility. Because if you hadn't done your therapy so well, instead of being in this predicament, I would be a crippled old man hiding in my apartment. Now I am out in the world and contemplating what I am now about to tell you."

As if he had unburdened himself of a heavy problem, Horowitz said, "So far, so good."

"And?" Mrs. Washington persisted.

"And . . ." He tried to continue but found himself at a loss for words. Finally he blurted out, "Mrs. Washington, I am in a terrible fix. I have made a proposal of marriage. . . . Yes, yes, a proposal to a woman, that very nice, wonderful woman, Molly Mendelsohn."

"What's the problem?" Mrs. Washington asked.

"The problem is, what if she says yes?" a troubled Samuel Horowitz replied.

"You don't want her to say yes?"

"The problem is, I don't know *what* I want her to say," Horowitz explained. "Sometimes I want her to say yes, sometimes no. There are dilemmas and there are dilemmas. This one, I think, is a wholesale dilemma."

"Of course, if she says no, your problem is solved," Mrs. Washington pointed out.

"Mrs. Washington, remember the early days when you first wheeled me out to sit in the sun in Central Park? We talked about your Horace and my Hannah. You told me you would never remarry. I felt the same way. You stuck to your word. But me, here I am asking another woman to marry me. That makes my love for Hannah seem very small compared to your love for Horace."

"Not so, Mr. Horowitz. There is a difference," she pointed out. "From the day Elysse's husband was shot down by those thugs who robbed that supermarket I had a new responsibility. My daughter. And her two little children. I had a family depending on me. I was needed. At least for the time being I am needed. You don't have that comfort."

"Right," Horowitz agreed sadly. "I could disappear or die tomorrow and nobody would really miss me. Marvin, Mona, the grandchildren would mourn for a while, but not really miss me. Mind you, I am not saying they don't love me. They do. But like you said, they don't *need* me. That is a big difference."

"Molly Mendelsohn is in the same situation," Mrs. Washington pointed out. "Alone. Wanting to be needed. Wanting to need someone."

"But there is always the feeling that Hannah might feel I am being disloyal," Horowitz admitted.

"I never met your beloved Hannah. But I have lived in her house, cooked in her kitchen, felt her presence. I feel I know her. I don't think she would resent your spending the later years of your life with a fine woman like Molly Mendelsohn."

Horowitz nodded thoughtfully. "Of course there are all the other problems. The practical problems. A million things. Like does she move in with me or do I move in with her? And if she moves in with me, what about her apartment, her furniture? How will she feel about giving them up? It would be a big step for her. She might not want to do that. And who could blame her? After all, she has lived there for thirty years. So you see, Mrs. Washington, how much easier it would be for her to say no."

"If that's the way you feel, call her, say you are sorry. You spoke too fast. You would like to withdraw your proposal."

"She could sue me for breach of promise," Horowitz argued.

"Legally, I don't think people can do that anymore in this state," Mrs. Washington replied.

"Still, I would hate to hurt her feelings. She is an unusual woman, Mrs. Washington. Just doing volunteer work with her you haven't had a chance to really know what she is like. She is a fine housekeeper. A wonderful baker. A good cook. A regular *ballabusteh*."

"Really," Mrs. Washington remarked, as if she were becoming aware of Molly Mendelsohn's virtues for the first time.

"She enjoys the same things I enjoy," Horowitz continued. "We laugh at the same places in the movies. And she defended me. One time when I got into a little argument at the Y she defended me. She is small but she is also strong. A woman of character. You just don't know her."

Mrs. Washington saw no purpose to be served by revealing her intensive research into the qualifications of Molly Mendelsohn.

She said only, "Obviously you have found a number of fine qualities in her."

"No question," Horowitz agreed. "Yet, there is still the question of Hannah. . . ."

"Yes, the question of Hannah." Mrs. Washington appeared to ponder. While she thought, *This is classic Samuel Horowitz, impulsive, then given to more sober second thoughts. And poor Molly, she must have been overwhelmed by such a sudden and unexpected proposal of marriage. It will take some delicate therapy to keep this on track to a richly deserved conclusion. The question is not Hannah, but Horowitz. Still, as long as he thinks it is . . .*

"Mr. Horowitz," she declared, "I can well understand that your darling Hannah would have some . . . shall we say . . . some problems with this sudden development. There's a good reason."

"Disloyalty," Horowitz anticipated. "She never expected that from me."

"Not disloyalty," Mrs. Washington corrected.

"Then what?"

"You made the same basic mistake that husbands always make, whether wives are alive or dead."

"And what is that?"

"You didn't give her time to become accustomed to a new idea," Mrs. Washington pointed out. "When she was alive, was your Hannah an unreasonable woman?"

"No, not generally, that is. Sometimes when it had to do

with the children she could be stubborn. But otherwise, she was a very reasonable, commonsense woman. She must have been. She agreed with me most of the time."

"Then what makes you think she would be unreasonable now? That is, if you gave her time to become used to the idea."

"Too impulsive again," Horowitz realized. "Too quick to jump to a decision. Hannah often used to say that."

"Give Hannah a little time. I'm sure she won't feel you are being disloyal."

"Maybe it would be a good idea if we *all* had more time to get used to the idea," Horowitz considered.

"You always told me what Hannah used to say about chicken soup for a cold: 'Couldn't hurt,' " Mrs. Washington pointed out. "Same thing with time. Couldn't hurt."

Horowitz nodded thoughtfully.

Tuesday, late afternoon. Molly Mendelsohn had been trying to avoid considering Samuel Horowitz's sudden proposal by busying herself. She gave great care and devotion to three more infants than her usual assigned group. She had lingered longer overhearing gossip at the coffee corner. Finally she realized she was overstaying her time at the hospital in order not to be home in case Mr. Horowitz called to press her for the answer she was not yet ready to give.

In fact, the more she had thought about the situation, the more questions, problems and doubts had beset her.

Finally, lest her dilatory tactics became too obvious to her fellow volunteers and the nursery staff, she decided to leave. She waited impatiently for the down elevator. Boarded it. When it stopped at the ground floor she was the first one out and on her way to the front doors of the hospital when she heard her name called.

"Mrs. Mendelsohn!"

Molly Mendelsohn stopped. Turned slowly to spy Samuel Horowitz hurrying across the lobby toward her.

He was breathless when he reached her.

"I was worried I might miss you," he began. "Thank God I didn't. We have to talk. Now."

"I . . . I . . ." She could not bring herself to say, *I am not ready to talk.*

But it was too late for that. For he took her by the hand and said, "I have it all arranged."

"All arranged? What is all arranged?" Molly asked, feeling a shortness of breath suddenly. She wanted to withdraw her hand but he held it too firmly.

"I have a cab waiting outside. It will take us to the pier on Forty-second Street," he announced.

"Forty-second Street pier? Are you crazy, Mr. Horowitz?"

"I warned you. I am sometimes a very impulsive man. Well, this time I am being impulsive in a very cautious way. As you will see. This evening we are going on a boat ride."

"Boat ride?" Molly Mendelsohn replied, trying to pull her hand free.

"Boat ride," Horowitz repeated, explaining, "Around Manhattan Island. We will have dinner on the boat. A little wine. Most important, we will talk."

"Talk?" Molly considered dubiously.

"One thing I promise you, my dear, you will not have to make any big decisions tonight."

Assured that she would not be forced to give her answer, Molly Mendelsohn relented and went with him.

Chapter 30

××××

THE CIRCLE LINE BOAT EASED AWAY FROM THE FORTY-SECOND Street pier smoothly and slowly. It backed into the middle of the Hudson River, then gracefully turned south.

Samuel Horowitz and Mrs. Molly Mendelsohn stood at the rail of the aft section of the vessel, looking west where the spring sun was setting between the new tall apartment houses ranged along the top of the New Jersey Palisades.

Still tense because of the uncertain purpose of this voyage, Molly Mendelsohn said nothing. Aware that he was responsible for her discomfort, Samuel Horowitz felt the need to make diversionary conversation to put her at ease.

"Remember when a person could look across the Hudson and see only the Palisades? No big overpriced condominiums. Just the Palisades, like nature intended palisades to be. I am all for nature, and against progress, if it means destroying such a view."

"Well . . ." Molly Mendelsohn ventured, but seemed to lose courage.

" 'Well,' " Horowitz chided gently, "is not exactly a whole sentence."

"The way I remember, it wasn't all just palisades. There was the big electric sign, PALISADES AMUSEMENT PARK. So bright you could read by it late at night." Then, fearing her statement had been too extravagant, she modified, "Well, you couldn't exactly read by it. But it was a big bright sign."

"You're right," Horowitz recalled. "There was the park, the big sign. Remember the ads in the papers: 'Palisades Amusement Park, where we make waves in our own swimming pool.' Remember?"

"Yes," Molly agreed, then pointed out shyly, "I don't think nature ever intended there should be an amusement park on top of the Palisades."

"No, no, you're right," Horowitz conceded.

They stared at the western sky where a few light clouds had begun to pick up the pink glow of the setting sun.

"Did you ever go there?" Horowitz asked. When Molly did not respond at once, he explained, "When you and Phil were going steady, did he ever take you there?"

"No," Molly admitted. "Coney Island. Brighton Beach. Rockaway sometimes."

"Me, too," Horowitz said. "Hannah and me, I mean Hannah and I, we never went to the Palisades Park either. Who needed fake waves in a pool when you could go to Coney Island or Rockaway and get all the real ocean waves you could want?"

They were silent for a long time, watching the pink clouds turn to gray.

"You are maybe hungry?" Horowitz suggested.

Though she was not, Molly replied, "I could do with a bite."

He had reserved a table at a window on the port side of the vessel so that while heading downriver lower Manhattan was just outside their window. He suggested a cocktail, she refused. He ordered his usual one drink before dinner, a Scotch and soda. By brand name. So that she should know he was a man of the world.

During their dinner, of which Molly ate little, they spoke only when Samuel Horowitz made comments about the passing scene.

"It's like a fairyland, this skyline." When Molly responded with a slight nervous smile of agreement, he felt somewhat encouraged. "No city in the world like it. Hannah and I, we went to

London, Paris, West Berlin, no city in the world like New York. We also went to Tel Aviv and Jerusalem. You and Phil ever went to Israel?"

"Oh, yes," she was relieved to reply. "Phil won a contest his trade association ran, for buying Israel bonds. The prize was a trip to Israel. What an experience! To see all the places that I only used to hear or read about in Sunday school."

"It was exciting," Horowitz agreed.

Conversation lagged after that, he failing to find topics that would stimulate her to talk. She, shy and tense, waiting for Horowitz to address the purpose of this impromptu voyage.

Samuel Horowitz was equally sensitive to her predicament.

Mistake, Horowitz, mistake. Again your impulsive nature and your big mouth have got you into trouble. Just because you think you are anxious to discuss the problem you think she should be, too. Just goes to show how insensitive you are. Why would any woman want a relationship with a man who is so lacking in tact and consideration?

He made no further attempt at conversation but applied himself to his broiled chicken and baked potato, margarine please, not butter.

They had rounded the southern end of Manhattan Island when he remarked over coffee, "Did you happen to notice when we passed them, the twin towers of the World Trade Center? Fantastic! That is what New York is all about. Where a few years ago there was nothing, suddenly two skyscrapers. And such skyscrapers! Build, build, build."

Molly Mendelsohn nodded, smiled, and agreed softly, "That's New York for you."

"Would you care to go up on deck?" he asked.

She nodded.

They were on the top deck, leaning against the rail facing west, passing the United Nations building when she finally spoke without prodding.

"All those windows," she said. "Sometimes I wonder how they keep them all clean."

"Considering what goes on there, sometimes I wonder how they keep them all unbroken. Of course, now that there is no Soviet Union things are a little quieter there."

They were passing that area of Manhattan where skyscraper office buildings had already given way to apartment houses. The skyline was darker now; the buildings seemed gaunt against the night sky. Beneath, the lights of the vessel reflected in the black waters of the East River.

They were both silent while Horowitz considered, *Do I let this evening end this way? Or do I say now what I invited her here to say? She has seemed so nervous all evening, she might resent it. And who can blame her? Being grabbed by the hand by a meshuganeh like me, hurried into a taxi and suddenly onto a boat going around Manhattan with a man she may not even like. This is the last chance I may ever have to talk to her alone. I will risk it. The worst can happen is she says no. She can't say no! She mustn't say no! See, there you go again, Horowitz, deciding what other people can and cannot do. Maybe you ought to keep your big mouth shut! No, start. Start like a man. You made a mistake, admit it.*

"My dear Mrs. Mendelsohn, I owe you an apology."

Taken aback, she replied, "Apology? For what?"

"The other day . . ."

Even more confused, she repeated, "The other day? What other day?"

"In the park," he explained. "After we came from the radiologist's office. When I asked you to marry me."

"Oh, that," Molly Mendelsohn replied, growing even more tense now.

Because he noticed, Horowitz was quick to reassure. "Please, there is no need to be nervous. I am not about to press you for an answer."

She appeared considerably more at ease now.

"But it would help if you knew why I said what I did," Horowitz explained, "I think it has to do with the babies."

"The babies?" Molly repeated, even more puzzled now.

"After what I proposed in the park, that night I couldn't sleep. I lay in bed twisting, turning—not tossing, though. And I asked myself, impulsive I am, but so impulsive? On the spur of the moment to ask a woman to marry me? Dos that make sense?

"So I argued with myself, yes, it does make sense. She may tell herself that she is not alone. But I know better. How do I know? I have children. She has children. I have grandchildren. She has grandchildren. But we are still alone. I maybe more even than she. I notice that the grandchildren used to come more often when Hannah was still alive. True, they were younger then. Also they loved her cooking. They loved her. I think they only put up with me. After all, what was there to love about me? I was the grandpa who gave them lectures on studying hard, getting a job in the summer, saving their money. Then, every once in a while, to bribe them to listen to me, I would slip them a few dollars. Sometimes more. I guess I gave them too *much* advice because they don't come around very often these days."

"After all, they have lives of their own now," Molly tried to excuse them.

"Is that what you tell yourself, too?" he asked.

After a moment of silence, she whispered, "Yes, yes I do."

"I wonder, my dear Mrs. Mendelsohn, if anyone has ever made a list of all the reasons grandparents invent to excuse the conduct of grandchildren? It would be taller than the Empire State Building."

"I think you are right. If anyone ever made such a list," Molly granted.

"When you had that scare about the lump in your breast you started to call your son, then hung up before he could answer."

"Did I tell you about that?" Molly tried to recall.

"Yes. But you didn't have to. Every one of us has done that. We don't want to be a burden to our kids. Did you hear me? Kids! They are in their late thirties, their early forties, and we still call them 'the kids' or 'the children.' The main point is, almost by choice we are both alone.

"Who do we have to laugh with when we see something funny on television? Not the children. Who do we have to nudge in the theater when the play or the movie makes a good point? Not the kids. When we get up in the morning, to whom can we say, 'You know what we should do today? Go to the museum to see that new exhibit they mentioned in the *Times* yesterday.' Not the kids. Comes evening, and we are tired of eating out, so we just want to stay home and have some simple thing, to whom do we say, 'Let's just get into our pajamas and robes and have a sandwich in front of the television set?' Not the kids.

"So while we have family and kids and grandkids, we are alone. With no one else to depend on."

Molly Mendelsohn had listened patiently throughout Horowitz's recitation. When she assumed that he had finished, perplexed by his prologue, she asked, a bit timidly. "I'm afraid I don't understand, Mr. Horowitz. What does this have to do with the babies?"

Reminded, and called to account, Horowitz explained, "That day, your problem, the radiologist, the mammogram, suddenly that made something clear to me. Without realizing it, I had seen in you a person with whom I could share the rest of my life. Together neither of us would have to be lonely any longer."

Quickly he added, "Look, as I told you, I am not exactly a bargain."

"I never thought any such . . ." Molly tried to protest.

"Of course not. You are too respectful of another person's feelings. So I will say it for you. I did have a stroke. But since that time, between Mrs. Washington and Dr. Tannenbaum, I am in very good shape. If not exactly tip-top, then not bad either. Still, it is something a woman in your situation must consider. So, consider. Just give me, as they say, a fair shake."

There was a moment of deep and pervading silence until a puzzled Molly asked, "But the babies. Where do the babies come in?"

"Once I began to feel that you and I, that we . . . you know? Then suddenly this thing happened with you, and the radiologist. And I had this feeling, no, this fear, that it would be like with the babies. We take care of them, learn to know them. To love them. Then suddenly we come to the nursery one day and they are gone. We never see them again. I felt the same way about you.

"Here was a woman I was beginning to know and . . . and have feelings for . . . deep feelings. And it felt that you would suddenly be taken away. Like the babies. With the babies I have no choice. But with you, I could do something. But I handled it very badly. Too quickly. I took you by surprise. I think I even frightened you. Didn't I?"

Her silence was confirmation enough.

"So the only thing I want to say tonight, give me another chance. Take time. As much time as you would like. Think it over. In fact, let me go back to what I had originally intended to ask you that day in the park. Let me pick you up every Tuesday and Thursday. Let us go up to the hospital together so that you don't feel like a potential mugging victim like poor Mrs. Robbins."

"Every Tuesday and Thursday," Molly Mendelsohn considered.

"I will pick you up at your apartment. Then we will walk over to Amsterdam and take the Number 11. Of course, on rainy days we will take a taxi."

Molly considered his suggestion but appeared still to have reservations.

"You are afraid of what the neighbors will think," he assumed.

"Well . . ." Molly began to say, but went no further.

"Very simple. Instead of coming up to your apartment, I will wait in the lobby. Your doorman will ring, you will come down. Certainly your neighbors, even that nosy one, cannot make a scandal out of that."

"It wasn't my neighbors I was thinking about," Molly replied.

"Aha!" Horowitz realized. "The other volunteers."

"Yes," Molly admitted. "You don't know how they talk."

"Half a dozen women around a coffee urn, I can imagine," Horowitz said. "We will find a way to avoid that, too. And in the meantime, if every once in a while I have an extra ticket to a show, a lecture, something, I hope you won't mind if I call."

"No . . . no, I won't mind," Molly said.

"Good! Then promise me one more thing. Every night before you go to sleep, practice."

"Practice?"

"The name."

"The name?" Molly asked.

"Sam. Just say it over and over. Until it becomes easy, natural-like. Promise?"

"I . . . I think I would like to start with 'Samuel' and see how that goes," Molly replied.

"Good. And take your time. From now on, no rushing into things. So long as we are making progress," Samuel Horowitz declared.

And not a moment too soon, since the vessel was docking at Forty-second Street.

Chapter 31

XXX

FOR SEVERAL WEEKS SAMUEL HOROWITZ AND MOLLY MENDELSOHN had followed their agreed-upon plan.

Every Tuesday and Thursday Horowitz walked over to Eighty-second Street and West End Avenue. There he announced himself to the doorman, who called up from the lobby. Molly Mendelsohn would come down, hand her foil-wrapped plate of *ruggaluch* to Horowitz. Together they would walk east to Amsterdam Avenue where they boarded the Number 11 bus, at senior citizens' fares, of course.

Surrounded by strangers, their conversation on the bus was limited to impersonal subjects such as the weather, the news, a bit of gossip about an anonymous member of the volunteer staff at the hospital.

If they had attended a lecture, a play or a film the night before they might discuss that on the bus. But never anything of a personal or intimate nature.

Faithful to his promise, Samuel Horowitz never pressed Molly Mendelsohn on the issue of marriage.

On the Thursday of the third week one news event occurred that dominated the conversation of not only Molly Mendelsohn and Samuel Horowitz but much of the citizenry of New York.

The night before, leading off the eleven o'clock television

news, was a shocking story, with accompanying film. An hours-old infant had been discovered after being dropped down the garbage chute of a project building on the Upper East Side. It had landed in the compactor. Were it not for the alert eye of the building superintendent, that fragile, tiny new life would have been crushed like so much garbage.

The infant, a girl with almost two feet of umbilical cord still attached, had been rushed to the same hospital where Molly and Samuel served as volunteers.

"How could any human being do such a thing?" Molly asked. "Especially a mother."

"In these times every day you wonder how so many terrible things can happen. But they do, they do," Horowitz replied sadly.

"I hope the little one lives," Molly said. After a moment, she added, "And is healthy. Healthy is very important when they put her up for adoption."

Unable to find words to express his outrage, Horowitz sighed. Twice he started to say, "What could possibly go through a woman's mind . . . What . . ." But he never did complete the thought.

As was their practice now, before entering the hospital, Horowitz dutifully handed the foil-wrapped package of *ruggaluch* back to Molly. To avoid gossip, she entered the hospital to take the first car up to the nurseries on the eleventh floor. Horowitz always took, not the next car, but the one after that.

During the time Molly was making up her mind, they did not wish to invite suspicion or anticipation. Nor did they wish to risk gossip in the event she eventually decided not to honor Samuel Horowitz's proposal.

Thus, as far as anyone in Volunteer Services was aware, Molly Mendelsohn and Samuel Horowitz arrived each Tuesday and Thursday as individual volunteers. While on duty, they were always courteous toward each other but reserved. They gave no hint of the fact that they shared a social life outside the hospital.

On this early afternoon, instead of following her usual routine of unpacking and setting out her pastries on the table in the coffee corner, Molly Mendelsohn stood outside Pediatric Intensive

Care. Her face was pressed against the glass wall as she stared at a group of white-coated doctors and uniformed nurses who crowded around one particular ICU isolette. The troubled infant who lay within that enclosure was obscured from Molly's view by the cluster of so much staff.

When Supervisor Flaherty emerged she informed Molly, "The infant who was on the news last night. From the compactor."

"Oh, God," Molly replied instinctively. "How is she?"

"They're not sure yet," Flaherty said and started back to her office.

Molly pressed closer against the glass in an effort to catch at least a glimpse of the tiny two-day-old. She was still in that position when Horowitz emerged from the elevator. Surprised to find her there, he joined her, asking, "Molly?"

"It's that little one," Molly replied in a whisper.

"The compactor baby," Horowitz realized. "Must be in bad shape to need such a large consultation."

They proceeded about their duties, each tending infants in separate nurseries. At odd moments, when their duties caused their paths to converge in search of additional supplies, tiny fresh shirts, bottles of formula, clean diapers, lotions, they exchanged quick glances. At some moments Molly betrayed a flicker of a minxlike smile, as if daring someone to suspect them. Horowitz would counter with the slightest eye response as if to say, *So what if they know! I would be very proud.*

During the remainder of their volunteer hours they went about their duties, feeding, caressing, rocking, whispering or humming to the little ones. They changed them into fresh, soft, clean shirts, wrapped them firmly in their blankets, tenderly returned them to their cribs.

Always Molly leaned into the crib to whisper a last soft assuring word before going on to the next crib to pick up another hungry little one.

Horowitz carried out his duties with the same degree of care and loving attention. Always, as he walked about with a little one in his arms, crooning to it, he would interrupt to whisper, "Don't you worry, little one, out there some nice people are waiting to snap you up. Some family that will love you. Mark my word!"

Knowing full well the infants could not understand, nevertheless Horowitz felt better giving them what little assurance was in his power to give by the sheer sound of promise and encouragement in his voice.

In order to be available to accompany Molly to the Number 11 bus for the ride back home, Horowitz no longer avoided the coffee corner. He would partake of coffee, even exchange an opinion or two, but he never chose one of Molly's *ruggaluch*, lest someone suspect.

On this particular afternoon, instead of making his usual stop at the coffee corner to wait for Molly, Horowitz went instead to Intensive Care to see if he could catch a glimpse of what everyone in Pediatrics now called the Compactor Baby.

This time there was no crowd of white coats to obscure the isolette from view. Only a single nurse hovered over the new little patient. Wearing his antiseptic smock and having scrubbed earlier, Horowitz felt he was not endangering any infant in ICU. He slipped in to get a closer look at the unfortunate infant.

To attract as little attention as possible he casually eased toward the isolette. Standing alongside the nurse, he stared down at the tiny body. The infant was asleep, eyes clenched, tiny face twisted into a frown, lips making a sucking motion. To monitor its condition sensors were taped to its body, which had the ruddy color of a newborn. An intravenous fed life-preserving sustenance into its pencil-thin arm.

Once the nurse took cognizance of Horowitz's presence, he felt called on to express his medical opinion.

"Considering its history, seems in pretty good condition."

When the nurse rewarded him with a superior glance, he identified, with military crispness, "Samuel Horowitz, Volunteer Services." Failing a response from the nurse, he asked, "This little one *is* in pretty good condition, right?"

"Considering everything," the nurse replied. "But we will keep her under intensive observation for a few days."

"Exactly what I would suggest," Horowitz said.

The nurse glanced at him, shook her head slightly in controlled disapproval, then slipped her hands through the protective portholes of the isolette to make sure all sensors were firmly affixed.

A bit sheepish, Horowitz asked, "Nurse, would you mind . . . I mean, since I am already scrubbed, would it be all right if I slipped *my* hands in?"

"For what reason, may I ask?" the nurse demanded.

"Just to touch her. After all, as we volunteers know, the human touch has beneficial qualities. Gives the little ones a sense that there are people who care."

Impressed more by Horowitz's concern than the medical efficacy of his argument, the nurse replied, "I'm sorry, but hospital rules . . ."

"Of course," Horowitz conceded. "Hospitals run on rules. Rules have to be obeyed. Then would it do any harm if I just stood here, watched a little while? I promise I won't touch anything."

The nurse seemed about to refuse, but the plea in his eyes caused her to say, "You may stay. But if any doctor or my supervisor comes by, don't you tell them I gave you permission."

"Wild horses couldn't drag it out of me," Horowitz promised.

The nurse went off to attend other little patients, for this was a usual hectic afternoon in an ICU that housed almost a dozen infants in various states of serious illness. Some were premature and physically unequipped for basic functions such as breathing without help. Others struggled to throw off the drug addiction that had been inflicted on them by their mothers.

Samuel Horowitz stood alone at the isolette of the tiny compactor baby.

Poor little one, so little there is hardly enough room on you for all the equipment they put on. Between the sensors and the intravenous all I can see is your little pinched face. The way you breathe, not easy, is it? The important thing is, keep breathing. Don't give up. So you had a bad start in life. Bad start? Small words for what happened to you. To be thrown out like so much garbage. And by your own mother.

But at least you are alive. You have a chance. Hold on to it. Keep fighting. Because there are other people in this world who worry about you. Who want to see you live. And grow healthy. All those doctors, these nurses here. Do you realize how much skill and care was gathered around your little crib before? Doctors, specialists, all here for one thing. To make sure you live. Now you have to do your part. And if you do, I promise you there will be other people who will care. You can have a long, happy life if you fight for it now. So keep breathing. Keep breathing.

"See, already you seem to be breathing better."

When Horowitz realized that he had spoken the last eight words aloud he became self-conscious. He glanced around to detect if anyone had overheard him. At a nearby isolette a nurse who had been replacing an empty IV bag with a fresh one was staring in his direction. He decided he had better leave before any embarrassing questions were asked.

After a whispered, "I have to go now. But I will be watching for you. I will be watching," Horowitz slipped out of ICU.

As had become their practice, Molly Mendelsohn and Samuel Horowitz each left the hospital alone to meet up at the corner of the street. Then they started down the block in the direction of the bus stop.

Once they were under way, in what he considered his seemingly offhand but provocative manner, Horowitz remarked, "In my professional opinion, she is in good shape. Not what I would call *very* good, but *pretty* good."

As he had intended, Molly Mendelsohn was immediately intrigued. "Good shape? Who?"

"The little one," Horowitz teased to heighten her curiosity.

"The Velez baby?" Molly asked. "Or little Corry?"

"The Compactor Baby!" Horowitz announced with a sense of triumph.

"The Compactor Baby?" Molly exclaimed. "How do you know? What happened? Tell me!"

With considerable pride Horowitz related his adventure into ICU, his closeness with the newsworthy, if unfortunate, baby.

"You dared to go into ICU?" Molly asked, half in admiration, half in trepidation.

"After all, I am part of the health care system, as they say. I was scrubbed. I was wearing my smock. . . ."

"You scrubbed hours before. And you held half a dozen little ones against that smock. You were hardly what I would call sterile," Molly pointed out.

"Granted," Horowitz agreed. "Still I had to do it," he confessed. "Doctors are all well and good. Also nurses. And all that equipment they stick in them and on them in ICU. An intravenous can feed nourishment and medication into a little one. But hope? Desire to live? I never heard of any intravenous could do that. That takes more. The closeness of another person. Words. A voice. Something that just by being there can give courage, hope, the will to live. So I thought, who needs that more than a little one who in its first few hours already almost lost its life? Nobody knows her, and the one person who does doesn't want her. So I watched a little. Thought a few thoughts, said a few words. What harm could that do?"

By that time the bus pulled up. They boarded. Since the bus was crowded, all discussion of what had transpired in ICU ended.

As they walked from Amsterdam Avenue toward West End, Molly Mendelsohn said, "I was just thinking, what if Ms. Flaherty finds out?"

"And if she did?"

"Remember little Cletus and the last time you broke the rules," Molly pointed out. "She said, one more time and you would be out for good."

"If I am, I am. I still had to do it," Horowitz persisted.

"Wouldn't be the same," Molly said.

"*What* wouldn't be the same?" Horowitz asked.

Molly Mendelsohn did not reply at once but then shyly said, "You ever see that show *My Fair Lady*?"

"Of course. Hannah and me, we took both kids. Terrific. What does that have to do with rules?"

"There was a song in there. Rex Harrison sang it. 'I've Grown Accustomed to Her Face.' "

"Yes. So?" Horowitz inquired almost impatiently.

"Well," Molly ventured to explain, "I have grown accustomed to our walks to the bus, from the bus. I . . . I would miss them. Very much."

Samuel Horowitz stopped walking suddenly. He stared down into Molly Mendelsohn's face.

My God, she is blushing, Horowitz realized. *Blushing. Like Hannah used to blush when we were going steady.*

Rather than blurt out something that might be misinterpreted, Samuel Horowitz resumed walking. Moments later he said, "Believe me, if I thought it would change things between us I wouldn't have done it. No, I must be very honest with you, I still would have done it, and hoped that Ms. Flaherty never found out."

They had arrived at the door of Molly's apartment house. He assumed that his last declaration had offended her for she had said nothing since. He sought some sign by asking, "Tuesday? Like usual?"

She assented, "Tuesday."

"And if before Tuesday something comes up? For instance, there is a lecture at the Ethical Culture Society this weekend," he proposed tentatively.

"Call me," Molly said.

Horowitz nodded but felt that he had been rebuffed. As he started to turn away, her voice reached out to him: "Samuel . . . Sam . . . that was a very thoughtful thing you did. Such a little one . . . starting out in life like that . . . Anything anyone can do, even words the little one can't hear . . . somehow we have to believe that it helps. . . ."

She had more to say but could not find the right words. But they both knew what she meant. Then she was gone.

On his circuitous route back to Central Park West and Eighty-fourth Street, Samuel Horowitz recalled, *First she called me Samuel . . . then Sam. At least she is practicing. A good sign. A very good sign.*

At that same time, Molly Mendelsohn was just slipping out of her dress to get into a comfortable housecoat. She stopped suddenly to consider, *All other men would have felt sympathy for that poor abandoned baby. But what other man would have done something about it? He is impulsive about things. His sudden proposal of marriage frightened me. But being impulsive about that little one, that kind of impulsive I like about him.*

*   *   *

After three days in ICU the Compactor Baby was moved into the nursery area. The chart that hung at the foot of its crib designated her Baby Jane. One of her nurses in ICU had suggested it. "Remember that picture with Bette Davis, *What Ever Happened to Baby Jane?* Well, isn't that what we're still doing, wondering what ever happened to make this little one end up here?" And so the infant was designated.

On its very first day in the nursery it fell to Molly Mendelsohn to care for her. Every other volunteer on the afternoon service came in to stare, study and coo over the little one. Though Horowitz fought the impulse, before the end of Molly's time with little Baby Jane he could no longer resist. He found Molly seated in the chair, cradling the little bundle in her arm and gently easing the nipple of the bottle into its tiny pursed mouth.

Horowitz stood over them studying closely, first from one angle, then from another, the tiny face that was barely visible within the folds of the white blanket.

"Pretty baby," he appraised.

"Very pretty," Molly replied, much more concerned with whether the little one was sucking hungrily enough.

Horowitz moved slightly to achieve a less obstructed view, since the infant had turned, the nipple slipping out of its mouth. At once he apologized, as if the fault was his. "Sorry. Maybe I am in the way here. I will leave you two to your business."

"Also," Molly pointed out, "people might notice that you are spending too much time with me."

"You're right," Horowitz said, turning away at once until Molly said:

"They'll have opportunity enough to find out later."

Slowly Horowitz turned back to stare down at her. Molly raised her face to him. They were staring into each other's eyes.

"Molly?" Horowitz dared to whisper.

"Not a word, not to anyone, until the children know first," she whispered.

Exercising every effort to restrain his delight, Horowitz replied in an equally soft voice, "The children. Of course. I will call Mona first thing in the morning."

"Do that. She should be the first to know. After all, she is Hannah's daughter."

Poor Molly, she doesn't know Mona. She has never even imagined such a woman as Mona. No wonder she was quick to say she should be the first to know. On the other hand, what choice do we have? Elope? Like Romeo and Juliet? That didn't turn out too well. Of course, naturally, tell Mona, tell the children.

And then?

We have survived hurricanes, blizzards, the Sixty-seven War in Israel, and then Desert Storm, we will survive this.

But in the mind of Samuel Horowitz all that paled in comparison with telling "the children," especially Mona.

By the end of Samuel Horowitz's tour of duty that afternoon it fell to him to feed and care for little Baby Jane. Careful as he was with all little ones, he took very special pains with this one. He cuddled her closer. He made sure she finished her bottle down to the last drop. Which was not easy, since, unlike other infants, this one would rather sleep than eat.

He carried her in his arms longer as he paced the small nursery. When he crooned to her he felt he was in such good voice he could have substituted for the cantor in synagogue on the High Holidays. If forced to assess his performance on this particular afternoon, he would have to rate himself perfect.

Not only was this little one deserving and needing such extra special care, but he would always consider that in some way she was the catalyst for making up Molly's mind.

He had stripped little Jane of her diaper, washed her clean with medicated gauze pads and was about to put on a fresh diaper. Instead, he took her hand in his, studied the perfectly formed tiny fingers. He examined her legs and her little pink toes, all ten perfect.

This miniature miracle, Horowitz thought, *what a precious thing it is. Yet some woman, whoever she is, threw it away.*

He applied the soothing lotion over her buttocks and between her nicely formed legs. Then he diapered her afresh and slipped a clean dry shirt over her.

As he returned her to her crib he thought, *Maybe God had a special eye out for this one. Not wanting His miracle destroyed, He directed that superintendent's attention to her before she disappeared into that compactor.*

Horowitz lingered over that crib, observing anxiously, *Is this little one pale, or is it my imagination? Seems two days ago it had better color. No, if there was something wrong one of the nurses would have noticed.*

On their way to the bus stop Samuel Horowitz and Molly Mendelsohn exchanged a torrent of ideas, plans and suggestions about the wedding.

"Tell no one yet" was Molly's firm suggestion.

"Until the children meet and approve, no one else must know," Horowitz agreed.

What about the hospital? At the hospital they would continue to follow their present routine, polite but casual.

Molly agreed instantly. How could they risk jeopardizing the work that had brought them together? Especially now with little Baby Jane. Her mother had still had not been found, so she would be staying on in the nursery longer than most infants.

About the wedding ceremony, whose synagogue, whose rabbi? His or hers? And when? What day? What time of day?

So much to plan, so much to do.

But first, the children. And first among firsts, Mona.

Chapter 32

XXX

SAMUEL HOROWITZ SAT IN HIS USUAL EASY CHAIR OVERLOOKING
Central Park, pretending to read his morning paper while uncomfortably conscious of the fact that Bernadine was vacuuming the
foyer carpet. It was not the noise she made that annoyed him but
her proximity.

*Damn it, why does this woman have to vacuum now of all times
when it is eleven o'clock in the morning here and eight o'clock in San
Diego? And if she must, why in the foyer where she can overhear every
word I say? Why not in the bedroom? Or the dining room? All I need
now, in addition to the firestorm I am sure to get from Mona, is another
epidemic of Bernadine's mumbling. Especially since somehow that woman
with her nosy nose knew what was going to happen even before I did.*

"For God's sake, Bernadine, if there is something wrong with
that vacuum have it fixed!"

"Ain't nothing wrong with this here machine," Bernadine
replied. She went right on propelling it back and forth over the
thick foyer carpet.

"Does it always make so much noise?" Horowitz asked.

"Ain't never been the soul of quiet," Bernadine replied.

"Then at least go vacuum in some other place," he suggested,
hoping she would oblige. But then, if she did, she would not be
Bernadine.

Horowitz continued to divide his attention between the pages of his newspaper and his wristwatch. Eight-fourteen. With Mona's busy schedule she could well be out of her house and on her way to another committee meeting in another ten minutes. To his great relief Bernadine unplugged the vacuum from the outlet, retracted the cord and wheeled the machine into the dining room.

Thank God! Finally! Horowitz thought, reaching for his phone to begin dialing the 800 number in Mona's husband's office. It was an arrangement Mona had worked out. Horowitz could call Albert's 800 number, reach his office switchboard and be put through to the house to Mona's private line, at no cost.

He dialed the number, heard the operator's response, asked for Mrs. Fields.

"Oh, hello, Mr. Horowitz! How are you this morning?" the operator greeted cheerily.

Bad enough Bernadine is practically breathing down my neck; now the operator will be in on it. Maybe this call should be on the satellite so the whole world will know! Samuel Horowitz is going to marry Molly Mendelsohn. What is next? CBS 60 Minutes?

While Horowitz held the phone in his right hand (restored to full use thanks to Mrs. Washington's excellent therapy), he continued to search for precisely the right words. Ever since he had left Molly yesterday he had been rehearsing. Now, at the crucial moment, none of those words sounded right to him.

"Mona darling, your father has news for you, good news. . . ." He had rehearsed and discarded that by one o'clock in the morning.

"Mona darling, something has happened to your father. . . ." *No, first thing Mona would assume that I have been mugged again.*

"Mona, you'll never guess what happened. . . ." *No. With my luck, Mona would guess and for the next hour and a half she would do all the talking and I wouldn't get a word in edgewise.*

How about, "Mona, there has been a wonderful development in your father's life. . . ." *No. Right away she would be suspicious. What kind of wonderful development could there be in the life of a seventy-year-old man? She would assume that something terrible hap-*

*pened and I am covering it up. Like I was hit by a car but I lived. Or else
I had a heart attack but I am still breathing.*

Maybe the best way would be to say in a nice calm voice, "Mona,
after several years of living alone your father has decided to get
married." *Short. Simple. The truth. Straight out.*

*Of course, what could follow, God alone knows. Maybe like the
great flood, forty days and nights of not rain but tears. Or worse, words.
Mona has a way with words. A way? She has nothing but words. And
she does not hesitate to use them.*

He was suddenly brought up short by Mona's voice on the
other end of the line.

"Dad! For a change *you're* calling *me*. What a delightful surprise!"

Surprise, Horowitz thought, *no question. But delightful? That is,
like they say, a horse of a different color.*

"Yes, Mona darling, a delightful surprise. With delightful
news."

"I knew it, I knew it," Mona greeted his announcement with
great joy.

Knew it? How could she know it? Horowitz wondered. *Aha!
Bernadine! Bernadine suspected even before I did what could happen. Of
course, Bernadine must have called her.*

Before his suspicion could harden into an accusation, he heard
Mona say, "So you've finally come to your senses?"

*Could that mean Mona doesn't mind my getting married? Could this
be my darling Mona talking? A miracle!*

But his hopes were dashed as she continued: "I knew it was
only a matter of time before you finally came to your senses. You
realize the best thing for you is to move out here to San Diego."

"Mona darling, who said anything about moving—"

Mona's many talents did not include listening. She swept
right over Horowitz's attempt to correct her.

"Now, Dad, don't worry about shipping any of Mother's
furniture out here. In the first place, it wouldn't blend in with
West Coast decor. Too heavy. Too—what shall I say—too 'city.'
And don't worry about disposing of the stuff there. I will find a
secondhand broker . . . though we can't expect the prices we

would have gotten if you'd moved out when I first suggested it— However . . ."

My Mona. One of her asides is longer than most people's speeches. But sooner or later she must stop to take a breath.

". . . we will do the best we can. Now, as to your own personal things, I will arrange a moving company to come in and pack everything. You are not to lift a finger!"

No, Horowitz lamented. *All I have to do is hold the phone and listen. Or else get her to shut up long enough to hear what I called to say.*

"Mona! Be quiet! And listen to your father!"

The commanding tone of his voice forced Mona to stop suddenly, gasp, and respond, "Dad? What's wrong?"

"Just because your father dares to get a word in edgewise does not mean there is something wrong," Horowitz pointed out. "I called because I have something important to tell you."

"Yes, I know. You have decided to move out to—"

"I have not decided any such thing. *Mona darling, your father has decided to get married.*"

For an instant there was a hush from the other end of the line. Then came the torrent he had expected. Plus one thing he had not expected.

"I knew it! I suspected it all along! That Mrs. Washington! Ever since that woman came into your life you have been her slave. So now she has decided to have it all. She is only marrying you for very obvious reasons. Your money!"

"Mona, Mona, please, don't go making wild accusations."

"Wild accusations? Tell me that marrying Mrs. Washington never crossed your mind!"

To provoke her he said, "It crossed *my* mind, but not *hers.*"

"But now, after getting a good idea of your financial worth, she has magnanimously consented to change her mind," Mona said sarcastically.

"Mona, stop making such outrageous accusations against a very fine woman! Instead, listen to what your father has to say. Yes, I have decided to get married. No, the bride to be is not Mrs. Washington. It is a woman named Mendelsohn."

With the suspicious attitude and disdain of a homicide detective, Mona repeated the name: "Mendelsohn?"

"If you don't like her name, don't worry. Because soon it will be Horowitz," he replied.

"Who is she? Where is she from? Is she a widow? Or a divorcée? And if not, why hasn't she been married before? Oh, just a minute! I am beginning to get it now. She is a young woman looking for a foolish old man to marry. So in a few years she will become his rich widow. Oh, Dad! How could you fall for such an obvious trick? My own father, my own—"

Tears took the place of words.

"Mona darling, she is not a twenty-year-old. She is a widow, only three years younger than your father. She is a very fine, reserved, neat little woman. She reminds me of your mother in many ways."

The mention of the word "mother" brought forth another rush of tears.

"Now, Mona, because I know how sensitive you are about your mother, I am calling you first before anyone else, even Marvin. What I would like is for you to come to New York. To meet this woman. I am sure you will like her."

"And if I *don't* like her?" Mona asked.

Horowitz's instinctive response was *I wouldn't be surprised.* But in the interest of peacemaking he said, "Don't make any judgment. Just see her. Is that asking too much?"

"Well, Dad, if you insist on being serious about this, the least I can do is come east to protect you from any impulsive and foolish action," Mona granted. "Don't do a thing until I get there! The earliest I can be there is Monday."

When he hung up the phone, Samuel Horowitz knew that his attempt to handle the situation in a harmonious manner had failed. Pursuing a suspicion, he dialed the 800 number once more, was greeted by the same operator. Again he asked for Mrs. Fields and, exactly as he had anticipated, was told that her line was busy. He hung up.

All I have to do is wait, he thought. *Minutes, maybe half an hour. No longer.*

If he had any question about how to occupy his time while he waited that was soon answered when he heard a familiar sound emanating from the dining room. It was a low mumble, which warned of more to come.

"Bernadine! Come in here!"

She reached the point where the foyer met the living room. There she stopped in the archway.

"Yes, Mr. Horowitz?" she asked, almost daring him to speak.

"Did you overhear my conversation with my daughter?"

"No, sir. I was in the dining room and your voice just reached in there. You know when you talk to your Mona ain't no such thing as a quiet conversation. So I wasn't overhearing. I was just not able to get out of the way of your conversation."

Thinking to confront the situation head-on, he asked, "So?"

"I didn' say anything," she replied in response to his challenge. "Didn' have to say anything. Ain't nothing different from what I expected. And, if you callin' me in now to give me my notice ain't no surprise. I guess the only thing remaining is when and how much termination pay."

"There is no when! There is no talk about termination. Understand?"

" 'S the way it always happens," Bernadine said. "I already told you . . ."

"Yes, yes, I know," Horowitz interrupted. "Your friend's boss got married and then she was out of a job. Well, that will not happen to you. I give you my word."

"Oh, sure, her boss give her his word too," Bernadine pointed out. "Always happens. New wife, new maid. Never seen it to fail."

"Bernadine, stop it! And stop crying! I have had enough tears for one day and it is not even twelve o'clock."

Which only brought forth another burst of tears from the black woman. She was about to make one last protest when, fortunately for Samuel Horowitz, his telephone intervened to rescue him. With great deliberation he picked up his phone and said, "Yes, Marvin?"

"How did you know . . ." Marvin Hammond started to ask.

"Elementary, my dear Watson," Samuel Horowitz responded. "Your darling sister got off the phone with me. Called you right away. And said, 'Call Dad. Talk to Dad. Tell him that he is a doddering old man who has lost his mind. Say anything you have to say, just talk him out of it.' Right?"

"Well, Dad," Marvin admitted a bit sheepishly, "you know your daughter. Now, tell me all about it."

As dispassionately as he could, Samuel Horowitz explained his situation to his son.

He ended by saying, "Son, between you and me there has never been anything but the truth. I tell you now in all honesty that there has never been any other woman in my life but your mother. No one will ever take her place. But she is no longer here. This is a chance for me to have a new life. With a very nice, very fine woman. As you will see."

"I understand, Dad. And I will do my best with Mona, but don't blame me if there are no miracles."

"You have five days, son. See what you can do," Horowitz said, with the same degree of apprehension his son had expressed.

"Just one question, Dad. If Mona doesn't agree, what will you do then?"

"What will I do?" Horowitz repeated sadly. "We'll see, we'll see."

Long after he hung up the phone, he pondered, *What will I do?*

Chapter 33

XXX

LATER THAT DAY, ON THEIR WALK TO THE BUS STOP ON AMSTERDAM Avenue, Samuel Horowitz informed Molly Mendelsohn that his daughter was coming to New York to meet her. To avoid alarming her he did not relate the details of his conversation with Mona.

"Wonderful!" Molly enthused. "I am anxious to meet her!"

To himself Horowitz observed, *Don't be so anxious. Because you are about to learn why the Weather Service used to name hurricanes after women.*

Aloud he remarked, "Molly dear, you have to realize that our news came as a bit of a shock to her."

"My Sybil didn't exactly react with great joy, either," Molly admitted. "As for Lawrence, he always had a very nervous stomach. However, once they meet you I'm sure they will feel much better. Especially Lawrence."

"I hope so," Horowitz replied, not without misgivings.

"I know," Molly exclaimed suddenly, "the Sunday after Mona arrives I will invite them all to dinner. Mona and Marvin, Sybil and Lawrence, you and I. A nice family group. Unless you think I should invite husbands and wives too?"

"No, I think just the children will be enough," Horowitz said, aware that "enough" was a small word for what might happen.

By that time the Number 11 bus pulled up.

*   *   *

Samuel Horowitz waited impatiently for his chance to care for little Baby Jane. Once he had the infant in his arms he cooed into its little ear, "Well, well, well, already I can feel you are heavier than on Tuesday. Not much. But some. Well, I shall feed you up. And this time, don't keep falling asleep on me. First, we get your bottle. Then we sit down and have a nice substantial lunch. After that, we have a little chat, and since I feel in good voice today, maybe a little concert."

He had just slipped the nipple of the bottle into little Jane's mouth, holding it there until she began to suck, when a woman dressed in street clothes and a man who carried an official-looking folio entered the nursery. The woman strode directly to Baby Jane's crib only to find it empty. She looked around impatiently. Horowitz anticipated her by announcing, "If you are looking for the compactor baby, this is her."

The woman and her colleague approached Horowitz, stared down at the infant. She reached out to move the blanket aside and obtain a closer look. Horowitz interdicted her with a sharp "You didn't scrub! And where is your smock? You two don't even belong in here!"

"Tell him," the man commanded the woman.

"Sir, we are from the Human Resources Administration. This infant is our responsibility."

"Maybe," Horowitz granted, then ordered, "but until you scrub, keep your hands off her."

The woman appeared about to dispute Horowitz but the man forbade it with a soft "It's good to see volunteers who are so protective of our infants."

As he turned to go, Horowitz called to him, "Mister! This little one? What happens now?"

"That's the reason we are here. To see the infant. To consult with the doctors. As you can guess, this is not the usual case. Without a mother to sign over permission, our hands are tied for the moment."

"Suppose they never find her. What then?" Horowitz asked.

"Depends" was all the man would say before they departed.

Once they had closed the door, Horowitz whispered to the

infant, "Don't you worry. It will all work out. All work out." He realized that the infant had stopped feeding again and had fallen asleep once more.

Holding the infant close, Horowitz rose from the chair. He began to pace slowly, not wishing to wake her. But he himself was greatly disturbed at the fate that awaited this little one. The absence of the mother would mean that it would remain here longer than babies usually did. But even that could not be permitted to continue too long. What then? Foster home? Or homes? Many infants and young children were shifted from foster home to foster home, uprooted many times, before they finally ended up either adopted or consigned to a home for homeless children. In the old days they called them orphan asylums. Now they had some new fancy-sounding name for them.

The thought caused Horowitz to hold the infant more closely. In so doing he unfortunately caused it to come awake. Its face, which had been clenched even in repose, began slowly to come to life. The eyes opened, then closed. The motion of its lips indicated it might feed again. Horowitz picked up a fresh bottle of formula, seated himself in the chair, held the nipple close to the infant's lips. This time the infant avoided the nipple. When Horowitz tried to carefully ease it between the infant's lips it would not accept it, but fell asleep again.

Strange, Horowitz thought, *first time this little one is hungry but won't eat.*

On their way home from the hospital, Horowitz asked Molly, "My dear, when you took care of little Jane today did you notice anything?"

"You mean she hasn't gained weight?" Molly assumed.

"She didn't? I thought she gained a little," Horowitz replied, perplexed.

"Believe me, when it comes to the weight of a baby I can tell. She hasn't gained," Molly reiterated. "What did you mean, if I noticed anything?"

"First time she refused the bottle," Horowitz replied.

"They don't always take the bottle," Molly pointed out.

"The others, no. But this little one, she has never refused. She never nurses long, but she never refused the bottle before. I wonder why."

"Don't worry, Sam; when she is hungry she will eat."

"Maybe," Horowitz speculated, "it was because I didn't sing to her. She seems to like my singing."

To please him she said, "That must be it."

Still Samuel Horowitz continued to brood. Until Molly asked, "Any further word from Mona?"

"Not since yesterday. Monday afternoon is D day," he replied.

"I'm sure you're exaggerating," Molly assured.

"I hope so," Horowitz said, "I hope so."

It was early Monday evening when Samuel Horowitz's doorbell rang with such determination that Bernadine raced out of the kitchen just as Horowitz came rushing out of the bedroom.

Such a forceful ring could only mean that Mona Fields had arrived.

Both Horowitz and Bernadine headed for the front door in such haste that they almost collided. Out of deference to a father's anxiety, Bernadine stepped aside to allow him to open the door.

Properly prepared, he greeted as a warm and loving father, "Mona darling!"

"Dad!" She embraced him and began to cry.

"Mona, Mona, please, no tears. This can be a very happy occasion," Horowitz reminded.

Mona sniffled back her tears, started into the apartment. At the same time she handed her overnight bag and the jacket of her costly Chanel suit to Bernadine. She did it with such a flourish that Bernadine said, "Yes, ma'am, Miss Scarlett."

With a puzzled glance at Bernadine, Mona started into the living room. She looked about and broke into fresh tears, exclaiming, "Mother's living room!"

While she buried her face in her handkerchief, Horowitz gestured Bernadine to leave them alone. Bernadine drifted toward the kitchen, not without looking back several times.

"Mona darling, I know it can be a shock to learn that your father is thinking of marrying another woman. All your life you have been used to thinking of Mother and Father, Mom and Dad, together forever. Unfortunately, the way life works out, most times one or the other is left behind. Living alone is no fun. You try to lose yourself in all kinds of activities. You search for things to do, places to go, lectures, concerts, classes, anywhere you will be with other people.

"But Mona darling, we are only fooling ourselves. It isn't other *people* we miss. It is one other person we need and want. Can you understand that?"

Slowly, gasping only slightly less, Mona appeared to regain possession of her feelings. She looked about the room. She sighed. "To think, some other woman in my mother's home. Every piece of furniture in this room I helped her select. The fabric on that sofa. It took us days to find it. Finally, an import. At Brunschwig. And now some other woman will enjoy it."

"Mona darling, if it will make you feel better I will have the sofa recovered."

"Naturally!" Mona exploded into tears once more. "Wipe out every trace of my mother! Next thing you know the only one who will remember her will be me!"

"Now, Mona"—Samuel Horowitz turned more severe—"I will not have you saying such things. I made it very clear to Molly how I feel about your mother. And she appreciates that. After all, she had a husband to whom she feels very loyal, too."

"Molly . . . You called her Molly. Not Mrs. Mendelsohn as you did on the phone."

"Mona, it is no crime for a man to call the woman he plans to marry by her first name," Horowitz pointed out.

"Of course not. And I'll bet you call her 'dear' and 'darling,' just like you called my mother."

"Mona, the way you say '*my* mother,' you would think that to me she was a stranger. Don't forget that before she was your mother she was *my* wife. For thirty-eight years."

"And we can see now how much loyalty that earned her," Mona rebuked.

"Mona, please listen to me. Sunday we are invited to dinner at Molly's—Mrs. Mendelsohn's—home. You and Marvin, Lawrence and Sybil."

"And just who are Lawrence and Sybil?"

"Molly's children," Horowitz explained.

"Ah, I see. That was *her* idea, wasn't it? *She* suggested it."

"Not 'her.' Not 'she.' Molly. Yes, Molly suggested it," Horowitz affirmed.

"And I am sure she said, 'We will all become one big happy family.' "

"Not in those words," Horowitz replied. "But she did hope it might help bring both sides together."

"Well, don't let her get her hopes up," Mona warned. "I can see it now, that woman and her two children rubbing their hands in anticipation of getting Samuel Horowitz's money. Well, over my dead body!"

"Mona, Mona, nobody has said anything about money," he pointed out.

"Of course not. Everything is lovey-dovey until after the wedding. Then she automatically claims half of everything you own. If not more."

"Mona, I don't think she needs any of my money."

"But what about her children?" Mona demanded.

"As I understand it, her daughter is married and very comfortable. And her son is a successful accountant."

Mona seized on the word. "An accountant! I knew it! I'm sure he has already looked you up in Dun and Bradstreet, checked you at every bank in the city, to say nothing of every brokerage house. An accountant!" She pronounced it as if it were a four-letter word.

"Come, Mona, you must be tired from such a long trip. After all, five hours on a plane and then the shlepp in from Kennedy. You need some sleep. Or maybe a little dinner?" Horowitz suggested.

With the air of a martyr, Mona replied, "How can anyone eat at a time like this?"

"To tell you the truth, myself, I could do with a little snack," Horowitz said.

"As long as you feel that way I'll have my driver run down to Petrossian and get us some caviar," Mona said.

"Driver? You have a driver waiting downstairs?" Horowitz asked.

"Albert never lets me come to a dangerous place like New York without making sure I have a limousine and driver."

"Of course," Horowitz said, *and Molly and I take the bus together, to safeguard her from being mugged. The "children" really know how to live.* "Okay, Petrossian!"

"As long as he's going I'll have him bring back some Scotch salmon and some champagne," Mona said.

My daughter certainly knows how to soothe a breaking heart, Horowitz thought.

In half an hour the uniformed chauffeur delivered to Horowitz's door an elegantly wrapped package of very expensive food, protected by dry ice and too cold to handle.

They ate caviar and smoked salmon and drank champagne. During the repast Mona said little. She interrupted spreading the lovely gray pearls of caviar only long enough to say, "Dad, have you thought this through? I mean, really thought this through?"

"I have thought, and thought, and thought, believe me," Horowitz reassured.

Mona continued to eat, then remarked, "When I look around this dining room and think that some day soon some other woman will be here . . ." She never did finish the thought but did finish her caviar.

At least she isn't crying anymore, Horowitz comforted himself. But that was to last only a very short time. When they had finished he suggested that for tonight and until she could install herself in a hotel she use the bedroom and he would sleep in the den.

She approached the bedroom, stopped suddenly in the doorway and exclaimed, "Mother's bedroom!" The tears started once more.

He could hear her sobbing all through undressing. When her sobbing became louder he rushed into the bedroom to discover her standing aloof from the bed.

"Mona darling, what happened?"

"Mother's bed. To think some day soon some other woman will be lying in it."

"You sleep in the den. I will sleep in here." He led her into the den where he had made up the couch as a bed.

Once he had closed the den door he hurried back to the kitchen. He dialed a Washington phone number, waited a moment, was relieved to hear the voice he sought.

"Marvin? Dad."

"I know," Marvin replied. "The eagle has landed. She is there."

"You think maybe you could come up to New York before Sunday?"

"I wish I could, Dad. But I am tied up in court the rest of the week."

"Marvin, tell me something: How do *you* feel about this?"

"To tell you the truth, Dad," Marvin confessed, "it's a shock. It shouldn't be. But it is."

"Of course, I understand," Samuel Horowitz said as he hung up the phone. Denied the answer he had hoped for, he considered calling Molly to suggest they cancel the plans for Sunday.

No, he decided, *no. Sooner or later we will have to face this. It might as well be Sunday. Thank God, tomorrow is Tuesday. Molly and me, we'll go up to the hospital, see little Jane and the other babies. At least there we have no problems, only the joy of taking care of the little ones.*

Chapter 34

XXX

ON THEIR WALK FROM MOLLY'S PLACE TO THE BUS STOP MOLLY noticed that Samuel Horowitz was unusually quiet on this day. Obviously deeply engrossed in a problem he was trying to avoid discussing. Though ordinarily Molly Mendelsohn would grant him his private thoughts, as she used to do when Phil had business problems he would rather not discuss, she felt so intimately at the center of this problem that she was forced to ask, "So? How did it go?"

"Go?" Horowitz replied, as if he had barely heard her question.

"Mona," Molly reminded.

"Oh, Mona," Horowitz echoed as if suddenly reminded.

"What else would have you so deep in thought this morning?" Molly asked.

"The honest truth, I was thinking about little Jane. I'm not a doctor. Certainly not a pediatrician. But I have this feeling something is wrong."

When Molly appeared skeptical, Horowitz said, "You know, considering the history of Jews in medicine, since we have been among the world's best for thousands of years, being doctors to kings and even popes, just being Jewish entitles a man to having a medical opinion."

"Still," Molly ventured to point out, "it doesn't hurt to also have a medical degree. And if the doctors haven't found anything wrong with her . . ."

"You're right, Molly dear, I worry too much. About everything."

"Including Mona?" Molly asked.

"Molly, you have that same knack that Hannah had. You can tell when I am avoiding. All right, I confess, worried about little Jane I surely am. So rather than talk about Mona I choose to talk about her. Yes, I am also worried about my darling daughter Mona."

"Don't be," Molly comforted. "I am sure on Sunday everything will turn out all right. It's just a matter of people getting to know each other."

"I hope so, Molly dear, I hope so."

As arranged, Molly Mendelsohn reached the nursery floor first. Samuel Horowitz followed by some minutes. At once, even before scrubbing, he went to the nursery where little Jane was kept. He was delighted to see that she was in the arms and in the care of his friend Homer Wesley. Horowitz gestured through the glass wall, inquiring, *Is she all right?* Wesley nodded, without interrupting the feeding. Horowitz gestured *Wait, I'll be right there.* He went off to scrub.

Once he had executed his intricate scrub routine, which exceeded all hospital requirements, Horowitz forced his now sterile hands through the elasticized cuffs of a fresh smock. He entered the nursery as Wesley was just changing little Jane from her damp shirt into a fresh one.

"Well, how is she today?"

"Not bad," Wesley said.

Horowitz detected that his black friend did not exhibit his usual degree of enthusiasm.

"Just not bad?" Horowitz pressed.

"She's a little off her feed today," Wesley said. "But it happens. Why do you ask?"

"I have this feeling there is something wrong," Horowitz confessed.

"She don't run a fever. She's not crying. She sleeps very good," Wesley pointed out. "What's got you worried?"

"Just a feeling. Maybe it's being Jewish. A Jew must always have something to worry about. When you don't, you make something up," Horowitz replied.

"If you're so concerned I'll keep a special lookout every time I'm here," Wesley promised.

"Thanks. If you notice anything let me know."

"Of course," Wesley said. "Meantime, how do you like your afternoon hours? Better than morning?"

"It has its compensations." Horowitz tried to avoid the issue.

"Well, I want you to know I miss you. The old team of Wesley and Horowitz breaking up was not easy to take."

"Wesley, believe me, nothing personal. I really enjoy working with you. But there are reasons . . . maybe one day soon it will all become clear."

"Horowitz, you remember a lot about the old-time vaudeville," Wesley said, an obvious prelude to a question.

"Sure. Some act you're trying to remember? Maybe the Howards, Will and Eugene? Or maybe Red Skelton's doughnut and coffee act?"

"Not an act. A song," Wesley said.

"You name it, I bet I can remember it," Horowitz boasted, ready for the challenge.

"Barbershop quartets used to sing it a lot. It went something like this. . . ." Wesley began to sing, "Dada da da dada da, that old gang of mine. Remember that one?"

"As they say, duck soup!" Horowitz replied. Instantly he began to sing, in his less-than-perfect pitch, "Wedding bells are breaking up that old gang . . ." He stopped. He looked up into Wesley's smiling black face. "You know?" Horowitz asked.

"Suspected," Wesley said.

"You mean it is obvious?" Horowitz asked. "Does anyone else know?"

"I don't think so. But since you and me, we got to be such good friends, I figured it had to be something like that to break up the old vaudeville team."

"Keep it a secret. For the time being. Okay?"

"Of course," Wesley promised. "Can I ask who?"

"Mrs. Mendelsohn."

"Ah. Good! Nice lady!" Wesley said. "Horowitz, I am very happy for you."

Wesley held out his hand and Horowitz shook it vigorously.

Thursday afternoon Samuel Horowitz assumed his usual volunteer duties, always keeping an eye on the nursery in which little Jane reposed. When she was due for her next feeding, he slipped in and took charge of her before any other volunteer could.

Throughout the feeding he tried to assess her condition by comparing in his mind her weight today against her weight on Tuesday when he had last held her, fed her, diapered her. He consulted the chart at the foot of her crib. According to the figures listed there she was gaining, not as fast as the others but still she was gaining. Yet the feeling nagged at him.

He spent more time than usual with her. Walked her more. Hummed to her more. Spoke words into her tiny pink ears more closely than before. He tried feeding her a second time but she fell asleep instead. Still he persisted until, between falling asleep and feeding, she had emptied the bottle.

Once she had been fed, changed into a clean, dry shirt and diaper, he placed her back in her crib, covered her with the light blanket, patted her on the head. He went out to see Ms. Haworth, the nurse in charge during the day shift.

"Any word?" he asked.

He had been asking that same question every Tuesday and Thursday since little Jane had been delivered to the nursery. Haworth knew what those words meant.

"No sign of the mother," Haworth informed.

"Any word from Human Resources?" Horowitz asked.

"No," Haworth replied, then added, "Mr. Horowitz, need I remind you what happened when you became too attached to little Cletus Simon. Don't let that happen again."

Disputatious as ever, Horowitz replied, "Me? Becoming too attached? Maybe *you* are becoming too suspicious!" He went off muttering, "Too attached . . . ridiculous!"

Chapter 35

✕✕✕

Molly Mendelsohn seemed to have four hands and eight eyes as she opened the oven door to see how her roast stuffed breast of veal was browning, lifted the cover of the large pot to see how the pea soup was bubbling away, glanced into another pot in which the green beans were gently simmering, checked the potato *kigel* in the toaster oven.

At the same time she was giving suggestions to Sophie, who usually came in twice a week to clean and dust. Since this was a special occasion, Sophie had agreed to come in on Sunday, serve dinner and clean up after.

"Please, Mrs. Mendelsohn, they will be here before you know it. Go in, take your bath, get dressed."

"Yes, Sophie, of course. It's just that everything has to be perfect for them. Especially for Mr. Horowitz's daughter. From what I've heard . . . Never mind what I've heard. But everything must be perfect."

"Don't worry, it will be," Sophie assured.

A big woman, with Slavic features and hair that had once been light blond and was now tinged with slight traces of gray, Sophie inspired sufficient confidence to assure that Molly would leave matters in her hands. After a final inspection of the dinner table, set for six, with her best Lenox china and her Royal Danish solid silver, Molly went off to take her bath.

She tried to relax in the warm, fragrant water. Another hour and they would be here. So many questions, so many doubts. If it had included only Samuel and herself, adjustment would have been difficult enough for two people set in their ways. Adding to the situation four other personalities, each with feelings of their own, multiplied the problem not by four but by forty.

Exactly what did Sybil say when I told her?, Molly tried to recall. *"Mother, are you* sure *you have given this enough thought?" Very formal for Sybil, calling me "Mother." Always it has been Ma or Mom. But "Mother"? And treating me like a naughty child. "Mother, are you sure you have given this enough thought?"*

Bad enough Sybil, but Lawrence. He made no bones about his reaction. "Ma, how could you? Moving in with a stranger. What would my father have said if he were here?"

She had tried to explain. "Lawrence, in the first place the situation arises precisely because your father is *not* here. And in the second place, Mr. Horowitz may be a stranger to you, but not to me."

"How long have you known him? Days? Weeks?"

"Almost two months."

"That's only another way of saying seven weeks," her son had pointed out. "I can see it now. I know what he's after," Lawrence declared.

She had detected in Lawrence the same emotional upset that always afflicted him in times of great stress. Final exams in college and when he took his State Boards to become certified as an accountant. Poor Lawrence. Since early high school days he did all his reacting through his sensitive colon.

By the time Molly stepped out of her warm tub she was even more tense than when she had stepped in. One thing comforted her as she dried herself with a big thick red towel that complemented her red and white bathroom. She stopped drying herself long enough to stand naked before the mirror. She studied her body. True, everything sagged a little. But, for a woman of sixty-eight, not bad. Exercise, an active life, had yielded its rewards. As long as she felt this way about herself, and about Samuel, she would weather the reactions of her children, and his.

Molly was clipping her small, simple gold earrings into place when she heard the doorbell. At once her hands began to tremble. She almost dropped one earring while she called out, "Sophie! Please?"

She was greatly relieved when she heard the cheerful voice of Samuel Horowitz say, "Ah, Sophie! Nice to see you."

Molly Mendelsohn came out of her bedroom to greet him. She started to say, "Samuel, I'm glad you got here first. I was worried . . ."

Before she could get all the words out, he held up both hands in a gesture that called for silence.

"First, my dear, let me look at you. Did I say 'look'? A small word for what I mean. Let me admire you. Please turn around. Slowly."

Smiling shyly she turned about.

"My dear Molly, if this is the way you modeled clothes in those days, no wonder Phil fell in love with you."

"Will they like me?" she asked.

"*They* will *like* you. *I* will *love* you," Samuel Horowitz said.

He took her hand, and drew her close. He pressed his cheek against hers. "Molly, Molly, I know we are both very nervous today. But if nervous makes you look so beautiful, do me a favor, stay nervous."

They were both laughing when the doorbell interrupted. Molly looked at him, shrugged a look that said *We might as well.* She went to the door and threw it open.

She was greeted by Sybil's judgmental "Mother?" Which was neither a greeting nor a question, but a comment that seemed to demand an explanation or an apology. At the same time Lawrence bent down to kiss Molly on the cheek. She could tell from the tension in his body that he was having one of his spastic-colon attacks.

Meantime, Samuel Horowitz pulled his navy blue blazer into place, straightened his Countess Mara tie and flattened the collar of his one-hundred-seventy-five-dollar Charvet shirt. He intended to present himself at his very best.

"Children, this is Samuel Horowitz. Samuel, this is Sybil and Lawrence," Molly introduced.

"How do you do," Sybil responded, staring at him with a disapproving look that reminded Horowitz of Charles Laughton as Captain Bligh in *Mutiny on the Bounty*.

"How do you do?" Horowitz responded.

Lawrence Mendelsohn held out his hand. Horowitz seized it and shook it heartily. At the same time thinking, *Tense, his hand is tense. Molly warned me he reacts strangely at times like this. But, then, my hand is not exactly loose either.*

"Well," Molly said, cheerfully as she could. "Let's all go into the living room and get acquainted."

They had started toward the living room when the doorbell rang once more. The very sound and length of the ring made Samuel Horowitz explain, "My daughter, Mona."

He was right, of course. Fortunately, Marvin was with her.

"Dad!" Mona greeted, embracing him but at the same time casting a critical glance over his shoulder at Molly.

Samuel Horowitz disengaged himself from his daughter's embrace to introduce, "Mona, Marvin, this is Sybil, this is Lawrence. And this, my dear children, is Molly!"

Molly Mendelsohn held out her hand to Mona, intending to draw her close and kiss her on the check. But Mona's arch gesture and brisk shake of her hand discouraged any intimacy. Marvin greeted Molly with a polite but reserved nod of the head.

Unnerved by the coolness of the greeting, Molly said, "Why don't we . . . why . . . let's all go into the living room and become better acquainted."

"Yes. Let's. By all means," Mona said, meaning, of course, the exact opposite.

They entered the living room. All remained standing, awkward and ill at ease.

"Please, please, sit down. Make yourselves comfortable," Molly invited.

Samuel Horowitz asked, "Anybody for a drink? Lawrence?

Sybil? Can I get you anything? Marvin? Scotch and soda? Mona? Vodka on ice? Molly made sure to have Absolut just for you."

"Absolut. How thoughtful," Mona said, as if her words too were on ice. "Well, Dad, you certainly seem to know your way around this place."

He was about to turn and rebuke her but he restrained himself, smiled and started toward the server that Molly had set up as a temporary bar. While he was mixing drinks for Mona and Marvin, he invited again, "Sybil? Lawrence?"

"No, thanks," they both responded at once.

Drinks served, Horowitz stood in the middle of the room. Hoping to stir up some friendly conversation, he said in his warmest tone, "Well?"

No one responded, until Molly said, "You know, the funniest thing . . ." She turned her attention to Mona and Marvin. "The first time your father and I met we didn't get along at all. In fact we had an argument about how to take care of the babies. Did he tell you that's how we met? Doing volunteer work?"

"I never liked the idea of his going up to that hospital," Mona said in a flat tone of voice.

Interrupted, but only for a moment, Molly pointed out, " 'That hospital' is where the need for volunteers is the greatest. Anyhow, that's how we met."

"Very interesting," Mona said. That was all she said.

Conversation lagging, Horowitz decided it was time to step in and take over. "Well, as it turned out, *she* was right. And I was wrong. But, you know your father, I didn't give in so easily. It took another man, a very fine black gentleman named Homer Wesley, to really teach me the ropes. Funny thing about him. I'm not allowed to call him Homer. Especially not *Mr.* Wesley. He insists on just Wesley. And Horowitz. Like we were a vaudeville team. Or else a law firm. Not a bad name for a law firm. Wesley and Horowitz. Right, Marvin?"

He had hoped to elicit some response from his son, perhaps even a smile. He failed.

"Well," Horowitz said, "I know you must all be curious about how we became closer. It really happened in a very strange way. Call it an act of God."

"A marriage made in heaven, no doubt," Mona commented.

"Mona, darling," Horowitz tried to warn, then continued: "Mrs. Robbins, one of our volunteers, was mugged within sight of the hospital. So I was worried about Molly." He turned to Sybil and Lawrence. "Your mother has a long walk from the Number Eleven bus stop to the hospital."

"Yes, we know," Lawrence replied. "Many times I have told her to take a cab."

"Well, she doesn't like to. Neither do I. So I thought if I came here and picked her up we could take the bus together, and she would be safe."

"Very thoughtful," Sybil remarked.

"But the next thing you know I am taking her to the doctor to have a mammogram."

"Mammogram?" both Sybil and Mona declared at the same time, each from her own disapproving point of view.

"Mother, you never told me about needing a mammogram."

Before Molly could respond, Mona turned on her father. "You never took *my* mother to the doctor for a mammogram."

"Mona, darling, your mother never had *need* for a mammogram," Horowitz explained. Then countered, "Sitting there in that doctor's office, waiting for the results, then going into the doctor's consultation room with her . . ."

Slowly, but with a commanding gesture, Mona turned back to confront her father. "You actually went into the consultation room with her?"

"She was nervous. What woman wouldn't be at such a time? She needed someone. I am glad I was there."

"You never showed such care and attention to my mother before *she* died."

Even Marvin could not abide his sister's attitude. He interrupted to rebuke, "Mona! Ma was sick a very short time. Dad had little chance to give her much care and attention!"

"Not so!" Horowitz disputed. Both children turned to him.

"Dad?" Marvin asked.

"Your mother was sick long before you knew," Samuel Horowitz confessed.

"And you never told us?" Mona challenged.

"You know your mother. 'Sam, why worry the children? Once I get better we'll call them.' But that time she didn't get better."

"You should have told us," Marvin said.

" 'Should have told you,' " Horowitz repeated sadly. "Children. Parents. We spend the first half of our married lives worrying about the children. And the last half trying to keep the children from worrying about us. Mona, take my word for it, your mother had the very best care and attention during her brief illness. By the time you and Marvin knew, it was too late. So never accuse your father of not loving and caring for your mother."

For once Mona had no response.

Horowitz directed his attention to Lawrence and Sybil, hoping they would be more receptive to the events that led up to this meeting.

"Your mother's scare started me thinking that maybe we needed each other. But we also needed time to get used to the idea. So the night I took your mother for dinner on the boat ride around Manhattan, I—"

Mona turned back to glare at her father. Before she could say a word, Horowitz anticipated, "I know. I never took your mother on a boat ride around Manhattan. It so happens that your mother, better known as my wife, did not trust boats. When we went to Europe and then to Israel we went by plane, not by boat. She had more confidence in planes. Especially planes flown by Israeli pilots. So, Mona, what did you want me to do? Chloroform your mother and drag her on board a boat?"

"Dad! Spare me your usual exaggerations," Mona said.

"Mona, you *are* right about one thing. During your mother's lifetime we did put off doing lots of things, trips, vacations, There never seemed to be enough time. I had a business to run. We had kids to bring up. After she died I can't tell you how guilty I felt about all the things we never did together."

"I know how that is," Molly joined in. "The regrets. In a way, that is what made me accept Samuel's proposal. The things we fail to do in the early years, we must rush to do now when time is so short."

"So everything my father deprived my mother of will now—" Mona started to say.

Fortunately, at that moment Sophie appeared in the doorway.

"Mrs. Mendelsohn, I am ready to put dinner on the table." This despite the fact that Molly had rehearsed her to say, "Dinner is served."

It did not escape Mona's critical eye that every dish Molly Mendelsohn served was one of her father's favorites.

The woman is obviously trying to prove she is a better cook than my mother. Of course, this is a special meal. God knows what she will feed him if they get married. That is, if she feeds him anything. She must be the type who loves to eat out all the time. And my father does not like to eat out. How this woman was able to twist him around her little finger . . .

Once dinner was over Horowitz assumed that Mona and Marvin were ready to leave. Gracefully, he hoped. So he was surprised to hear Mona order, "Marvin, this is the time!"

"Time?" Horowitz asked. "Time for what?"

"Marvin, tell him!" Mona replied.

"Tell me what?" Horowitz demanded.

"Dad, we think, and I as an attorney insist, that Lawrence and I have a talk. A very frank talk."

"About what?" Horowitz demanded. "Everything is agreed. Molly and I are getting married. At my synagogue. But both rabbis will preside. So what is there to talk about?"

Lawrence Mendelsohn intruded. "Mr. Horowitz . . ."

"Can't you even *try* to call me Samuel?" he asked.

"That may come later. Once we get *certain* things out of the way."

"Certain things?" Horowitz started to question until it dawned on him. "Aha! I see. 'Certain *financial* things.' Right?"

"Samuel, please?" Molly intervened. "I don't blame them for being curious."

"Are we allowed to be present?" Horowitz asked. "Or are we too old and feebleminded to understand what is going on?"

"Dad!" Mona rebuked. "*Now*, Marvin!" She ordered her brother to proceed with a plan they had obviously rehearsed.

"Lawrence, can you and I go into the living room and have a little frank talk?"

"By all means," Lawrence Mendelsohn replied.

Chapter 36

XXX

MARVIN HAMMOND STEPPED POLITELY ASIDE TO ALLOW LAWRENCE Mendelsohn to precede him into the living room. Though not invited, Mona Fields followed, which immediately caused Sybil to do the same.

Left in the dining room, Samuel Horowitz looked the length of the table to Molly Mendelsohn who sat in the hostess chair.

"You think we should also?" she asked.

"Not yet, my dear," Horowitz advised. "I have a feeling they will need us later."

Molly called toward the kitchen, "Sophie, is there any more decaf left?"

Once served, Molly Mendelsohn and Samuel Horowitz glanced lovingly at each other across the length of the table. With a philosophic and indulgent smile she observed, "Children."

To which Samuel Horowitz added, with a sad shake of his head, "Children."

They both sat back to enjoy their fresh hot coffee.

In the living room Marvin and Mona had taken up positions on the sofa. Across the room Lawrence and Sybil had settled into the two matching armchairs. There was a long moment of silence, each side waiting for the other to commence the discussions.

287

Not unexpectedly, it was Mona who fired the first salvo.

"You understand I am not interested in any of this for myself. It's only my children I'm thinking of."

"Naturally," Sybil remarked sarcastically.

Before the moment could flare into a conflict between the two women, Marvin took over.

"I suggest we all remain calm. This is a situation which I often face in my law practice. So I know the more emotional the situation, the more necessary it is to keep our minds on the practicalities."

"Agreed!" Lawrence said, with the attitude of a man who only awaits the enemy's first thrust so he can counterthrust.

"Now, as I see it," Marvin began, "my father and your mother are intent on coming together to share the rest of their lives."

"So it would seem," Lawrence agreed, already feeling a slight queasiness in his colon.

"Whatever their private emotional arrangements might be—" Marvin started to say.

Lawrence interrupted frantically, "What did you mean by that? Exactly *what did you mean*?"

He was up out of his armchair, almost looming over Mona and Marvin.

"All I meant was that emotions, sentiment, are one thing."

"Meaning?" Lawrence demanded.

Even his sister intervened. "Larry, please, give him a chance to say what he means."

Driven by private jealousies of his own, Lawrence Mendelsohn persisted, "What did your father say to you?"

"About what?" Marvin asked.

"You know about what!" Lawrence accused.

"No, I don't know!" Marvin insisted.

"Did he say anything to you about having . . ." Lawrence faltered before continuing, "having . . . sex with my mother?"

"He never mentioned any such thing," Marvin insisted.

Lawrence Mendelsohn glared at Marvin Hammond, debating whether to believe him. Finally he sank back into his chair. But only for an instant. Suddenly he was up again, racing past the dining room door and on his way to the bathroom.

Whereupon Molly remarked to Samuel, "I think I told you. My Lawrence has a very sensitive stomach. Once he tried psychiatry. And it helped."

"But evidently not enough," Horowitz replied.

"Do you think we should go in?" Molly asked.

"Not yet," Horowitz said.

When Lawrence returned, the meeting resumed in earnest.

"The way I see it," Marvin Hammond started out, "we—my sister and I—on behalf of the grandchildren, have no objection whatsoever to my father paying for the support of this marriage during his lifetime."

"That's very noble of you," Sybil remarked acidly.

"However . . ." Mona took command. "However, we insist on a clear, written premarital agreement stating that at the time of my father's demise all his assets shall revert to his estate. To which his grandchildren shall be the sole heirs."

"I see," Lawrence Mendelsohn said.

"After all," Mona persisted, "my father did not work all his life building up a business and accumulating assets for the benefit of some strange woman's children and grandchildren!"

"You won't call *my* mother 'some strange woman'!" Sybil fought back.

In the dining room, Molly instinctively started to rise to intervene. But Samuel Horowitz gestured her patiently back into her chair.

"Later," he counseled. Then he shook his head. "That Mona. Marvin doesn't know, but sometimes when he is trying a case in New York federal court I sneak in. I sit in the back. Just to watch him in action. He's terrific. He dominates witnesses, other lawyers, sometimes even judges. But when it comes to his sister, Mona, he doesn't stand a chance. Oh, that Mona."

"Samuel, don't explain, don't apologize. When you meet my cousin Shirley you'll realize there's a Mona in every family."

In the living room, Marvin tried to placate his sister by putting a firm grip on her arm to prevent any rebuttal to Sybil's last outburst. In his most professional, lawyerly manner he proceeded calmly, "I am sure you can understand that by any concept of equity the fruits of a man's labor rightfully belong to his own flesh and blood."

To cut through the rhetoric, Lawrence replied, "Look, I'm an accountant. All I understand are figures. Exactly how much are we talking about here?"

Marvin glanced at Mona, Mona at Marvin, his look asking, *Shall we tell him? And if we do, shall I tell him how much we discussed settling for?* Mona's look dictated, *See how far you can get without stating any figure!*

"What difference do the figures make?" Marvin replied. "It's the concept of equity that is paramount here."

To which Lawrence Mendelsohn responded, "I notice that whenever lawyers want to hide the figures they talk about equity. So I'll tell you what. You take the equity. I'll take the figures. How much are we talking about?"

"You have no right to ask that question!" Mona protested.

"Mona, please." Her brother tried to calm her. He turned back to Lawrence and Sybil. "If we are to proceed with a good-faith discussion the amount should not matter."

"Okay," Lawrence conceded. "No figures."

Mona and Marvin exchanged sly glances at their first negotiating victory.

Until Lawrence Mendelsohn added, "No figures. Not yours. Not ours."

"Not 'ours'?" Mona echoed sharply.

"That is very important," Sybil intervened. "After all, we do not want any fortune-hunting stranger coming into our mother's life and . . ."

In outrage, Mona exclaimed, "How dare you! My father has been an honorable, hardworking man all his life. If there is any fortune hunter in this situation it is *your* mother. Well, I can promise you now, she won't get her hands on a dime of *my* father's money!"

"My father left my mother very well fixed, thank you!" Lawrence Mendelsohn shouted in return. "She doesn't need your father's money! All we want to do is protect what's ours!"

Samuel Horowitz looked across the table at Molly Mendelsohn and said, "Now."

He walked the length of the table, politely helped her out of her chair. Clasping hands, they started toward the living room.

At the moment they entered, all four voices were raised in a bedlam of accusations, counteraccusations and refutations. Raising his voice above all the others, Samuel Horowitz exclaimed, "Silence! *Zull zein sha!* There shall be quiet!"

He continued: "All right, now. We are sitting in there listening to what you four have said. And you know what it sounds like? Are you fighting over equity? No! Or over our welfare? Definitely no! You are fighting over what will be left for you after we are dead.

"Well, *we* are interested in what happens while we are still *alive*. This discussion about money, Molly and me, we talked all that through. We discovered that, yes, I am comfortably fixed. It happens she is even *more* comfortably fixed. Her Phil was a very good businessman. So she doesn't need what I have. And I don't need what she has. There's enough for everybody.

"Now that we have settled that, let me say a word to all four of you. I hope none of you ever has to experience what we have been through. To live your life with a dear one and then suddenly to be left alone.

"Well, Molly and me, we are *tired* of being alone. We want someone to share with. The good. And just as important, the bad. The pain. And, if it should happen, the sickness. So all this talk about money, and who gets what, to us that is not nice. Not . . . how shall I say? Not *decent*. Very distasteful. *We* are dealing with living, with sharing days and hours. We will leave the greed and selfishness to you."

"Dad, that is unfair!" Mona responded at once. "You know very well that ever since Mom died I have been after you to move out to our house in San Diego. Where we can offer you every comfort."

"And also ship me off to the Hebrew Home for the Aged, whenever you think I have become a nuisance," Horowitz replied.

"I never said any such thing!" Mona protested.

"You didn't have to, because I know you, Mona. You are a

born manager. Of other people's lives. You would like to be president of everything and everybody. I often said to your mother, God rest her, 'It's a good thing Mona isn't Catholic. Otherwise the pope would be out of a job.' "

"Well, if that's the way you feel, I won't trouble you any longer. Go ahead. Marry that woman. But don't expect me to attend or approve!"

So saying, Mona Fields strode toward the door. Molly Mendelsohn hurried after her, calling, "Mona! Please! Don't do this to your father!"

The slam of the door ended Molly's plea. She turned back to Horowitz.

"I'm sorry, Samuel. I would never want to be the cause of such bitterness between a father and his daughter. Maybe this is all a mistake."

"Molly . . . Molly dear . . . What are you saying?" Horowitz asked.

"Maybe we have both been too . . . too impulsive. I think we should take time, think this over."

To which not Horowitz but Molly's son, Lawrence, responded at once. "A very wise decision, Mother."

"Molly, please," Horowitz protested. "We can't let Mona decide the rest of our lives for us."

"There can't be a wedding unless all the children are there. It wouldn't be right." Molly Mendelsohn started to weep silently.

Marvin said softly, "Pa, give her time to get over it. Don't press her for an answer now."

"Yes," Samuel Horowitz conceded reluctantly. "You're right." He approached Molly, put his arms around her and said, "I will call you in the morning."

He followed Marvin to the door. While they waited for the elevator, Marvin said, "Pa, I'll do what I can. But you know Mona."

"I know, I know," Horowitz agreed sadly. "When it comes to stubborn, mules could take lessons from your sister."

Horowitz arrived home. He had just inserted his key in the door when he heard the phone ringing. Hoping it was Mona with an apology, or at least a change of heart, he hurried to the phone to greet anxiously, "Mona darling?"

Instead of Mona, he heard the voice of Mrs. Washington. In their usual shorthand, she asked, "So?"

Meaning so, how did it go? The dinner. The attitude. The young ones, did they seem to get along? Did they like Molly? Did she like them? All tightly packed into that single syllable.

Responding in equivalent shorthand, Samuel Horowitz replied, "Disaster."

"Good God, what happened?" Mrs. Washington asked, fearing the match she had so carefully guided was suddenly doomed.

Samuel Horowitz reviewed the entire evening, from the first anxious moments to the last bitter words.

"Oh, too bad, too bad," Mrs. Washington commiserated.

"Maybe Molly is right," Horowitz said. "We should have taken things slower. Maybe I should have expected what Mona did. On the other hand, Mrs. Washington, tell me, am I being too hard on her? After all, the thought of another woman living in her mother's house could be an emotional shock. All I know, I never wanted anything to succeed more. And I never had anything fail so miserably. Mona won't come to the wedding. And Molly says there can't be a wedding next Sunday unless all the children are there."

With considerable sorrow, Mrs. Washington hung up. Her first consoling hope was, *Tomorrow, once Mona has had a chance to think things over, she will change her mind.* But then she realized, *I know Mona well. Too well. Give her a night to think things over and she will wake up doubly convinced that she is right.*

Something must be done. Something. Lemonade time again!

Chapter 37

XXX

MRS. HARRIET WASHINGTON SAT BY HER PHONE, DEEP IN TROUBLED thought. Her fingers drummed nervously on the instrument as she considered the plight of her dearest former patient, Samuel Horowitz.

Considering at which hotel Mona Fields might be staying, Mrs. Washington knew that only the newest and the most expensive would do for a woman of her taste and means. She picked up the Manhattan phone book. She started to make a list. She began with the St. Regis, which had recently reopened after a three-year multimillion-dollar refurbishing. Where the smallest room now cost three hundred and seventy-five dollars a night. And Mona Fields was never content with the smallest of anything.

Of course there was the new Essex House, and the Peninsula, and four others equally expensive. Since it was late at night, Mrs. Washington knew that she would have no trouble extracting the information she sought from the clerk at the registration desk of any hotel. She commenced to place her calls. Her intuition was, as usual, flawless. She scored a bull's-eye on her first call. Mona Fields was, of course, registered at the St. Regis.

But Mrs. Fields had given strict instructions not to be disturbed until morning. Mrs. Washington left a pointed message:

Before you do anything, call me in the morning. Urgent! She added the
phone number of her present patient.

Just before nine o'clock the next morning, while Mrs. Washington was instructing her patient in the art of converting from a
metal walker to a quad cane, the phone rang.

"Mrs. Washington, *this* is Mona Fields. I am making this call
only out of courtesy. I do not have much time. My limousine is
waiting. I am on my way to the airport. What did you wish?"

"First thing, cancel your flight!"

"Mrs. Washington, I am only too familiar with your habit of
taking charge, and giving orders. But I have plans I cannot
change."

"If you love your father, you'll change them," Mrs. Washington insisted.

"I have never given you or anyone cause to doubt my love for
my father. Or my mother," Mona replied. "But that does not
mean I must indulge all his whims. Especially at this late stage in
his life when men have been known to make foolish decisions."

"Mrs. Fields, if you get on that plane and something terrible
happens to your father you will never forgive yourself," Mrs.
Washington warned.

Startled as much by Mrs. Washington's solemn tone as by her
ominous words, Mona asked, "Mrs. Washington, do you know
something about my father that I don't?"

"I know something about your father that even *he* doesn't
know," Mrs. Washington asserted.

"To precisely what are you referring?" Mona demanded.

"Cancel your flight. Meet me here Wednesday afternoon at
two-thirty. My patient will be having his after-lunch nap. I will be
free to tell you what I know."

"Wednesday, two-thirty?" Mona considered. "Can't we do it
today?"

"Wednesday," Mrs. Washington ruled.

There was a long moment of silence.

But Mrs. Washington knew that, for all Mona's eccentrici-
ties, and her need to dominate in all situations, she loved her

father. Mrs. Washington's analysis proved accurate. After some thought, Mona Fields replied, "Wednesday. Yes, yes, I will stay over. What is the address?"

Once Mrs. Washington gave Mona the address, she hung up, thinking, *I have delayed her departure two days. I must find a way to keep her here until Sunday.*

Tuesday morning at ten o'clock Samuel Horowitz appeared at Molly Mendelsohn's building. This time the doorman had no need to call up since Molly was already waiting in the lobby. Though they had spoken on the phone several times since that unfortunate dinner, this was the first time they had seen each other.

At once, Horowitz realized that Molly had spent two rather sleepless nights since Sunday. By sheer habit he took from her hands the aluminum-foil–wrapped platter of pastries.

This package was far heavier than Molly's usual contribution to the coffee corner. Though he said nothing, his look of surprise called for an explanation.

"Aggravation," Molly confessed sadly. "Whenever I have a really serious problem I find it helps to keep busy in the kitchen. Cooking. Baking. I made and have in the refrigerator a beef stew, a chicken fricassee and a *luchen kigel*. And as for *ruggaluch* and cheese strudel, a freezer full."

"I'm sorry," Horowitz apologized. "Whatever else, I didn't expect Mona to walk out."

"Have you heard from her since?" Molly asked.

"Not a word. She must have gone back to San Diego," Horowitz replied. "Maybe once she gets back there, talks to her husband, he is a pretty commonsense person, maybe she will change her mind." Then, in the interest of truth and the need to be completely honest with Molly, he admitted, "Commonsense as Albert is, he has never had much influence on Mona."

They continued walking toward Amsterdam Avenue in silence. Just before they arrived at the bus stop, Horowitz asked suddenly, "If Mona doesn't change her mind, would you?"

"Would I what?" Molly asked.

"Change *your* mind about the wedding without all the children being there?" Horowitz asked.

"Samuel, much as I want to marry you, I wouldn't feel right to come between a father and his only daughter. I would never forgive myself."

They boarded the bus and were on their way up to the hospital in complete silence.

When Molly Mendelsohn laid out her pastries on the counter in the coffee corner, Mrs. Braun asked, "What are we celebrating today? The birth of another grandchild? Or a graduation?"

"Celebrating?" Molly asked glumly.

"So many *ruggaluch,*" Mrs. Braun observed, "enough to share with the whole eleventh floor."

Molly did not explain but continued laying out her tasty little pastries.

Minutes later Samuel Horowitz arrived on the eleventh floor, went to the scrub room where he performed his usual surgical cleansing, but with somewhat less than his usual enthusiasm. Having slipped into his smock, he started for the nursery where tiny Baby Jane's crib was housed. Even looking forward to that enjoyable duty did not arouse in Samuel Horowitz his usual sense of anticipation.

He was relieved to see Homer Wesley sitting in his usual chair with the bundle of white blanket in his arm. In his other hand Wesley held a formula bottle to the lips of the infant, whose face was obscured from view.

Horowitz entered, greeted Wesley with a weary wave of his hand. Wesley knew his colleague well enough to read that gesture accurately. His friend Horowitz was depressed today, lacking the exuberance of their last meeting on Thursday. But Wesley did not pry. For he also knew that if Horowitz wanted to share his problem he would, without any prodding.

Horowitz approached, leaned over to stare down at the infant Wesley was feeding.

"Aha. Baby Jane," Horowitz realized. "How is she doing today?"

"Sleeps more," Wesley said. "Almost like this life is taking more out of her than she can bear."

"I know," Horowitz agreed. "Seems almost like just feeding is too much. Takes a little, then falls asleep. Wakes up hungry, eats a little more, falls asleep again."

"Takes almost twice as long to feed her as most of the others," Wesley replied.

Horowitz stood over her, observing closely. "Ah. There. She did it again. Stopped sucking and fell asleep." He watched a moment, then remarked, "Tell me, Wesley, does she seem to you to have trouble breathing?"

"Breathes a little heavy," Wesley confirmed. "But regular."

"Well, I got to get on to my other little friends," Horowitz said. "I will catch up with this one later."

As Horowitz started away, Wesley asked casually, "Horowitz? Sunday. How did it go?"

"Not good. Not good at all." But he chose not to explain. Nor did Wesley pry.

For the next two hours, Samuel Horowitz carried out his duties, cuddling, feeding, and changing several little ones. Even though his personal concerns diminished his enjoyment he hummed and crooned to them with all the enthusiasm and warmth he could summon.

He saved his last efforts for Baby Jane, who had now had two hours of sleep and should be hungry again. He lifted her from her crib, whispering, "Well, look who's here, Janie. Samuel Horowitz! And are we about to have a delicious meal!" he enthused, despite the fact that he had once, on the sly, sampled the formula and found it a little less than delicious.

Little Jane in his left arm, he lifted the fresh bottle of formula in his right hand and made his way to the armchair. Settled in, he parted the blanket sufficiently to give him access to the infant's face. He studied it closely. Still wrinkled from sleep, it appeared not so ruddy as it had been that first day. But Horowitz had confidence that with his urging, and once she was fully awake, her color would improve.

"Well, now, little one, open up. Lunch is served!" he coaxed.

He held the nipple to her lips. The infant did not respond. As he had done many times before, Horowitz very carefully eased the nipple between the tiny pale lips and past the pink gums. The infant finally began to suck.

"Now we're getting somewhere," Horowitz tried to enthuse. Having started the little one feeding he was content to just watch. But soon, sooner than he expected, she was asleep once more.

So I'll wait, Horowitz decided. *After all, the way things have worked out, what have I got but time to wait? She gets hungry she will wake up.*

Several times, the infant woke, fed very little, feel asleep once more. Twice Horowitz spoke closely into her little pink ear but she was fast asleep almost at once. He hummed to her, one of the songs of his childhood on which he prided himself, but stopped when he realized she had been asleep almost from his first note.

He had overstayed his time in the nursery by more than an hour. He looked up to discover Molly staring through the glass wall. She was obviously ready to leave, and had been for some time. He carried sleeping Jane back to her crib, changed her into a fresh shirt, wrapped her securely in her blanket, placed her in the crib, patted her on the backside and started for the door. Halfway there he stopped, turned back to take one more look, then left.

As he came out of the nursery, he whispered to Molly, "Wait for me on the corner. I might be late."

"Late? Why? Something wrong?"

"I have to talk to one of the doctors," Horowitz explained.

At once Molly responded with controlled alarm. "Samuel, what is it? Don't you feel well? It's these last few days . . . my fault . . . that dinner . . . a big mistake."

"Molly, please. I'm fine. It's little Janie I want to ask about."

"Volunteers are not supposed to bother the medical staff," Molly reminded.

"So, they can call it a consultation and send me a bill," Horowitz said. "You wait. I will be down shortly."

Molly made one last effort. "Samuel . . . Don't do . . . ."

But he had started along the line of nurseries until he arrived at the neonate ICU. He stared through the glass, searching among the personnel for a doctor. He zeroed in on a young, tall black woman, with a stethoscope hung around her neck and a plastic badge pinned to her white lab coat that was different from the ones that the nurses wore. Horowitz entered. He waited a short distance from the small group of nurses whom the doctor was instructing.

Once she had given her last order and started out, Horowitz stepped between her and the door. With much on her mind, the doctor glared at him impatiently, then tried to avoid him to get to the door. But he moved to prevent it, at the same time he apologized.

"Doctor . . ." He strained to read her badge. . . . "Doctor Buford, could you possibly spare me a minute? It is very important."

"Sir, I can tell from your smock that you are one of our volunteers. And we appreciate the fine work you do. But I am a pediatrician, not a general practitioner. You would do much better going down to Emergency."

"Oh, it's not for me," Horowitz explained. "It's one of the little ones."

"They are weighed and tested periodically. If there were something wrong I'm sure one of us would have picked it up. Now I am due down in Pediatric Clinic . . ."

As she started to go around him to get to the door, Horowitz asked, "Tell me, Doctor, what does it mean when a little one would rather sleep than eat?"

For the first time, Dr. Leitha Buford seemed more intrigued by what Horowitz was saying than by the need to race down to the clinic. She gestured Horowitz to follow her out to the corridor. Once there, she asked, "Exactly what did you mean—she would rather sleep than eat?"

"Well, most little ones, they either are awake and hungry for the bottle. Or once I wake them they eat until they are full, then fall asleep. This one, she eats a little, falls asleep, wakes up hungry. Again eats very little, falls asleep again," Horowitz explained.

"Tell me, her breathing . . ." the doctor inquired.

"Takes a little . . . a little effort, you might say," Horowitz replied.

"I see," the young doctor replied, much more concerned than she had been. "Which infant is it?"

"Baby Jane."

"The Compactor Baby," the doctor identified.

"So if you could spare a minute, take a look, I would appreciate," Horowitz said.

Without hesitation, Dr. Buford started for the nursery, Horowitz trailing alongside.

She had examined the infant very carefully, applied her stethoscope over its chest and back, peered at the lower lids of its eyes. All the while, Horowitz stood by, asking from time to time, "Well, Doctor, anything?" Buford did not reply until she had slipped the infant's shirt back on, wrapped it in its blanket.

"Well, Doctor?"

"I will have her moved into ICU. Immediately!" Buford said.

"It's serious," Horowitz concluded grimly. "Very serious or just pretty serious?"

"We won't know that until we've done all the tests," Buford replied, then admitted with considerable concern, "Damn it. We should have picked it up on EKG when she was first brought in. I'm ordering an echocardiograph. Stat."

"Very serious, then?" Horowitz asked.

"We'll know more in a day or two. Now I'd better go set up those tests."

"So when will I know?" Horowitz asked.

Buford looked at him with a sudden realization that this man had taken a proprietary interest in this infant. While she did not approve, she did understand. "Call me in a day or two."

"Yes. Sure. I'll call you tomorrow," Horowitz said.

"I think Thursday or Friday would be better."

"I'll be on duty here Thursday," Horowitz informed.

"Good. See me on Thursday," Dr. Buford said.

Chapter 38

XXX

PROMPTLY AT TWO-THIRTY ON WEDNESDAY, MONA FIELDS RANG the doorbell of the apartment of Matthew Milligan, who at the time he suffered his stroke was a surrogate court judge in the city of New York.

Mrs. Washington greeted Mona with a hushed, "Mrs. Fields, we must keep our voices down so we won't disturb the judge's nap."

Adopting an equally, though for her unaccustomed, soft tone of voice, Mona replied, "No one has ever accused me of being loud or difficult to talk to."

Well aware of her tendency to dramatic explosions, having heard Horowitz refer to his daughter as "the Sarah Bernhardt of San Diego," Mrs. Washington nevertheless permitted Mona's statement to pass unchallenged.

She showed the way into the living room, where Mona was confronted by the same instruments and articles of therapy Mrs. Washington had introduced into her father's home during his recovery several years ago. The aluminum walker, the box of buttons and marbles for relearning hand coordination, the crumpled newspapers, the residue of exercises to rebuild strength in stroke-afflicted hands.

Ready on the coffee table was a tray with a pot of hot tea, cups, saucers, and little cakes. Mrs. Washington invited Mona to be seated. Mona assumed a stiff pose on the edge of the couch. Without a word, Mrs. Washington began to pour her a cup of tea.

With evident impatience, Mona asked, "Well, Mrs. Washington?"

Blithely Mrs. Washington responded, "Sugar? Sweet 'n Low? Cream?"

"Mrs. Washington, I did not come here for afternoon tea. I came to find out what you know about my father that I don't!" Mona declared forthrightly and in full voice.

Gesturing for quiet, Mrs. Washington whispered quickly, "Please, Mrs. Fields! The judge!"

"Oh, sorry," Mona whispered in return. "Now, what about my father?"

Unperturbed, Mrs. Washington finished serving tea, then set herself to the business at hand. "Mrs. Fields, as you know, I have long experience with stroke patients, especially men. I challenge them to recover by putting obstacles in their way. I defy them, I bully them. Some haven't the inner strength to meet the challenge. They just give up, content to remain crippled. Some fight back. The more I challenge them, the harder they fight. They complain and rant and rave but they do their exercises faithfully. Eventually they recover most or almost all of their faculties."

Impatiently, Mona Fields anticipated, "Yes, yes, I know what you did for my father. I was very impressed. So there is no need to tell me. Now about my father's present—"

"Please, Mrs. Fields! Your voice! The judge needs his afternoon nap," Mrs. Washington interrupted.

"Yes, of course. Sorry," Mona apologized in a whisper.

"I was about to say, after those men have gone through all the torture and pain of therapy they finally recover. That's when the crucial problem sets in. Your father's problem."

"My father had no problem until he met that Mendelsohn woman. She is a widow on the prowl, looking to pounce on the first vulnerable man. Being a widower, my father was defenseless. Natural prey for such a predatory female."

Mrs. Washington permitted Mona to vent her hostility before she startled her with "Mrs. Fields, have you ever heard of *senile depression*?

"My father is not senile!" Mona declared in full voice.

"Mrs. Fields, unless you keep your voice down I must ask you to leave!" Mrs. Washington warned sternly.

"Sorry. Just don't call my father senile," Mona replied, this time in a hoarse whisper.

Indulgently, Mrs. Washington replied, "Mrs. Fields, you don't seem to know the meaning of the word *senile*. It only means *old*. So there is senile dementia. But there is also senile wisdom. And, unfortunately, there is senile depression as well. You can look it up in Webster's."

"Yes. I will do that. Someday when I have more time," Mona shot back. "Right now I want to know about my father!"

"As far as your father is concerned, the important word is not *senile* but *depression*."

"He doesn't sound depressed when he talks to me on the phone," Mona protested.

"Of course not. He doesn't want to upset you. But I am an experienced hand at this. I have seen it all before. Many times. A patient struggles to recover from his stroke. He finally succeeds. However, once he does, unless he has a rewarding life waiting for him, he becomes depressed. Extremely depressed. Why not? Who wants to look forward to a life of nothing to do? Would you?"

There was no need for Mona to reply, not with her overactive life-style.

"I detected these signs in your father months ago. I knew that unless I could involve him in some worthwhile activity he would begin that slow deterioration."

"So," Mona accused, "it was you got him involved in volunteer work in that hospital up in Harlem!"

"Yes. Best thing that's happened to him since he recovered from his stroke, and he's very good at it. A very caring man. Sometimes too caring."

"How is it possible to be *too* caring?"

Mrs. Washington related the events that culminated in Samuel Horowitz tracking down little Cletus Simon to make sure he was being properly cared for.

"That sounds like my father," Mona admitted.

"But no matter how devoted a man is, volunteer work takes only three hours two days a week. Yes, he and I have dinner occasionally, or go to a concert. That still leaves more than a hundred and fifty hours a week with nothing to do. More important, no one to do it *with*. That's when terminal depression sets in. Fortunately, I caught your father in time. Fortunately, too, just by chance, he happened to meet Molly Mendelsohn. They have a great deal in common."

By now, Mona Fields began to suspect. "Mrs. Washington, do I detect a personal interest on your part in all this?"

"If by a personal interest you mean, do I feel a kinship with your father? Do I appreciate and sympathize with his situation? Indeed I do. With Conrad almost ready to go off to college, with Louise only two years behind, I ask myself, how will I spend my retirement and the rest of my days with no one needing me? So, yes, I guess I do have a strong personal interest. Did I help arrange all this? I most certainly did. Your father and Molly Mendelsohn have much in common. Best of all, they are good for each other. Those two people belong together!"

"Really?" Mona challenged. "Well, I can tell you now that I will never accept that woman in *my* mother's house!"

"Shhh," Mrs. Washington warned. "The judge."

"Of course. Sorry. But soft or loud, my feelings are still the same! I will never accept her as my father's wife!" Mona declared in such strong voice that Mrs. Washington had to gesture her to quiet once more.

"Mona, if you go back to San Diego feeling this way, your father will be dead within a year. Maybe less," Mrs. Washington warned.

Mona looked questioningly into Mrs. Washington's bright black eyes, which stared back at her intensely.

"Is that what you meant about something you know that I don't? That he doesn't?"

"Yes, Mona, something we in my profession have observed

for years. But the statistical proof of it has become public only recently. Older people who live alone die years before those who have a companion. Living alone can be a terminal illness. Even having a pet can make a difference. Best of all is having a mate. In your father's case, a wife. That won't happen if you refuse to go to that wedding. So you have a choice. Do you go back to San Diego and endanger your father's life? Or do you stay until Sunday, go to that wedding and wish your father a longer and happy life?"

When Mona hesitated, Mrs. Washington urged, "Call Dr. Tannenbaum. Ask him. Who lives longer, people who live alone or people who live together?"

Mona Fields was silent for a long moment before she admitted, in a very soft voice, "I never realized . . ."

"Then why not . . . No, no, I have no right—" Mrs. Washington pretended to refrain from intervening.

But as she intended, Mona Fields insisted. "What were you about to suggest?"

"An impulsive thought. But knowing your father as I do, I'll bet he's home right now, brooding. What a wonderful gesture it would be if as a loving daughter you were to call him. And say something like 'Dad, I've been thinking things over. Your happiness is the most important thing in the world to me. So I have changed my mind. I *will* come to the wedding on Sunday!' "

Mona Fields appeared tempted, but not yet convinced.

"Can't you just see his face when he hears you say that?" Mrs. Washington continued: "His impish smile. That glow in his eyes. Like when he catches *The New York Times* in a mistake."

Mona had to concede, "Nothing gives him greater pleasure."

"Until you call and tell him you are coming to the wedding," Mrs. Washington pointed out, at the same time indicating the telephone on the end table alongside the judge's old leather easy chair.

"Do it," Mrs. Washington urged. "But softly; after all, we don't want to disturb the judge's nap, do we?"

Mona tiptoed to the phone, dialed her father's number, waited. Then, to Mrs. Washington's relief and delight, she heard Mona exclaim in a whisper, "Dad! I'm so glad you're home!"

A dispirited Samuel Horowitz replied, "After Sunday, where else would I be? Out dancing?"

Mona turned to nod to Mrs. Washington, confirming her grim diagnosis.

"Dad, that's why I'm calling. I'm afraid I was a bit hasty Sunday night. The emotion of the moment. But I have been thinking things over. And I have decided, if this woman is the person who will make you happy, I *will* come to your wedding."

"Mona darling, nothing in this world would make me happier."

Mona cast a glance and a nod to Mrs. Washington to confirm her strategy. "And, Dad, you know what I thought? Since Albert knows Ivana so well?"

"Ivana? Who's Ivana?"

"Ivana Trump, of course. She runs the Plaza Hotel. I will have Albert call her at once. And though it is on short notice he can have her cater an intimate wedding reception in one of the smaller ballrooms."

"Really, Mona darling, I don't like to impose on anyone."

"Nonsense, Dad! After all, what are contacts for?" Mona insisted.

Oh, my God, Mrs. Washington groaned silently, *that woman will never change.*

"Mona," Horowitz declared, "we have already decided all that. The ceremony in the rabbi's study. Then a small party at the house. Just family and a few friends."

Disappointed, Mona asked sadly, "No reception? No caterer? An announcement in the *Times* perhaps?"

"Just the love and closeness of our children around us."

"Well, I guess if that's the way you want it . . ." Mona whispered reluctantly.

"That's the way," Horowitz said, then asked, "Mona? Mona darling, are you all right?"

"Yes. Why?"

"I never heard you sound like this before. You maybe have a cold? Or laryngitis?"

"No cold, no laryngitis."

"The way you are whispering, I thought . . ."

"Oh, that," Mona explained. "The judge."

"The judge?" Horowitz asked, even more baffled than before.

"He's napping."

"The judge is napping," Horowitz repeated, then hung up, happy but more puzzled than he had ever been.

Mona Fields turned to Mrs. Washington and in full voice started to say, "Mrs. Washington, you were so right. To hear his delight . . ."

Mrs. Washington interrupted with a broad, forbidding gesture of both her big black hands.

At once, Mona dropped her voice to a whisper. "Oh. Of course. Sorry. But my father did sound very happy. I can't thank you enough. You *will* come to the wedding, won't you?"

"My professional duty. I never feel a case is closed until the patient has made a complete and affirmative adjustment to life."

"See you Sunday. At the synagogue," Mona whispered as she headed in the direction of the front door.

As that door closed, the bedroom door opened slightly. An elderly gray-haired man peeked out.

"She's gone," Mrs. Washington assured. "You can come out now, Judge. But watch that left leg."

Judge Matthew Milligan started out of the bedroom on his quad cane, measuring every step. Once he felt secure enough, he permitted himself the luxury of talking as he walked.

"Mrs. Washington, if both my hands were free, right now I would be applauding. Since they are not, all I can do is say 'Bravo!' Or, when addressed to a woman, is the correct form 'Brava'?"

"I wouldn't know," Mrs. Washington said.

"Bravo or brava, I know one thing. Your strategy worked to perfection. As you said, if you could keep that woman from shouting you could talk sense into her. And you did."

"Were you eavesdropping on our conversation?" Mrs. Washington demanded indignantly.

"You exile me to my bedroom. You forbid me to turn on the television set because I am supposedly taking a nap. What else did I have to do but eavesdrop? I found it fascinating. The way you made her keep her voice down to a whisper."

"Let that woman raise her voice and she takes charge. Of everything in sight. Mostly of other people's lives," Mrs. Washington said.

"It didn't take her long to try to run that wedding," the judge agreed. "Well, now, Mrs. Washington, since, as we agreed, I played my part in your little plan, don't you think I have earned the right to watch the Mets? They are playing the Los Angeles Dodgers and I can catch the last few innings."

"As long as you practice picking up your marbles and buttons at the same time," she ruled.

"Tyrant!" the judge growled.

But he diligently began to pick up the small buttons with his damaged left hand, while using his right to turn on the television set by remote control.

At that moment, Samuel Horowitz was dialing his phone. He heard it ring through once, twice. By the third ring he was resigned to the fact that Molly was not home. But the fourth ring was interrupted by her disheartened "Hello?"

"Molly, my dear, I have the great pleasure to inform you that on Sunday next, in the study of Rabbi Ellenstein, there will be the wedding of Molly Mendelsohn and Samuel Horowitz."

"Not unless the children are all there. I will not break up a family," Molly replied.

"Mona just called. She will be there," Horowitz informed.

"Oh, Samuel . . . Sam . . ." And Molly broke down and wept.

Chapter 39

XXX

THIS THURSDAY, DIFFERENT FROM ALL OTHER RECENT THURSDAYS, Samuel Horowitz suggested that he and Molly leave for the hospital earlier than usual. For Dr. Buford had promised him the report on the condition of little Baby Jane.

On the walk to the bus, like all prospective brides and grooms, Molly and Samuel made and unmade many plans.

"Tell them or not?" Horowitz asked.

"First, I was thinking, we would make an announcement at the coffee corner," Molly said. "Get it over with, all at once."

"But then?" he asked.

"I thought if we do that, they will think we are asking for presents."

"I wouldn't want them to feel obligated to give any presents. After all, a few of them couldn't afford it. I wouldn't want to hurt their feelings," Horowitz agreed.

"You think we should invite any of them?" Molly asked.

"From the hospital? Ms. Flaherty maybe. After all, if she didn't give me a second chance this whole thing never would have happened," Horowitz said.

"And Mrs. Washington," Molly suggested.

"Goes without saying. Without her I would be long gone

from this world," Horowitz said. "Also, she was the one made me become a volunteer."

"If not for her I would never have made those posters to reinstate you," Molly explained.

"Mrs. Washington did that?" Horowitz realized. "That woman, that woman. Maybe we should also have her perform the wedding ceremony."

They both paid her the tribute of their silent admiration until the bus arrived to carry them up to the hospital.

As usual, and until their relationship became public knowledge, Molly arrived in the nursery area first. Horowitz appeared some minutes later. While Molly laid out her *ruggaluch* in the coffee corner, Horowitz went at once to the scrub room. He scrubbed with added vigor on this day. For he did not wish to be challenged when he entered the neonate intensive care unit.

Properly scrubbed, garbed in a sterile smock, Samuel Horowitz stood outside ICU, surveying the entire efficient active staff, but seeking Dr. Buford. When he could not find her, he entered and started toward the isolette in which little Baby Jane lay.

Even from some feet away he became aware and disturbed by the fact that it was empty. Startled, he stopped, Then, braced to confront the truth, though not resigned to accept it, Samuel Horowitz drew close to the isolette, stared down into it. It was lined with used, wrinkled linen. The sensors that had once been attached to her little body lay discarded as if haphazardly abandoned. Alongside on the IV pole a plastic IV bag hung half empty, its needle dangling.

Too late, Horowitz thought, *too late. I should not have waited until today. I should have been here yesterday. So what if yesterday was a Wednesday? There is no law that says a volunteer can't show up on a day he is not scheduled. There is always a need for another pair of hands. But no, I was too involved with my own troubles, with Mona, with the wedding, with all kinds of personal things. And if I was, would it hurt me to call and ask for Dr. Buford to find out how the little one was doing? Who else is there to call about her? The mother who dumped her out like so much garbage?*

Samuel Horowitz, you have failed in your duty as a human being. A decent person, a Jew most of all, should have greater reverence for life, especially new life. You should not have allowed any personal problems to interfere with that.

What now? What do they do with a little body like that? There is no one to claim it. Do they use it for research? Or bury it in that place on that island in the East River. Potter's Field? Well, not little Baby Jane. At least one thing I can do, make sure she has a proper burial. I must ask, I must find out. Right away.

How like life it is, to give a man a moment of happiness about Mona coming to the wedding, about all the happy plans, when the biggest problem is who to invite. Then to afflict a man with this tragic news.

Horowitz, do what needs doing! First, whatever they are planning to do with that little one, stop them! Right now!

He turned away from the isolette to address the first nurse in his view.

"Tell me, Nurse, the little one, Baby Jane, from that isolette, where is her body now?"

The nurse turned on him abruptly. "Sir, what are you doing in ICU?"

"Never mind that. What about that little one?" Horowitz persisted.

"That isolette was empty when this shift came on duty. Now, get out. Or else I will call Security!"

"All right, all right," Horowitz yielded grudgingly.

He came out of ICU, started past the glass walls of the small nurseries until he found the one in which Homer Wesley was just changing an infant before putting him down to sleep.

Wesley caught a glimpse of him and waved him in.

"Gone," Horowitz said. "Baby Jane. Gone."

"She was moved to ICU," Wesley corrected.

"Gone also from ICU," Horowitz informed.

"Oh, too bad, too bad," Wesley consoled. "Of course she was never too strong. Sometimes I wonder if we are doing the right thing trying to save them if they have no chance at a good healthy life."

"Who knows, who knows," Horowitz replied. "But I have things to do now. Sad things that must be done."

After he informed Molly, and she had cautioned, "Samuel, don't do anything impulsive," he set out to track down the body of little unidentified Baby Jane.

The place to start? he wondered. *What department has charge of when patients die with no one to claim them? Who to ask? Surely not Ms. Flaherty, a nice lady but who would surely tell me to mind my own business. Maybe Haworth, the nurse in charge? No. She is even more a stickler than Flaherty. Of course, there is Dr. Buford. A nice woman. Very sympathetic. She promised to tell me today. Yes, Dr. Buford. But where to find her?*

Careful not to be observed, Samuel Horowitz slipped into the scrub room to use the wall phone. Adopting his conception of a formal official voice, he instructed "Operator, please page Dr. Buford!"

"May I ask . . ." the operator started to ask.

Horowitz interrupted, "My dear woman, this is Dr. Horowitz. I have no time to argue. Page Dr. Buford!"

"Dr. Horowitz?" the operator questioned.

"Operator! Will you page Dr. Buford or must I report you for insubordination?" Horowitz demanded.

"Yes, Doctor, of course."

"Tell her to report to neonate ICU at once," Horowitz instructed.

He hung up the phone with a sign of great relief. Whatever rules he had broken, whatever the punishment might be, he was willing to endure it in this good cause. He slipped out of the scrub room, took up a position opposite ICU. Soon the door of one of the elevators opened. Dr. Buford came charging out. Before she could reach the door of ICU, Horowitz called to her.

"Doctor!"

Buford swung about impatiently, her pretty lean black face moist with the sweat of agitation and concern. She took a moment to place Horowitz in the scheme of things, then recalled, "Oh, yes, you. I remember. But I have an emergency first." She spun around to enter ICU.

"Doctor, the emergency is *me*," Horowitz felt forced to confess.

"You? What the hell do you mean you are an emergency?" the young doctor exploded.

"Doctor, I don't blame you for losing your temper. Just give me a minute to explain. Please? It is very important. If you believe in human dignity, give me a chance."

Buford was ready to reject his plea. It was his moist eyes that stopped her.

"Okay. But make it quick."

He had barely begun to explain his obligation to provide a decent burial for little Baby Jane when Dr. Buford's face slowly relaxed into a smile.

"What's the matter? You don't think even such a little one deserves a decent farewell?"

"Yes. But let's wait until her life is over," Buford said.

"Her empty isolette . . . What do you mean exactly?"

"Right now she is the subject of a series of intensive tests, including an MRI, a sonogram. Dr. Spence in Cardiology thinks she may be a good candidate for the heart repair she needs in order to survive. The tests will determine that."

"And if she is?"

"They will schedule her for surgery on Sunday morning."

"Aha!" Horowitz exclaimed with great relief. "Here I was thinking the worst." Then he added, "Tell me, Doctor, would it help if there was . . . I mean would the little one have a better chance if someone was willing to pay?"

"That won't be necessary," Buford said. "Spence looks on this case as a challenge to this hospital. So he has asked for a volunteer team of anesthesiologists, nurses and heart surgeons to assist him. That's why surgery is scheduled for Sunday."

"As long as she will be getting the best," Horowitz replied.

"She will get the best. But in a case like this, even the best is no guarantee. This is very high-risk surgery," Buford warned.

"Doctor, will you be there?"

"Yes."

"Good enough for me," Horowitz said.

Reassured, Samuel Horowitz returned to the nursery to assume his volunteer duties. As he passed the first nursery he found Molly just burping the infant she had finished feeding. Through the glass, he smiled his broadest smile and nodded confidently.

When he entered the next nursery he informed Wesley, "As they say, everything is A-OK!" Then he proceeded to explain.

"Well, goes to show. I always say, expect the worst and all your surprises will be good ones," Wesley said.

"Tell me, Wesley, by any chance could you be part Jewish?" Horowitz joked.

While Wesley laughed, Horowitz asked, "By the way, you happen to be free on Sunday?"

"Sunday?" Wesley tried to recall. "Nothing special. Why?"

"How would you like to go to a wedding?" Horowitz asked.

"*Your* wedding?" Wesley asked.

"Yep!" Horowitz responded.

"It would be my pleasure, Horowitz," Wesley replied.

Chapter 40

×××

Samuel Horowitz had had a very restless night. Numerous times, more than usual, he woke, then dozed off again. Shortly after four he woke with a start. *Today,* it struck him, *today is Sunday. The day that little Baby Jane has her surgery. I must call and find out how it is going. Just before I go to the wedding.* The *wedding?* My *wedding!*

Today, Sunday May 24, 1992, is the day I get married for the second time in my life!

Samuel Horowitz sat up in bed suddenly to ask himself, *Is this what I really want to do?*

He had suffered those same last-minute doubts that first time, when he had married little Hannah Siegel. Then, too, he had almost been overwhelmed by doubts. Doubts as to whether he was ready for marriage. Doubts about the whole idea of marriage, since he had just started a new business which had not yet begun to pay him as much as the job he had quit. Doubts about the kind of husband he would make. Some people, even his own family, considered him too quick to reach decisions. He had strong opinions. Sometimes too strong. And sometimes wrong, as well.

Could a woman, even a very loving and indulgent woman like Hannah, put up with such a man day after day? He had never had any doubts about his ability to stand her. He had never had enough of her, her warmth, her laughter. God, how that woman loved to laugh. An easy laugh, hearty. Her presence lit up a home. But in those days Samuel Horowitz had doubts about himself.

Now, on this day, he would be entering a new kind of relationship. He would be a *second* husband. How would he compare with Phil, Molly's first husband? From what she had told him, Phil was a fine man, a good husband, a good father. A very clever designer and businessman. She idolized him. Quite a standard to live up to.

Horowitz argued on his own behalf: *Hannah loved and idolized me, too. But were their standards for husbands the same, Hannah and Molly?*

Even though, thanks to Mrs. Washington, Mona was now resigned to his marriage, her initial reaction, her accusation that he was being disloyal to her mother, had left a deeper wound than he had realized.

Oh, Hannah, Hannah, could I use a little of your wisdom and counsel on this day.

He had not realized how long he had been pondering his dilemma until the phone rang. As he reached for it, he glanced at the clock radio. *Ten after seven on a Sunday morning. Who could be calling so early? . . . Oh-oh, I know, Dr. Buford. And it can't be good news. Not so early in the morning. Or maybe it's Mona. She has changed her mind again. No, it's Molly! She's the one who has changed her mind. Like me, she must have lain awake in bed pondering and at the last moment decided this is a mistake.*

Molly, Mona, Dr. Buford, whoever. I better answer the phone.

"Hello?" he greeted with some trepidation.

He was surprised, almost relieved to hear the voice of the sexton of the synagogue. A question about the wedding ceremony, Horowitz assumed.

Instead, the sexton said, "Mr. Horowitz, I am sorry to trouble you on such an important day when you have so many things to take care of. But I never realized this is the Memorial Day weekend."

"Of course," Horowitz replied. "Congress has decided that every holiday must now come on a weekend. When I was a boy we didn't know any better, so Memorial Day came on Memorial

Day. A good thing we have separation of Church and State, otherwise Congress could decide that Yom Kippur should also be on a weekend.''

After abiding Horowitz's complaint, the sexton continued: "The point is, usually on a Sunday there is no trouble gathering a *minyan*. But since so many members are away for the weekend, we are short one man. So, if you don't mind, I would appreciate if you could join us this morning.''

"This morning . . .'' Horowitz considered. "I am not yet showered and dressed, and I have an important call to make to the hospital . . .''

"So we will wait a little,'' the sexton conceded.

"Okay. I will be there as soon as I can,'' Horowitz agreed.

Early as it was, he decided to call the hospital at once. The operator informed him that she could not page Dr. Buford. She was in surgery.

So the surgery has started, Horowitz realized. *I hope it goes well. In fact, while I am in synagogue I will say the prayer asking for the recovery of the sick. Couldn't hurt.*

At seventeen minutes to eight, Samuel Horowitz hurried into the synagogue, paused at the back bench to pick up a prayer book and a tallith. As he started down the aisle he silently spoke the prayer that accompanied wrapping himself in the sacred shawl. He was ready to join the *minyan* and round out the ten men required.

Throughout, he spoke the prayers, responded when indicated. They reached the part of the service that was the reason why most men attended. To say the *kaddish* in memory of close relatives who had died during the past year, or whose anniversary of death fell on this day. Samuel Horowitz did not qualify on either count, yet today he stood with the other mourners and spoke the words, beginning *yiskadal, veyiskadash*. . . .

The prayer ended, the service concluded, Samuel Horowitz did not do as the others did, shake hands with the men close around them, then start toward the doors. Instead, he stood silent, facing the Ark in which the scrolls of the Torah were kept.

Must have been the hand of God made the sexton call me this morning of all mornings. Yes, true, it is a holiday Sunday. Still, why this

Sunday of all Sundays? This day when I am about to be married for the second time in my life?

Have I been called before God to justify my conduct? Or am I called to explain to Hannah? Or to receive her permission before I can do this? If only I could end this feeling that I am being disloyal to Hannah.

And am I being fair to Molly, to have such doubts and feelings on the very morning of the day we are to be married? She deserves better. Maybe I should call her and be frank with her. Even if it makes her decide that now she wants to call it off. Or is that what I really want? To call it off but not be the one to do it?

Oh, Hannah, Hannah, what have I gotten myself into? It was at times like this that I used to depend on you.

I remember our earliest days together, when the business first got started. I would come home at the end of a long day, tired and discouraged. I would say to you, "Hannah, darling, it was a mistake. Working for someone else, you always think the easiest thing in the world is to be a boss. Well, that's not true. Being a boss is tougher. I think I should pack it in. Get a job. Forget the dream about having a business of my own." You were the one who said, "Samuel, I won't let you do that! Just because it isn't easy doesn't mean it isn't right."

Hannah, what you said then applies to now. Just because what happens today isn't as easy as I thought doesn't mean it isn't right. If you were against it you would have found some way to let me know. I think the sexton's call this morning was your way to bring me here to tell me you approve. Thank you, my darling.

Now, Hannah, as long as I am here, there is something else. A little infant, whose own mother tried to get rid of her as soon as she was born, this morning she is having heart surgery. A very delicate operation. Dangerous. Right now she is on the operating table. So if you could intercede with God, ask for help for this poor little infant, I would appreciate.

Silently, Samuel Horowitz recited the prayer for relief of the very sick, then started out of the synagogue, ready for the day's events.

The first of which was to call the hospital once more.

"Sorry," the operator said. "I cannot page Dr. Buford while she is in the O.R."

Slowly, Horowitz hung up the phone. *Still in the O.R.? Can't be good. Nine o'clock. Still three hours to the wedding. I will go up there! I will find out what is happening. And if it is the worst, then I can at least make sure the little one has a decent funeral.*

He started toward the corner to wait for the Number 10 bus. In his anxiety he decided, today every minute counts. He hailed a cab. As he struggled to get in he instructed the driver: "The hospital! And don't spare the horses!"

When the cab did not take off at once, Horowitz growled, "I told you. I am in a hurry! A little child's life could depend on it."

"*Which* hospital?" the driver pointed out.

"Which hospital?" Horowitz suddenly realized. "City Hospital. Up in Harlem!"

"Okay, Doctor!" The cab took off with such speed that Horowitz was flattened against the back of his seat. Instead of bristling angrily, he consoled himself: *He called me Doctor. All those weeks of scrubbing must finally be showing.*

Unlike all previous days when Horowitz arrived at the bustling hospital, on this early Sunday morning there were hardly any people entering or leaving. A few nurses, white uniforms protruding from under their coats, were arriving. A few tearful relatives were leaving after an unsuccessful nighttime vigil.

Horowitz hurried into the lobby, studied the bulletin board with its many directions and colored arrows pointing to various departments and services.

SURGERY, Horowitz finally located. And under SURGERY, PEDIATRIC. He followed the arrow toward the elevators.

On the surgical floor he slipped out of the elevator, pursued the blue arrow that pointed to PEDIATRIC. As he approached the double doors that granted access to the surgical wing, a nurse who was coming out stopped, glared at him and asked, "Sir, are you looking for someone?"

Not a man to be caught unaware, Horowitz responded by producing his volunteer's pass. While the nurse studied it skeptically he ventured, "Dr. Buford asked me to come just in case . . ."

"Just in case what?" the nurse demanded.

Put to the test, any test, Samuel Horowitz was not a man to be found wanting. "In case a transfusion is necessary," he ad-libbed.

"You're to be a donor?" the nursed asked, openly dubious. "At your age?"

"Unusual-type blood," Horowitz explained. While the nurse considered that, Horowitz stressed the urgency of his situation. "Look, if Dr. Buford called, who am I to question?"

Once more the nurse stared at his pass, stared at him, finally relented. "Must be a very unusual case."

Relieved to be granted admission to the surgical area, Horowitz hurried along the corridor, trying to identify the operating room in which little Janie's surgery was taking place. He saw several men and women in surgical greens clustered outside one door. When he asked, he discovered they were interns and residents who had just witnessed a complicated pediatric kidney transplant.

Horowitz continued along the corridor. He spied a solitary figure seated on a bench at the far end. Straining to identify the person, this was one of those times when he regretted his vanity, which prevented him from wearing his distance glasses except at the movies. The more he strained the more blurred the figure became.

He drew closer. He stopped, startled to recognize—*Molly . . . It's Molly.*

Breathless from hurry, he whispered, "Molly? Molly, what are you doing here? Today of all days."

"The same as you, I'm afraid."

Horowitz sank down on the bench beside her. Reached for her hand. Cold. Cold as his own.

"Any word yet?" he asked.

"Doctors, nurses keep going in. Some come out. When I ask, they say it's too early to tell. From their faces, it doesn't look good."

"I was asked to come to *shul* this morning. For a *minyan*."

"So that's where you were when I called," Molly realized.

"Long as I was there, I put in a word for the little one."

"Good. Everyone, especially such a little one, needs someone to speak for them," Molly replied.

"That's what made you come here," he assumed.

"Not exactly."

"Then what?" Horowitz asked.

"I didn't want you to wait alone."

"You knew I would be here?" Horowitz asked. "How?"

"Where else would you be at a time like this?"

"Getting ready for the wedding," Horowitz pointed out.

"Not *you* . . ." Molly replied.

Startled, Horowitz wondered, *Does she know or even suspect the doubts that woke me early this morning?*

He dared to ask, "What do you mean, not *me*?"

"When such a little one's life is in danger, weddings can wait. That's the kind of man you are. So I knew you would be here. I didn't want you to wait alone."

He clasped her hand even more tightly.

After some minutes had elapsed, Molly said, "You'd think there would be some word by now."

"So long as they are still in there it's a good sign," he tried to comfort.

"Reminds me of when my Sybil was in a riding accident in camp. They took her to the local hospital. Phil and I, we rushed up to the country. When we got there they were operating on her for a concussion. Nowadays it's not so serious. But in those days . . . And Phil and I, all we could do was wait. And wait. And wait. Until finally the surgeon came out. We both jumped up from the bench at the same moment and both asked, 'Doctor?'

"Before he said a word, he smiled. I would pay a million dollars for a picture of that smile. The weight of the world dropped from my shoulders. The pain in my stomach was suddenly gone. I started to cry. Just cry. So I know what waiting is like," Molly said.

"Waiting?" Horowitz responded. "Believe me, on waiting I am an expert. I told you the time my Marvin was lost in a heavy fog with a troop of Boy Scouts on Mount Washington. Hannah and me started to wait. But you know me. Next thing I hire a small private plane. A little puddle jumper. To fly us up there to the mountains in New Hampshire. I wanted to climb up and look for them myself. State troopers wouldn't let me. Said they had trouble enough without more people getting lost. So we waited. Hannah and me. All the time I was blaming myself. For giving Marvin permission to go mountain climbing. I was the one said, a boy needs adventure, a boy needs to experience nature. If anything happens to that boy, Hannah will blame me forever. Those were the worst eleven hours of my life. In the morning the state troopers came. Told us the fog was beginning to lift on the mountain. Maybe they could locate them now. So, again we waited. Four more hours. Felt like four years. Finally came one of the troopers. With that same smile you described. They found them. All of them. And all safe. And I . . . that time *I* cried. So I don't need lessons in waiting."

They were silent for a time. Suddenly Horowitz could bear it no longer. He was up from the bench. "I'm going in there! I'm going to find out!"

"Samuel! You will do no such thing. Sit down!" Molly ordered.

He turned to stare at her. "The only one ever talked to me that way was Hannah. And in the same tone of voice. It's like you two knew each other. She was always right. And you are, too. Wait. We wait."

He sank back onto the bench. He reached out. Molly took his hand.

After a time Molly asked, "What will they do if we're late? For the wedding, I mean."

"What will they do?" Horowitz echoed. "They will do what we are doing. Wait." He looked at his watch. "Already ten-fifty-five. We have a whole hour. How much longer can it take?"

"I have to get home, change. I bought such a lovely dress especially for today."

"Me, too. A new suit. Tropical worsted. Navy blue," Horowitz said.

Moments later he asked, "So what if we don't have time to change? As they say in the movies, 'Will you take me to be your lawful wedded husband, even in this old suit'?"

"As they say in the movies, I do," Molly replied.

At that moment the door to the operating room opened. A stream of young doctors, male and female, emerged, chattering among themselves. Molly and Samuel caught only a phrase, a word.

"Fantastic technique . . . worth getting up early to see . . . As brilliant as his reputation . . ."

Emboldened, Horowitz rose to confront them. "Tell me, the patient. Is she all right?"

"Considering what she's been through," one of the young women replied, "she has a chance. Which is more than she had before."

At that moment two nurses wheeled a gurney out of the O.R., one in command of the rolling stretcher, the other tending the IV pole that was attached to the tiny infant who was almost hidden from view by blankets and bandages.

Horowitz caught only a glimpse of her as they went by. He followed, Molly at his side. At the door marked RECOVERY the gurney was pushed in. But the door was abruptly closed to shut them out. They pressed up against the glass panel in the door trying to see what the nurses were doing to little Janie, but they could not.

From behind them came a stern female voice, "Pardon me!"

Horowitz swung about, ready to confront whoever it was until he realized she was Dr. Buford, still in O.R. greens.

"Doctor, tell me, how did it go, what happens now?"

"The operation was very tricky. Dr. Hesseltine had to replace not only the mitral value but one other."

"But, as they say, bottom line?" Horowitz asked anxiously.

Buford smiled. "As they say, bottom line, she now has an excellent chance for a long, healthy life!"

"Thank God, thank God," Horowitz whispered.

Molly said, "Doctor, someday I would like a picture of you smiling the way you did just now."

Puzzled but affable, Buford replied, "Of course. Anytime. Now, they need me in there."

Before Horowitz would give way, asked. "Can we see her?" When Buford hesitated, he said, "Just a look, that's all. Just . . . just to make sure."

Buford considered his plea. "Quietly. One look. Then out!"

They both nodded. Buford opened the door, permitting them

to precede her. They slipped in, tiptoeing to the isolette where the two nurses were still affixing instrumentation to the tiny body. Horowitz and Molly both peeked in, at the same time trying not to impede the nurses at their duties.

They stared down at the tiny body, at all the equipment being affixed to it, at the bandage that covered the surgical wound that ran the length of her tiny body.

Horowitz turned to Buford, whispered, "She breathes better."

Buford nodded, not only agreeing but by her silence cautioning him not to speak.

Horowitz nodded in turn, indicating he knew it was time for them to leave.

As they emerged from Recovery, Molly said, "Her color, much better."

"The operation is a success, thank God."

Horowitz held out his hand. Molly put her hand in his. "Now, Molly Mendelsohn, I think it is time to go get married."

Chapter 41

XXX

ATTIRED IN HIS NEW BLUE SUIT, SAMUEL HOROWITZ ARRIVED AT the rabbi's study accompanied by his daughter, Mona, and son, Marvin, along with Marvin's wife. Minutes thereafter, Molly Mendelsohn, in her pretty new dress, arrived in the company of her son, Lawrence, his wife, her daughter, Sybil, and her husband.

After the greetings and introductions, the families separated into two distinct groups, Horowitzes to one side of the study, Mendelsohns to the other. Samuel and Molly glanced at each other from moment to moment to send signals of anticipation, and at the same time hints of regret that the younger generation had not yet been able to bridge the strangeness which the two of them had long overcome.

Through his eyes alone Horowitz tried to reassure Molly, *It is going to be all right. Everything will be fine.* Her eyes answered with equally encouraging glances. Both felt an eagerness to have the formalities over with.

Other members of the small wedding company began to arrive. Administrator of Volunteer Services Catherine Flaherty was first, followed by Homer Wesley.

As Horowitz had explained to Molly, "After all, Wesley and me, we are like buddies who served together in the same war.

Wesley and Horowitz, the old vaudeville team. As the song goes, you can't have one without the other."

He did not inform Molly that, aside from his friendship with Homer, he had in mind another reason for this particular invitation.

Mrs. Washington was last to arrive, since before she was free she had to settle her patient, Judge Milligan, so he would be comfortable for the rest of the day.

The wedding party assembled. Horowitz's rabbi invited Marvin and Lawrence, and Mona and Sybil, to hold up the four corners of the *chupah,* the ceremonial canopy under which all Jewish weddings must be conducted.

He beckoned Molly and Samuel to stand side by side under it. They held hands as he intoned the holy words. When the ritual had been completed, Molly Mendelsohn's rabbi delivered a brief word to the newlyweds.

"In the course of a year I perform many marriages. Young marriages, which mean the start of new families. They are always encouraging. But I take most pleasure from marriages between older couples. Because, having known the problems as well as the joys of marriage, they choose marriage once more as the finest expression of the relationship between man and woman. They enter it with memories, but no illusions. The burning love of youth is replaced by the tenderness and caring that only those who have experienced life can bring."

Having said that, he placed on the floor the napkin within which had been wrapped the ceremonial wineglass. In keeping with Jewish tradition, Samuel Horowitz brought his foot down hard, smashing the glass. With cries of *Mazel tov,* the ceremony was over.

Horowitz turned to kiss his new bride.

When they arrived at the apartment, Bernadine was waiting for them. She had set the dining-room table for a buffet lunch that presented some of Samuel Horowitz's favorite delicacies. Smoked salmon with bagels and cream cheese. Pungent corned beef, pastrami and bologna with potato salad and coleslaw. And pickles fragrant with garlic that dominated the air.

Mona took one look and shook her head sadly. *Ah, what one of my caterers could have produced for such an occasion.* But all the other guests seemed quite pleased.

Horowitz presented glasses of wine, and proposed a toast.

"To my new bride. With whom I have an agreement. We do not compare grandchildren. And we do not talk about the past. Only the future."

Lawrence Mendelsohn felt it his duty to respond on behalf of Molly's side of the family.

"To Samuel Horowitz and my mother. May they enjoy together the long, happy life they so richly deserve."

All the guests drank to that. They then felt free to partake of the buffet. Samuel Horowitz left Molly's side and with his forefinger gestured Mrs. Washington to follow him.

He led the way to the den. He closed the door and motioned her to be seated. But she remained standing.

"Mrs. Washington, I am not very good with words." Her look of amused reproach made him admit, "I know, I use a lot of words. That's only because I am not very good with them."

"Mr. Horowitz, exactly what are you trying to say?"

"After today things will not be the same."

"I hope not. I hope this is the start of a new and more enjoyable life for both of you," Mrs. Washington said.

"You don't see the problem there?" Horowitz asked.

"It always takes time for newly married couples to adjust."

"That is not the problem I am talking about," Horowitz said.

"So?" she asked in their accustomed shorthand, meaning, so what is the problem?

"What I am talking about is, I would like certain things to continue as they now are. For example, Conrad and Louise, I won't be cut off from them, will I?"

"Of course not," Mrs. Washington assured.

"The tuition . . . and Conrad's college money can continue?"

"As you wish."

"It would give me great pride for people one day to say, 'You see that young man, graduating with honors and going on to medical school, Samuel Horowitz had a hand in his education.' You wouldn't deprive me of that pleasure, would you?"

"You've been a great influence in Conrad's life. I've heard him say, 'A man like Mr. Horowitz couldn't even speak English when he came to this country. If he made it, I can make it.' "

"He said that?" Horowitz asked, starting to beam a little.

"More than once," she assured.

"That's nice to hear. Very nice." Horowitz savored the feeling. But only for a moment. "Comes time Conrad graduates, would you possibly have an extra ticket? I remember when Marvin graduated the school allowed four tickets. Two for parents, two for grandparents. And if all four grandparents were still alive, don't ask what kind of trouble there was. But always there were at least two tickets for grandparents."

"When Conrad graduates, I promise you will be there. He will insist on it. And so will I."

"Thanks. And after, suppose Molly and me want to give a little party for him. We could all go up to Alice's. Conrad and Louise like it. You like it. I like it. And I think Molly will like it too."

"I'm sure she will," Mrs. Washington agreed.

Horowitz breathed a deep sigh of relief. "So far so good." He paused before he said, "Now comes the hard part."

"And that is?"

"I told you, I am not very good with words." Uneasiness caused him to change the subject. "Mrs. Washington, remember the first few days you were here, I wanted to fire you?"

"I'll never forget it," she replied.

"But you were a tough cookie even then. You wouldn't budge. And I demanded, 'I would like already to hear Mrs. Washington's Farewell Address.' Remember?"

"Indeed I do," she replied, puzzled by his recalling that event from her early days in this household.

"Well, today I am in the same position. What I am trying to say, comes now time for Horowitz's Farewell Address."

"Horowitz's Farewell Address?" she considered, still puzzled.

"Mrs. Washington, I don't know how to say this."

"Mr. Horowitz, whatever you have to say, is it really so difficult?"

"Very difficult. But I will try." He set himself and ventured,

"You. Me. Us. Together we had a . . . what they call these days . . . a relationship. Dinner every so often. Occasionally a Broadway show. A movie. A lecture. Which we both enjoyed. Now, with Molly, things will be different."

"Of course they will," she was quick to agree. "So?"

"So I feel in some way I will be losing a friend. A very close, very precious friend. My dear Mrs. Washington, what I am trying to say, I would not want to lose you from my life."

It was a confession of deep feeling, a touching plea.

"Mr. Horowitz, for the rest of my days you will not only be my star patient, but my very dear friend."

"Thank you, Mrs. Washington," he said. "Then you will maybe come to dinner from time to time?"

"I will come to dinner," she promised.

"And occasionally, if there is a movie which I know you would especially enjoy, you would join us?"

"If I can."

"Oh, that's good, that's very good," Horowitz said.

She thought she had reassured him on all his doubts and questions, but he had yet another request to make.

"Mrs. Washington, one thing more. Just once, I would like to kiss you. On the cheek, of course. Would you mind?"

She considered his request, then her big brown face slowly expanded into a warm smile.

Permission granted, Samuel Horowitz put his arms around Mrs. Washington in a tender and affectionate embrace. He pressed his cheek against hers, then kissed her.

She thought she detected a slight gasp.

"Mr. Horowitz?" she asked softly.

He sniffled a bit. His eyes moist with emotion, he explained, "You remember once I said, the teary eyes of age. Leaky valves."

As she did years ago, she corrected him now. "Ducts."

"Of course. Leaky ducts," he agreed. He drew back, brushing the moistness from his eyes. "Now go, my dear, go enjoy the party."

Mrs. Washington stared into his eyes. He tried to make light of his emotions, saying, "Like I said, just the teary eyes of age. Go, go, enjoy."

Mrs. Washington had started for the door when Horowitz called, "Mrs. Washington."

She looked back. He held out his handkerchief.

"What for?" she asked.

"You also have the teary eyes of age," he said softly.

"Who, me?" she challenged in her domineering voice.

"Of course not. But as they say, couldn't hurt to dry your eyes anyhow."

She glared, then smiled, took his handkerchief, dabbed at her eyes. She sniffled back a tear; then, the ruling tyrant once more, she started out of the room.

When Mrs. Washington and Mr. Horowitz returned to the dining room they found the guests had all served themselves and were separated into little groups. Horowitz noticed that his volunteer buddy Wesley was off by himself. He edged over to comment, as if in passing, "You know, Wesley, if you are as smart as I think you are, you will not allow this chance to escape. That Mrs. Washington, a fine woman. Very fine."

A short time later, Samuel Horowitz drifted from guest to guest, stopping long enough to make a friendly joke with Ms. Flaherty.

"I will never be able to thank you enough."

"Me? What did I do?" the baffled administrator asked.

"If you didn't fire me from the volunteer staff, Molly and I would never have met," Horowitz remarked.

"Oh, that. Yes," Catherine Flaherty replied with a knowing smile that puzzled Horowitz.

Since no explanation was forthcoming, he moved on to chat with the other guests. Which was his subtle manner of working his way toward Mrs. Washington, who was chatting with Mona on what seemed to him surprisingly friendly terms. Horowitz sidled up to interrupt softly, "Mona darling, would you excuse me? I need a moment with Mrs. Washington."

Once Mona had started in Molly's direction, Horowitz whispered, "Mrs. Washington, I'm afraid I have to impose on you for a favor."

"If it doesn't take too much time," Mrs. Washington said.

"I know. You have to be home in time to make dinner for Louise and Calvin," Horowitz said. "But this won't take long."

He angled very slightly to bring into his view Homer Wesley across the room. "Homer Wesley, my buddy from the hospital, is here alone. I mean, aside from me and Molly and Ms. Flaherty, he doesn't know anyone here. So would you kind of . . . make him feel at home? As a personal favor to me?"

Mrs. Washington turned from watching Wesley to stare into Horowitz's blue, trying-to-seem-innocent, eyes.

"Samuel Horowitz, since when have you become a *shadchen*?"

"You know, Mrs. Washington, sometimes I think you take too much advantage of the fact that you know a little Yiddish," Horowitz rebuked, embarrassed that his ploy had been so transparent. "It is not a matter of matchmaking. It is simply a little common courtesy. But if you refuse, you refuse. What can I do?"

"I didn't say I refuse. I just don't want you to think you're putting one over on me," Mrs. Washington said. "On the other hand, no reason Mr. Wesley should be deprived, because of your lack of tact." She smiled and started in Wesley's direction.

Suddenly, Samuel Horowitz was struck by the similarity between Ms. Flaherty's knowing smile and Mrs. Washington's.

Good God, no! That Mrs. Washington, did she . . . No, she couldn't have. True, she was the one got me started on volunteer work. And turns out she was behind the protest. What else could she have done to bring about this day? That woman! There is no limit to what she is capable of. Well, I can't let her think she put one over on Samuel Horowitz.

Just before the guests started to leave, Samuel Horowitz raised his glass for a toast. "To my new bride. And to all of you who came here today to help us celebrate. Thank you all. Especially you, Mrs. Washington, I was onto your little tricks right from the start."

He pointed his glass in Mrs. Washington's direction and then drank. As he did so, Mona Fields called out, "Your attention, please! I want you all to know I insist the newlyweds spend their honeymoon out in San Diego! Two weeks of seeing all the sights of the West Coast. Including a private tour of Disneyland. Albert has important contacts at the Disney company."

With all the regret that she could muster, Molly replied, "Oh, how I wish we could. But, you see, Mona darling, we have a very sick little patient in the hospital. She needs us. Tomorrow and the day after and, if God is good, for many days after that. So, much as we would love to spend our honeymoon with you in San Diego, I'm afraid we can't."

"Then the first moment that you two are free," Mona insisted.

"I promise you, the moment the hospital runs out of babies we will come out," Molly promised.

Samuel Horowitz listened to their conversation, thinking, *That Molly, a born diplomat. I couldn't have handled it better myself.* That crisis past, he urged, "Marvin, aren't you going to see your sister to the airport? I wouldn't want her to miss her plane."

The other guests decided it was time to leave as well.

There were kisses and hugs and bright predictions all around.

Samuel and Molly Horowitz stood in the doorway of the apartment watching the last of the guests load into the elevator, Mrs. Washington and Homer Wesley among them.

Once the elevator door closed, Samuel shut their front door. "I got to see!" Horowitz said.

"See? What?" Molly asked.

He took her by the hand, and led her to the living room that overlooked the street. He opened the window so he could lean out to look down at the canopy of the building. In moments their departing guests appeared from under it. Some flagged taxis, some walked down Central Park West.

"Samuel, what in the world—"

"Shhh. Wait and see. There. Now!"

Molly joined him in looking down the street. She saw Harriet Washington and Homer Wesley appear from under the canopy. They stopped to exchange some words. Then, instead of separating, they started strolling north together.

"There!" Samuel Horowitz exclaimed. "I could give that woman lessons in matchmaking!"

"I wonder," Molly Horowitz said, with that same knowing smile.